KEN LIU

THE
PAPER
MENAGERIE
AND
OTHER STORIES

HEAD
ZEUS

First published in the USA in 2016 by Saga Press, an imprint
of Simon & Schuster, Inc.

First published in the UK in 2016 by Head of Zeus Ltd.
This paperback edition published in the UK in 2016 by Head of Zeus Ltd.

Previously published in *Lightspeed*: "Simulacrum" (2011), "The Bookmaking
Habits of Select Species" and "The Perfect Match" (2012), and "The Litigation
Master and the Monkey King" (2013); in *Polyphony 4*: "State Change" (2004);
in *Strange Horizons*: "Good Hunting" (2012); in *Fantasy & Science Fiction*:
"The Literomancer" (2010), "The Paper Menagerie" (2011), and "A Brief
History of the Trans-Pacific Tunnel" (2012); in *Upgraded*: "The Regular"
(2014); in *Asimov's Science Fiction*: "The Waves" (2012); in *The Future
Is Japanese*: "Mono no aware" (2012); in *GigaNotoSaurus*: "All the
Flavors" (2012); and *Panverse 3*: "The Man Who Ended History:
A Documentary" (2011). Calligraphy for "The Literomancer" and
"Mono no aware" copyright © 2016 by Mingmei Yip

9 7 5 3 1 2 4 6 8

A catalogue record for this book is available from the British Library.

ISBN (PB) 9781784975692
ISBN (E) 9781784975661

Typeset by Adrian McLaughlin

Printed and bound in Great Britain by
CPI Group (UK) Ltd, Croydon CR0 4YY

Head of Zeus Ltd
Clerkenwell House
45–47 Clerkenwell Green
London EC1R 0HT

WWW.HEADOFZEUS.COM

Contents

Preface

I started my career as a short story writer. Although I no longer write dozens of short stories every year since shifting most of my creative efforts to long-form fiction, short fiction still holds a special place in my heart.

This collection thus has the flavor of a retrospective for me. It includes some of my most popular works (as judged by award nominations and wins) as well as works that I'm proud of but didn't seem to get much recognition. I think they're a good, representative sample of my interests, obsessions, and creative goals.

I don't pay much attention to the distinction between fantasy and science fiction—or between "genre" and "mainstream" for that matter. For me, all fiction is about prizing the logic of metaphors—which is the logic of narratives in general—over reality, which is irreducibly random and senseless.

We spend our entire lives trying to tell stories about ourselves—they're the essence of memory. It is how we make living in this unfeeling, accidental universe tolerable. That we call such a tendency "the narrative fallacy" doesn't mean it doesn't also touch upon some aspect of the truth.

Some stories simply literalize their metaphors a bit more explicitly.

I'm also a translator, and translation offers a natural metaphor for how I think about writing in general.

Every act of communication is a miracle of translation.

At this moment, in this place, the shifting action potentials in my neurons cascade into certain arrangements, patterns, thoughts; they flow down my spine, branch into my arms, my fingers, until muscles twitch and thought is translated into motion; mechanical levers are pressed; electrons are rearranged; marks are made on paper.

At another time, in another place, light strikes the marks, reflects into a pair of high-precision optical instruments sculpted by nature after billions of years of random mutations; upside-down images are formed against two screens made up of millions of light-sensitive cells, which translate light into electrical pulses that go up the optic nerves, cross the chiasm, down the optic tracts, and into the visual cortex, where the pulses are reassembled into letters, punctuation marks, words, sentences, vehicles, tenors, thoughts.

The entire system seems fragile, preposterous, science fictional.

Who can say if the thoughts you have in your mind as you read these words are the same thoughts I had in my mind as I typed them? We are different, you and I, and the qualia of our consciousnesses are as divergent as two stars at the ends of the universe.

And yet, whatever has been lost in translation in the long journey of my thoughts through the maze of civilization to your mind, I think you do understand me, and you think you do understand me. Our minds managed to touch, if but briefly and imperfectly.

Does the thought not make the universe seem just a bit kinder, a bit brighter, a bit warmer and more human?

We live for such miracles.

I am forever grateful to the many beta readers, fellow writers, and editors who have helped me along the way. Every story here represents, in some measure, the sum of all my experiences, all the books I've read, all the conversations I've had, all the successes and failures and joys and sorrows and wonder and despair I've shared—we are but vertices in Indra's web.

I also want to thank everyone at Saga Press, my publisher, for helping me put together such a beautiful book. Among them are Jeannie Ng, for catching all those errors in the manuscript; Michael McCartney, for the lovely jacket design; Mingmei Yip, for accommodating unorthodox requests for calligraphy; and Elena Stokes and Katy Hershberger, for the thoughtful publicity campaign. I'm especially thankful to Joe Monti, my editor at Saga Press, for championing and shaping this book with his good judgment (and saving me from myself); Russ Galen, my agent, for seeing the possibilities in these stories; and most of all, to Lisa, Esther, and Miranda, for the millions of ways in which they make the story of my life complete and meaningful.

And finally, thank you, dear reader. It is the possibility of our minds touching that makes writing a worthwhile endeavor at all.

The Bookmaking Habits
of Select Species

There is no definitive census of all the intelligent species in the universe. Not only are there perennial arguments about what qualifies as intelligence, but each moment and everywhere, civilizations rise and fall, much as the stars are born and die.

Time devours all.

Yet every species has its unique way of passing on its wisdom through the ages, its way of making thoughts visible, tangible, frozen for a moment like a bulwark against the irresistible tide of time.

Everyone makes books.

It is said by some that writing is just visible speech. But we know such views are parochial.

A musical people, the Allatians write by scratching their thin, hard proboscis across an impressionable surface, such as a metal tablet covered by a thin layer of wax or hardened clay. (Wealthy Allatians sometimes wear a nib made of precious metals on the tip of the nose.) The writer speaks his thoughts as he writes, causing the proboscis to vibrate up and down as it etches a groove in the surface.

To read a book inscribed this way, an Allatian places his nose into the groove and drags it through. The delicate proboscis vibrates in sympathy with the waveform of the groove, and a hollow chamber in the Allatian skull magnifies the sound. In this manner, the voice of the writer is re-created.

The Allatians believe that they have a writing system superior to all others. Unlike books written in alphabets, syllabaries, or logograms, an Allatian book captures not only words, but also the writer's tone, voice, inflection, emphasis, intonation, rhythm. It is simultaneously a score and recording. A speech sounds like a speech, a lament a lament, and a story re-creates perfectly the teller's breathless excitement. For the Allatians, reading is literally hearing the voice of the past.

But there is a cost to the beauty of the Allatian book. Because the act of reading requires physical contact with the soft, malleable surface, each time a text is read, it is also damaged and some aspects of the original irretrievably lost. Copies made of more durable materials inevitably fail to capture all the subtleties of the writer's voice, and are thus shunned.

In order to preserve their literary heritage, the Allatians have to lock away their most precious manuscripts in forbidding libraries where few are granted access. Ironically, the most important and beautiful works of Allatian writers are rarely read, but are known only through interpretations made by scribes who attempt to reconstruct the original in new books after hearing the source read at special ceremonies.

For the most influential works, hundreds, thousands of interpretations exist in circulation, and they, in turn, are interpreted and proliferate through new copies. The Allatian scholars spend much of their time debating the relative authority of competing versions and inferring, based on the multiplicity of imperfect copies, the imagined voice of their antecedent, an ideal book uncorrupted by readers.

The Quatzoli do not believe that thinking and writing are different things at all.

They are a race of mechanical beings. It is not known if they began as mechanical creations of another (older) species, if they are shells hosting the souls of a once-organic race, or if they evolved on their own from inert matter.

A Quatzoli's body is made out of copper and shaped like an hourglass. Their planet, tracing out a complicated orbit between three stars, is subjected to immense tidal forces that churn and melt its metal core, radiating heat to the surface in the form of steamy geysers and lakes of lava. A Quatzoli ingests water into its bottom chamber a few times a day, where it slowly boils and turns into steam as the Quatzoli periodically dips itself into the bubbling lava lakes. The steam passes through a regulating valve—the narrow part of the hourglass—into the upper chamber, where it powers the various gears and levers that animate the mechanical creature.

At the end of the work cycle, the steam cools and condenses against the inner surface of the upper chamber. The droplets of water flow along grooves etched into the copper until they are collected into a steady stream, and this stream then passes through a porous stone rich in carbonate minerals before being disposed of outside the body.

This stone is the seat of the Quatzoli mind. The stone organ is filled with thousands, millions of intricate channels, forming a maze that divides the water into countless tiny, parallel flows that drip, trickle, wind around each other to represent simple values which, together, coalesce into streams of consciousness and emerge as currents of thought.

Over time, the pattern of water flowing through the stone changes. Older channels are worn down and disappear or become blocked and closed off—and so some memories are forgotten. New channels are created, connecting previously separated flows—an epiphany—and the departing water deposits new mineral growths at the far, youngest end of the stone, where the tentative, fragile miniature stalactites are the newest, freshest thoughts.

When a Quatzoli parent creates a child in the forge, its final act is to gift the child with a sliver of its own stone mind, a package of received wisdom and ready thoughts that allow the child to begin its life. As the child accumulates experiences, its stone brain grows around that core, becoming ever more intricate and elaborate, until it can, in turn, divide its mind for the use of its children.

And so the Quatzoli *are* themselves books. Each carries within its stone brain a written record of the accumulated wisdom of all its ancestors: the most durable thoughts that have survived millions of years of erosion. Each mind grows from a seed inherited through the millennia, and every thought leaves a mark that can be read and seen.

Some of the more violent races of the universe, such as the Hesperoe, once delighted in extracting and collecting the stone brains of the Quatzoli. Still displayed in their museums and libraries, the stones—often labeled simply "ancient books"—no longer mean much to most visitors.

Because they could separate thought from writing, the conquering races were able to leave a record that is free of blemishes and thoughts that would have made their descendants shudder.

But the stone brains remain in their glass cases, waiting for water to flow through the dry channels so that once again they can be read and live.

The Hesperoe once wrote with strings of symbols that represented sounds in their speech, but now no longer write at all.

They have always had a complicated relationship with writing, the Hesperoe. Their great philosophers distrusted writing. A book, they thought, was not a living mind yet pretended to be one. It gave sententious pronouncements, made moral judgments, described purported historical facts, or told exciting stories . . . yet it could not be interrogated like a real person, could not answer its critics or justify its accounts.

The Hesperoe wrote down their thoughts reluctantly, only when they could not trust the vagaries of memory. They far preferred to live with the transience of speech, oratory, debate.

At one time, the Hesperoe were a fierce and cruel people. As much as they delighted in debates, they loved even more the glories of war. Their philosophers justified their conquests and slaughter in the name of forward motion: War was the only way to animate the ideals embedded in the static text passed down through the ages, to ensure that they remained true, and to refine them for the future. An idea was worth keeping only if it led to victory.

When they finally discovered the secret of mind storage and mapping, the Hesperoe stopped writing altogether.

In the moments before the deaths of great kings, generals, philosophers, their minds are harvested from the failing bodies. The paths of every charged ion, every fleeting electron, every strange and charming quark, are captured and cast in crystal-line matrices. These minds are frozen forever in that moment of separation from their owners.

At this point, the process of mapping begins. Carefully, meticulously, a team of master cartographers—assisted by numerous apprentices—trace out each of the countless minus-cule tributaries, impressions, and hunches that commingle into the flow and ebb of thought, until they gather into the tidal forces, the ideas that made their originators so great.

Once the mapping is done, they begin the calculations to project the continuing trajectories of the traced-out paths so as to simulate the next thought. The charting of the courses taken by the great, frozen minds into the vast, dark terra incognita of the future consumes the efforts of the most brilliant scholars of the Hesperoe. They devote the best years of their lives to it, and when they die, their minds, in turn, are charted indefinitely into the future as well.

In this way, the great minds of the Hesperoe do not die. To converse with them, the Hesperoe only have to find the answers on the mind maps. Thus, they no longer have a need for books as they used to make them—which were merely dead symbols—for the wisdom of the past is always with them, still thinking, still guiding, still exploring.

And as more and more of their time and resources are devoted to the simulation of ancient minds, the Hesperoe have also grown less warlike, much to the relief of their neighbors. Perhaps it is true that some books do have a civilizing influence.

The Tull-Toks read books they did not write.

They are creatures of energy. Ethereal, flickering patterns of shifting field potentials, the Tull-Toks are strung out among the stars like ghostly ribbons. When the starships of the other species pass through, the ships barely feel a gentle tug.

The Tull-Toks claim that everything in the universe can be read. Each star is a living text, where the massive convection currents of superheated gas tell an epic drama, with the starspots serving as punctuation, the coronal loops extended figures of speech, and the flares emphatic passages that ring true in the deep silence of cold space. Each planet contains a poem, written out in the bleak, jagged, staccato rhythm of bare rocky cores or the lyrical, lingering, rich rhymes—both masculine and feminine—of swirling gas giants. And then there are the planets with life, constructed like intricate jeweled clockwork, containing a multitude of self-referential literary devices that echo and re-echo without end.

But it is the event horizon around a black hole where the Tull-Toks claim the greatest books are to be found. When a Tull-Tok is tired of browsing through the endless universal library, she drifts toward a black hole. As she accelerates toward the point of no return, the streaming gamma rays and X-rays unveil more and more of the ultimate mystery for which all the other books are but glosses. The book reveals itself to be ever more complex, more nuanced, and just as she is about to be overwhelmed by the immensity of the book she is reading, her companions, observing from a distance, realize with a start that time seems to have slowed down to a standstill for her, and she will have eternity to read it as she falls forever toward a center that she will never reach.

Finally, a book has triumphed over time.

Of course, no Tull-Tok has ever returned from such a journey, and many dismiss their discussion of reading black holes as pure myth. Indeed, many consider the Tull-Toks to be nothing more than illiterate frauds who rely on mysticism to disguise their ignorance.

Still, some continue to seek out the Tull-Toks as interpreters of the books of nature they claim to see all around us. The interpretations thus produced are numerous and conflicting, and lead to endless debates over the books' content and—especially—authorship.

In contrast to the Tull-Toks, who read books at the grandest scale, the Caru'ee are readers and writers of the minuscule.

Small in stature, the Caru'ee each measure no larger than the period at the end of this sentence. In their travels, they seek from others only to acquire books that have lost all meaning and could no longer be read by the descendants of the authors.

Due to their unimpressive size, few races perceive the Caru'ee as threats, and they are able to obtain what they want with little trouble. For instance, at the Caru'ee's request, the people of Earth gave them tablets and vases incised with Linear A, bundles of knotted strings called *quipus*, as well as an assortment of ancient magnetic disks and cubes that they no longer knew how to decipher. The Hesperoe, after they had ceased their wars of conquest, gave the Caru'ee some ancient stones that they believed to be books looted from the Quatzoli. And even the reclusive Untou, who write with fragrances and flavors, allowed them to have some old bland books whose scents were too faint to be read.

The Caru'ee make no effort at deciphering their acquisitions. They seek only to use the old books, now devoid of meaning, as a blank space upon which to construct their sophisticated, baroque cities.

The incised lines on the vases and tablets were turned into thoroughfares whose walls were packed with honeycombed rooms that elaborate on the pre-existing outlines with fractal beauty. The fibers in the knotted ropes were teased apart, re-woven, and re-tied at the microscopic level, until each original knot had been turned into a Byzantine complex of thousands of smaller knots, each a kiosk suitable for a Caru'ee merchant just starting out or a warren of rooms for a young Caru'ee family. The magnetic disks, on the other hand, were used as arenas of entertainment, where the young and adventurous careened across their surface during the day, delighting in the shifting push and pull of local magnetic potential. At night, the place was lit up by tiny lights that followed the flow of magnetic forces, and long-dead data illuminated the dance of thousands of young people searching for love, seeking to connect.

Yet it is not accurate to say that the Caru'ee do no interpretation at all. When members of the species that had given these artifacts to the Caru'ee come to visit, inevitably they feel a sense of familiarity with the Caru'ee's new construction.

For example, when representatives from Earth were given a tour of the Great Market built in a *quipu*, they observed—via the use of a microscope—bustling activity, thriving trade, and an incessant murmur of numbers, accounts, values, currency. One of Earth's representatives, a descendant of the people who had once knotted the string books, was astounded. Though he could not read them, he knew that the *quipus* had been made to keep track of accounts and numbers, to tally up taxes and ledgers.

Or take the example of the Quatzoli, who found the Caru'ee repurposing one of the lost Quatzoli stone brains as a research complex. The tiny chambers and channels, where ancient, watery thoughts once flowed, were now laboratories, libraries, teaching rooms, and lecture halls echoing with new ideas. The Quatzoli delegation had come to recover the mind of their ancestor, but left convinced that all was as it should be.

It is as if the Caru'ee were able to perceive an echo of the past, and unconsciously, as they built upon a palimpsest of books written long ago and long forgotten, chanced to stumble upon an essence of meaning that could not be lost, no matter how much time had passed.

They read without knowing they are reading.

Pockets of sentience glow in the cold, deep void of the universe like bubbles in a vast, dark sea. Tumbling, shifting, joining and breaking, they leave behind spiraling phosphorescent trails, each as unique as a signature, as they push and rise toward an unseen surface.

Everyone makes books.

State Change

Every night, before going to bed, Rina checked the refrigerators.

There were two in the kitchen, on separate circuits, one with a fancy ice dispenser on the door. There was one in the living room holding up the TV, and one in the bedroom doubling as a nightstand. A small cubical unit meant for college dorm rooms was in the hallway, and a cooler that Rina refilled with fresh ice every night was in the bathroom, under the sink.

Rina opened the door of each refrigerator and looked in. Most of the refrigerators were empty most of the time. This didn't bother Rina. She wasn't interested in filling them. The checks were a matter of life and death. It was about the preservation of her soul.

What she was interested in were the freezer compartments. She liked to hold each door open for a few seconds, let the cold mist of condensation dissipate, and feel the chill on her fingers, breasts, face. She closed the door when the motor kicked in.

By the time she was done with all of the refrigerators, the apartment was filled with the bass chorus of all the motors, a low, confident hum that to Rina was the sound of safety.

In her bedroom, Rina got into bed and pulled the covers over her. She had hung some pictures of glaciers and icebergs on the walls, and she looked at them as pictures of old friends. There was also a framed picture on the refrigerator by her bed, this one of Amy, her roommate in college. They had lost touch over the years, but Rina kept her picture there, anyway.

Rina opened the refrigerator next to her bed. She stared into the glass dish that held her ice cube. Every time she looked, it seemed to get smaller. Rina closed the refrigerator and picked up the book lying on top of it.

Edna St. Vincent Millay:
A Portrait in Letters by Friends, Foes, and Lovers

New York, January 23, 1921

MY DEAREST VIV,—

Finally got up the courage to go see Vincent at her hotel today. She told me she wasn't in love with me anymore. I cried. She became angry and told me that if I couldn't keep myself under control then I might as well leave. I asked her to make me some tea.

It's that boy she's been seen with. I knew that. Still, it was terrible to hear it from her own lips. The little savage.

She smoked two cigarettes and offered me the box. I couldn't stand the bitterness so I stopped after one. Afterward she gave me her lipstick so I could fix my lips, as if nothing had happened, as if we were still in our room at Vassar.

"Write a poem for me," I said. She owed me at least that.

She looked as if she wanted to argue, but stopped herself. She took out her candle, put it in that candleholder I made for her, and lit it at both ends. When she lit her soul like that she was at her most beautiful. Her face glowed. Her pale skin was lit from within like a Chinese paper lantern about to burst into flame. She paced around the room as if she would tear down the walls. I drew up my feet on the bed, and wrapped her scarlet shawl around me, staying out of her way.

Then she sat down at her desk and wrote out her poem. As soon as it was done she blew out her candle, stingy with what remained of it. The smell of hot wax made me all teary-eyed again. She made out a clean copy for herself and gave the original to me.

"I did love you, Elaine," she said. "Now be a good girl and leave me alone."

This is how her poem starts:

What lips my lips have kissed, and where, and why,
I have forgotten, and what arms have lain
Under my head till morning, but the rain
Is full of ghosts tonight, that tap and sigh—

Viv, for a moment I wanted to take her candle and break it in half, to throw the pieces into the fireplace and melt her soul into nothing. I wanted to see her writhing at my feet, begging me to let her live.

But all I did was to throw that poem in her face, and I left.

I've been wandering around the streets of New York all day. I can't keep her savage beauty out of my mind. I wish my soul was heavier, more solid, something that could weigh itself down. I wish my soul wasn't this feather, this ugly wisp of goose down in my pocket, lifted up and buffeted about by the wind around her flame. I feel like a moth.

Your Elaine

Rina put the book down.

To be able to set your soul afire, she thought, *to be able to draw men and women to you at your will, to be brilliant, fearless of consequences, what would she not give to live a life like that?*

Millay chose to light her candle at both ends, and lived an incandescent life. When her candle ran out, she died sick, addicted, and much too young. But each day of her life she could decide, "Am I going to be brilliant today?"

Rina imagined her ice cube in the dark, cold cocoon of the freezer. *Stay calm,* she thought. *Block it out. This is your life. This bit of almost-death.*

Rina turned out the light.

When Rina's soul finally materialized, the nurse in charge of watching the afterbirth almost missed it. All of a sudden, there, in the stainless steel pan, was an ice cube, the sort you would find clinking around in glasses at cocktail parties. A pool of water was already forming around it. The edges of the ice cube were becoming rounded, indistinct.

An emergency refrigeration unit was rushed in, and the ice cube was packed away.

"I'm sorry," the doctor said to Rina's mother, who looked into the serene face of her baby daughter. No matter how careful they were, how long could they keep the ice cube from melting? It wasn't as if they could just keep it in a freezer somewhere and forget about it. The soul had to be pretty close to the body; otherwise the body would die.

Nobody in the room said anything. The air around the baby was awkward, still, silent. Words froze in their throats.

Rina worked in a large building downtown, next to the piers and docked yachts she had never been on. On each floor, there were offices with windows around the sides, the ones overlooking the harbor being bigger and better furnished than the others.

In the middle of the floor were the cubicles, one of which was Rina's. Next to her were two printers. The hum of the printers was a bit like the hum of refrigerators. Lots of people passed by her cubicle on the way to pick up their printouts. Sometimes they stopped, thinking they would say hello to the quiet girl sitting there, with her pale skin and ice-blonde hair, and always a sweater around her shoulders. Nobody knew what color her eyes were because she did not look up from her desk.

But there was a chill in the air around her, a fragile silence that did not want to be broken. Even though they saw her every day, most people did not know Rina's name. After a while, it became too embarrassing to ask. While the chattering life of the office ebbed and flowed around her, people left her alone.

Under Rina's desk was a small freezer that the firm had installed just for her. Each morning Rina would rush into her cubicle, unzip her insulated lunch bag, and from her thermos stuffed with ice cubes, she would carefully pull out the sandwich bag holding her one special ice cube and put it into the freezer. She would sigh, and sit in her chair, and wait for her heart to slow down.

The job of the people in the smaller offices away from the harbor was to look up, on their computers, the answers to questions asked by people in the offices facing the harbor. Rina's job was to take those answers and use the right fonts to squeeze them into the right places on the right pieces of paper to be sent back to the people in the harbor offices. Sometimes the people in the smaller offices were too busy, and they would dictate their answers onto cassette tapes. Rina would then type up the answers.

Rina ate her lunch at her cubicle. Even though one could go some distance away from one's soul for short periods of time without getting sick, Rina liked to be as close to the freezer as possible. When she had to be away sometimes to deliver an envelope to some office on another floor, she had visions of sudden power failures. Out of breath, she would then hurry through the halls to get back to the safety of her freezer.

Rina tried not to think that life was unfair to her. Had she been born before the invention of the Frigidaire she would not have survived. She didn't want to be ungrateful. But sometimes it was difficult.

After work, instead of going dancing with the other girls or getting ready for a date, she spent her nights at home, reading biographies to lose herself in other lives.

* * * *

Between 1958 and 1963, Eliot was a member of the Commission for the Revised Psalter of the Book of Common Prayer. He was rather frail by this time, and avoided tapping into his tin of coffee altogether.

One exception was when the commission came to revise Psalm 23. Four centuries earlier, Bishop Coversdale had been rather free with his translation from the Hebrew. The correct English rendition for the central metaphor in the psalm, the commission agreed, was "the valley of deep darkness."

At the meeting, for the first time in months, Eliot brewed a cup of his coffee. The rich, dark aroma was unforgettable to me.

Eliot took a sip of his coffee, and then, in that same mesmerizing voice he used to read *The Waste Land*, he recited the traditional version that had infused itself into the blood of every Englishman: "Though I walk through the valley of the shadow of death, I shall fear no evil."

The vote was unanimous to keep Coversdale's version, embellished though it might have been.

I think it always surprised people how deep was Eliot's devotion to tradition, to the Anglican Church, and also how thoroughly his soul had been imbibed by the English.

I believe that was the last time Eliot tasted his soul, and often since then I have wished that I could again smell that aroma: bitter, burned, and restrained. It was not only the spirit of a true Englishman, but also that of the genius of poetry.

To measure out a life with coffee spoons, Rina thought, *must have seemed dreadful sometimes. Perhaps that was why Eliot had no sense of humor.*

But a soul in a coffee tin was also lovely in its own way. It enlivened the air around him, made everyone who heard his voice alert, awake, open and receptive to the mysteries of his difficult, dense verse. Eliot could not have written, and the world would have understood, *Four Quartets* without the scent of Eliot's soul, the edge it gave to every word, the sharp tang of having drunk something deeply significant.

I would love to have the mermaids sing to me, Rina thought. *Was that what Eliot dreamed of after drinking his coffee before sleep?*

Instead of mermaids, she dreamed of glaciers that night. Miles and miles of ice that would take a hundred years to melt. Though there was no life in sight, Rina smiled in her sleep. It was her life.

On the first day the new man showed up at work, Rina could tell that he was not going to be in his office for long.

His shirt was a few years out of style, and he did not take care to polish his shoes that morning. He was not very tall, and his chin was not very sharp. His office was down the hall from Rina's cubicle, and it was small, with only one window facing the building next to this one. The name tag outside the office said JIMMY KESNOW. By all signs he should have been just another one of the anonymous, ambitious, disappointed young men passing through the building every day.

But Jimmy was the most comfortable person Rina had ever seen. Wherever he was, he acted like he belonged. He was not loud and he did not talk fast, but conversations and crowds opened up places for him. He would say only a few words, but people would laugh and afterward feel a little wittier themselves. He would smile at people, and they would feel happier, more handsome, more beautiful. He popped in and out of his office all morning, managing to look purposeful and relaxed enough to stop and chat at the same time. Offices remained open after he had left, and their occupants felt no desire to close the doors.

Rina saw that the girl in the cubicle next to hers primped herself when she heard Jimmy's voice coming down the hall.

It seemed difficult to even remember what life in the office was like before Jimmy.

Rina knew that young men like that did not stay in small offices with only one window facing an alley for very long. They moved into offices facing the harbor, or maybe on the next floor. Rina imagined that his soul was probably a silver spoon, effortlessly dazzling and desirable.

The Trial of Joan of Arc

"At night the soldiers and Joan slept together on the ground. When Joan took off her armor, we could see her breasts, which were beautiful. And yet never once did she awake in me carnal desires.

"Joan would become angry when the soldiers swore in her presence or spoke of the pleasures of the flesh. She always chased away the women who followed soldiers with her sword unless a soldier promised to marry such a woman.

"Joan's purity came from her soul, which she always carried on her body whether she was riding into battle or getting ready to sleep for the night. This was a beech branch. Not far from Domrémy, her home village, there was an old beech tree called the Ladies' Tree by a spring. Her soul came from that tree, for the branch gave off a smell that those who knew Joan in her childhood swore was the same smell given off by the spring by the Ladies' Tree.

"Whoever came into Joan's presence with a sinful thought would instantly have that flame extinguished by the influence of her soul. Thus, she remained pure, as I do swear to tell the truth, even though she would sometimes be naked as the rest of the soldiers."

"Hey," Jimmy said. "What's your name?"

"Joan," Rina said. She blushed and put her book down. "Rina, I meant." Instead of looking at him she looked down at the half-eaten salad on her desk. She wondered if there was anything at the corners of her mouth. She thought about wiping her mouth with the napkin but decided that would draw too much attention.

"You know, I've been asking around the office all morning, and no one could tell me your name."

Even though Rina already knew this was true, she felt a little sad, as if she had disappointed him. She shrugged.

"But now I know something no one else here knows," Jimmy said, and sounded as if she had told him a wonderful secret.

Did they finally turn down the air-conditioning? Rina thought. *It didn't feel as cold as it usually did.* She thought about taking off her sweater.

"Hey, Jimmy," the girl in the cubicle next to Rina's called out. "Come over here. Let me show you those pictures I was telling you about."

"See you later," Jimmy said, and smiled at her. She knew because she was looking up, looking into his face, which she realized could be handsome.

Legends of the Romans

Cicero was born with a pebble. Therefore, no one expected him to amount to much.

Cicero practiced public speaking with the pebble in his mouth. Sometimes he almost choked on it. He learned to use simple words and direct sentences. He learned to push his voice past the pebble in his mouth, to articulate, to speak clearly even when his tongue betrayed him.

He became the greatest orator of his age.

★ ★ ★ ★

"You read a lot," Jimmy said.

Rina nodded. Then she smiled at him.

"I've never seen eyes with your shade of blue," Jimmy said, looking directly into her eyes. "It's like the sea, but through a layer of ice." He said this casually, as if he was talking about a vacation he had taken, a movie he had seen. This was why Rina knew he was being sincere, and she felt as if she had given him another secret, one she didn't even know she had.

Neither of them said anything. This would usually be awkward. But Jimmy simply leaned against the wall of the cubicle, admiring the stack of books on Rina's desk. He settled into the silence, relaxed into it. And so Rina felt content to let the silence go on.

"Oh, Catullus," Jimmy said. He picked up one of the books. "Which poem is your favorite?"

Rina pondered this. It seemed too bold to say that it was "Let us live, my Lesbia, and let us love." It seemed too coy to say that it was "You ask me how many kisses."

She agonized over the answer.

He waited, not hurrying her.

She couldn't decide. She began to say something, anything, but nothing came out. A pebble was in her throat, an ice-cold pebble. She was angry with herself. She must have looked like such an idiot to him.

"Sorry," Jimmy said. "Steve is waving at me to come to his office. I'll catch up with you later."

Amy was Rina's roommate in college. She was the only person Rina ever pitied. Amy's soul was a pack of cigarettes.

But Amy did not act like she wanted to be pitied. By the time Rina met her, Amy had less than half a pack left.

"What happened to the rest of them?" Rina was horrified. She could not imagine herself being so careless with her life.

Amy wanted Rina to go out with her at nights, to dance, to drink, and to meet boys. Rina kept on saying no.

"Do it for me," Amy said. "You feel sorry for me, right? Well, I'm asking you to come with me, just once."

Amy took Rina to a bar. Rina hugged her thermos to her the whole way. Amy pried it out of her hand, dropped Rina's ice cube into a shot glass, and told the bartender to keep it chilled in the freezer.

Boys came up to try to pick them up. Rina ignored them. She was terrified. She wouldn't take her eyes off the freezer.

"Try to act like you are having fun, will you?" Amy said.

The next time a boy came up to them, Amy took out one of her cigarettes.

"You see this?" she said to the boy, her eyes flashing in the glow from the neon lights behind the bar. "I'm going to start smoking it right now. If you can get my friend here to laugh before I finish it, I will go home with you tonight."

"How about both of you come home with me tonight?"

"Sure," Amy said. "Why not? You better get cracking, though." She flicked her lighter and took a long drag on her cigarette. She threw her head back and blew the smoke high into the air.

"This is what I live for," Amy whispered to Rina, her pupils unfocused, wild. "All life is an experiment." Smoke drifted from her nostrils and made Rina cough.

Rina stared at Amy. Then she turned around to face the boy. She felt a little light-headed. The crooked nose on the boy's face seemed funny and sad at the same time.

Amy's soul was infectious.

"I'm jealous," Amy said to Rina the next morning. "You have a very sexy laugh." Rina smiled when she heard that.

Rina found the shot glass with her ice cube in the boy's freezer. She took the shot glass home with her.

Still, that was the last time Rina agreed to go with Amy.

They lost touch after college. When Rina thought about Amy, she wished that her pack of cigarettes would magically refill itself.

★ ★ ★ ★

Rina had been paying attention to the flow of paper out of the printers next to her. She knew that Jimmy was going to move to an office upstairs soon. She didn't have a lot of time.

She went shopping over the weekend. She made her choices carefully. Her color was ice blue. She had her nails done, to go with her eyes.

Rina decided on Wednesday. People tended to have more to talk about at the beginning of the week and the end of the week, either about what they had done over the weekend or what they were about to do the next weekend. There was not so much to talk about on Wednesdays.

Rina brought her shot glass with her, for good luck, and because the glass was easy to chill.

She made her move after lunch. There was still a lot of work in the afternoon, and the gossip tended to die down then.

She opened the freezer door, took out the chilled shot glass and the sandwich bag with her ice cube. She took the ice cube out of the bag and put it into the shot glass. Condensation immediately formed on the outside of the glass.

She took off her sweater, picked up the glass in her hand, and began to walk around the office.

She walked wherever there were groups of people—in the hallways, by the printers, next to the coffee machines. As she approached, people felt a sudden chill in the air, and there would be a lull in the conversation. Witticisms sounded flat and stupid. Arguments died. Suddenly everyone would remember how much work was left to do and make up some excuse to get away. Office doors closed as she passed them.

She walked around until the halls were quiet, and the only office with its door open was Jimmy's.

She looked down into the glass. There was a small pool of water at the bottom of the glass; soon the ice cube would be floating.

She still had time, if she hurried.

Kiss me, before I disappear.

She put the shot glass down outside the door to Jimmy's office. *I am not Joan of Arc.*

She walked into Jimmy's office and closed the door behind her.

"Hello," she said. Now that she was alone with him, she didn't know what else to do.

"Hey," he said. "It's so quiet around here today. What's going on?"

"*Si tecum attuleris bonam atque magnam cenam, non sine candida puella,*" she said. "If you bring with you a good meal and lots of it, and not without a pretty girl. That's the one. That's my favorite poem."

She felt shy, but warm. There was no weight on her tongue, no pebble in her throat. Her soul was outside that door, but she was not anxious. She was not counting down the seconds. The shot glass with her life in it was in another time, another place.

"*Et uino et sale et omnibus cachinnis,*" he finished for her. "And wine and salt and all the laughter."

She saw that there was a saltshaker on his desk. Salt made the blandest food palatable. Salt was like wit and laughter in conversation. Salt made the plain extraordinary. Salt made the simple beautiful. Salt was his soul.

And salt made it harder to freeze.

She laughed.

She unbuttoned her blouse. He began to get up, to stop her. She shook her head and smiled at him.

I have no candle to burn at both ends. I won't measure my life with coffee spoons. I have no spring water to quiet desire, because I have left behind my frozen bit of almost-death. What I have is my life.

"All life is an experiment," she said.

22

She shook off her blouse and stepped out of her skirt. He could now see what she had bought over the weekend.

Ice blue was her color.

She remembered laughing, and she remembered him laughing back. She worked hard to memorize every touch, every quickened breath. What she didn't want to remember was the time.

The noise of the people outside the door gradually rose and then gradually settled down. They lingered in his office.

What lips my lips have kissed, she thought, and realized that it was again completely quiet outside the office. Sunlight in the room was taking on a red tinge.

She got up, stepping away from his grasp, and put on her blouse, stepped into her skirt. She opened the door to his office and picked up the shot glass.

She looked, and looked frantically, for a sliver of ice. Even the tiniest crystal would suffice. She would keep it frozen and eke out the rest of her life on the memory of this one day, this one day when she was alive.

But there was only water in the glass; clear, pure water.

She waited for her heart to stop beating. She waited for her lungs to stop breathing. She walked back into his office so that she could die looking into his eyes.

It would be hard to freeze salty water.

She felt warm, inviting, open. Something flowed into the coldest, quietest, and emptiest corners of her heart and filled her ears with the roar of waves. She thought she had so much to say to him that she would never have time to read again.

Rina,

I hope you are well. It has been a long time since we last saw each other.

I would imagine the immediate question on your mind is how many cigarettes I have left. Well, the good news is that

23

I have quit smoking. The bad news is that my last cigarette was finished six months ago.

But as you can see, I am still alive.

Souls are tricky things, Rina, and I thought I had it all figured out. All my life I thought my fate was to be reckless, to gamble with each moment of my life. I thought that was what I was meant to do. The only moments when I felt alive were those times when I lit up a bit of my soul, daring for something extraordinary to happen before the flame and ashes touched my fingers. I would be alert during those times, sensitive to every vibration in my ears, every bit of color in my eyes. My life was a clock running down. The months between my cigarettes were just dress rehearsals for the real performance, and I was engaged for twenty showings.

I was down to my last cigarette, and I was terrified. I had planned for some big final splash, to go out with a bang. But when it came time to smoke that last cigarette, I lost my courage. When you realize you are going to die after you have finished that last breath, suddenly your hands start to shake, and you cannot hold a match steady or flick a lighter with your thumb.

I got drunk at a beach party, passed out. Someone needed a nicotine fix, pawed through my purse and found my last cigarette. By the time I woke up the empty box was on the sand next to me, and a little crab had crawled into it and made it its home.

Like I said, I didn't die.

All my life I thought my soul was in those cigarettes, and I never even thought about the box. I never paid any attention to that paper shell of quiet, that enclosed bit of emptiness.

An empty box is a home for lost spiders you want to carry outside. It holds loose change, buttons that have fallen off, needles and thread. It works tolerably well for lipstick, eye pencil, and a bit of blush. It is open to whatever you'd like to put in it.

And that is how I feel: open, careless, adaptable. Yes, life is now truly just an experiment. What can I do next? Anything.

But to get here, I first had to smoke my cigarettes.

What happened to me was a state change. When my soul turned from a box of cigarettes to a box, I grew up.

I thought of writing to you because you remind me of myself. You thought you understood your soul, and you thought you knew how you needed to live your life. I thought you were wrong then, but I didn't have the right answer myself.

But now I do. I think you are ready for a state change.

Your friend always, Amy

The Perfect Match

Sai woke to the rousing first movement of Vivaldi's violin concerto in C minor, "Il Sospetto."

He lay still for a minute, letting the music wash over him like a gentle Pacific breeze. The room brightened as the blinds gradually opened to the sunlight. Tilly had woken him right at the end of a light sleep cycle, the optimal time. He felt great: refreshed, optimistic, ready to jump out of bed.

Which is what he did next. "Tilly, that's an inspired choice for a wake-up song."

"Of course." Tilly spoke from the camera/speaker in the nightstand. "Who knows your tastes and moods better than I?" The voice, though electronic, was affectionate and playful.

Sai went into the shower.

"Remember to wear the new shoes today." Tilly now spoke to him from the camera/speaker in the ceiling.

"Why?"

"You have a date after work."

"Oh, the new girl. Shoot, what's her name? I know you told me—"

"I'll bring you up to speed after work. I'm sure you'll like her. The compatibility index is very high. I think you'll be in love for at least six months."

Sai looked forward to the date. Tilly had also introduced him to his last girlfriend, and that relationship had been wonderful. The breakup afterward was awful, of course, but it helped that Tilly had guided him through it. He felt that he had matured emotionally and, after a month on his own, was ready start a new relationship.

But first he still had to get through the workday. "What do you recommend for breakfast this morning?"

"You are scheduled to attend the kickoff meeting for the Davis case at eleven, which means you'll get a lunch paid for by the firm. I suggest you go light on the breakfast, maybe just a banana."

Sai was excited. All the paralegals at Chapman Singh Stevens & Rios lived for client lunches made by the firm's own executive chef. "Do I have time to make my own coffee?"

"You do. Traffic is light this morning. But I suggest you go to this new smoothie place along the way instead—I can get you a coupon code."

"But I really want coffee."

"Trust me, you'll love the smoothie."

Sai smiled as he turned off the shower. "Okay, Tilly. You always know best."

Although it was another pleasant and sunny morning in Las Aldamas, California—sixty-eight degrees Fahrenheit—Sai's neighbor Jenny was wearing a thick winter coat, ski goggles, and a long, dark scarf that covered her hair and the rest of her face.

"I thought I told you I didn't want that thing installed," she said as he stepped out of his apartment. Her voice was garbled through some kind of electronic filter. In response to his questioning look, she pointed to the camera over Sai's door.

Talking to Jenny was like talking to one of his grandmother's friends who refused to use Centillion e-mail or get a ShareAll account because they were afraid of having "the computer" know "all their business"—except that as far as he could tell, Jenny was his age. She had grown up a digital native, but somehow had missed the ethos of sharing.

"Jenny, I'm not going to argue with you. I have a right to install anything I want over *my* door. And I want Tilly to keep an eye on my door when I'm away. Apartment three-oh-eight was just burglarized last week."

"But your camera will record visitors to my place too, because we share this hallway."

"So?"

"I don't want Tilly to have any of my social graph."

Sai rolled his eyes. "What do you have to hide?"

"That's not the point—"

"Yeah, yeah, civil liberties, freedom, privacy, blah blah blah . . ."

Sai was sick of arguing with people like Jenny. He had made the same point countless times: *Centillion is not some big, scary government. It's a private company, whose motto happens to be "Make things better!" Just because you want to live in the dark ages doesn't mean the rest of us shouldn't enjoy the benefits of ubiquitous computing.*

He dodged around her bulky frame to get to the stairs.

"Tilly doesn't just tell you what you want!" Jenny shouted. "She tells you what to *think*. Do you even know what you really want anymore?"

Sai paused for a moment.

"Do you?" she pressed.

What a ridiculous question. Just the kind of pseudo-intellectual antitechnology rant that people like her mistake for profundity.

He kept on walking.

"Freak," he muttered, expecting Tilly to chime in from his phone earpiece with some joke to cheer him up.

But Tilly said nothing.

Having Tilly around was like having the world's best assistant:
—"Hey, Tilly, do you remember where I kept that Wyoming

filing with the weird company name and the F merger from maybe six months ago?"

—"Hey, Tilly, can you get me a form for Section 131 Articles? Make sure it's a form that associates working with Singh use."

—"Hey, Tilly, memorize these pages. Assign them the tags: 'Chapman,' 'favors buyer,' 'only use if associate is nice to me.'"

For a while, Chapman Singh had resisted the idea of allowing employees to bring Tilly into the office, preferring their proprietary corporate AI system. But it proved too difficult to force employees to keep their personal calendars and recommendations rigidly separate from work ones, and once the partners started to violate the rules and use Tilly for work, IT had to support them.

And Centillion had then pledged that they would encrypt all corporate-derived information in a secure manner and never use it for competitive purposes—only to give better recommendations to employees of Chapman Singh. After all, the mission statement of Centillion was to "arrange the world's information to ennoble the human race," and what could be more ennobling than making work more efficient, more productive, more pleasant?

As Sai enjoyed his lunch, he felt very lucky. He couldn't even imagine what drudgery work would have been like before Tilly came along.

After work, Tilly guided Sai to the flower shop—of course Tilly had a coupon—and then, on the way to the restaurant, she filled Sai in on his date, Ellen: educational background, ShareAll profile, reviews by previous boyfriends/girlfriends, interests, likes, dislikes, and of course, pictures—dozens of photos recognized and gathered by Tilly from around the Net. Sai smiled. Tilly was right. Ellen was exactly his type.

It was a truism that what a man wouldn't tell his best friend, he'd happily search for on Centillion. Tilly knew all about what kind of women Sai found attractive, having observed the pictures and videos he perused late at nights while engaging the Just-for-Me mode in his browser.

And, of course, Tilly would know Ellen just as well as she knew him, so Sai knew that he would be exactly Ellen's type too.

As predicted, it turned out they were into the same books, the same movies, the same music. They had compatible ideas about how hard one should work. They laughed at each other's jokes. They fed off each other's energy.

Sai marveled at Tilly's accomplishment. Four billion women on Earth, and Tilly seemed to have found the perfect match for him. It was just like hitting the "I Trust You" button on Centillion search back in the early days and how it knew just the right web page to take you to.

Sai could feel himself falling in love, and he could tell that Ellen wanted to ask him to come home with her.

Although everything had gone exceedingly well, if he was being completely honest with himself, it wasn't *quite* as exciting and lovely as he had expected. Everything was indeed going smoothly, but maybe just a tad *too* smoothly. It was as if they already knew everything there was to know about each other. There were no surprises, no thrill of finding the truly new.

In other words, the date was a bit boring.

As Sai's mind wandered, there was a lull in the conversation. They smiled at each other and just tried to enjoy the silence.

In that moment, Tilly's voice burst into his earpiece. "You might want to ask her if she likes contemporary Japanese desserts. I know just the place."

Sai realized that though he hadn't been aware of it until just then, he did suddenly have a craving for something sweet and delicate.

Tilly doesn't just tell you what you want. She tells you what to think.

Sai paused.

Do you even know what you really want anymore?

He tried to sort out his feelings. Did Tilly just figure out what he hadn't even known he wanted? Or did she put the thought into his head?

Do you?

The way Tilly filled in that lull . . . it was as if Tilly didn't trust that he would be able to manage the date on his own, as if Tilly thought he wouldn't know what to say or do if she didn't jump in.

Sai suddenly felt irritated. The moment had been ruined.

I'm being treated like a child.

"I know you'll like it. I have a coupon."

"Tilly," he said, "please stop monitoring and terminate auto-suggestions."

"Are you sure? Gaps in sharing can cause your profile to be incomplete—"

"Yes, please cease."

With a beep, Tilly turned herself off.

Ellen stared at him, eyes and mouth wide open in shock.

"Why did you do that?"

"I wanted to talk to you alone, just the two of us." Sai smiled. "It's nice sometimes to just be ourselves, without Tilly, don't you think?"

Ellen looked confused. "But you know that the more Tilly knows, the more helpful she can be. Don't you want to be sure we don't make silly mistakes on a first date? We're both busy, and Tilly—"

"I know what Tilly can do. But—"

Ellen held up a hand, silencing him. She tilted her head, listening to her headset.

"I have the perfect idea," Ellen said. "There's this new club, and I know Tilly can get us a coupon."

Sai shook his head, annoyed. "Let's try to think of something to do without Tilly. Would you please turn her off?"

Ellen's face was unreadable for a moment.

"I think I should head home," she said. "Early workday tomorrow." She looked away.

"Did Tilly tell you to say that?"

She said nothing and avoided looking into his eyes.

"I had a great time," Sai added quickly. "Would you like to go out again?"

Ellen paid half the bill and did not ask him to walk her home.

With a beep, Tilly came back to life in his ear.

"You're being very antisocial tonight," Tilly said.

"I'm not antisocial. I just didn't like how you were interfering with everything."

"I have every confidence you would have enjoyed the rest of the date had you followed my advice."

Sai drove on in silence.

"I sense a lot of aggression in you. How about some kickboxing? You haven't gone in a while, and there's a twenty-four-hour gym coming up. Take a right here."

Sai drove straight on.

"What's wrong?"

"I don't feel like spending more money."

"You know I have a coupon."

"What exactly do you have against me saving my money?"

"Your savings rate is right on target. I simply want to make sure you're sticking to your regimen for consumption of leisure. If you oversave, you'll later regret that you didn't make the most of your youth. I've plotted the optimum amount of consumption you should engage in daily."

"Tilly, I just want to go home and sleep. Can you shut yourself off for the rest of the night?"

"You know that in order to make the best life recommendations, I need to have complete knowledge of you. If you shut me out of parts of your life, my recommendations won't be as accurate—"

Sai reached into his pocket and turned off the phone. The earpiece went silent.

When Sai got home, he saw that the light over the stairs leading up to his apartment had gone out, and several dark shapes skulked around the bottom.

"Who's there?"

Several of the shadows scattered, but one came toward him: Jenny.

"You're back early."

He almost didn't recognize her; this was the first time he'd heard her voice without the electronic filter she normally used. It sounded surprisingly . . . happy.

Sai was taken aback. "How did you know I was back early? You stalking me?"

Jenny rolled her eyes. "Why would I need to stalk you? Your phone automatically checks in and out of everywhere you go with a status message based on your mood. It's all on your ShareAll lifecast for anyone to see."

He stared at her. In the faint glow from the streetlights he could see that she wasn't wearing her thick winter coat or ski goggles or scarf. Instead, she was in shorts and a loose white T-shirt. Her black hair had been dyed white in streaks. In fact, she looked very pretty, if a bit nerdy.

"What, surprised that I *do* know how to use a computer?"

"It's just that you usually seem so . . ."

"Paranoid? Crazy? Say what's on your mind. I won't be offended."

"Where's your coat and goggles? I've never even seen you without them."

"Oh, I taped over your door camera so my friends could come for a visit tonight, so I'm not wearing them. I'm sorry—"

"You did what?"

"—and I came out here to meet you because I saw that you

turned off Tilly, not once, but *twice*. I'm guessing you're finally ready for the truth."

Stepping into Jenny's apartment was like stepping into the middle of a fishing net.

The ceiling, floor, and walls were all covered with a fine metal mesh, which glinted like liquid silver in the flickering light from the many large, high-definition computer monitors stacked on top of each other around the room, apparently the only sources of illumination.

Besides the monitors, the only other visible furniture appeared to be bookshelves—full of books (the paper kind, strangely enough). A few upside-down, ancient milk crates covered with cushions served as chairs.

Sai had been feeling restless, had wanted to do something strange. But he now regretted his decision to accept her invitation to come in. She was indeed eccentric, perhaps too much so.

Jenny closed the door and reached up and plucked the earpiece out of Sai's ear. Then she held out her hand. "Give me your phone."

"Why? It's already off."

Jenny's hand didn't move. Reluctantly, Sai took out his phone and gave it to her.

She looked at it contemptuously. "No removable battery. Just what you'd expect of a Centillion phone. They should call these things tracking devices, not phones. You can never be sure they're really off." She slipped the phone inside a thick pouch, sealed it, and dropped it on the desk.

"Okay, now that your phone is acoustically and electromagnetically shielded, we can talk. The mesh on the walls basically makes my apartment into a Faraday cage, so cellular signals can't get through. But I don't feel comfortable around a Centillion phone until I can put a few layers of shielding around it."

"I'm just going to say it. You are *nuts*. You think Centillion spies on you? Their privacy policy is the best in the business. Every bit of information they gather has to be given up by the user voluntarily, and it's all used to make the user's life better—"

Jenny tilted her head and looked at him with a smirk until he stopped talking.

"If that's all true, why did you turn Tilly off tonight? Why did you agree to come up here with me?"

Sai wasn't sure he himself knew the answers.

"Look at you. You've agreed to have cameras observe your every move, to have every thought, word, interaction recorded in some distant data center so that algorithms could be run over them, mining them for data that marketers pay for.

"Now you've got nothing left that's private, nothing that's yours and yours alone. Centillion owns all of you. You don't even know who you are anymore. You buy what Centillion wants you to buy; you read what Centillion suggests you read; you date who Centillion thinks you should date. But are you really happy?"

"That's an outdated way to look at it. Everything Tilly suggests to me has been scientifically proven to fit my taste profile, to be something I'd like."

"You mean some advertiser paid Centillion to pitch it at you."

"That's the point of advertising, isn't it? To match desire with satisfaction. There are thousands of products in this world that would have been perfect for me, but I might never have known about them. Just like there's a perfect girl out there for me, but I might never have met her. What's wrong with listening to Tilly so that the perfect product finds the perfect consumer, the perfect girl finds the perfect boy?"

Jenny chuckled. "I love how you're so good at rationalizing your state. I ask you again: If life with Tilly is so wonderful, why did you turn her off tonight?"

"I can't explain it," Sai said. He shook his head. "This is a mistake. I think I'll head home."

"Wait. Let me show you a few things about your beloved Tilly first," Jenny said. She went to the desk and started typing, bringing up a series of documents on a monitor. She talked as Sai tried to scan and get their gist.

"Years ago, they caught Centillion's traffic-monitoring cars sniffing all the wireless traffic from home networks on the streets they drove through. Centillion also used to override the security settings on your machine and track your browsing habits before they shifted to an opt-in monitoring policy designed to provide better 'recommendations.' Do you think they've really changed? They hunger for data about you—the more the better—and damned if they care about how they get it."

Sai flicked through the documents skeptically. "If this is all true, why hasn't anyone brought it up in the news?"

Jenny laughed. "First, everything Centillion did was arguably legal. The wireless transmissions were floating in public space, for example, so there was no violation of privacy. And the end-user agreement could be read to allow everything Centillion did to 'make things better' for you. Second, these days, how do you get your news except through Centillion? If Centillion doesn't want you to see something, you won't."

"So how did you find these documents?"

"My machine is connected to a network built on top of the Net, one that Centillion can't see inside. Basically, we rely on a virus that turns people's computers into relaying stations for us, and everything is encrypted and bounced around so that Centillion can't see our traffic."

Sai shook his head. "You're really one of those tinfoil-hat conspiracy theorists. You make Centillion sound like some evil repressive government. But it's just a company trying to make some money."

Jenny shook her head. "Surveillance is surveillance. I can never understand why some people think it matters whether it's the government doing it to you or a company. These days, Centillion is bigger than governments. Remember, it managed to topple three countries' governments just because they dared to ban Centillion within their borders."

"Those were repressive places—"

"Oh, right, and you live in the land of the free. You think Centillion was trying to promote freedom? They wanted to be able to get in there and monitor everyone and urge them to all consume more so that Centillion could make more money."

"But that's just business. It's not the same thing as evil."

"You say that, but that's only because you don't know what the world really looks like anymore, now that it's been remade in Centillion's image."

Although Jenny's car was heavily shielded liked her apartment, as she and Sai drove, she whispered anyway, as if she were afraid that their conversation would be overheard by people walking by on the sidewalk.

"I can't believe how decrepit this place looks," Sai said as she parked the car on the side of the street. The surface of the road was pockmarked with potholes, and the houses around them were in ill repair. A few had been abandoned and were falling apart. In the distance they could hear the fading sound of a police siren. This was not a part of Las Aldamas that Sai had ever been to.

"It wasn't like this even ten years ago."

"What happened?"

"Centillion noticed a certain tendency for people—some people, not all—to self-segregate by race when it came to where they wanted to live. The company tried to serve this need by prioritizing different real estate listings to searchers based on their race. Nothing illegal about what they were doing, since they were just satisfying a need and desire in their users. They weren't hiding any listings, just pushing them far down the list, and in any event, you couldn't ever pick apart their algorithm and prove that they were looking at race when it was just one out of hundreds of factors in their magical ranking formula.

"After a while, the process began to snowball, and the segregation got worse and worse. It became easier for the politicians to gerrymander districts based on race. And so here we are. Guess who got stuck in these parts of the town?"

Sai took a deep breath. "I had no idea."

"If you ask Centillion, they'll say that their algorithms just reflected and replicated the desire to self-segregate in some of their users, and that Centillion wasn't in the business of policing thoughts. Oh, they'd claim that they were actually increasing freedom by giving people just what they wanted. They'd neglect to mention that they were profiting off it through real estate commissions, of course."

"I can't believe no one ever says anything about this."

"You're forgetting again that everything you know now comes filtered through Centillion. Whenever you do a search, whenever you hear a news digest, it's been curated by Centillion to fit what it thinks you want to hear. Someone upset by the news isn't going to buy anything sold by the advertisers, so Centillion adjusts things to make it all okay.

"It's like we're all living in Oz's Emerald City. Centillion puts these thick green goggles over our eyes, and we all think everything is a beautiful shade of green."

"You're accusing Centillion of censorship."

"No. Centillion is an algorithm that's gotten out of hand. It just gives you more of what it thinks you want. And we—people like me—think that's the root of the problem. Centillion has put us in little bubbles, where all we see and hear are echoes of ourselves, and we become ever more stuck in our existing beliefs and exaggerated in our inclinations. We stop asking questions and accept Tilly's judgment on everything.

"Year after year, we become more docile and grow more wool for Centillion to shave off and grow rich with. But I don't want to live that way."

"And why are you telling me all this?"

"Because, neighbor, we're going to kill Tilly," Jenny said, giving Sai a hard look, "and you're going to help us do it."

Jenny's apartment, with all its windows tightly shut and curtained, felt even more stifling after the car ride. Sai looked around at the flickering screens showing dancing, abstract patterns, suddenly wary. "And just how are you planning to kill Tilly?"

"We're working on a virus, a cyber weapon, if you want to get all macho about it."

"What exactly would it do?"

"Since the lifeblood of Tilly is data—the billions of profiles Centillion has compiled on every user—that's how we have to take it down.

"Once inside the Centillion data center, the virus will gradually alter every user profile it encounters and create new, fake profiles. We want it to move slowly to avoid detection. But eventually, it will have poisoned the data so much that it will no longer be possible for Tilly to make creepy, controlling predictions about users. And if we do it slowly enough, they can't even go to backups because they'll be corrupted too. Without the data it's built up over the decades, Centillion's advertising revenue will dry up overnight, and poof, Tilly'll be gone."

Sai imagined the billions of bits in the cloud: his tastes, likes and dislikes, secret desires, announced intentions, history of searches, purchases, articles and books read, pages browsed.

Collectively, the bits made up a digital copy of him, literally. Was there anything that was a part of *him* that wasn't also up there in the cloud, curated by Tilly? Wouldn't unleashing a virus on that be like suicide, like murder?

But then he remembered how it had felt to have Tilly lead him by the nose on every choice, how he had been content, like a pig happily wallowing in his enclosure.

The bits were his, but not *him*. He had a will that could not be captured in bits. And Tilly had almost succeeded in making him forget that.

"How can I help?" Sai asked.

Sai woke to Miles Davis's rendition of "So What."

For a moment, he wondered if the memory of the night before wasn't a dream. It felt so good to be awake, listening to just the song he wanted to hear.

"Are you feeling better, Sai?" Tilly asked.

Am I?

"I thought I turned you off, Tilly, with a hardware switch."

"I was quite concerned that you stopped all Centillion access to your life last night and forgot to turn it back on. You might have missed your wake-up call. However, Centillion added a system-level fail-safe to prevent just such an occurrence. We thought most users such as yourself would want such an over-ride so that Centillion could regain access to your life."

"Of course," Sai said. *So it's impossible to turn Tilly off and keep her off. Everything Jenny said last night was true.* He felt a chill tingle on his back.

"There's a gap of about twelve hours during which I couldn't acquire data about you. To prevent degradation in my ability to help you, I recommend that you fill me in."

"Oh, you didn't miss much. I came home and fell asleep. Too tired."

"There appears to have been vandalism last night of the new security cameras you installed. The police have been informed. Unfortunately, the camera did not capture a good image of the perpetrator."

"Don't worry about it. There's nothing here worth stealing, anyway."

"You sound a bit down. Is it because of the date last night? It seems that Ellen wasn't the right match for you after all."

"Um, yeah. Maybe not."

"Don't worry: I know just the thing that will put you in a good mood."

Over the next few weeks, Sai found it extremely difficult to play his assigned role.

Maintaining the pretense that he still trusted Tilly was crucial, Jenny had emphasized, if their plan was to succeed. Tilly couldn't suspect anything was going on at all.

It seemed simple enough at first, but it was nerve-racking, keeping secrets from Tilly. Could she detect the tremors in his voice? Sai wondered. Could she tell that he was faking enthusiasm for the commercial consumption transactions she suggested?

Meanwhile, he also had a much bigger puzzle to solve before John P. Rushgore, Assistant General Counsel of Centillion, came to Chapman Singh in another week.

Chapman Singh is defending Centillion in a patent dispute with ShareAll, Jenny had said. *This is our opportunity to get inside Centillion's network. All you have to do is to get someone from Centillion to plug this into his laptop.*

And she had then handed him a tiny thumb drive.

Though he still hadn't figured out a plan for plugging the thumb drive into a Centillion machine, Sai was glad to have come to the end of another long day of guarding himself against Tilly.

"Tilly, I'm going jogging. I'll leave you here."

"You know that it's best to carry me with you," Tilly said. "I can track your heart rate and suggest an optimal route for you."

"I know. But I just want to run around on my own a bit, all right?"

"I'm growing quite concerned with your latest tendencies toward hiding instead of sharing."

"There's no tendency, Tilly. I just don't want you to be stolen if I get mugged. You know this neighborhood has become more unsafe lately."

And he turned off the phone and left it in his bedroom.

He closed the door behind him, made sure that the taped-over camera was still taped-over, and gently knocked on Jenny's door.

Getting to know Jenny was the oddest thing he'd ever done, Sai realized.

He couldn't count on Tilly to have made sure ahead of time that they would have topics to talk about. He couldn't rely on Tilly's always apropos suggestions when he was at a loss for words. He couldn't even count on being able to look up Jenny's ShareAll profile.

He was on his own. And it was exhilarating.

"How did you figure out everything Tilly was doing to us?"

"I grew up in China," Jenny said, wiping a strand of hair behind her ear. Sai found the gesture inexplicably endearing. "Back then, the government watched everything you did on the Network and made no secret of it. You had to learn how to keep the insanity at bay, to read between the lines, to speak without being overheard."

"I guess we were lucky, over here."

"No." And she smiled at his surprise. He was learning that she preferred to be contrarian, to disagree with him. He liked that about her. "You grew up believing you were free, which made it even harder for you to see when you weren't. You were like frogs in the pot being slowly boiled."

"Are there many like you?"

"No. It's hard to live off the grid. I've lost touch with my old friends. I have a hard time getting to know people because so much of their lives are lived inside Centillion and ShareAll. I can peek in on them once in a while through a dummy profile, but I can never *be* a part of their lives. Sometimes I wonder if I'm doing the right thing."

"You are," Sai said, and, though there was no Tilly to prompt him, he took Jenny's hand in his. She didn't pull away.

"I never really thought of you as my type," she said.

Sai's heart sank like a stone.

"But who thinks only in terms of 'types' except Tilly?" she said quickly, then smiled and pulled him closer.

Finally, the day had come. Rushgore had come to Chapman Singh to prepare for a deposition. He was huddled up with the firm's lawyers in one of their conference rooms all day long.

Sai sat down in his cubicle, stood up, and sat down again. He found himself full of nervous energy as he contemplated the best way to deliver the payload, as it were.

Maybe he could pretend to be tech support, there to perform an emergency scan of his system?

Maybe he could deliver lunch to him and plug the drive in slyly?

Maybe he could pull the fire alarm and hope that Rushgore would leave his laptop behind?

Not a single one of his ideas passed the laugh test.

"Hey." The associate who had been with Rushgore in the conference room all day was suddenly standing next to Sai's cubicle. "Rushgore needs to charge his phone—you got a Centillion charging cable over here?"

Sai stared at him, dumbfounded by his luck.

The associate held up a phone and waved it at him.

"Of course!" Sai said. "I'll bring one right to you."

"Thanks." The associate went back to the conference room.

Sai couldn't believe it. This was it. He plugged the drive into a charging cable and added an extension on the other end. The whole thing looked only a little odd, like a thin python that had swallowed a rat.

But suddenly he felt a sinking feeling in the pit of his stomach, and he almost swore aloud: He had forgotten to turn off the webcam above his computer—*Tilly's eyes*—before preparing the cable. If Tilly raised questions about the weird cable he was carrying, he would have no explanation, and then all his efforts at misdirection, at hiding, would be for naught.

But there was nothing he could do about it now but proceed as planned. As he left his cubicle, his heart was almost in his throat.

He stepped into the hallway and strode down to the conference room.

Still nothing from his earpiece.

He opened the door. Rushgore was too busy with his computer even to look up. He grabbed the cable from Sai and plugged one end into his computer and the other end into his phone.

And Tilly remained silent.

Sai woke to—what else?—"We Are the Champions."

The previous night of drinking and laughing with Jenny and her friends had been a blur, but he did remember coming home and telling Tilly, right before he fell asleep, "We did it! We won!"

Ah, if Tilly only knew what we were celebrating.

The music faded, stopped.

Sai stretched lazily, turned to his side, and stared into the eyes of four burly, very serious men.

"Tilly, call the police!"

"I'm afraid I can't do that, Sai."

"Why the hell not?"

"These men are here to help you. Trust me, Sai. You know I know just what you need."

When the strange men had appeared in his apartment, Sai had imagined torture chambers, mental hospitals, faceless guards parading outside of dark cells. He had not imagined that he

44

would be sitting across the table from Christian Rinn, Founder and Executive Chairman of Centillion, having white tea.

"You got pretty close," Rinn said. The man was barely in his forties and looked fit and efficient—*kind of like how I picture a male version of Tilly,* Sai thought. He smiled. "Closer than almost anyone."

"What was the mistake that gave us away?" Jenny asked.

She was sitting to Sai's left, and Sai reached out for her hand. They intertwined their fingers, giving each other strength.

"It was his phone, on that first night he visited you."

"Impossible. I shielded it. It couldn't have recorded anything."

"But you left it on your desk, where it could still make use of its accelerometer. It detected and recorded the vibrations from your typing. There's a very distinctive way we strike the keys on a keyboard, and it's possible to reconstruct what someone was typing based on the vibration patterns alone. It's an old technology we developed for catching terrorists and drug dealers."

Jenny cursed under her breath, and Sai realized that until that moment, on some level he still hadn't quite believed Jenny's paranoia.

"But I didn't bring my phone after that first day."

"True, but we didn't need it. After Tilly picked up what Jenny was typing, the right alert algorithms were triggered and we focused surveillance on you. We parked a traffic observation vehicle a block away and trained a little laser on Jenny's window. It was enough to record your conversations through the vibrations in the glass."

"You're a very creepy man, Mr. Rinn," Sai said. "And despicable too."

Rinn didn't seem bothered by this. "I think you might feel differently by the end of our conversation. Centillion was not the first company to stalk you."

Jenny's fingers tightened around Sai's. "Let him go. I'm the one you really want. He doesn't know anything."

Rinn shook his head and smiled apologetically. "Sai, did

you realize that Jenny moved into the apartment next to yours a week after we retained Chapman Singh to represent us in the suit against ShareAll?"

Sai didn't understand what Rinn was getting at, but he sensed that he would not like what he was about to find out. He wanted to tell Rinn to shut up, but he held his tongue.

"Curious, aren't you? You can't resist the pull of information. If it's possible, you always want to learn something new; we're hardwired that way. That's the drive behind Centillion, too."

"Don't believe anything he says," Jenny said.

"Would it surprise you to find out that the five other paralegals in your firm also had new neighbors move in during that same week? Would it also surprise you to learn that the new neighbors have all sworn to destroy Centillion, just like Jenny here? Tilly is very good at detecting patterns."

Sai's heart beat faster. He turned to Jenny. "Is this true? You planned from the start to use me? You got to know me just so you'd have a chance to deliver a virus?"

Jenny turned her face away.

"They know that there's no way to hack into our systems from the outside, so they had to sneak a trojan in. You were used, Sai. She and her friends guided you, led you by the nose, made you do things—just like they accuse *us* of doing."

"It's not like that," Jenny said. "Listen, Sai, maybe that was how it started. But life's full of surprises. I was surprised by you, and that's a good thing."

Sai let go of Jenny's hand and turned back to Rinn. "Maybe they *did* use me. But they're right. You've turned the world into a panopticon and all the people in it into obedient puppets that you nudge this way and that just so you'd make more money."

"You yourself pointed out that we were fulfilling desires, lubricating the engine of commerce in an essential way."

"But you also fulfill dark desires." He remembered again the abandoned houses by the side of the road, the pockmarked pavement.

"We unveil only the darkness that was already inside people," Rinn said. "And Jenny didn't tell you about how many child pornographers we've caught, how many planned murders we've stopped, or how many drug cartels and terrorists we've exposed. And all the dictators and strongmen we've toppled by filtering out their propaganda and magnifying the voices of those who oppose them."

"Don't make yourself sound so noble," Jenny said. "After you topple governments, you and the other Western companies get to move in and profit. You're just propagandists of a different ilk—for making the world flat, turning everywhere into copies of suburban America studded with malls."

"It's easy to be cynical like that," Rinn said. "But I'm proud of what we've done. If cultural imperialism is what it takes to make the world a better place, then we'll happily arrange the world's information to ennoble the human race."

"Why can't you just be in the business of neutrally offering up information? Why not go back to being a simple search engine? Why all the surveillance and filtering? Why all the manipulation?" Sai asked.

"There's no such thing as neutrally offering up information. If someone asks Tilly about the name of a candidate, should Tilly bring them to his official site or a site that criticizes him? If someone asks Tilly about 'Tiananmen,' should Tilly tell them about the hundreds of years of history behind the place or just tell them about June 4, 1989? The 'I Trust You' button is a heavy responsibility that we take very seriously.

"Centillion is in the business of organizing information, and that requires choices, direction, inherent subjectivity. What is important to you—what is true to you—is not as important or as true to others. It depends on judgment and ranking. To search for what matters to you, we must know all about you. And that, in turn, is indistinguishable from filtering, from manipulation."

"You make it sound so inevitable."

"It *is* inevitable. You think destroying Centillion will free you, whatever 'free' means. But let me ask you, can you tell me the requirements for starting a new business in the State of New York?"

Sai opened his mouth and realized that his instinct was to ask Tilly. He closed his mouth again.

"What's your mother's phone number?"

Sai resisted the urge to reach for his phone.

"How about you tell me what happened in the world yesterday? What book did you buy and enjoy three years ago? When did you start dating your last girlfriend?"

Sai said nothing.

"You see? Without Tilly, you can't do your job, you can't remember your life, you can't even call your mother. We are now a race of cyborgs. We long ago began to spread our minds into the electronic realm, and it is no longer possible to squeeze all of ourselves back into our brains. The electronic copies of yourselves that you wanted to destroy are, in a literal sense, actually you.

"Since it's impossible to live without these electronic extensions of ourselves, if you destroy Centillion, a replacement will just rise to take its place. It's too late; the genie has long left the bottle. Churchill said that we shape our buildings, and afterward our buildings shape us. We made machines to help us think, and now the machines think for us."

"So what do you want with us?" Jenny asked. "We won't stop fighting you."

"I want you to come and work for Centillion."

Sai and Jenny looked at each other. *"What?"*

"We want people who can see through Tilly's suggestions, detect her imperfections. For all that we've been able to do with AI and data mining, the Perfect Algorithm remains elusive. Because you can see her flaws, you'll be the best at figuring out what Tilly's still missing and where she's gone too far. It's the perfect match. You'll make her better, more compelling, so that Tilly will do a better job."

"Why would we do that?" Jenny asked. "Why would we want to help you run people's lives with a machine?"

"Because as bad as you think Centillion is, any replacement is likely worse. It was not a mere PR move that I made ennobling the human race the mission of this company, even if you don't agree with how I've gone about it.

"If we fail, who do you think will replace us? ShareAll? A Chinese company?"

Jenny looked away.

"And that is why we've gone to such extraordinary lengths to be sure that we have all the data we need to stop competitors as well as well-meaning, but naive, individuals like you from destroying all that Centillion has accomplished."

"What if we refuse to join you but tell the world what you've done?"

"No one would believe you. We will make it so that whatever you say, whatever you write, no one will ever find it. On the Net, if it can't be found by Centillion, it doesn't exist."

Sai knew that he was right.

"You thought Centillion was just an algorithm, a machine. But now you know that it's built by people—people like me, people like you. You've told me what I've done wrong. Wouldn't you rather be part of us so that you can try to make things better?

"In the face of the inevitable, the only choice is to adapt."

Sai closed the door of the apartment behind him. The camera overhead followed.

"Will Jenny be coming over tomorrow for dinner?" Tilly asked.

"Maybe."

"You really need to get her to start sharing. It will make planning much easier."

"I wouldn't count on it, Tilly."

"You're tired," Tilly said. "How about I order you some hot organic cider for delivery and then you go to bed?"

That does sound perfect.

"No," Sai said. "I think I prefer to just read for a while, in bed."

"Of course. Would you like me to suggest a book?"

"I'd rather you take the rest of the night off, actually. But first, set the wake-up song to Sinatra's 'My Way.'"

"An unusual choice, given your taste. Is this a one-time experiment or would you like me to incorporate it into your music recommendations for the future?"

"Just this once, for now. Good night, Tilly. Please turn yourself off."

The camera whirred, followed Sai to bed, and shut off.

But a red light continued to blink, slowly, in the darkness.

Good Hunting

Night. Half-moon. An occasional hoot from an owl.

The merchant and his wife and all the servants had been sent away. The large house was eerily quiet.

Father and I crouched behind the scholar's rock in the court-yard. Through the rock's many holes I could see the bedroom window of the merchant's son.

"Oh, Hsiao-jung, my sweet Hsiao-jung . . ."

The young man's feverish groans were pitiful. Half-deliri-ous, he was tied to his bed for his own good, but Father had left a window open so that his plaintive cries could be carried by the breeze far over the rice paddies.

"Do you think she really will come?" I whispered. Today was my thirteenth birthday, and this was my first hunt.

"She will," Father said. "A *hulijing* cannot resist the cries of the man she has bewitched."

"Like how the Butterfly Lovers cannot resist each other?" I thought back to the folk opera troupe that had come through our village last fall.

"Not quite," Father said. But he seemed to have trouble explaining why. "Just know that it's not the same."

I nodded, not sure I understood. But I remembered how the merchant and his wife had come to Father to ask for his help.

"How shameful!" the merchant had muttered. "He's not even nineteen. How could he have read so many sages' books and still fall under the spell of such a creature?"

"There's no shame in being entranced by the beauty and wiles of a hulijing," Father had said. "Even the great scholar Wong Lai once spent three nights in the company of one, and he took first place at the Imperial Examinations. Your son just needs a little help."

"You must save him," the merchant's wife had said, bowing like a chicken pecking at rice. "If this gets out, the matchmakers won't touch him at all."

A *hulijing* was a demon who stole hearts. I shuddered, worried if I would have the courage to face one.

Father put a warm hand on my shoulder, and I felt calmer. In his hand was Swallow Tail, a sword that had first been forged by our ancestor, General Lau Yip, thirteen generations ago. The sword was charged with hundreds of Daoist blessings and had drunk the blood of countless demons.

A passing cloud obscured the moon for a moment, throwing everything into darkness.

When the moon emerged again, I almost cried out.

There, in the courtyard, was the most beautiful lady I had ever seen.

She had on a flowing white silk dress with billowing sleeves and a wide, silvery belt. Her face was pale as snow, and her hair dark as coal, draping past her waist. I thought she looked like the paintings of great beauties from the Tang Dynasty the opera troupe had hung around their stage.

She turned slowly to survey everything around her, her eyes glistening in the moonlight like two shimmering pools.

I was surprised to see how sad she looked. Suddenly, I felt sorry for her and wanted more than anything else to make her smile.

The light touch of my father's hand against the back of my neck jolted me out of my mesmerized state. He had warned me about the power of the *hulijing*. My face hot and my heart hammering, I averted my eyes from the demon's face and focused on her stance.

The merchant's servants had been patrolling the courtyard every night this week with dogs to keep her away from her victim. But now the courtyard was empty. She stood still, hesitating, suspecting a trap.

"Hsiao-jung! Have you come for me?" The son's feverish voice grew louder.

The lady turned and walked—no, glided, so smooth were her movements—toward the bedroom door.

Father jumped out from behind the rock and rushed at her with Swallow Tail.

She dodged out of the way as though she had eyes on the back of her head. Unable to stop, my father thrust the sword into the thick wooden door with a dull thunk. He pulled but could not free the weapon immediately.

The lady glanced at him, turned, and headed for the courtyard gate.

"Don't just stand there, Liang!" Father called. "She's getting away!"

I ran at her, dragging my clay pot filled with dog piss. It was my job to splash her with it so that she could not transform into her fox form and escape.

She turned to me and smiled. "You're a very brave boy." A scent, like jasmine blooming in spring rain, surrounded me. Her voice was like sweet, cold lotus paste, and I wanted to hear her talk forever. The clay pot dangled from my hand, forgotten.

"Now!" Father shouted. He had pulled the sword free.

I bit my lip in frustration. *How can I become a demon hunter if I am so easily enticed?* I lifted off the cover and emptied the clay pot at her retreating figure, but the insane thought that I shouldn't dirty her white dress caused my hands to shake, and my aim was wide. Only a small amount of dog piss got onto her.

But it was enough. She howled, and the sound, like a dog's but so much wilder, caused the hairs on the back of my neck to stand up. She turned and snarled, showing two rows of sharp, white teeth, and I stumbled back.

I had doused her while she was in the midst of her transformation. Her face was thus frozen halfway between a woman's and a fox's, with a hairless snout and raised, triangular ears that twitched angrily. Her hands had turned into paws, tipped with sharp claws that she swiped at me.

She could no longer speak, but her eyes conveyed her venomous thoughts without trouble.

Father rushed by me, his sword raised for a killing blow. The *hulijing* turned around and slammed into the courtyard gate, smashing it open, and disappeared through the broken door.

Father chased after her without even a glance back at me. Ashamed, I followed.

The *hulijing* was swift of foot, and her silvery tail seemed to leave a glittering trail across the fields. But her incompletely transformed body maintained a human's posture, incapable of running as fast as she could have on four legs.

Father and I saw her dodging into the abandoned temple about a *li* outside the village.

"Go around the temple," Father said, trying to catch his breath. "I will go through the front door. If she tries to flee through the back door, you know what to do."

The back of the temple was overgrown with weeds and the wall half-collapsed. As I came around, I saw a white flash darting through the rubble.

Determined to redeem myself in my father's eyes, I swallowed my fear and ran after it without hesitation. After a few quick turns, I had the thing cornered in one of the monks' cells.

I was about to pour the remaining dog piss on it when I realized that the animal was much smaller than the *hulijing* we had been chasing. It was a small white fox, about the size of a puppy.

I set the clay pot on the ground and lunged.

The fox squirmed under me. It was surprisingly strong for

such a small animal. I struggled to hold it down. As we fought, the fur between my fingers seemed to become as slippery as skin, and the body elongated, expanded, grew. I had to use my whole body to wrestle it to the ground.

Suddenly, I realized that my hands and arms were wrapped around the nude body of a young girl about my age.

I cried out and jumped back. The girl stood up slowly, picked up a silk robe from behind a pile of straw, put it on, and gazed at me haughtily.

A growl came from the main hall some distance away, followed by the sound of a heavy sword crashing into a table. Then another growl, and the sound of my father's curses.

The girl and I stared at each other. She was even prettier than the opera singer that I couldn't stop thinking about last year.

"Why are you after us?" she asked. "We did nothing to you."

"Your mother bewitched the merchant's son," I said. "We have to save him."

"*Bewitched? He's* the one who wouldn't leave *her* alone."

I was taken aback. "What are you talking about?"

"One night about a month ago, the merchant's son stumbled upon my mother, caught in a chicken farmer's trap. She had to transform into her human form to escape, and as soon as he saw her, he became infatuated.

"She liked her freedom and didn't want anything to do with him. But once a man has set his heart on a *hulijing*, she cannot help hearing him no matter how far apart they are. All that moaning and crying he did drove her to distraction, and she had to go see him every night just to keep him quiet."

This was not what I learned from Father.

"She lures innocent scholars and draws on their life essence to feed her evil magic! Look how sick the merchant's son is!"

"He's sick because that useless doctor gave him poison that was supposed to make him forget about my mother. My mother is the one who's kept him alive with her nightly visits. And stop using the word *lure*. A man can fall in love with a *hulijing* just like he can with any human woman."

I didn't know what to say, so I said the first thing that came to mind. "I just know it's not the same."

She smirked. "Not the same? I saw how you looked at me before I put on my robe."

I blushed. "Brazen demon!" I picked up the clay pot. She remained where she was, a mocking smile on her face. Eventually, I put the pot back down.

The fight in the main hall grew noisier, and suddenly there was a loud crash, followed by a triumphant shout from Father and a long, piercing scream from the woman.

There was no smirk on the girl's face now, only rage turning slowly to shock. Her eyes had lost their lively luster; they looked dead.

Another grunt from Father. The scream ended abruptly.

"Liang! Liang! It's over. Where are you?"

Tears rolled down the girl's face.

"Search the temple," my father's voice continued. "She may have pups here. We have to kill them, too."

The girl tensed.

"Liang, have you found anything?" The voice was coming closer.

"Nothing," I said, locking eyes with her. "I didn't find anything."

She turned around and silently ran out of the cell. A moment later, I saw a small white fox jump over the broken back wall and disappear into the night.

It was *Qingming*, the Festival of the Dead. Father and I went to sweep Mother's grave and to bring her food and drink to comfort her in the afterlife.

"I'd like to stay here for a while," I said. Father nodded and left for home.

I whispered an apology to my mother, packed up the chicken we had brought for her, and walked the three *li* to the other side of the hill, to the abandoned temple.

I found Yan kneeling in the main hall, near the place where my father had killed her mother five years ago. She wore her hair up in a bun, in the style of a young woman who had had her *jijili*, the ceremony that meant she was no longer a girl.

We'd been meeting every *Qingming*, every *Chongyang*, every *Yulan*, every New Year's, occasions when families were supposed to be together.

"I brought you this," I said, and handed her the steamed chicken.

"Thank you." And she carefully tore off a leg and bit into it daintily. Yan had explained to me that the *hulijing* chose to live near human villages because they liked to have human things in their lives: conversation, beautiful clothes, poetry and stories, and, occasionally, the love of a worthy, kind man.

But the *hulijing* remained hunters who felt most free in their fox form. After what happened to her mother, Yan stayed away from chicken coops, but she still missed their taste.

"How's hunting?" I asked.

"Not so great," she said. "There are few Hundred-Year Salamanders and Six-Toed Rabbits. I can't ever seem to get enough to eat." She bit off another piece of chicken, chewed, and swallowed. "I'm having trouble transforming, too."

"It's hard for you to keep this shape?"

"No." She put the rest of the chicken on the ground and whispered a prayer to her mother.

"I mean it's getting harder for me to return to my true form," she continued, "to hunt. Some nights I can't do it at all. How's hunting for you?"

"Not so great either. There don't seem to be as many snake spirits or angry ghosts as a few years ago. Even hauntings by suicides with unfinished business are down. And we haven't had a proper jumping corpse in months. Father is worried about money."

We also hadn't had to deal with a *hulijing* in years. Maybe Yan had warned them all away. Truth be told, I was relieved. I didn't relish the prospect of having to tell my father that he was wrong about something. He was already very irritable, anxious that he was losing the respect of the villagers now that his knowledge and skill didn't seem to be needed as much.

"Ever think that maybe the jumping corpses are also misunderstood?" she asked. "Like me and my mother?"

She laughed as she saw my face. "Just kidding!"

It was strange, what Yan and I shared. She wasn't exactly a friend. More like someone who you couldn't help being drawn to because you shared the knowledge of how the world didn't work the way you had been told.

She looked at the chicken bits she had left for her mother. "I think magic is being drained out of this land."

I had suspected that something was wrong, but didn't want to voice my suspicion out loud, which would make it real.

"What do you think is causing it?"

Instead of answering, Yan perked up her ears and listened intently. Then she got up, grabbed my hand, and pulled until we were behind the buddha in the main hall.

"Wha—"

She held up her finger against my lips. So close to her, I finally noticed her scent. It was like her mother's, floral and sweet, but also bright, like blankets dried in the sun. I felt my face grow warm.

A moment later, I heard a group of men making their way into the temple. Slowly, I inched my head out from behind the buddha so I could see.

It was a hot day, and the men were seeking some shade from the noon sun. Two men set down a cane sedan chair, and the passenger who stepped off was a foreigner, with curly yellow hair and pale skin. Other men in the group carried tripods, levels, bronze tubes, and open trunks full of strange equipment.

"Most Honored Mister Thompson." A man dressed like a

mandarin came up to the foreigner. The way he kept on bowing and smiling and bouncing his head up and down reminded
me of a kicked dog begging for favors. "Please have a rest and
drink some cold tea. It is hard for the men to be working on the
day when they're supposed to visit the graves of their families,
and they need to take a little time to pray lest they anger the
gods and spirits. But I promise we'll work hard afterward and
finish the survey on time."

"The trouble with you Chinese is your endless superstition,"
the foreigner said. He had a strange accent, but I could understand him just fine. "Remember, the Hong Kong–Tientsin Railroad is a priority for Great Britain. If I don't get as far as Botou
Village by sunset, I'll be docking all your wages."

I had heard rumors that the Manchu Emperor had lost a
war and been forced to give up all kinds of concessions, one
of which involved paying to help the foreigners build a road of
iron. But it had all seemed so fantastical that I didn't pay much
attention.

The mandarin nodded enthusiastically. "Most Honored
Mister Thompson is right in every way. But might I trouble
your gracious ear with a suggestion?"

The weary Englishman waved impatiently.

"Some of the local villagers are worried about the proposed
path of the railroad. You see, they think the tracks that have
already been laid are blocking off veins of *qi* in the earth. It's
bad *feng shui*."

"What are you talking about?"

"It is kind of like how a man breathes," the mandarin said,
huffing a few times to make sure the Englishman understood.
"The land has channels along rivers, hills, ancient roads that
carry the energy of *qi*. It's what gives the villages prosperity
and maintains the rare animals and local spirits and household
gods. Could you consider shifting the line of the tracks a little,
to follow the *feng shui* masters' suggestions?"

Thompson rolled his eyes. "That is the most ridiculous thing

I've yet heard. You want me to deviate from the most efficient path for our railroad because you think your idols would be angry?"

The mandarin looked pained. "Well, in the places where the tracks have already been laid, many bad things are happening: people losing money, animals dying, household gods not responding to prayers. The Buddhist and Daoist monks all agree that it's the railroad."

Thompson strode over to the buddha and looked at it appraisingly. I ducked back behind the statue and squeezed Yan's hand. We held our breaths, hoping that we wouldn't be discovered.

"Does this one still have any power?" Thompson asked.

"The temple hasn't been able to maintain a contingent of monks for many years," the mandarin said. "But this buddha is still well respected. I hear villagers say that prayers to him are often answered."

Then I heard a loud crash and a collective gasp from the men in the main hall.

"I've just broken the hands off this god of yours with my cane," Thompson said. "As you can see, I have not been struck by lightning or suffered any other calamity. Indeed, now we know that it is only an idol made of mud stuffed with straw and covered in cheap paint. This is why you people lost the war to Britain. You worship statues of mud when you should be thinking about building roads from iron and weapons from steel."

There was no more talk about changing the path of the railroad.

After the men were gone, Yan and I stepped out from behind the statue. We gazed at the broken hands of the buddha for a while.

"The world's changing," Yan said. "Hong Kong, iron roads, foreigners with wires that carry speech and machines that belch smoke. More and more, storytellers in the teahouses speak of these wonders. I think that's why the old magic is leaving. A more powerful kind of magic has come."

She kept her voice unemotional and cool, like a placid pool

of water in autumn, but her words rang true. I thought about my father's attempts to keep up a cheerful mien as fewer and fewer customers came to us. I wondered if the time I spent learning the chants and the sword dance moves was wasted.

"What will you do?" I asked, thinking about her, alone in the hills and unable to find the food that sustained her magic.

"There's only one thing I *can* do." Her voice broke for a second and became defiant, like a pebble tossed into the pool.

But then she looked at me, and her composure returned. "There's only one thing *we* can do: learn to survive."

The railroad soon became a familiar part of the landscape: the black locomotive huffing through the green rice paddies, puffing steam and pulling a long train behind it, like a dragon coming down from the distant hazy, blue mountains. For a while it was a wondrous sight, with children marveling at it, running alongside the tracks to keep up.

But the soot from the locomotive chimneys killed the rice in the fields closest to the tracks, and two children playing on the tracks, too frightened to move, were killed one afternoon. After that, the train ceased to fascinate.

People stopped coming to Father and me to ask for our services. They either went to the Christian missionary or the new teacher who said he'd studied in San Francisco. Young men in the village began to leave for Hong Kong or Canton, moved by rumors of bright lights and well-paying work. Fields lay fallow. The village itself seemed to consist only of the too-old and too-young, their mood one of resignation. Men from distant provinces came to inquire about buying land for cheap.

Father spent his days sitting in the front room, Swallow Tail over his knee, staring out the door from dawn to dusk, as though he himself had turned into a statue.

Every day, as I returned home from the fields, I would see the glint of hope in Father's eyes briefly flare up.

"Did anyone speak of needing our help?" he would ask.

"No," I would say, trying to keep my tone light. "But I'm sure there will be a jumping corpse soon. It's been too long."

I would not look at my father as I spoke because I did not want to look as hope faded from his eyes.

Then, one day, I found Father hanging from the heavy beam in his bedroom. As I let his body down, my heart numb, I thought that he was not unlike those he had hunted all his life: They were all sustained by an old magic that had left and would not return, and they did not know how to survive without it.

Swallow Tail felt dull and heavy in my hand. I had always thought I would be a demon hunter, but how could I when there were no more demons, no more spirits? All the Daoist blessings in the sword could not save my father's sinking heart. And if I stuck around, perhaps my heart would grow heavy and yearn to be still too.

I hadn't seen Yan since that day six years ago, when we hid from the railroad surveyors at the temple. But her words came back to me now.

Learn to survive.

I packed a bag and bought a train ticket to Hong Kong.

The Sikh guard checked my papers and waved me through the security gate.

I paused to let my gaze follow the tracks going up the steep side of the mountain. It seemed less like a railroad track than a ladder straight up to heaven. This was the funicular railway, the tram line to the top of Victoria Peak, where the masters of Hong Kong lived and the Chinese were forbidden to stay.

But the Chinese were good enough to shovel coal into the boilers and grease the gears.

Steam rose around me as I ducked into the engine room. After five years, I knew the rhythmic rumbling of the pistons and the staccato grinding of the gears as well as I knew my own breath and heartbeat. There was a kind of music to their orderly cacophony that moved me, like the clashing of cymbals and gongs at the start of a folk opera. I checked the pressure, applied sealant on the gaskets, tightened the flanges, replaced the worn-down gears in the backup cable assembly. I lost myself in the work, which was hard and satisfying.

By the end of my shift, it was dark. I stepped outside the engine room and saw a full moon in the sky as another tram filled with passengers was pulled up the side of the mountain, powered by my engine.

"Don't let the Chinese ghosts get you," a woman with bright blonde hair said in the tram, and her companions laughed.

It was the night of *Yulan*, I realized, the Ghost Festival. *I should get something for my father, maybe pick up some paper money at Mongkok.*

"How can you be done for the day when we still want you?" a man's voice came to me.

"Girls like you shouldn't tease," another man said, and laughed.

I looked in the direction of the voices and saw a Chinese woman standing in the shadows just outside the tram station. Her tight western-style cheongsam and the garish makeup told me her profession. Two Englishmen blocked her path. One tried to put his arms around her, and she backed out of the way.

"Please. I'm very tired," she said in English. "Maybe next time."

"Now, don't be stupid," the first man said, his voice hardening. "This isn't a discussion. Come along now and do what you're supposed to."

I walked up to them. "Hey."

The men turned around and looked at me.

"What seems to be the problem?"

"None of your business."

"Well, I think it *is* my business," I said, "seeing as how you're talking to my sister."

I doubt either of them believed me. But five years of wrangling heavy machinery had given me a muscular frame, and they took a look at my face and hands, grimy with engine grease, and probably decided that it wasn't worth it to get into a public tussle with a lowly Chinese engineer.

The two men stepped away to get in line for the Peak Tram, muttering curses.

"Thank you," she said.

"It's been a long time," I said, looking at her. I swallowed the *you look good*. She didn't. She looked tired and thin and brittle. And the pungent perfume she wore assaulted my nose.

But I did not think of her harshly. Judging was the luxury of those who did not need to survive.

"It's the night of the Ghost Festival," she said. "I didn't want to work anymore. I wanted to think about my mother."

"Why don't we go get some offerings together?" I asked.

We took the ferry over to Kowloon, and the breeze over the water revived her a bit. She wet a towel with the hot water from the teapot on the ferry and wiped off her makeup. I caught a faint trace of her natural scent, fresh and lovely as always.

"You look good," I said, and meant it.

On the streets of Kowloon, we bought pastries and fruits and cold dumplings and a steamed chicken and incense and paper money, and caught up on each other's lives.

"How's hunting?" I asked. We both laughed.

"I miss being a fox," she said. She nibbled on a chicken wing absentmindedly. "One day, shortly after that last time we talked, I felt the last bit of magic leave me. I could no longer transform."

"I'm sorry," I said, unable to offer anything else.

"My mother taught me to like human things: food, clothes, folk opera, old stories. But she was never dependent on them. When she wanted, she could always turn into her true form and hunt. But now, in this form, what can I do? I don't have claws. I don't have sharp teeth. I can't even run very fast. All I have is

64

my beauty, the same thing that your father and you killed my mother for. So now I live by the very thing that you once falsely accused my mother of doing: I *lure* men for money."

"My father is dead too."

Hearing this seemed to drain some of the bitterness out of her. "What happened?"

"He felt the magic leave us, much as you. He couldn't bear it."

"I'm sorry." And I knew that she didn't know what else to say either.

"You told me once that the only thing we can do is to survive. I have to thank you for that. It probably saved my life."

"Then we're even," she said, smiling. "But let us not speak of ourselves anymore. Tonight is reserved for the ghosts."

We went down to the harbor and placed our food next to the water, inviting all the ghosts we had loved to come and dine. Then we lit the incense and burned the paper money in a bucket.

She watched bits of burned paper being carried into the sky by the heat from the flames. They disappeared among the stars. "Do you think the gates to the underworld still open for the ghosts tonight, now that there is no magic left?"

I hesitated. When I was young I had been trained to hear the scratching of a ghost's fingers against a paper window, to distinguish the voice of a spirit from the wind. But now I was used to enduring the thunderous pounding of pistons and the deafening hiss of high-pressured steam rushing through valves. I could no longer claim to be attuned to that vanished world of my childhood.

"I don't know," I said. "I suppose it's the same with ghosts as with people. Some will figure out how to survive in a world diminished by iron roads and steam whistles, some will not."

"But will any of them thrive?" she asked.

She could still surprise me.

"I mean," she continued, "are you happy? Are you happy to

keep an engine running all day, yourself like another cog? What do you dream of?"

I couldn't remember any dreams. I had let myself become entranced by the movement of gears and levers, to let my mind grow to fit the gaps between the ceaseless clanging of metal on metal. It was a way to not have to think about my father, about a land that had lost so much.

"I dream of hunting in this jungle of metal and asphalt," she said. "I dream of my true form leaping from beam to ledge to terrace to roof, until I am at the top of this island, until I can growl in the faces of all the men who believe they can own me."

As I watched, her eyes, brightly lit for a moment, dimmed.

"In this new age of steam and electricity, in this great metropolis, except for those who live on the Peak, is anyone still in their true form?" she asked.

We sat together by the harbor and burned paper money all night, waiting for a sign that the ghosts were still with us.

Life in Hong Kong could be a strange experience: From day to day, things never seemed to change much. But if you compared things over a few years, it was almost like you lived in a different world.

By my thirtieth birthday, new designs for steam engines required less coal and delivered more power. They grew smaller and smaller. The streets filled with automatic rickshaws and horseless carriages, and most people who could afford them had machines that kept the air cool in houses and the food cold in boxes in the kitchen—all powered by steam.

I went into stores and endured the ire of the clerks as I studied the components of new display models. I devoured every book on the principle and operation of the steam engine I could find. I tried to apply those principles to improve the machines I was in charge of: trying out new firing cycles, testing new kinds of lubricants for the pistons, adjusting the gear ratios. I found a measure of satisfaction in the way I came to understand the magic of the machines.

One morning, as I repaired a broken governor—a delicate bit of work—two pairs of polished shoes stopped on the platform above me.

I looked up. Two men looked down at me.

"This is the one," said my shift supervisor.

The other man, dressed in a crisp suit, looked skeptical. "Are you the man who came up with the idea of using a larger flywheel for the old engine?"

I nodded. I took pride in the way I could squeeze more power out of my machines than dreamed of by their designers.

"You did not steal the idea from an Englishman?" His tone was severe.

I blinked. A moment of confusion was followed by a rush of anger. "No," I said, trying to keep my voice calm. I ducked back under the machine to continue my work.

"He is clever," my shift supervisor said, "for a Chinaman. He can be taught."

"I suppose we might as well try," said the other man. "It will certainly be cheaper than hiring a real engineer from England."

Mr. Alexander Findlay Smith, owner of the Peak Tram and an avid engineer himself, had seen an opportunity. He foresaw that the path of technological progress would lead inevitably to the use of steam power to operate automata: mechanical arms and legs that would eventually replace the Chinese coolies and servants.

I was selected to serve Mr. Findlay Smith in his new venture.

I learned to repair clockwork, to design intricate systems of gears and devise ingenious uses for levers. I studied how to plate metal with chrome and how to shape brass into smooth curves. I invented ways to connect the world of hardened and ruggedized clockwork to the world of miniaturized and regulated piston and clean steam. Once the automata were finished, we connected them to the latest analytic engines shipped from Britain and fed them with tape punched with dense holes in Babbage-Lovelace code.

It had taken a decade of hard work. But now mechanical arms served drinks in the bars along Central and machine hands fashioned shoes and clothes in factories in the New Territories. In the mansions up on the Peak, I heard—though I'd never seen—that automatic sweepers and mops I designed roamed the halls discreetly, bumping into walls gently as they cleaned the floors like mechanical elves puffing out bits of white steam. The expats could finally live their lives in this tropical paradise free of reminders of the presence of the Chinese.

I was thirty-five when she showed up at my door again, like a memory from long ago.

I pulled her into my tiny flat, looked around to be sure no one was following her, and closed the door.

"How's hunting?" I asked. It was a bad attempt at a joke, and she laughed weakly.

Photographs of her had been in all the papers. It was the biggest scandal in the colony: not so much because the Governor's son was keeping a Chinese mistress—it was expected that he would—but because the mistress had managed to steal a large sum of money from him and then disappear. Everyone tittered while the police turned the city upside down, looking for her.

"I can hide you for tonight," I said. Then I waited, the unspoken second half of my sentence hanging between us.

She sat down in the only chair in the room, the dim light-bulb casting dark shadows on her face. She looked gaunt and exhausted. "Ah, now you're judging me."

"I have a good job I want to keep," I said. "Mr. Findlay Smith trusts me."

She bent down and began to pull up her dress.

"Don't," I said, and turned my face away. I could not bear to watch her try to ply her trade with me.

"Look," she said. There was no seduction in her voice. "Liang, look at me."

I turned and gasped.

Her legs, what I could see of them, were made of shiny chrome. I bent down to look closer: the cylindrical joints at the knees were lathed with precision, the pneumatic actuators along the thighs moved in complete silence, the feet were exquisitely molded and shaped, the surfaces smooth and flowing. These were the most beautiful mechanical legs I had ever seen.

"He had me drugged," she said. "When I woke up, my legs were gone and replaced by these. The pain was excruciating. He explained to me that he had a secret: he liked machines more than flesh, couldn't get hard with a regular woman."

I had heard of such men. In a city filled with chrome and brass and clanging and hissing, desires became confused.

I focused on the way light moved along the gleaming curves of her calves so that I didn't have to look into her face.

"I had a choice: let him keep on changing me to suit him, or he could remove the legs and throw me out on the street. Who would believe a legless Chinese whore? I wanted to survive. So I swallowed the pain and let him continue."

She stood up and removed the rest of her dress and her evening gloves. I took in her chrome torso, slatted around the waist to allow articulation and movement; her sinuous arms, constructed from curved plates sliding over each other like obscene armor; her hands, shaped from delicate metal mesh, with dark steel fingers tipped with jewels where the fingernails would be.

"He spared no expense. Every piece of me is built with the best craftsmanship and attached to my body by the best surgeons—there are many who want to experiment, despite the law, with how the body could be animated by electricity, nerves replaced by wires. They always spoke only to him, as if I was already only a machine.

"Then, one night, he hurt me and I struck back in desperation. He fell like he was made of straw. I realized, suddenly, how much strength I had in my metal arms. I had let him do all this to me, to replace me part by part, mourning my loss all the while without understanding what I had gained. A terrible thing had been done to me, but I could also be *terrible*.

"I choked him until he fainted, and then I took all the money I could find and left.

"So I come to you, Liang. Will you help me?"

I stepped up and embraced her. "We'll find some way to reverse this. There must be doctors—"

"No," she interrupted me. "That's not what I want."

It took us almost a whole year to complete the task. Yan's money helped, but some things money couldn't buy, especially skill and knowledge.

My flat became a workshop. We spent every evening and all of Sundays working: shaping metal, polishing gears, reattaching wires.

Her face was the hardest. It was still flesh.

I pored over books of anatomy and took casts of her face with plaster of Paris. I broke my cheekbones and cut my face so that I could stagger into surgeons' offices and learn from them how to repair these injuries. I bought expensive jeweled masks and took them apart, learning the delicate art of shaping metal to take on the shape of a face.

Finally, it was time.

Through the window, the moon threw a pale white parallelogram on the floor. Yan stood in the middle of it, moving her head about, trying out her new face.

Hundreds of miniature pneumatic actuators were hidden under the smooth chrome skin, each of which could be controlled independently, allowing her to adopt any expression. But her eyes were still the same, and they shone in the moonlight with excitement.

"Are you ready?" I asked.

She nodded.

I handed her a bowl filled with the purest anthracite coal, ground into a fine powder. It smelled of burned wood, of the heart of the earth. She poured it into her mouth and swallowed. I could hear the fire in the miniature boiler in her torso grow hotter as the pressure of the steam built up. I took a step back.

She lifted her head to the moon and howled: it was a howl made by steam passing through brass piping, and yet it reminded me of that wild howl long ago, when I first heard the call of a *hulijing*.

Then she crouched to the floor. Gears grinding, pistons pumping, curved metal plates sliding over each other—the noises grew louder as she began to transform.

She had drawn the first glimmers of her idea with ink on paper. Then she had refined it, through hundreds of iterations until she was satisfied. I could see traces of her mother in it, but also something harder, something new.

Working from her idea, I had designed the delicate folds in the chrome skin and the intricate joints in the metal skeleton. I had put together every hinge, assembled every gear, soldered every wire, welded every seam, oiled every actuator. I had taken her apart and put her back together.

Yet, it was a marvel to see everything working. In front of my eyes, she folded and unfolded like a silvery origami construction, until finally, a chrome fox as beautiful and deadly as the oldest legends stood before me.

She padded around the flat, testing out her sleek new form, trying out her stealthy new movements. Her limbs gleamed in the moonlight, and her tail, made of delicate silver wires as fine as lace, left a trail of light in the dim flat.

She turned and walked—no, glided—toward me, a glorious hunter, an ancient vision coming alive. I took a deep breath and smelled fire and smoke, engine oil and polished metal, the scent of power.

"Thank you," she said, and leaned in as I put my arms around her true form. The steam engine inside her had warmed her cold metal body, and it felt warm and alive.

"Can you feel it?" she asked.

I shivered. I knew what she meant. The old magic was back but changed: not fur and flesh, but metal and fire.

"I will find others like me," she said, "and bring them to you. Together, we will set them free."

Once, I was a demon hunter. Now, I am one of them.

I opened the door, Swallow Tail in my hand. It was only an old and heavy sword, rusty, but still perfectly capable of striking down anyone who might be lying in wait.

No one was.

Yan leapt out of the door like a bolt of lightning. Stealthily, gracefully, she darted into the streets of Hong Kong, free, feral, a *hulijing* built for this new age.

. . . *once a man has set his heart on a* hulijing, *she cannot help hearing him no matter how far apart they are.* . . .

"Good hunting," I whispered.

She howled in the distance, and I watched a puff of steam rise into the air as she disappeared.

I imagined her running along the tracks of the funicular railway, a tireless engine racing up, and up, toward the top of Victoria Peak, toward a future as full of magic as the past.

The Literomancer

September 18, 1961

Lilly Dyer anticipated and also dreaded three o'clock in the afternoon, more than any other moment of the day. That was when she returned home from school and checked the kitchen table for new mail.

The table was empty. But Lilly thought she'd ask, anyway. "Anything for me?"

"No," Mom said from the living room. She was giving English lessons to Mr. Cotton's new Chinese bride. Mr. Cotton worked with Dad and was important.

A full month had passed since Lilly's family moved to Taiwan, and no one from Clearwell, Texas, where she had been the third-most-popular girl in the fourth grade, had written to her, even though all the girls had promised that they would.

Lilly did not like her new school at the American military base. All of the other children's fathers were in the armed forces, but Dad worked in the city, in a building with the picture of Sun Yat-sen in the lobby and the red, white, and blue flag of the Republic of China flying on top. That meant Lilly was strange, and the other kids did not want to sit with her at lunch. Earlier that morning, Mrs. Wyle finally lectured them about their treatment of Lilly. That made things worse.

Lilly sat at her own table, quietly eating by herself. The other girls chattered at the next table.

"The Chinese whores are crafty, always hanging around the Base," Suzie Randling said. Suzie was the prettiest girl in

73

the class, and she always had the best gossip. "I heard Jennie's mom telling my mom that as soon as one gets her hands on an American soldier, she'll use her nasty tricks to hook him. She wants him to marry her so that she can steal all his money, and if he won't marry her, she'll make him sick."

The girls broke out in laughter. "When an American man rents a house for his family outside the Base, you can imagine what the husband is really chasing after," Jennie added darkly, trying to impress Suzie. The girls giggled, throwing looks over at Lilly. Lilly pretended not to hear.

"They are unbelievably dirty," Suzie said. "Mrs. Taylor was saying how when she took a car trip to Tainan during the summer, she couldn't eat any of the dishes the Chinese were serving her. One time they tried to give her some fried frog legs. She thought it was chicken and almost ate them. Disgusting!"

"My mom said that it's a real shame that you can't get any decent Chinese food except back in America," Jennie added.

"That's not true," Lilly said. As soon as she spoke up she regretted it. Lilly had brought *kòng-uân* pork balls and rice for lunch. Lin Amah, their Chinese maid, had packed the leftovers from dinner the night before. The pork balls were delicious, but the other girls wrinkled their noses at the smell.

"Lilly is eating smelly Chinaman slops again," Suzie said menacingly. "She really seems to like it."

"Lilly, Lilly, she's gonna have a stinky gook baby," the other girls began to chant.

Lilly had tried to not cry; she had almost succeeded.

Mom came into the kitchen and lightly stroked Lilly's hair. "How was school?"

Lilly knew that her parents must never know about what happened at school. They would try to help. That would only make things worse.

"Good," she said. "I'm just getting to know the girls." Mom nodded and went back into the living room.

She didn't want to go to her room. There was nothing to do

there after she had finished all the Nancy Drew books that she brought with her. She also didn't want to stay in the kitchen, where Lin Amah was cooking and would try to talk to her in her broken English. Lilly was mad at Lin Amah and her *kòng-uân* pork balls. She knew it was unfair, but she couldn't help herself. She wanted to get out of the house.

Rain earlier in the day had cooled off the humid subtropical air, and Lilly enjoyed a light breeze as she walked. She shook her red, curly hair out of the ponytail she wore for school, and she felt comfortable in a light blue tank top and a pair of tan shorts. West of the small Chinese-style farmhouse the Dyers were renting, the rice paddies of the village stretched out in neat grids. A few water buffalo lazed about in muddy wallows, gently scratching the rough, dark hide on their backs with their long, curved horns. Unlike the longhorns that she had been familiar with back home in Texas, whose long, thin horns curved dangerously forward, like a pair of swords, the water buffalos' horns curved backward, perfect for back scratching.

The largest and oldest one had his eyes closed and was half submerged in the water.

Lilly held her breath. She wanted to take a ride on him.

Back when she was a little girl and before Dad got his new job that was so secret that he couldn't even tell her what he did, Lilly had wanted to be a cowgirl. She envied her friends, whose parents were not from back East and thus knew how to ride, drive, and ranch. She was a regular at the county rodeos, and when she was five, by telling the man at the sign-up table that she had her mom's permission, she entered the mutton-busting competition.

She had held on to the bucking sheep for a full thrilling and terrifying twenty-eight seconds, a record that stunned the whole county. Her picture, showing her in a wide-brimmed cowboy hat with her tight ponytail flapping behind her, had been in all the newspapers. There was no fear on the face of the little girl in the picture, only wild glee and stubbornness.

"You were too stupid to be afraid," Mom had said. "What

in the world made you do a thing like that? You could have broken your neck."

Lilly did not answer her. She dreamed about that ride for months afterward. *Just hold on for another second,* she had told herself on the back of the sheep, *just hold on.* For those twenty-eight seconds, she wasn't just a little girl, whose day was filled with copybooks and chores and being told what to do. There was a clear purpose to her life and a clear way to accomplish it.

If she were older, she would have described that feeling as *freedom.*

Now, if she could ride the old water buffalo, maybe she'll get that feeling back and her day would be all right after all.

Lilly began to run toward the shallow wallow, where the old water buffalo was still obliviously chewing cud. Lilly got to the edge of the wallow and leapt toward the buffalo's back.

Lilly landed on the back of the buffalo with a soft thud, and the buffalo sank momentarily. She was prepared for bucking and lunging, and she kept her eyes on the long, curved horns, ready to grab them if the buffalo used them to try to pry her off. Adrenaline pumped through her, and she was determined to hold on for dear life.

Instead, the old buffalo, disturbed from his nap, simply opened his eyes and snorted. He turned his head and stared accusingly at Lilly with his left eye. He shook his head in disapproval, got up, and began to amble out of the wallow. The ride on the back of the buffalo was smooth and steady, like the way Dad used to carry Lilly on his shoulders when she was little.

Lilly grinned sheepishly. She patted the back of the buffalo's neck in apology.

She sat lightly, leaving the buffalo to choose his own path and watching the rows of rice stalks pass by her. The buffalo came to the end of the fields, where there was a clump of trees, and turned behind them. Here the ground dipped toward the bank of a river, and the buffalo walked toward it, where several Chinese boys about Lilly's age were playing and washing their families' water buffalo. As Lilly and the old buffalo approached them, the laughter among the boys died down, and one by one they turned to look at her.

Lilly became nervous. She nodded at the boys and waved. They didn't wave back. Lilly knew, in the way that all children know, that she was in trouble.

Suddenly something wet and heavy landed against Lilly's face. One of the boys had thrown a fistful of river mud at her.

"Adoah, adoah, adoah!" the boys shouted. And more mud flew at Lilly. Mud hit her face, her arms, her neck, her chest. She didn't understand what they were shouting, but the hostility and glee in their voices needed no translation. The mud stung her eyes, and she couldn't stop the tears that followed. She covered her face with her arms, determined not to give the boys the satisfaction of hearing her cry out.

"Ow!" Lilly couldn't help herself. A rock hit her shoulder, followed by another against her thigh. She tumbled down from the back of the buffalo and tried to hide behind him by crouching down, but the boys only chanted louder and circled around the buffalo to continue tormenting her. She began to grab fistfuls of mud from around her and threw them back at the boys, blindly, angrily, desperately.

"Kâu-gín-á, khòai-cháu, khòai-cháu!" An old man's voice, full of authority, came to her. The rain of mud stopped. Lilly wiped the mud from her face with her sleeves and looked up. The boys were running away. The old man's voice yelled at them some more, and the boys picked up their speed, their water buffalo following them at a more leisurely pace.

Lilly stood up and looked around her old buffalo. An elderly Chinese man stood a few paces away, smiling kindly at her. Beside him stood another boy about Lilly's age. As Lilly watched, the boy threw a pebble after the rapidly diminishing figures of the fleeing boys. His throw was strong, and the pebble arched high into the air, landing just behind the last boy as he rounded a copse of trees and disappeared. The boy grinned at Lilly, revealing two rows of crooked teeth.

"Little miss," the old man said in accented but clear English. "Are you all right?"

Lilly stared at her rescuers, speechless.

"What were you doing with Ah Huang?" the boy asked. The old water buffalo gently walked over to him, and the boy reached up to pat him on the nose.

"I . . . uh . . . I was riding him." Lilly's throat felt dry. She swallowed. "I'm sorry."

"They are not bad kids," the old man said, "just a little rowdy and suspicious of strangers. As their teacher, it is my fault that I did not teach them better manners. Please accept my apology for them." He bowed to Lilly.

Lilly awkwardly bowed back. As she bent down, she saw that her shirt and pants were covered with mud, and she felt the throbbing in her shoulder and legs, where she had been hit with rocks. She was going to get an earful from Mom; that was for sure. She could just imagine what a sight she must have made, covered in mud from hair to toe.

Lilly had never felt so alone.

"Let me help you clean up a little," the old man offered. They walked to the bank of the river, and the old man used a handkerchief to wipe the mud from Lilly's face and rinsed it out in the clear river water. His touch was gentle.

"I'm Kan Chen-hua, and this is my grandson, Ch'en Chia-feng."

"You can call me Teddy," the boy added. The old man chuckled.

"It's nice to meet you," Lilly said. "I'm Lillian Dyer."

"So what do you teach?"

"Calligraphy. I teach the children how to write Chinese

characters with a brush so that they don't frighten everyone, including their ancestors and wandering spirits, with their horrible chicken scratch."

Lilly laughed. Mr. Kan was not like any Chinese she had ever met. But her laugh did not last long. School was never far from her mind, and she knitted her brows as she thought about tomorrow.

Mr. Kan pretended not to notice. "But I also do some magic."

This piqued Lilly's interest. "What kind of magic?"

"I'm a literomancer."

"A *what*?"

"Grandpa tells people's fortunes based on the characters in their names and the characters they pick," Teddy explained.

Lilly felt as though she had walked into a wall of fog. She looked at Mr. Kan, not understanding.

"The Chinese invented writing as an aid to divination, so Chinese characters always had a deep magic to them. From characters, I can tell what's bothering people and what lies in their past and future. Here, I'll show you. Think of a word, any word."

Lilly looked around her. They were sitting on some rocks by the side of the river, and she could see that the leaves on the trees were starting to turn gold and red, and the rice stalks were heavy with grain, soon to be ready for the harvest.

"Autumn," she said.

Mr. Kan took a stick and wrote a character in the soft mud near their feet.

"You'll have to excuse the ugliness of writing with a stick in mud, but I don't have paper and brush with me. This is the character *ch'iu*, which means 'autumn' in Chinese."

"How do you tell my fortune from that?"

"Well, I have to take the character apart and put it back together. Chinese characters are put together from more Chinese characters, like building blocks. *Ch'iu* is composed of two other characters. The one on the left is the character *he*, which means 'millet' or 'rice' or any grain plant. Now, what you see there is stylized, but in ancient times, the character used to be written this way."

He drew on the mud.

"See how it looks like the drawing of a stalk bent over with the weight of a ripe head of grain on top?"

Lilly nodded, fascinated.

"Now, the right side of *ch'iu* is another character, *huo*, which means 'fire.' See how it looks like a burning flame, with sparks flying up?"

"In the northern part of China, where I'm from, we don't have rice. Instead, we grow millet, wheat, and sorghum. In autumn, after we've harvested and threshed out the grain, we pile the stalks in the fields and burn them so that the ashes will fertilize the fields for the coming year. Golden stalks and red flame, you put them together and you get *ch'iu*, autumn."

Lilly nodded, imagining the sight.

"But what does it tell me that you picked *ch'iu* as your character?" Mr. Kan paused in thought. He drew a few more strokes beneath *ch'iu*.

"Now, I've written the character for 'heart,' *hsin*, under *ch'iu*. It's a drawing of the shape of your heart. Together, they make a new character, *ch'ou*, and it means 'worry' and 'sorrow.'"

Lilly felt her heart squeeze, and suddenly everything looked blurry through her eyes. She held her breath.

"There's a lot of sorrow in your heart, Lilly, a lot of worry. Something is making you very, very sad."

Lilly looked up at his kind and wrinkled face, the neat white hair, and she walked over to him. Mr. Kan opened his arms and Lilly buried her face in his shoulders as he hugged her, lightly, gently.

As she cried, Lilly told Mr. Kan about her day at school, about the other girls and their chant, about the kitchen table empty of mail from friends.

"I'll teach you how to fight," Teddy said when Lilly had finished her story. "If you punch them hard enough, they won't bother you again."

Lilly shook her head. Boys were simple, and fists could do the talking for them. The magic of words between girls was much more complicated.

"There's a lot of magic in the word *gook*," Mr. Kan said after Lilly had wiped her tears and calmed down a little. Lilly looked up at him in surprise. She knew that the word was ugly and was afraid that he would be angry at hearing her say it, but Mr. Kan was not angry at all.

"Some people think that the word has a dark magic that can be used to slice into the hearts of the people of Asia and hurt them and those who would befriend them," Mr. Kan said. "But they do not understand its true magic. Do you know where the word comes from?"

"No."

"When American soldiers first went to Korea, they often heard the Korean soldiers say *miguk*. They thought the Koreans were saying 'me, gook.' But really they were talking about the Americans, and *miguk* means 'America.' The Korean word *guk* means 'country.' So when the American soldiers began calling the people of Asia 'gooks,' they didn't understand that they were in a way really just speaking about themselves."

"Oh," Lilly said. She wasn't sure how this information helped.

"I'll show you a bit of magic that you can use to protect yourself." Mr. Kan turned to Teddy. "Can I have that mirror that you use to tease the cats with?"

Teddy took out a small bit of glass from his pocket. It was broken from a larger mirror and the jagged edges had been wrapped in masking tape. Some Chinese characters had been written in ink on the masking tape.

"The Chinese have been using mirrors to ward off harm for millennia," Mr. Kan said. "Don't underestimate this little mirror. It has great magic in it. Next time, when the other girls tease you, bring out this mirror and shine it in their faces."

Lilly took the mirror. She didn't really believe what Mr. Kan was saying. He was kind and nice, but what he was saying sounded preposterous. Still, she needed a friend, and Mr. Kan and Teddy were the closest thing to friends she had on this side of the Pacific Ocean.

"Thank you," she said.

"Miss Lilly." Mr. Kan stood up and solemnly shook her hand. "When there is such a large gap of years between two friends, we Chinese call it *wang nien chih chiao*, a friendship that forgets the years. It's destiny that brings us together. I hope you will always think of me and Teddy as your friends."

Lilly explained her muddy appearance by blaming it all on Ah Huang, the "stubborn water buffalo" that she eventually subdued with her Texan cowgirl skills. Of course Mom was angry, seeing Lilly's ruined clothes. She gave Lilly a long lecture, and even Dad sighed and explained that her days of being a tomboy really needed to come to an end, now that she was a young lady. But on the whole, Lilly thought she had gotten off easy.

Lin Amah made Three-Cup Chicken, which was Dad's favorite. The sweet smell of sesame oil, rice wine, and soy sauce filled the kitchen and living room, and Lin Amah smiled and nodded as Mr. and Mrs. Dyer praised the food. She wrapped the leftovers into two rice balls and put them in the lunch box for Lilly. Lilly was apprehensive about bringing Three-Cup Chicken to lunch, but she fingered the mirror in her pocket and thanked Lin Amah.

"Good night," Lilly said to her parents, and went to her room.

In the hallway Lilly found a couple of sheets of paper lying on the floor. She picked them up and saw that they were filled with dense typescript:

have successfully sabotaged numerous factories, railroads, bridges, and other infrastructure. Agents have also assassinated several local ChiCom cadres. We have captured dozens of ChiCom individuals on these raids, and their interrogation yielded valuable intelligence concerning Red China's internal conditions. The covert program has been conducted with plausible deniability, and so far no elements of the US press have questioned our denials of ChiCom accusations of American involvement. (It should be noted that even if US involvement is revealed, we can legally justify our intervention under the Sino-American Mutual Defense Treaty as the ROC's sovereignty claims extend over all the territory of the PRC.)

Interrogations of ChiCom prisoners suggest that this program of harassment and terror, combined with the threat of an ROC invasion of the mainland, has pushed the ChiCom to further intensify internal repression and tighten domestic control. The ChiCom have increased military spending, and this likely has shifted scarce resources away from economic development and increased the suffering of the masses at a time when the PRC is experiencing great famines after the Great Leap Forward. As a result, there is a great deal of dissatisfaction with the regime.

President Kennedy has reoriented us toward a more confrontational stance with the ChiCom. I suggest that we weaken the PRC by all means short of all-out, general war. In addition to our continued support of ROC interdiction and harassment of PRC shipping and our support and direction of the insurgency in Tibet, we should increase our joint covert operations with the ROC in the PRC. I believe that by intensifying our covert operations against the ChiCom, we can force the ChiCom to curtail its support for North Viet Nam. In the best case, we may even provide the proverbial straw to break the camel's back, and successfully induce a domestic popular revolt to support a ChiNat invasion force from Taiwan and Burma. The Generalissimo is quite eager.

Should the PRC be provoked into a general war with us, it will be necessary to use atomic weapons to ensure the credibility of American resolve to our allies. The President should be prepared to manage popular perception in America and to induce our allies to accept atomic warfare as the means to victory.

At the same time, there is no question that the ChiCom would step up their efforts to infiltrate Taiwan and establish a network of agents and sympathizers within Taiwan. ChiCom propaganda and psywar techniques are not as sophisticated as ours, but appear to have been effective (at least in the past), especially among the native Taiwanese, by exploiting conflicts between the native-born <u>penshengjen</u> and the Nationalist <u>waishengjen</u>.

The maintenance of ChiNat morale is vital to our hold on Taiwan, the most vital link in the chain of islands that form the bulwark of American thalassocracy in the Western Pacific and the perimeter defense of the Free World. We must assist the ROC in counterespionage efforts on the island. Current ROC policy suppresses sensitive issues such as the so-called 228 Incident to avoid giving the ChiCom an opportunity to exploit <u>penshengjen</u> resentment, and we should give this policy our full support. We should also give all possible assistance to root out, suppress, and punish ChiCom agents, sympathizers, and other

They seemed to belong to Dad from work. Lilly stumbled over the many words that she didn't know, and finally stopped at "thalassocracy," whatever that meant. She quietly put the papers back down on the ground. Suzie Randling and tomorrow's lunch were far more pressing and worrisome to Lilly than whatever was typed on those sheets.

As expected, Suzie Randling and her gaggle of loyal lieutenants kept a watchful eye on Lilly as she sat at the other table with her back to the girls.

Lilly delayed taking out her lunch as long as she could, hoping that the girls would be distracted by their gossip and ignore her. She drank her juice and nibbled on the grapes that she brought for dessert, taking as long as she could, peeling the skin off each grape and carefully chewing on the sweet, juicy flesh inside.

But eventually, Lilly finished all the grapes. She willed her hands not to tremble as she took out the rice balls. She unwrapped the banana leaves from the first rice ball and bit into it. The sweet smell of sesame oil and chicken wafted across to the other table, and Suzie perked up right away.

"I smell Chinaman slops again," Suzie said. She sniffed the

air exaggeratedly. The corners of her mouth turned up in a nasty grin. She loved the way Lilly seemed to shrink and cower at her voice. She took pleasure in it.

Suzie and the flock of girls around her took up the chant from yesterday again. Laughter was in their voices, the laughter of girls drunk on power. There was desire in their eyes, a lust for blood, a craving to see Lilly cry.

Well, it won't hurt to try, Lilly thought.

She turned around to face the girls, and in her raised right hand was the mirror that Mr. Kan had given her. She turned the mirror to Suzie.

"What's that in your hand?" Suzie laughed, thinking that Lilly was offering something as tribute, a peace offering. Silly girl. What could she offer besides her tears?

Suzie looked into the mirror.

Instead of her beautiful face, she saw a pair of bloodred lips, grinning like a clown, and instead of a tongue, an ugly, wormy mess of tentacles writhed inside the mouth. She saw a pair of blue eyes, opened wide as teacups, filled half with hatred and half with surprise. It was easily the most ugly and frightening sight she had ever seen. She saw a monster.

Suzie screamed and covered her mouth with her hands. The monster in the mirror lifted a pair of hairy paws in front of its bloody lips, and the long, daggerlike claws seemed to reach out of the mirror.

Suzie turned around and ran, and the chant stopped abruptly, replaced by the screams of the other girls as they, too, saw the monster inside the mirror.

Later, Mrs. Wyle had to send a hysterical Suzie home. Suzie had insisted that Mrs. Wyle take the mirror from Lilly, but after a minute of careful examination, Mrs. Wyle concluded that the mirror was perfectly ordinary and handed it back to Lilly. She sighed as she tried to pen a note to Suzie's parents. She suspected that Suzie had made up the whole episode as a way to get out of school, but the girl was a good actress.

Lilly fingered the mirror in her pocket and smiled to herself as she sat through the afternoon's lessons.

"You are really good at baseball," Lilly said from her perch on top of Ah Huang.

Teddy shrugged. He was walking ahead of Ah Huang, leading him by the nose and carrying a baseball bat over this shoulder. He walked slowly, so that Lilly's ride was smooth.

Teddy was quiet, and Lilly was getting used to that. At first Lilly thought it was because his English wasn't as good as Mr. Kan's. But then she found that he spoke just as little to the other Chinese children.

Teddy had introduced her to the other kids from the village, some of whom had thrown mud at Lilly the day before. The boys nodded at Lilly, but then looked away, embarrassed.

They played a game of baseball. Only Teddy and Lilly knew all the rules, but all the children were familiar with it from watching the American soldiers at the Base nearby. Lilly loved baseball, and one of the things she missed the most about home was playing baseball with Dad and watching games together on TV. But since they moved to Taiwan, there were no more games on TV, and he no longer seemed to be able to find the time.

When it was Lilly's turn to bat, the pitcher, one of the boys from yesterday, lobbed her a soft and slow pitch that Lilly turned into a gentle groundball that rolled into right field. The outfielders ran over and suddenly all of them seemed to have trouble locating the ball in the grass. Lilly easily circled the bases.

Lilly understood that that was the way the boys apologized. She smiled at them and bowed, showing that all was forgiven. The boys grinned back at her.

"Grandpa would say, '*pu ta pu hsiang shih.*' It means that sometimes you can't become friends until you've fought each other."

Lilly thought that was a very good philosophy, but she doubted that it worked among girls.

Teddy was by far the best player among all the children. He was a good pitcher, but he was a great hitter. Every time he came up to bat, the opposing team fanned out, knowing that he would hit it way out.

"Someday, when I'm older, I'm going to move to America, and I'll play for the Red Sox," Teddy suddenly said, without looking back at Lilly on the water buffalo.

Lilly found the notion of a Chinese boy from Taiwan playing baseball for the Red Sox pretty ridiculous, but she kept herself from laughing because Teddy didn't seem to be joking. She was partial to the Yankees because her mother's family was from New York. "Why Boston?"

"Grandpa went to school in Boston," Teddy said.

"Oh." *That must be how Mr. Kan learned English,* Lilly thought.

"I wish I were older. Then I could have gotten to play with Ted Williams. Now I will never get to see him play in person. He retired last year."

There was such sadness in his voice that neither spoke for a few minutes. Only Ah Huang's loud, even breathing accompanied their silent walk.

Lilly suddenly understood something. "Is that why you call yourself Teddy?"

Teddy didn't answer, but Lilly could see that his face was red. She tried to distract him from his embarrassment. "Maybe he'll come back to coach someday."

"Williams was the best hitter ever. He'll definitely show me how to improve my swing. But the guy they replaced him with, Carl Yaz, is really good too. Me and Yaz, someday we'll beat the Yankees and take the Sox to the World Series."

Well, it is called the World Series, Lilly thought. *Maybe a Chinese boy will really make it.*

"That's a really grand dream," Lilly said. "I hope it happens."

"Thanks," Teddy said. "When I'm successful in America, I'll buy the biggest house in Boston, and Grandpa and I will live there. And I'll marry an American girl, because American girls are the best and prettiest."

"What's she going to look like?"

"Blonde." Teddy looked back at Lilly, riding on Ah Huang, with her loose red curls and hazel eyes. "Or red-haired," he added quickly, and turned his face away, flushed.

Lilly smiled.

As they walked past the other houses in the village, Lilly noticed that many of the houses had slogans painted on their walls and doors. "What do those signs say?"

"That one says, 'Beware of Communist bandit spies. It is everyone's responsibility to keep secrets.' That one over there says, 'Even if we by mistake kill three thousand, we can't let a single Communist spy slip through our fingers.' And that one over there says, 'Study hard and work hard, we must rescue our mainland brothers from the Red bandits.'"

"That's frightening."

"The Communists are scary," Teddy agreed. "Hey, that's my house down there. You want to come in?"

"Am I going to meet your parents?"

Teddy suddenly slumped his shoulders. "It's just Grandpa and me. He's not my real grandpa, you know. My parents died when I was just a baby, and Grandpa took me in as an orphan."

Lilly didn't know what to say. "How . . . how did your parents die?"

Teddy looked around them to make sure that no one was nearby. "They tried to leave a wreath on an empty lot on February 28, 1952. My uncle and aunt had died there back in 1947." He seemed to think that was all that needed to be said.

Lilly had no idea what he was talking about, but she couldn't probe any further. They had arrived at Teddy's home.

★ ★ ★ ★

The cottage was tiny. Teddy opened the door and showed Lilly in while he went to take care of Ah Huang. Lilly found herself standing in the kitchen. Through a doorway she could see a larger room—the only other room in the cottage, really—lined with tatami mats. That was evidently where Teddy and Mr. Kan slept.

Mr. Kan showed her to a seat by the small table in the kitchen and gave her a cup of tea. He was cooking something on the stove, and it smelled delicious.

"If you like," Mr. Kan said, "you are welcome to share some stew with us. Teddy likes it, and I think you would too. You'll have a hard time finding Mongolian-style mutton stewed in Shantung-style milkfish soup anywhere else in the world, ha-ha."

Lilly nodded. Her stomach growled as she breathed in the wonderful cooking fumes. She was feeling relaxed and comfortable.

"Thank you for the mirror. It worked." Lilly took out the mirror and put it on the table. "What do the words on the tape mean?"

"It's a quote from the *Analects*. Jesus said something that means exactly the same thing: 'Do unto others as you would have them do unto you.'"

"Oh." Lilly was disappointed. She was hoping that the words were some secret magical chant.

Mr. Kan seemed to know what Lilly was thinking about. "Magic words are often misunderstood. When those girls and you all thought 'gook' was a magic word, it held a kind of power. But it was an empty magic based on ignorance. Other words also hold magic and power, but they require reflection and thought."

Lilly nodded, not sure she really understood.

"Can we do more literomancy?" she asked.

"Sure." Mr. Kan put the lid on the pot and wiped his hands. He retrieved some paper, ink, and a brush. "What word would you like?"

"It would be more impressive if you can do it in English," said Teddy as he came into the kitchen.

"Yes, can you do it in English?" Lilly clapped her hands.

"I can try." Mr. Kan laughed. "This will be a first." He handed the brush to Lilly.

Lilly slowly wrote out the first word that came into her head, a word she didn't understand: *thalassocracy*.

Mr. Kan was surprised. "Oh, I don't know that word. This is going to be difficult." He frowned.

Lilly held her breath. *Was the magic not going to work in English?*

Mr. Kan shrugged. "Well, I'll just have to give it a try. Let's see . . . in the middle of the word is another word: 'lass.' That means you." He tipped the end of the brush toward Lilly. "The lass has an *o*, a circle of rope, trailing after her, and that makes 'lasso.' Hmm, Lilly, do you want to grow up to be a cowgirl?"

Lilly nodded, smiling. "I was born in Texas. We are born knowing how to ride."

"And what letters do we have left after 'lasso'? We have 'tha'-space-'cracy.' Hmm, if you rearrange them, you can spell 'Cathay,' with a *c* and an *r* left over. *C* is just a way to say 'sea,' and Cathay is an old name for China. But what is *r*?

"Ah, I've got it! The way you've written the *r*, it looks like a bird flying. So, Lilly, this means that you are the lass with a lasso who was destined to fly across the sea and come to China. Ha-ha! It was fate that we should be friends!"

Lilly clapped and laughed with joy and amazement.

Mr. Kan ladled out mutton and fish stew into two bowls for Teddy and Lilly. The stew was good, but very different from anything Lin Amah made. It was savory, smooth, laced with the sharp fresh scent of scallions. Mr. Kan watched the children eat and happily sipped his tea.

"You've found out a lot about me, Mr. Kan, but I don't know much about you."

"True. Why don't you pick another word? We'll see what the characters want you to know."

Lilly thought about it. "How about the word for America? You lived there, didn't you?"

Mr. Kan nodded. "Good choice." He wrote with his brush.

"This is *mei*. It's the character for 'beauty,' and America, *Meikuo*, is the Beautiful Country. See how it's composed of two characters stacked on top of each other? The one on the top means 'sheep.' Can you see the horns of the ram sticking up? The one on the bottom means 'great,' and it's shaped like a person standing up, legs and arms spread out, feeling like a big man."

Mr. Kan stood up to demonstrate.

"The ancient Chinese were a simple people. If they had a great, big, fat sheep, that meant wealth, stability, comfort, and happiness. They thought that was a beautiful sight. And now, in my old age, I understand how they felt." Lilly thought about mutton busting, and she understood too.

Mr. Kan sat down and closed his eyes as he continued.

"I come from a family of salt merchants in Shantung. We were considered wealthy. When I was a boy, people praised me for being clever and good with words, and my father hoped that I would do something great to glorify the Kan name. When I was old enough, he borrowed a large sum of money to send me to study in America. I chose to study law because I liked words and their power."

Mr. Kan wrote another character on the paper. "Let's see what I can tell you with more characters formed from 'sheep.'"

"The first time I had this stew, I was a law student in Boston. My friend and I, we shared a room together. We had no money, and every meal we ate nothing but bread and water. But this one time, our landlord, the owner of a restaurant in Chinatown, took pity on us. He gave us some rotting fish and mutton scraps that he was going to throw away. I knew how to make a good fish stew, and my friend, who was from Manchuria, knew how to make good Mongolian mutton.

"I thought, since the character for 'savory' is made from 'fish' and 'lamb,' maybe if we put our dishes together, it would taste pretty good. And it worked! I don't think we'd ever been that happy. Literomancy is even useful for cooking." Mr. Kan chuckled like a kid.

Then his face turned more serious.

"Later, in 1931, Japan invaded Manchuria, and my friend left America to defend his home. I heard that he became a Communist guerrilla to fight the Japanese, and the Japanese killed him a year later."

Mr. Kan sipped his tea. His hands trembled.

"I was a coward. I had a job then and a comfortable life in America. I was safe, and I did not want to go to war. I made excuses, telling myself that I could do more to help if I waited for the war to be over.

"But Japan was not content with Manchuria. A few years later, it invaded the rest of China, and one day I woke up to find that my hometown had been captured, and I stopped getting any letters from my family. I waited and waited, trying to reassure myself that they had escaped south and that everything was all right. But eventually, a letter from my baby sister arrived, bringing with it the news that the Japanese army had killed everyone in our clan, including our parents, when the town fell. My sister was the only one who survived by playing dead. Because I dithered, I had let my parents die.

"I left for China. I asked to sign up for the army as soon as I stepped off the boat. The Nationalist officer couldn't care less that I had gone to school in America. What China needed were men who could shoot, not men who knew how to read and write and could interpret the laws. I was given a gun and ten bullets, and told that if I wanted more bullets, I had to get them from the dead bodies."

Mr. Kan wrote another character on the paper.

"Here's another character also built from 'sheep.' It looks a lot like *mei*. I just changed the 'great' on the bottom a bit. Do you recognize it?"

Lilly thought back to the drawings from a day earlier. "That's the character for 'fire.'"

Mr. Kan nodded. "You are a very smart girl."

"So this is a character for roasting mutton over fire?"

"Yes. But when 'fire' is on the bottom of a character, usually we change its shape to show that it's cooking at low heat. Like this."

"Originally, roasted lamb was an offering to the gods, and this character, *kao*, came to mean lamb in general."

"Like a sacrificial lamb?"

Mr. Kan nodded. "I guess so. We had no training and no support, and we lost more than we won. Behind you, officers with machine guns would shoot you if you tried to run. In front of you, the Japanese charged at you with bayonets. When you used

94

up your bullets, you looked for more from your dead comrades. I wanted revenge for my dead family, but how could I get my revenge? I didn't even know which Japanese soldiers killed them.

"That was when I began to understand another kind of magic. Men spoke of the glory of *Japan* and the weakness of *China*, that *Japan* wants the best for Asia, and that *China* should accept what *Japan* wants and give up. But what do these words mean? How can '*Japan*' *want* something? 'Japan' and 'China' do not exist. They are just words, fiction. An individual Japanese may be glorious, and an individual Chinese may want something, but how can you speak of 'Japan' or 'China' *wanting, believing, accepting* anything? It is all just empty words, myths. But these myths have powerful magic, and they require sacrifices. They require the slaughter of men like sheep.

"When America finally entered the war, I was so happy. I knew that China was saved. Ah, see how powerful that magic is, that I can speak of these nonexistent things as though they are real. No matter. As soon as the war with Japan was over, I was told that we Nationalists now had to fight the Communists, who were our brothers-in-arms just days earlier against the Japanese. The Communists were evil and had to be stopped."

Mr. Kan wrote another character.

"This is the character *yi*, which used to mean 'righteousness,' and now also means '-ism,' as in Communism, Nationalism, Imperialism, Capitalism, Liberalism. It's formed from the character for 'sheep,' which you know, on top, and the character for 'I,' on the bottom. A man holds up a sheep for sacrifice, and he thinks he has truth, justice, and the magic that will save the world. It's funny, isn't it?

"But here's the thing. Even though the Communists had even worse equipment than we did, and less training, they kept on winning. I couldn't understand it until one day, my unit was ambushed by the Communists, and I surrendered and joined them. You see, the Communists really were bandits. They would take the land from the landlords and distribute it to the landless peasants, and this made them very popular. They couldn't care less about the fiction of laws and property rights. Why should they? The rich and educated had made a mess of things, so why shouldn't the poor and illiterate have a chance at it? No one before the Communists had ever thought much of the lowly peasants, but when you have nothing, not even shoes for your feet, you are not afraid to die. The world had many more people who were poor and therefore fearless than people who were rich and afraid. I could see the logic of the Communists.

"But I was tired. I had been fighting for almost a decade of my life, and I was alone in the world. My family had been rich, and the Communists would have killed them, too. I did not want to fight for the Communists, even if I could understand them. I wanted to stop. A few friends and I slipped away in the middle of the night and stole a boat. We were going to try to get to Hong Kong and leave all this slaughter behind.

"But we did not know navigation, and the waves took us into the open sea. We ran out of water and food and waited to die. But a week later, we saw land on the horizon. We rowed with our last bits of strength until we came ashore, and we found ourselves in Taiwan.

"We swore each other to secrecy about our time with the Communists and our desertion. We each went about our own ways, determined to never have to fight again. Because I was good with the abacus and the brush, I was hired by a Taiwanese couple who owned a small general store, and I kept their books and ran the place for them.

"Most of Taiwan had been settled by immigrants from Fukien several centuries earlier, and after Japan took Taiwan from

China in 1885, the Japanese tried to Japanize the island, much as they had done in Okinawa, and remake the *penshengjen* into loyal subjects of the Emperor. Many of the men fought in Japan's armies during the war. After Japan lost, Taiwan was to be given back to the Republic of China. The Nationalists came to Taiwan and brought a new wave of immigrants with them, the *waishengjen*. The *penshengjen* hated the Nationalist *waishengjen*, who took away the best jobs, and the Nationalist *waishengjen* hated the *penshengjen*, who had been traitors to their race during the war.

"I was working in the shop one day when a mob gathered in the streets. They shouted in Fukienese, and so I knew they were *penshengjen*. They stopped everyone they met, and if the person spoke Mandarin, they knew him to be a *waishengjen* and attacked him. There was no reasoning and no hesitation. They wanted blood. I was terrified and tried to hide under the counter."

"The character for 'mob' is formed from the character for 'nobility' on one side and the character for 'sheep' on the other. So that's what a mob is, a herd of sheep that turns into a pack of wolves because they believe themselves to be serving a noble cause.

"The *penshengjen* couple tried to protect me, saying that I was a good man. Someone in the mob shouted that they were traitors, and they attacked all of us and burned the shop down. I managed to crawl out of the fire, but the couple died."

"They were my uncle and aunt," Teddy said. Mr. Kan nodded and put a hand on his shoulder.

"The *penshengjen* rebellion began on February 28, 1947,

and lasted for months. Because some of the rebels were led by Communists, the Nationalists were especially brutal. It took the Nationalists a long time to finally put down the rebellion, and thousands were killed.

"In those killings a new kind of magic was born. Now, no one is allowed to talk about the 228 Massacre. The number 228 is taboo.

"I took Teddy in after his parents were executed for trying to commemorate that day. I came here, away from the city, so that I could live in a small cottage and drink my tea in peace. The villagers respect those who have read books, and they come to me to ask my advice on picking names for their children that will bring good fortune. Even after so many men died because of a few magic words, we continue to have faith in the power of words to do good.

"I have not heard from my baby sister for decades. I believe she is still alive on the mainland. Someday, before I die, I hope to see her again."

The three sat around the table, and no one said anything for a while. Mr. Kan wiped his eyes.

"I'm sorry to have told you such a sad story, Lilly. But the Chinese have not had happy stories to tell for a long time."

Lilly looked at the paper before Mr. Kan, filled with characters made from sheep. "Can you look into the future? Will there be good stories then?"

Mr. Kan's eyes brightened. "Good idea. What character should I write?"

"What about the character for China?"

Mr. Kan thought about this. "That's a difficult request, Lilly. 'China' may be a simple word in English, but it is not so easy in Chinese. We have many words for China and the people who call themselves Chinese. Most of these words are named after ancient dynasties, and the modern words are empty shells, devoid of real magic. What is the People's Republic? What is the Republic? These are not true words. Only more altars for sacrifices."

After thinking some more, he wrote another character.

"This is the character *hua*, and it is the only word for China and for the Chinese that has nothing to do with any Emperor, any Dynasty, anything that demands slaughter and sacrifice. Although both the People's Republic and the Republic put it in their names, it is far older than they and belongs to neither of them. *Hua* originally meant 'flowery' and 'magnificent,' and it is the shape of a bunch of wildflowers coming out of the ground. See?

"The ancient Chinese were called *huajen* by their neighbors because their dress was magnificent, made of silk and fine tulle. But I think that's not the only reason. The Chinese are like wildflowers, and they will survive and make joy wherever they go. A fire may burn away every living thing in a field, but after the rain the wildflowers will reappear as though by magic. Winter may come and kill everything with frost and snow, but when spring comes the wildflowers will blossom again, and they will be magnificent.

"For now, the red flames of revolution may be burning on the mainland, and the white frost of terror may have covered this island. But I know that a day will come when the steel wall of the Seventh Fleet will melt away, and the *penshengjen* and the *waishengjen* and all the other *huajen* back in my home will blossom together in magnificence."

"And I will be a *huajen* in America," Teddy added.

Mr. Kan nodded. "Wildflowers can bloom anywhere."

Lilly didn't have much of an appetite for dinner. She had had too much fish and mutton stew.

"Well, this Mr. Kan is no true friend of yours, if he's going to ruin your appetite with snacks," said Mom.

"It's all right," said Dad. "It's good for Lilly to make some native friends. You should invite them over for dinner sometime. Mom and I should get to know them if you are going to spend a lot of time with this family."

Lilly thought this a splendid idea. She couldn't wait to show Teddy her Nancy Drew books. She knew that he'd like the beautiful pictures on the covers.

"Dad, what does 'thalassocracy' mean?"

Dad paused. "Where did you hear that word?"

Lilly knew that she wasn't supposed to look at things from Dad's work. "I just read it somewhere."

Dad stared at Lilly, but then he relented. "It comes from the Greek word for sea, *thalassa*. It means 'rule by the sea.' You know, like 'Rule, Britannia! Rule the waves.'"

Lilly was disappointed at this. She thought Mr. Kan's explanation was much better, and said so.

"Why were you and Mr. Kan talking about thalassocracy?"

"No reason. I just wanted to see him do some magic."

"Lilly, there's no such thing as magic," Mom said.

Lilly wanted to argue but thought better of it.

"Dad, I don't understand why Taiwan is free if they can't talk about 228."

Dad put down his fork and knife. "What did you say?"

"Mr. Kan said that they can't talk about 228."

Dad pushed his plate away and turned to Lilly. "Now, from the beginning, tell me everything that you talked about with Mr. Kan today."

Lilly waited by the river. She was going to invite Teddy and Mr. Kan to come for dinner.

The village boys showed up, one after another, with their water buffalo. But none of them knew where Teddy was.

Lilly got into the river and joined the boys as they splashed water on each other. But she couldn't help feeling uneasy. Teddy always showed up at the river after school to wash Ah Huang. Where was he?

When the boys started to go back to the village, she went with them. *Maybe Teddy was sick and stayed home?*

Ah Huang was pacing in front of Mr. Kan's cottage, and he snorted at Lilly when he saw her, coming closer to nuzzle her as she petted his forehead.

"Teddy! Mr. Kan!" There was no answer.

Lilly knocked on the door. No one answered. The door was not locked, and Lilly pushed it open.

The cottage had been ransacked. The tatami mats were overturned and slashed apart. Tables and chairs were broken and the pieces scattered around the cottage. Pots, broken dishes, chopsticks littered the floor. There were papers and torn books everywhere. Teddy's baseball bat was carelessly lying on the ground.

Lilly looked down and saw that Mr. Kan's magic mirror had been shattered into a thousand little pieces scattered about her feet.

Did Communist bandits do this?

Lilly ran to the neighboring houses, frantically knocking on their doors and pointing at Mr. Kan's cottage. The neighbors either refused to answer the door or shook their heads, their faces full of fear.

Lilly ran home.

Lilly could not sleep.

Mom had refused to go to the police. Dad was working late, and Mom said if it wasn't just Lilly's imagination and there really were bandits about, then the best thing to do was to stay home and wait for Dad to come back. Eventually, Mom sent Lilly to bed because it was a school night, and she promised that she would tell Dad about Mr. Kan and Teddy. Dad would know what to do.

Lilly heard the front door open and close, and the sound of chairs sliding on the tile floor in the kitchen. Dad was home, and Mom was going to heat up some food for him.

She knelt up on her bed and opened the window. A cool, humid breeze carried the smell of decaying vegetation and night-blooming flowers into the room. Lilly crawled out the window.

Once she landed on the muddy ground, she quietly made her way around the house to the back, where the kitchen was. Inside, Lilly could see Mom and Dad sitting across from each other at the kitchen table. There was no food on the table. In front of Dad was a small glass, and he poured an amber liquid into it from a bottle. He drained the glass in one gulp and filled it again.

The bright, golden light inside the kitchen cast a trapezoid of illumination upon the ground outside the kitchen window. She stayed beyond its edge and crouched below the open window to listen.

Amid the sound of the fluttering wings of moths striking against the screened window, she listened to her father's voice

In the morning, David Cotton told me that the man I had referred to them had been arrested. If I wanted to, I could go help with the interrogation. I went over to the detention compound with two Chinese interrogators, Chen Pien and Li Hui.

"He's a tough nut to crack," Chen said. "We've tried a few things, but he's very resistant. We still have some heightened interrogation techniques we can try."

"The Communists are very good at psychological manipulation and resistance," I said. "It's not surprising. We need to get him to tell us who his accomplices are. I believe he came to Taiwan with a team of operatives."

We got to the holding cell, and I saw that they had worked him over pretty good. Both of his shoulders had been dislocated, and his face was bloody. His right eye was swollen almost completely shut.

I asked that he be given some medical attention. I wanted to have him understand that I was the kind one, and that I could protect him if he trusted me. They fixed his shoulders and a nurse bandaged his face. I gave him some water.

"I'm not a spy," he said, in English.

"Tell me what your orders were," I said.

"I don't have any orders."

"Tell me who came to Taiwan with you," I said.

"I came to Taiwan alone."

"I know that's a lie."

He shrugged, wincing with the pain.

I nodded to Chen and Li, and they started pushing small, sharpened bamboo sticks under his fingernails. He tried to stay silent. Chen began to hit the base of the bamboo sticks with a small hammer, as though he were hammering nails into a wall. The man screamed like an animal. Eventually he passed out.

Chen hosed him down with cold water until he woke up. I asked him the same questions. He shook his head, refusing to talk.

"We just want to talk to your friends," I said. "If they are innocent, nothing will happen to them. They won't blame you."

He laughed.

"Let's try the Tiger Bench," Li said.

They brought over a narrow long bench and laid one end against a supporting column in the room. They sat him down on the bench so that his back was straight against the column. Bending his arms back and wrapping them around the column, they tied his hands together. Then they strapped his thighs and knees down to the top of the bench with thick leather straps. Finally, they tied his ankles together.

"We'll see if Communists have knees that can bend forward," Chen said to him.

They lifted his feet and placed a brick under his heels, then another one.

Because his thighs and knees were strapped tight to the bench, the bricks forced his feet and lower legs up and began to bend his knees at an impossible angle. Sweat dripped from his face and forehead, mixed with the blood from his wounds. He tried to squirm along the bench to relieve the stress on his knees but there was nowhere to go. He rubbed his arms, moving them up and down helplessly on the column until he broke the skin on his wrists and arms and blood streaked the whitewash on the column.

They put in another two bricks, and I could hear the bones in his knees crack. He began to moan and shout, but said nothing that we wanted to hear.

"I can't stop this if you won't talk," I said to him.

They brought in a long wooden wedge and pushed the thin end under the brick at the bottom. Then they took turns to strike a hammer against the thick end of the wedge. With each strike, the wedge moved in a little under the bricks and lifted his feet higher. He screamed and screamed. They forced a stick into his mouth so he wouldn't bite down on his tongue.

"Just nod if you are ready to talk."

He shook his head.

Suddenly, his knees broke at the next hammer strike, and his feet and lower legs jumped up, the broken bones sticking through the flesh and skin. He fainted again.

I was getting nauseous. If the Communists could train and prepare their agents to this degree, how could we possibly hope to win this war?

"This is not going to work," I said to the Chinese interrogators. "I have an idea. He has a grandson. Do we have him?" They nodded.

We brought the doctor in again to bandage his legs. The doctor gave him an injection so that he would stay awake.

"Kill me, please," he said to me. "Kill me."

We brought him out to the courtyard and sat him in a chair. Li brought in his grandson. He was a small boy, but seemed very bright. He was scared and tried to run to his grandfather. Li pulled him back, stood him against the wall and pointed a pistol at him.

"We are not going to kill you," I said. "But if you won't confess, we will execute your grandson as an accomplice."

"No, no," he begged. "Please. He doesn't know anything. We don't know anything. I'm not a spy. I swear."

Li stood back and held the pistol with both hands.

"You are making me do this," I said. "You have given me no choice. I don't want to kill your grandson, but you are going to make him die."

"I came here on a boat with four others," he said. He kept his eyes on the boy, and I could see that I was finally getting to him. "They are all good people. None of us are Communist spies."

"That's another lie," I said. "Tell me who they are."

Just then the boy jumped and grabbed Li's hands, and the boy tried to bite him. "Let my grandfather go," he yelled as he struggled with Li.

There were two gunshots, and the boy fell in a heap. Li dropped his gun and I rushed over. The boy had bitten his finger to the bone, and he was howling with pain. I picked up the gun.

I looked up and saw that the old man had fallen out of his chair. He was crawling to us, to the body of his grandson. He was crying, and I couldn't tell what language he was crying in.

Chen went to help Li while I watched the man crawl to the boy. He turned his body until he was sitting and lifted the boy's body into his lap, hugging the dead child to his chest. "Why, why?" he said to me. "He was just a boy. He didn't know anything. Kill me, please kill me."

I looked into his eyes: dark, glistening, like mirrors. In them I saw the reflections of my own face, and it was such a strange face, so full of crazed fury that I did not recognize myself.

Many things went through my head at that moment. I thought back to when I was a little boy in Maine, and the mornings when my grandfather would take me hunting. I thought about my sinology professor, and the stories he told of his boyhood in Shanghai and his Chinese friends and servants. I thought about yesterday morning, when David and I taught the class on counterintelligence to the Nationalist agents. I thought about Lilly, who is about the boy's age. What does she know about Communism and freedom? Somewhere, the world had gone horribly wrong.

"Please kill me, please kill me."

I pointed the pistol at the man and squeezed the trigger. I kept on squeezing the trigger, again and again, after the gun was empty.

"He was resisting," Chen said, later. "Trying to escape." It wasn't a question.

I nodded anyway.

"You had no choice," Mrs. Dyer said. "He forced you to do it. Freedom isn't without its price. You were trying to do the right thing."

He did not respond to this. After a while, he drained the glass again.

"You've told me how hardened these Communist agents are, and we've all heard the tales from Korea. But only now do I really understand. They must have really brainwashed him and made him without human feeling, without remorse. The blood of his grandson is on him. Just think what he could have done to Lilly."

He did not respond to this either. He looked across the table at her, and it seemed that there was a gulf between them, as wide as the Taiwan Strait.

"I don't know," he said finally. "I don't really know anything anymore."

Dad walked with Lilly next to the river, their feet sinking into the soft mud. Both stopped and took off their shoes, continuing barefoot. They did not speak to each other. Ah Huang followed behind them, and every once in a while Lilly stopped to pet him on the nose as he snorted into her palm.

"Lilly." Dad broke the silence. "Mom and I have decided to move back to Texas. I've gotten a transfer for work."

Lilly nodded without speaking. Autumn had settled over her heart. The trees along the river waved at their own reflections in the moving, rippling water, and Lilly wished she still had Mr. Kan's magic mirror.

"We have to find a new home for your water buffalo. We can't take him back to Texas."

Lilly stopped. She refused to look at him.

"It's too dry back there," Dad tried. "He won't be happy. He won't have a river to bathe in and rice paddies to wallow in. He won't be free."

Lilly wanted to tell him that she was no longer a little girl, and he did not need to speak to her that way. But instead she just stroked Ah Huang some more.

"Sometimes, Lilly, adults have to do things that they don't want to do, because it's the right thing to do. Sometimes we do things that seem wrong, but are really right."

Lilly thought about Mr. Kan's arms, and the way he held her the first time they met. She thought about the way his voice had sounded when he scared the boys away. She thought about the way the tip of his brush moved on paper, writing the character for "beautiful." She wished that she knew how to write his name. She wished she knew more about the magic of words and characters.

Even though it was a pleasant autumn afternoon, Lilly felt cold. She imagined the fields around her covered in white, a frost of terror that had come to freeze over the subtropical island.

The word "freeze" seemed to call for her attention. She closed her eyes and pictured the word in her head, examining it carefully the way she thought Mr. Kan would have. The letters jiggled and nudged against each other. The z took on the shape of a kneeling, supplicating man, the e the fetal curl of a dead child. And then the z and e disappeared, leaving *free* in its place.

It's okay, Lilly. Teddy and I are free now. Lilly tried to concentrate, to hold on to the fading smile and warm voice of Mr. Kan in her mind. *You are a very smart girl. You are destined to become a literomancer too, in America.*

Lilly squeezed her eyes tight so that no tears would fall out.

"Lilly, are you all right?" Dad's voice brought her back.

She nodded. She felt a little warmer.

They continued to walk, looking at the hunched-over figures of the women in the rice paddies harvesting the heavy grain with sickles.

"It's difficult to know how the future will turn out," Dad continued. "Things have a way of working themselves out to the surprise of everyone. Sometimes the most ugly things can turn out to be the cause for something wonderful. I know you haven't had a good time here, Lilly, and it's unfortunate. But this is a beautiful island. Formosa means 'most beautiful' in Latin."

Like America, Meikuo, *the Beautiful Country,* Lilly thought. *The wildflowers will bloom again when it is spring.*

In the distance, they could see the children from the village playing a game of baseball.

"Someday you'll see that our sacrifices here were worth it. This place will be free, and you'll see its beauty and remember your time here fondly. Anything is possible. Maybe one day we'll even see a boy from here playing baseball in America. Now wouldn't that be something, Lilly, a Chinese boy from Formosa playing at Yankee Stadium?"

Lilly focused on the scene in her head.

Teddy steps up to the plate in a Red Sox helmet, his calm eyes staring at the pitcher on the mound, the N crossed with a Y on his cap. *He swings at the first pitch, and there is a crisp, loud thwack. It's a hit. The ball floats high into the cold October air, into the dark sky and the bright lights, an arc that will end somewhere in the grandstands beyond right field. The crowd stands. Teddy begins to trot along the baselines, his face breaking into a wide grin, searching the crowd for Mr. Kan and Lilly. And the wild cheers shake the stadium as the pennant is clinched. The Red Sox are going to the World Series.*

"I've been thinking," Dad continued. "Maybe we should take a vacation before we go back to Clearwell. I was thinking that we can stop by New York to visit Grandma. The Yankees are playing the Reds in the World Series. I'll try to get tickets, and we can go see them and cheer them on."

Lilly shook her head and looked up at him. "I don't like the Yankees anymore."

★ ★ ★ ★

Author's Notes

For a variety of reasons, this text does not use pinyin to romanize Chinese. Instead, Mandarin phrases and words are generally romanized using the Wade-Giles system, and Taiwanese Minnan (Fukienese) phrases and words are romanized using either the Pėh-ōe-jī system or English phonetic spelling.

An introductory account of the history of joint American-ROC covert operations against the PRC during the Cold War may be found in John W. Garver's *The Sino-American Alliance: Nationalist China and American Cold War Strategy in Asia.*

The art of literomancy is greatly simplified in this story. As well, the folk etymologies and decompositions used here are understood to have little relationship with academic conclusions.

Simulacrum

*[A] photograph is not only an image (as a painting is
an image), an interpretation of the real; it is also
a trace, something directly stenciled off the real,
like a footprint or a death mask.*
—SUSAN SONTAG

PAUL LARIMORE:

You are already recording? I should start? Okay.

Anna was an accident. Both Erin and I were traveling a lot for work, and we didn't want to be tied down. But you can't plan for everything, and we were genuinely happy when we found out. We'll make it work somehow, we said. And we did.

When Anna was a baby, she wasn't a very good sleeper. She had to be carried and rocked as she gradually drifted to sleep, fighting against it the whole time. You couldn't be still. Erin had a bad back for months after the birth, and so it was me who walked around at night with the little girl's head against my shoulder after feedings. Although I know I must have been very tired and impatient, all I remember now is how close I felt to her as we moved back and forth for hours across the living room, lit only by moonlight, while I sang to her.

I wanted to feel that close to her, always.

I have no simulacra of her from back then. The prototype machines were very bulky, and the subject had to sit still for hours. That wasn't going to happen with a baby.

This is the first simulacrum I *do* have of her. She's about seven.

—Hello, sweetheart.
—*Dad!*
—Don't be shy. These men are here to make a documentary movie about us. You don't have to talk to them. Just pretend they're not here.
—*Can we go to the beach?*
—You know we can't. We can't leave the house. Besides, it's too cold outside.
—*Will you play dolls with me?*
—Yes, of course. We'll play dolls as long as you want.

ANNA LARIMORE:

My father is a hard person for the world to dislike. He has made a great deal of money in a way that seems like an American fairy tale: Lone inventor comes up with an idea that brings joy to the world, and the world rewards him deservedly. On top of it all, he donates generously to worthy causes. The Larimore Foundation has cultivated my father's name and image as carefully as the studios airbrush the celebrity sex simulacra that they sell.

But I know the real Paul Larimore.

One day, when I was thirteen, I had to be sent home because of an upset stomach. I came in the front door, and I heard noises from my parents' bedroom upstairs. They weren't supposed to be home. No one was.

A burglar? I thought. In the fearless and stupid way of teenagers, I went up the stairs, and I opened the door.

My father was naked in bed, and there were four naked women with him. He didn't hear me, and so they continued what they were doing, there in the bed that my mother shared with him.

After a while, he turned around, and we looked into each other's eyes. He stopped, sat up, and reached out to turn off the projector on the nightstand. The women disappeared.

I threw up.

When my mother came home later that night, she explained to me that it had been going on for years. My father had a weakness for a certain kind of woman, she said. Throughout their marriage, he had trouble being faithful. She had suspected this was the case, but my father was very intelligent and careful, and she had no evidence.

When she finally caught him in the act, she was furious, and wanted to leave him. But he begged and pleaded. He said that there was something in his makeup that made real monogamy impossible for him. But, he said, he had a solution.

He had taken many simulacra of his conquests over the years, more and more lifelike as he improved the technology. If my mother would let him keep them and tolerate his use of them in private, he would try very hard to not stray again.

So this was the bargain that my mother made. He was a good father, she thought. She knew that he loved me. She did not want to make me an additional casualty of a broken promise that was only made to her.

And my father's proposal did seem like a reasonable solution. In her mind, his time with the simulacra was no different from the way other men used pornography. No touching was involved. They were not real. No marriage could survive if it did not contain some room for harmless fantasies.

But my mother did not look into my father's eyes the way I did when I walked in on him. It was more than a fantasy. It was a continuing betrayal that could not be forgiven.

★ ★ ★ ★

PAUL LARIMORE:

The key to the simulacrum camera is *not* the physical imaging process, which, while not trivial, is ultimately not much more than the culmination of incremental improvements on technologies known since the days of the daguerreotype.

My contribution to the eternal quest of capturing reality is the oneiropagida, through which a snapshot of the subject's mental patterns—a representation of her personality—could be captured, digitized, and then used to reanimate the image during projection. The oneiropagida is at the heart of all simulacrum cameras, including those made by my competitors.

The earliest cameras were essentially modified medical devices, similar to those legacy tomography machines you still see at old hospitals. The subject had to have certain chemicals injected into her body and then lie still for a long time in the device's imaging tunnel until an adequate set of scans of her mental processes could be taken. These were then used to seed AI neural models, which then animated the projections constructed from detailed photographs of her body.

These early attempts were very crude, and the results were described variously as robotic, inhuman, or even comically insane. But even these earliest simulacra preserved something that could not be captured by mere videos or holography. Instead of replaying verbatim what was captured, the animated projection could interact with the viewer in the way that the subject would have.

The oldest simulacrum that still exists is one of myself, now preserved at the Smithsonian. In the first news reports, friends and acquaintances who interacted with it said that although they knew that the image was controlled by a computer, they elicited responses from it that seemed somehow "Paul": "That's something only Paul would say" or "That's a very Paul facial expression." It was then that I knew I had succeeded.

ANNA LARIMORE:

People find it strange that I, the daughter of the inventor of simulacra, write books about how the world would be better off without them, more authentic. Some have engaged in tiresome pop psychology, suggesting that I am jealous of my "sibling," the invention of my father that turned out to be his favorite child.

If only it were so simple.

My father proclaims that he works in the business of capturing reality, of stopping time and preserving memory. But the real attraction of such technology has never been about capturing reality. Photography, videography, holography . . . the progression of such "reality-capturing" technology has been a proliferation of ways to lie about reality, to shape and distort it, to manipulate and fantasize.

People shape and stage the experiences of their lives for the camera, go on vacations with one eye glued to the video camera. The desire to freeze reality is about avoiding reality.

The simulacra are the latest incarnation of this trend, and the worst.

PAUL LARIMORE:

Ever since that day, when she . . . well, I expect that you have already heard about it from her. I will not dispute her version of events.

We have never spoken about that day to each other. What she does not know is that after that afternoon, I destroyed all the simulacra of my old affairs. I kept no backups. I expect that knowing this will not make any difference to her. But I would be grateful if you can pass this knowledge on to her.

Conversations between us after that day were civil, careful

performances that avoided straying anywhere near intimacy. We spoke about permission slips, the logistics of having her come to my office to solicit sponsors for walkathons, factors to consider in picking a college. We did not speak about her easy friendships, her difficult loves, her hopes for and disappointments with the world.

Anna stopped speaking to me completely when she went off to college. When I called, she would not pick up the phone. When she needed a disbursement from her trust to pay tuition, she would call my lawyer. She spent her vacations and summers with friends or working overseas. Some weekends she would invite Erin up to visit her in Palo Alto. We all understood that I was not invited.

—*Dad, why is the grass green?*
—It's because the green from the leaves on the trees drips down with the spring rain.
—*That's ridiculous.*
—All right, it's because the grass is on the other side of the fence. But if you were standing on the other side, it wouldn't look so green.
—*You are not funny.*
—Okay. It's because of chlorophyll in the grass. The chlorophyll has rings in it that absorb all colors of light except green.
—*You're not making this up, are you?*
—Would I ever make anything up, sweetheart?
—*It's very hard to tell with you sometimes.*

I began to play this simulacrum of her often when she was in high school, and over time it became a bit of a habit. Now I keep her on all the time, every day.

There were later simulacra when she was older, many of them with far better resolution. But this one is my favorite. It reminded me of better times, before the world changed irrevocably.

The day I took this, we finally managed to make an oneirop-agida that was small enough to fit within a chassis that could be carried on your shoulder. That later became the prototype for the Carousel Mark I, our first successful home simulacrum camera. I brought it home and asked Anna to pose for it. She stood still next to the sun porch for two minutes while we chatted about her day.

She was perfect in the way that little daughters are always perfect in the eyes of their fathers. Her eyes lit up when she saw that I was home. She had just come back from day camp, and she was full of stories she wanted to tell me and questions she wanted to ask me. She wanted me to take her to the beach to fly her new kite, and I promised to help her with her sunprint kit. I was glad to have captured her at that moment.

That was a good day.

ANNA LARIMORE:

The last time my father and I saw each other was after my mother's accident. His lawyer called, knowing that I would not have answered my father.

My mother was conscious, but barely. The other driver was already dead, and she was going to follow soon after.

"Why can't you forgive him?" she said. "I have. A man's life is not defined by one thing. He loves me. And he loves you."

I said nothing. I only held her hand and squeezed it. He came in and we both spoke to her but not to each other, and after half an hour she went to sleep and did not wake up.

The truth was, I was ready to forgive him. He looked old—a quality that children are among the last to notice about their parents—and there was a kind of frailty about him that made me question myself. We walked silently out of the hospital together. He asked if I had a place to stay in the city, and I said no. He opened the passenger-side door, and after hesitating for only a second, I slipped into his car.

We got home, and it was exactly the way I remembered it, even though I hadn't been home in years. I sat at the dinner table while he prepared frozen dinners. We spoke carefully to each other, the way we used to when I was in high school.

I asked him for a simulacrum of my mother. I don't take simulacra or keep them, as a rule. I don't have the same rosy view of them as the general public. But at that moment, I thought I understood their appeal. I wanted a piece of my mother to be always with me, an aspect of her presence.

He handed me a disk, and I thanked him. He offered me the use of his projector, but I declined. I wanted to keep the memory of my mother by myself for a while before letting the computer's extrapolations confuse real memories with made-up ones.

(And as things turned out, I've never used that simulacrum. Here, you can take a look at it later, if you want to see what she looked like. Whatever I remember of my mother, it's all real.)

It was late by the time we finished dinner, and I excused myself.

I walked up to my room.

And I saw the seven-year-old me sitting on my bed. She had on this hideous dress that I must have blocked out of my memory—pink, flowery—and there was a bow in her hair.

—*Hello, I'm Anna. Pleased to meet you.*

So he had kept this thing around for years, this naive, helpless caricature of me. During the time I did not speak to him, did he turn to this frozen trace of me and contemplate this shadow of my lost faith and affection? Did he use this model of my childhood to fantasize about the conversations that he could not have with me? Did he even edit it, perhaps, to remove my petulance, to add in more saccharine devotion?

I felt violated. The little girl was undeniably me. She acted like me, spoke like me, laughed and moved and reacted like me. But she was not *me*.

I had grown and changed, and I'd come to face my father as an adult. But now I found a piece of myself had been taken and locked into this *thing*, a piece that allowed him to maintain a sense of connection with me that I did not want, that was not real.

The image of those naked women in his bed from years ago came rushing back. I finally understood why for so long they had haunted my dreams.

It is the way a simulacrum replicates the essence of the subject that makes it so compelling. When my father kept those simulacra of his women around, he maintained a connection to them, to the man he was when he had been with them, and thus committed a continuing emotional betrayal that was far worse than a momentary physical indiscretion. A pornographic image is a pure visual fantasy, but a simulacrum captures a state of mind, a dream. But *whose* dream? What I saw in his eyes that day was not sordid. It was too intimate.

By keeping and replaying this old simulacrum of my childhood, he was dreaming himself into reclaiming my respect and love, instead of facing the reality of what he had done and the real me.

Perhaps it is the dream of every parent to keep their child in that brief period between helpless dependence and separate selfhood, when the parent is seen as perfect, faultless. It is a dream of control and mastery disguised as love, the dream that Lear had about Cordelia.

I walked down the stairs and out of the house, and I have not spoken to him since.

PAUL LARIMORE:

A simulacrum lives in the eternal now. It remembers, but only hazily, since the oneiropagida does not have the resolution to discern and capture the subject's every specific memory. It learns, up to a fashion, but the further you stray from the moment the subject's mental life was captured, the less accurate the computer's extrapolations. Even the best cameras we offer can't project beyond a couple of hours.

But the oneiropagida is exquisite at capturing her mood, the emotional flavor of her thoughts, the quirky triggers for her smiles, the lilt of her speech, the precise, inarticulable quality of her turns of phrase.

And so, every two hours or so, Anna resets. She's again coming home from day camp, and again she's full of questions and stories for me. We talk, we have fun. We let our chat wander wherever it will. No conversation is ever the same. But she's forever the curious seven-year-old who worshipped her father, and who thought he could do no wrong.

> —*Dad, will you tell me a story?*
> —Yes, of course. What story would you like?
> —*I want to hear your cyberpunk version of Pinocchio again.*
> —I'm not sure if I can remember everything I said last time.
> —*It's okay. Just start. I'll help you.*

I love her so much.

Erin Larimore:

My baby, I don't know when you'll get this. Maybe it will only be after I'm gone. You can't skip over the next part. It's a recording. I want you to hear what I have to say.

Your father misses you.

He's not perfect, and he has committed his share of sins, the same as any man. But you have let that one moment, when he was at his weakest, overwhelm the entirety of your life together. You have compressed him, the whole of his life, into that one frozen afternoon, that sliver of him that was most flawed. In your mind, you traced that captured image again and again, until the person was erased by the stencil.

During all these years when you have locked him out, your father played an old simulacrum of you over and over, laughing, joking, pouring his heart out to you in a way that a seven-year-old would understand. I would ask you on the phone if you'd speak to him, and then I couldn't bear to watch as I hung up while he went back to play the simulacrum again.

See him for who he really is.

—Hello there. Have you seen my daughter Anna?

The Regular

"This is Jasmine," she says.

"It's Robert."

The voice on the phone is the same as the one she had spoken to earlier in the afternoon.

"Glad you made it, sweetie." She looks out the window. He's standing at the corner, in front of the convenience store, as she asked. He looks clean and is dressed well, like he's going on a date. A good sign. He's also wearing a Red Sox cap pulled low over his brow, a rather amateurish attempt at anonymity. "I'm down the street from you, at 27 Moreland. It's the gray stone condo building converted from a church."

He turns to look. "You have a sense of humor."

They all make that joke, but she laughs, anyway. "I'm in unit twenty-four, on the second floor."

"Is it just you? I'm not going to see some linebacker type demanding that I pay him first?"

"I told you. I'm independent. Just have your donation ready, and you'll have a good time."

She hangs up and takes a quick look in the mirror to be sure she's ready. The black stockings and garter belt are new, and the lace bustier accentuates her thin waist and makes her breasts seem larger. She's done her makeup lightly, but the eye shadow is heavy to emphasize her eyes. Most of her customers like that. Exotic.

The sheets on the king-size bed are fresh, and there's a small wicker basket of condoms on the nightstand, next to a clock that says 5:58. The date is for two hours, and afterward she'll have enough time to clean up and shower and then sit in front of the TV to catch her favorite show. She thinks about calling her mom later that night to ask about how to cook porgy.

She opens the door before he can knock, and the look on his face tells her that she's done well. He slips in; she closes the door, leans against it, and smiles at him.

"You're even prettier than the picture in your ad," he says. He gazes into her eyes intently. "Especially the eyes."

"Thank you."

As she gets a good look at him in the hallway, she concentrates on her right eye and blinks rapidly twice. She doesn't think she'll ever need it, but a girl has to protect herself. If she ever stops doing this, she thinks she'll just have it taken out and thrown into the bottom of Boston Harbor, like the way she used to, as a little girl, write secrets down on bits of paper, wad them up, and flush them down the toilet.

He's good-looking in a nonmemorable way: over six feet, tanned skin, still has all his hair, and the body under that crisp shirt looks fit. The eyes are friendly and kind, and she's pretty sure he won't be too rough. She guesses that he's in his forties, and maybe works downtown in one of the law firms or financial services companies, where his long-sleeved shirt and dark pants make sense with the air-conditioning always turned high. He has that entitled arrogance that many mistake for masculine attractiveness. She notices that there's a paler patch of skin around his ring finger. Even better. A married man is usually safer. A married man who doesn't want her to know he's married is the safest of all: he values what he has and doesn't want to lose it.

She hopes he'll be a regular.

"I'm glad we're doing this." He holds out a plain white envelope.

She takes it and counts the bills inside. Then she puts it on top of the stack of mail on a small table by the entrance without saying anything. She takes him by the hand and leads him toward the bedroom. He pauses to look in the bathroom and then the other bedroom at the end of the hall.

"Looking for your linebacker?" she teases.

"Just making sure. I'm a nice guy."

He takes out a scanner and holds it up, concentrating on the screen.

"Geez, you *are* paranoid," she says. "The only camera in here is the one on my phone. And it's definitely off."

He puts the scanner away and smiles. "I know. But I just wanted to have a machine confirm it."

They enter the bedroom. She watches him take in the bed, the bottles of lubricants and lotions on the dresser, and the long mirrors covering the closet doors next to the bed.

"Nervous?" she asks.

"A little," he concedes. "I don't do this often. Or, at all."

She comes up to him and embraces him, letting him breathe in her perfume, which is floral and light, so that it won't linger on his skin. After a moment, he puts his arms around her, resting his hands against the naked skin on the small of her back.

"I've always believed that one should pay for experiences rather than things."

"A good philosophy," he whispers into her ear.

"What I give you is the girlfriend experience, old-fashioned and sweet. And you'll remember this and relive it in your head as often as you want."

"You'll do whatever I want?"

"Within reason," she says. Then she lifts her head to look up at him. "You have to wear a condom. Other than that, I won't say no to most things. But like I told you on the phone, for some you'll have to pay extra."

"I'm pretty old-fashioned myself. Do you mind if I take charge?"

He's made her relaxed enough that she doesn't jump to the

worst conclusion. "If you're thinking of tying me down, that will cost you. And I won't do that until I know you better."

"Nothing like that. Maybe hold you down a little."

"That's fine."

He comes up to her, and they kiss. His tongue lingers in her mouth, and she moans. He backs up, puts his hands on her waist, turning her away from him. "Would you lie down with your face in the pillows?"

"Of course." She climbs onto the bed. "Legs up under me or spread out to the corners?"

"Spread out, please." His voice is commanding. And he hasn't stripped yet, not even taken off his Red Sox cap. She's a little disappointed. Some clients enjoy the obedience more than the sex. There's not much for her to do. She just hopes he won't be too rough and leave marks.

He climbs onto the bed behind her and knee-walks up between her legs. He leans down and grabs a pillow from next to her head. "Very lovely," he says. "I'm going to hold you down now."

She sighs into the bed, the way she knows he'll like.

He lays the pillow over the back of her head and pushes down firmly to hold her in place. He takes the gun out from where it's hidden against the small of his back, and in one swift motion, sticks the barrel—thick and long with the silencer—into the back of the bustier and squeezes off two quick shots into her heart. She dies instantly.

He removes the pillow, stores the gun away. Then he takes a small steel surgical kit out of his jacket pocket, along with a pair of latex gloves. He works efficiently and quickly, cutting with precision and grace. He relaxes when he's found what he's looking for; sometimes he picks the wrong girl—not often, but it has happened. He's careful to wipe off any sweat on his face with his sleeves as he works, and the hat helps to prevent any hair from falling on her. Soon, the task is done.

He climbs off the bed, takes off the bloody gloves, and leaves them and the surgical kit on the body. He puts on a fresh pair of gloves and moves through the apartment, methodically searching for places where she hid cash: inside the toilet tank, the back of the freezer, the nook above the door of the closet.

He goes into the kitchen and returns with a large plastic trash bag. He picks up the bloody gloves and the surgical kit and throws them into the bag. Picking up her phone, he presses the button for her voice mail. He deletes all the messages, including the one he had left when he first called her number. There's not much he can do about the call logs at the phone company, but he can take advantage of that by leaving his prepaid phone somewhere for the police to find.

He looks at her again. He's not sad, not exactly, but he does feel a sense of waste. The girl was pretty, and he would have liked to enjoy her first, but that would leave behind too many traces, even with a condom. And he can always pay for another, later. He likes paying for things. Power flows to *him* when he pays.

Reaching into the inner pocket of his jacket, he retrieves a sheet of paper, which he carefully unfolds and leaves by the girl's head.

He stuffs the trash bag and the money into a small gym bag he found in one of the closets. He leaves quietly, picking up the envelope of cash next to the entrance on the way out.

Because she's meticulous, Ruth Law runs through the numbers on the spreadsheet one last time, a summary culled from credit card and bank statements, and compares them against the numbers on the tax return. There's no doubt. The client's husband has been hiding money from the IRS, and more importantly, from the client.

Summers in Boston can be brutally hot. But Ruth keeps the air conditioner off in her tiny office above a butcher shop in Chinatown. She's made a lot of people unhappy over the years, and there's no reason to make it any easier for them to sneak up on her with the extra noise.

She takes out her cell phone and starts to dial from memory. She never stores any numbers in the phone. She tells people it's for safety, but sometimes she wonders if it's a gesture, however small, of asserting her independence from machines.

She stops at the sound of someone coming up the stairs. The footfalls are crisp and dainty, probably a woman, probably one with sensible heels. The scanner in the stairway hasn't been set off by the presence of a weapon, but that doesn't mean anything—she can kill without a gun or knife, and so can many others.

Ruth deposits her phone noiselessly on the desk and reaches into her drawer to wrap the fingers of her right hand around the reassuring grip of the Glock 19. Only then does she turn slightly to the side to glance at the monitor showing the feed from the security camera mounted over the door.

She feels very calm. The Regulator is doing its job. There's no need to release any adrenaline yet.

The visitor, in her fifties, is in a blue short-sleeve cardigan and white pants. She's looking around the door for a button for the doorbell. Her hair is so black that it must be dyed. She looks Chinese, holding her thin, petite body in a tight, nervous posture.

Ruth relaxes and lets go of the gun to push the button to open the door. She stands up and holds out her hand. "What can I do for you?"

"Are you Ruth Law, the private investigator?" In the woman's accent, Ruth hears traces of Mandarin rather than Cantonese or Fukienese. Probably not well-connected in Chinatown, then.

"I am."

The woman looks surprised, as if Ruth isn't quite who she expected. "Sarah Ding. I thought you were Chinese."

As they shake hands, Ruth looks Sarah level in the eyes:

They're about the same height, five foot four. Sarah looks well maintained, but her fingers feel cold and thin, like a bird's claw.

"I'm half-Chinese," Ruth says. "My father was Cantonese, second generation; my mother was white. My Cantonese is barely passable, and I never learned Mandarin."

Sarah sits down in the armchair across from Ruth's desk. "But you have an office here."

She shrugs. "I've made my enemies. A lot of non-Chinese are uncomfortable moving around in Chinatown. They stick out. So it's safer for me to have my office here. Besides, you can't beat the rent."

Sarah nods wearily. "I need your help with my daughter." She slides a collapsible file across the desk toward her.

Ruth sits down but doesn't reach for the file. "Tell me about her."

"Mona was working as an escort. A month ago she was shot and killed in her apartment. The police think it's a robbery, maybe gang related, and they have no leads."

"It's a dangerous profession," Ruth says. "Did you know she was doing it?"

"No. Mona had some difficulties after college, and we were never as close as . . . I would have liked. We thought she was doing better the last two years, and she told us she had a job in publishing. It's difficult to know your child when you can't be the kind of mother she wants or needs. This country has different rules."

Ruth nods. A familiar lament from immigrants. "I'm sorry for your loss. But it's unlikely I'll be able to do anything. Most of my cases now are about hidden assets, cheating spouses, insurance fraud, background checks—that sort of thing. Back when I was a member of the force, I did work in Homicide. I know the detectives are quite thorough in murder cases."

"They're not!" Fury and desperation strain and crack her voice. "They think she's just a Chinese whore and she died because she was stupid or got involved with a Chinese gang who

127

wouldn't bother regular people. My husband is so ashamed that he won't even mention her name. But she's my daughter, and she's worth everything I have, and more."

Ruth looks at her. She can feel the Regulator suppressing her pity. Pity can lead to bad business decisions.

"I keep on thinking there was some sign I should have seen, some way to tell her that I loved her that I didn't know. If only I had been a little less busy, a little more willing to pry and dig and to be hurt by her. I can't stand the way the detectives talk to me, like I'm wasting their time but they don't want to show it."

Ruth refrains from explaining that the police detectives are all fitted with Regulators that should make the kind of prejudice she's implying impossible. The whole point of the Regulator is to make police work under pressure more regular, less dependent on hunches, emotional impulses, appeals to hidden prejudice. If the police are calling it a gang-related act of violence, there are likely good reasons for doing so.

She says nothing because the woman in front of her is in pain, and guilt and love are so mixed up in her that she thinks paying to find her daughter's killer will make her feel better about being the kind of mother whose daughter would take up prostitution.

Her angry, helpless posture reminds Ruth vaguely of something she tries to put out of her mind.

"Even if I find the killer," she says, "it won't make you feel better."

"I don't care." Sarah tries to shrug, but the American gesture looks awkward and uncertain on her. "My husband thinks I've gone crazy. I know how hopeless this is; you're not the first investigator I've spoken to. But a few suggested you because you're a woman and Chinese, so maybe you care just enough to see something they can't."

She reaches into her purse and retrieves a check, sliding it across the table to put on top of the file. "Here's eighty thousand dollars. I'll pay double your daily rate and all expenses. If you use it up, I can get you more."

Ruth stares at the check. She thinks about the sorry state of her finances. At forty-nine, how many more chances will she have to set aside some money for when she'll be too old to do this?

She still feels calm and completely rational, and she knows that the Regulator is doing its job. She's sure that she's making her decision based on costs and benefits and a realistic evaluation of the case, and not because of the hunched-over shoulders of Sarah Ding, looking like fragile twin dams holding back a flood of grief.

"Okay," she says. "Okay."

The man's name isn't Robert. It's not Paul or Matt or Barry, either. He never uses the name John, because jokes like that will only make the girls nervous. A long time ago, before he had been to prison, they had called him the Watcher, because he liked to observe and take in a scene, finding the best opportunities and escape routes. He still thinks of himself that way when he's alone.

In the room he's rented at the cheap motel along Route 128, he starts his day by taking a shower to wash off the night sweat.

This is the fifth motel he's stayed in during the last month. Any stay longer than a week tends to catch the attention of the people working at the motels. He watches; he does not get watched. Ideally, he supposes he should get away from Boston altogether, but he hasn't exhausted the city's possibilities. It doesn't feel right to leave before he's seen all he wants to see.

The Watcher got about sixty thousand dollars in cash from the girl's apartment, not bad for a day's work. The girls he picks are intensely aware of the brevity of their careers, and with no bad habits, they pack away money like squirrels preparing for the winter. Since they can't exactly put it into the bank without raising the suspicion of the IRS, they tuck the money away in stashes in their apartments, ready for him to come along and claim them like found treasure.

The money is a nice bonus, but not the main attraction.

He comes out of the shower, dries himself, and wrapped in a towel, sits down to work at the nut he's trying to crack. It's a small, silver half sphere, like half of a walnut. When he had first gotten it, it had been covered in blood and gore, and he had wiped it again and again with paper towels moistened under the motel sink until it gleamed.

He pries open an access port on the back of the device. Opening his laptop, he plugs one end of a cable into it and the other end into the half sphere. He starts a program he had paid a good sum of money for and lets it run. It would probably be more efficient for him to leave the program running all the time, but he likes to be there to see the moment the encryption is broken.

While the program runs, he browses the escort ads. Right now he's searching for pleasure, not business, so instead of looking for girls like Jasmine, he looks for girls he craves. They're expensive, but not too expensive, the kind that remind him of the girls he had wanted back in high school: loud, fun, curvaceous now but destined to put on too much weight in a few years, a careless beauty that was all the more desirable because it was fleeting.

The Watcher knows that only a poor man like he had been at seventeen would bother courting women, trying desperately to make them like him. A man with money, with power, like he is now, can buy what he wants. There's purity and cleanliness to his desire that he feels is nobler and less deceitful than the desire of poor men. They only wish they could have what he does.

The program beeps, and he switches back to it.

Success.

Images, videos, sound recordings are being downloaded onto the computer.

The Watcher browses through the pictures and video recordings. The pictures are face shots or shots of money being handed over—he immediately deletes the ones of him.

But the videos are the best. He settles back and watches the screen flicker, admiring Jasmine's camera work.

He separates the videos and images by client and puts them into folders. It's tedious work, but he enjoys it.

The first thing Ruth does with the money is to get some badly needed tune-ups. Going after a killer requires that she be in top condition.

She does not like to carry a gun when she's on the job. A man in a sport coat with a gun concealed under it can blend into almost any situation, but a woman wearing the kind of clothes that would hide a gun would often stick out like a sore thumb. Keeping a gun in a purse is a terrible idea. It creates a false sense of security, but a purse can be easily snatched away, and then she would be disarmed.

She's fit and strong for her age, but her opponents are almost always taller and heavier and stronger. She's learned to compensate for these disadvantages by being more alert and by striking earlier.

But it's still not enough.

She goes to her doctor. Not the one on her HMO card.

Doctor B had earned his degree in another country and then had to leave home forever because he pissed off the wrong people. Instead of doing a second residency and becoming licensed here, which would have made him easily traceable, he had decided to simply keep on practicing medicine on his own. He would do things doctors who cared about their licenses wouldn't do. He would take patients they wouldn't touch.

"It's been a while," Doctor B says.

"Check over everything," she tells him. "And replace what needs replacement."

"Rich uncle die?"

"I'm going on a hunt."

Doctor B nods and puts her under.

He checks the pneumatic pistons in her legs, the replacement composite tendons in her shoulders and arms, the power cells and artificial muscles in her arms, the reinforced finger bones. He recharges what needs to be recharged. He examines the results of the calcium-deposition treatments (a counter to the fragility of her bones, an unfortunate side effect of her Asian heritage), and makes adjustments to her Regulator so that she can keep it on for longer.

"Like new," he tells her. And she pays.

Next, Ruth looks through the file Sarah brought.

There are photographs: the prom, high school graduation, vacations with friends, college commencement. She notes the name of the school without surprise or sorrow, even though Jess had dreamed of going there as well. The Regulator, as always, keeps her equanimous, receptive to information, only useful information.

The last family photo Sarah selected was taken at Mona's twenty-fourth birthday earlier in the year. Ruth examines it carefully. In the picture, Mona is seated between Sarah and her husband, her arms around her parents in a gesture of careless joy. There's no hint of the secret she was keeping from them, and no sign, as far as Ruth can tell, of bruises, drugs, or other indications that life was slipping out of her control.

Sarah had chosen the photos with care. The pictures are designed to fill in Mona's life, to make people care for her. But she didn't need to do that. Ruth would have given it the same amount of effort, even if she knew nothing about the girl's life. She's a professional.

There's a copy of the police report and the autopsy results. The report mostly confirms what Ruth has already guessed: no sign of drugs in Mona's systems, no forced entry, no indication there was a struggle. There was pepper spray in the drawer of the nightstand, but it hadn't been used. Forensics had vacuumed the scene, and the hair and skin cells of dozens, maybe hundreds, of men had turned up, guaranteeing that no useful leads will result.

Mona had been killed with two shots through the heart, and then her body had been mutilated, with her eyes removed. She hadn't been sexually assaulted. The apartment had been ransacked of cash and valuables.

Ruth sits up. The method of killing is odd. If the killer had intended to mutilate her face, anyway, there was no reason not to shoot her in the back of the head, a cleaner, surer method of execution.

A note in Chinese was found at the scene, which declared that Mona had been punished for her sins. Ruth can't read Chinese, but she assumes the police translation is accurate. The police had also pulled Mona's phone records. There were a few numbers whose cell tower data showed their owners had been to Mona's place that day. The only one without an alibi was a prepaid phone without a registered owner. The police had tracked it down in Chinatown, hidden in a Dumpster. They hadn't been able to get any further.

A rather sloppy kill, Ruth thinks, *if the gangs did it.*

Sarah had also provided printouts of Mona's escort ads. Mona had used several aliases: Jasmine, Akiko, Sinn. Most of the pictures are of her in lingerie, a few in cocktail dresses. The shots are framed to emphasize her body: a side view of her breasts half-veiled in lace, a back view of her buttocks, lounging on the bed with her hand over her hip. Shots of her face have black bars over her eyes to provide some measure of anonymity.

Ruth boots up her computer and logs on to the sites to check out the other ads. She had never worked in vice, so she takes a while to familiarize herself with the lingo and acronyms. The Internet had apparently transformed the business, allowing women to get off the streets and become "independent providers" without pimps. The sites are organized to allow customers to pick out exactly what they want. They can sort and filter by price, age, services provided, ethnicity, hair and eye colors, time of availability, and customer ratings. The business is competitive, and there's a brutal efficiency to the sites that Ruth might have found depressing without the Regulator: You can measure, if you apply statistical software to it, how much a girl depreciates with each passing year; how much value men place on each pound, each inch of deviation from the ideal they're seeking; how much more a blonde really is worth than a brunette; and how much more a girl who can pass as Japanese can charge than one who cannot.

Some of the ad sites charge a membership fee to see pictures of the girls' faces. Sarah had also printed these "premium" photographs of Mona. For a brief moment, Ruth wonders what Sarah must have felt as she paid to unveil the seductive gaze of her daughter, the daughter who had seemed to have a trouble-free, promising future.

In these pictures, Mona's face was made up lightly, her lips curved in a promising or innocent smile. She was extraordinarily pretty, even compared to the other girls in her price range. She dictated incalls only, perhaps believing them to be safer, with her being more in control.

Compared to most of the other girls, Mona's ads can be described as "elegant." They're free of spelling errors and overtly crude language, hinting at the kind of sexual fantasies that men here harbor about Asian women while also promising an American wholesomeness, the contrast emphasizing the strategically placed bits of exoticism.

The anonymous customer reviews praised her attitude and willingness to "go the extra mile." Ruth supposes that Mona had earned good tips.

Ruth turns to the crime scene photos and the bloody, eyeless shots of Mona's face. Intellectually and dispassionately, she absorbs the details in Mona's room. She contemplates the contrast between them and the eroticism of the ad's photos. This was a young woman who had been vain about her education, who had believed that she could construct, through careful words and images, a kind of filter to attract the right kind of clients. It was naive and wise at the same time, and Ruth can almost feel, despite the Regulator, a kind of poignancy to her confident desperation.

Whatever caused her to go down this path, she had never hurt anyone, and now she was dead.

Ruth meets Luo in a room reached through long underground tunnels and many locked doors. It smells of mold and sweat and spicy foods rotting in trash bags.

Along the way she saw a few other locked rooms behind which she guessed were human cargo, people who indentured themselves to the snakeheads for a chance to be smuggled into this country so they could work for a dream of wealth. She says nothing about them. Her deal with Luo depends on her discretion, and Luo is kinder to his cargo than many others.

He pats her down perfunctorily. She offers to strip to show that she's not wired. He waves her off.

"Have you seen this woman?" she asks in Cantonese, holding up a picture of Mona.

Luo dangles the cigarette from his lips while he examines the picture closely. The dim light gives the tattoos on his bare shoulders and arms a greenish tint. After a moment, he hands it back. "I don't think so."

"She was a prostitute working out of Quincy. Someone killed her a month ago and left this behind." She brings out the photograph of the note left at the scene. "The police think the Chinese gangs did it."

Luo looks at the photo. He knits his brow in concentration and then barks out a dry laugh. "Yes, this is indeed a note left behind by a Chinese gang."

"Do you recognize the gang?"

"Sure." Luo looks at Ruth, a grin revealing the gaps in his

teeth. "This note was left behind by the impetuous Tak-Kao, member of the Forever Peace Gang, after he killed the innocent Mai-Ying, the beautiful maid from the mainland, in a fit of jealousy. You can see the original in the third season of *My Hong Kong, Your Hong Kong*. You're lucky that I'm a fan."

"This is copied from a soap opera?"

"Yes. Your man either likes to make jokes or doesn't know Chinese well and got this from some Internet search. It might fool the police, but no, we wouldn't leave a note like that." He chuckles at the thought and then spits on the ground.

"Maybe it was just a fake to confuse the police." She chooses her words carefully. "Or maybe it was done by one gang to sic the police onto the others. The police also found a phone, probably used by the killer, in a Chinatown Dumpster. I know there are several Asian massage parlors in Quincy, so maybe this girl was too much competition. Are you sure you don't know anything about this?"

Luo flips through the other photographs of Mona. Ruth watches him, getting ready to react to any sudden movements. She thinks she can trust Luo, but one can't always predict the reaction of a man who often has to kill to make his living.

She concentrates on the Regulator, priming it to release adrenaline to quicken her movements if necessary. The pneumatics in her legs are charged, and she braces her back against the damp wall, in case she needs to kick out. The sudden release of pressure in the air canisters installed next to her tibia will straighten her legs in a fraction of a second, generating hundreds of pounds of force. If her feet connect with Luo's chest, she will almost certainly break a few ribs—though Ruth's back will ache for days afterward, as well.

"I like you, Ruth," Luo says, noting her sudden stillness out of the corner of his eyes. "You don't have to be afraid. I haven't forgotten how you found that bookie who tried to steal from me. I'll always tell you the truth or tell you I can't answer. We have nothing to do with this girl. She's not really competition.

The men who go to massage parlors for sixty dollars an hour and a happy ending are not the kind who'd pay for a girl like this."

The Watcher drives to Somerville, just over the border from Cambridge, north of Boston. He parks in the back of a grocery store parking lot, where his Toyota Corolla, bought with cash off a lot, doesn't stick out.

Then he goes into a coffee shop and emerges with an iced coffee. Sipping it, he walks around the sunny streets, gazing from time to time at the little gizmo attached to his key chain. The gizmo tells him when he's in range of some unsecured home wireless network. Lots of students from Harvard and MIT live here, where the rent is high but not astronomical. Addicted to good wireless access, they often get powerful routers for tiny apartments and leak the network onto the streets without bothering to secure them (after all, they have friends coming over all the time who need to remain connected). And since it's summer, when the population of students is in flux, there's even less likelihood that he can be traced from using one of their networks.

It's probably overkill, but he likes to be safe.

He sits down on a bench by the side of the street, takes out his laptop, and connects to a network called "INFORMATION_WANTS_TO_BE_FREE." He enjoys disproving the network owner's theory. Information doesn't want to be free. It's valuable and wants to earn. And its existence doesn't free anyone; possessing it, however, can do the opposite.

The Watcher carefully selects a segment of video and watches it one last time.

Jasmine had done a good job, intentionally or not, with the framing, and the man's sweaty grimace is featured prominently in the video. His movements—and as a result, Jasmine's—made the video jerky, and so he's had to apply software image stabilization. But now it looks quite professional.

The Watcher had tried to identify the man, who looks Chinese, by uploading a picture he got from Jasmine into a search engine. They are always making advancements in facial recognition software, and sometimes he gets hits this way. But it didn't seem to work this time. That's not a problem for the Watcher. He has other techniques.

The Watcher signs on to a forum where the expat Chinese congregate to reminisce and argue politics in their homeland. He posts the picture of the man in the video and writes below in English, "Anyone famous?" Then he sips his coffee and refreshes the screen from time to time to catch the new replies.

The Watcher doesn't read Chinese (or Russian, or Arabic, or Hindi, or any of the other languages where he plies his trade), but linguistic skills are hardly necessary for this task. Most of the expats speak English and can understand his question. He's just using these people as research tools, a human flesh-powered, crowdsourced search engine. It's almost funny how people are so willing to give perfect strangers over the Internet information, would even compete with each other to do it, to show how knowledgeable they are. He's pleased to make use of such petty vanities.

He simply needs a name and a measure of the prominence of the man, and for that, the crude translations offered by computers are sufficient.

From the almost-gibberish translations, he gathers that the man is a prominent official in the Chinese Transport Ministry, and like almost all Chinese officials, he's despised by his countrymen. The man is a bigger deal than the Watcher's usual targets, but that might make him a good demonstration.

The Watcher is thankful for Dagger, who had explained Chinese politics to him. One evening, after he had gotten out of jail the last time, the Watcher had hung back and watched a Chinese man rob a few Chinese tourists near San Francisco's Chinatown.

The tourists had managed to make a call to 911, and the robber had fled the scene on foot down an alley. But the Watcher had seen something in the man's direct, simple approach that he liked. He drove around the block, stopped by the other end of the alley, and when the man emerged, he swung open the passenger-side door and offered him a chance to escape in his car. The man thanked him and told him his name was Dagger.

Dagger was talkative and told the Watcher how angry and envious people in China were of the Party officials, who lived an extravagant life on the money squeezed from the common people, took bribes, and funneled public funds to their relatives. He targeted those tourists who he thought were the officials' wives and children and regarded himself as a modern-day Robin Hood.

Yet, the officials were not completely immune. All it took was a public scandal of some kind, usually involving young women who were not their wives. Talk of democracy didn't get people excited, but seeing an official rubbing their graft in their faces made them see red. And the Party apparatus would have no choice but to punish the disgraced officials, as the only thing the Party feared was public anger, which always threatened to boil out of control. If a revolution were to come to China, Dagger quipped, it would be triggered by mistresses, not speeches.

A light had gone on in the Watcher's head then. It was as if he could see the reins of power flowing from those who had secrets to those who knew secrets. He thanked Dagger and dropped him off, wishing him well.

The Watcher imagines what the official's visit to Boston had been like. He had probably come to learn about the city's experience with light rail, but it was likely in reality just another state-funded vacation, a chance to shop at the luxury stores on Newbury Street, to enjoy expensive foods without fear of poison or pollution, and to anonymously take delight in quality female companionship without the threat of recording devices in the hands of an interested populace.

He posts the video to the forum, and as an extra flourish, adds a link to the official's biography on the Transport Ministry's website. For a second, he regrets the forgone revenue, but it's been a while since he's done a demonstration, and these are necessary to keep the business going.

He packs up his laptop. Now, he has to wait.

Ruth doesn't think there's much value in viewing Mona's apartment, but she's learned over the years not to leave any stone unturned. She gets the key from Sarah Ding and makes her way to the apartment around six in the evening. Viewing the site at approximately the time of day when the murder occurred can sometimes be helpful.

She passes through the living room. There's a small TV facing a futon, the kind of furniture that a young woman keeps from her college days when she doesn't have a reason to upgrade. It's a living room that was never meant for visitors.

She moves into the room in which the murder happened. The forensics team has cleaned it out. The room—it wasn't Mona's real bedroom, which was a tiny cubby down the hall, with just a twin bed and plain walls—is stripped bare, most of the loose items having been collected as evidence. The mattress is naked, as are the nightstands. The carpet has been vacuumed. The place smells like a hotel room: stale air and faint perfume.

Ruth notices the line of mirrors along the side of the bed, hanging over the closet doors. Watching arouses people.

She imagines how lonely Mona must have felt living here, touched and kissed and fucked by a stream of men who kept as much of themselves hidden from her as possible. She imagines her sitting in front of the small TV to relax and dressing up to meet her parents so that she could lie some more.

Ruth imagines the way the murderer had shot Mona and then cut her after. Was there more than one of them so that Mona thought a struggle was useless? Did they shoot her right away, or did they ask her to tell them where she had hidden her money first? She can feel the Regulator starting up again, keeping her emotions in check. Evil has to be confronted dispassionately.

She decides she's seen all she needs to see. She leaves the apartment and pulls the door closed. As she heads for the stairs, she sees a man coming up, keys in hand. Their eyes briefly meet, and he turns to the door of the apartment across the hall.

Ruth is sure the police have interviewed the neighbor. But sometimes people will tell things to a nonthreatening woman that they are reluctant to tell the cops.

She walks over and introduces herself, explaining that she's a friend of Mona's family, here to tie up some loose ends. The man, whose name is Peter, is wary but shakes her hand.

"I didn't hear or see anything. We pretty much keep to ourselves in this building."

"I believe you. But it would be helpful if we can chat a bit, anyway. The family didn't know much about her life here."

He nods reluctantly and opens the door. He steps in and waves his arms up and around in a complex sequence as though he's conducting an orchestra. The lights come on.

"That's pretty fancy," Ruth says. "You have the whole place wired up like that?"

His voice, cautious and guarded until now, grows animated. Talking about something other than the murder seems to relax him. "Yes. It's called EchoSense. They add an adapter to your wireless router, and a few antennas around the room, and then it uses the Doppler shifts generated by your body's movements in the radio waves to detect gestures."

"You mean it can see you move with just the signals from your Wi-Fi bouncing around the room?"

"Something like that."

Ruth remembers seeing an infomercial about this. She notes how small the apartment is and how little space separates it from Mona's. They sit down and chat about what Peter remembers about Mona.

"Pretty girl. Way out of my league, but she was always pleasant."

"Did she get a lot of visitors?"

"I don't pry into other people's business. But yeah, I remember lots of visitors, mostly men. I did think she might have been an escort. But that didn't bother me. The men always seemed clean, business types. Not dangerous."

"No one who looked like a gangster, for example?"

"I wouldn't know what gangsters look like. But no, I don't think so."

They chat on inconsequentially for another fifteen minutes, and Ruth decides that she's wasted enough time.

"Can I buy the router from you?" she asks. "And the Echo-Sense thing."

"You can just order your own set online."

"I hate shopping online. You can never return things. I know this one works; so I want it. I'll offer you two thousand, cash."

He considers this.

"I bet you can buy a new one and get another adapter yourself from EchoSense for less than a quarter of that."

He nods and retrieves the router, and she pays him. The act feels somehow illicit, not unlike how she imagines Mona's transactions were.

Ruth posts an ad to a local classifieds site, describing in vague terms what she's looking for. Boston is blessed with many good colleges and lots of young men and women who would relish a technical challenge even more than the money she offers. She looks through the résumés until she finds the one she feels has the right skills: jailbreaking phones, reverse-engineering proprietary protocols, a healthy disrespect for acronyms like DMCA and CFAA.

She meets the young man at her office and explains what she wants. Daniel—dark-skinned, lanky, and shy—slouches in the chair across from hers as he listens without interrupting.

"Can you do it?" she asks.

"Maybe," he says. "Companies like this one will usually

send customer data back to the mothership anonymously to help improve their technology. Sometimes the data is cached locally for a while. It's possible I'll find logs on there a month old. If it's there, I'll get it for you. But I'll have to figure out how they're encoding the data and then make sense of it."

"Do you think my theory is plausible?"

"I'm impressed you even came up with it. Wireless signals can go through walls, so it's certainly possible that this adapter has captured the movements of people in neighboring apartments. It's a privacy nightmare, and I'm sure the company doesn't publicize that."

"How long will it take?"

"As little as a day or as much as a month. I won't know until I start. It will help if you can draw me a map of the apartments and what's inside."

Ruth does as he asked. Then she tells him, "I'll pay you three hundred dollars a day, with a five-thousand-dollar bonus if you succeed this week."

"Deal." He grins and picks up the router, getting ready to leave.

Because it never hurts to tell people what they're doing is meaningful, she adds, "You're helping to catch the killer of a young woman who's not much older than you."

Then she goes home because she's run out of things to try.

The first hour after waking up is always the worst part of the day for Ruth.

As usual, she wakes from a nightmare. She lies still, disoriented, the images from her dream superimposed over the sight of the water stains on the ceiling. Her body is drenched in sweat.

The man holds Jessica in front of him with his left hand while the gun in his right hand is pointed at her head. She's terrified, but not of him. He ducks so that her body shields his, and he whispers something into her ear.

"Mom! Mom!" she screams. "Don't shoot. Please don't shoot!"

Ruth rolls over, nauseated. She sits up at the edge of the bed, hating the smell of the hot room, the dust that she never has time to clean filling the air pierced by bright rays coming in from the east-facing window. She shoves the sheets off her and stands up quickly, her breath coming too fast. She's fighting the rising panic without any help, alone, her Regulator off.

The clock on the nightstand says six o'clock.

She's crouching behind the opened driver's-side door of her car. Her hands shake as she struggles to keep the man's head, bobbing besides her daughter's, in the sight of her gun. If she turns on her Regulator, she thinks her hands may grow steady and give her a clear shot at him.

What are her chances of hitting him instead of her? Ninety-five percent? Ninety-nine?

"Mom! Mom! No!"

She gets up and stumbles into the kitchen to turn on the coffeemaker. She curses when she finds the can empty and throws it clattering into the sink. The noise shocks her, and she cringes.

Then she struggles into the shower, sluggishly, painfully, as though the muscles that she conditions daily through hard exercise were not there. She turns on the hot water, but it brings no warmth to her shivering body.

Grief descends on her like a heavy weight. She sits down in the shower, curling her body into itself. Water streams down her face so she does not know if there are tears as her body heaves.

She fights the impulse to turn on the Regulator. It's not time yet. She has to give her body the necessary rest.

The Regulator, a collection of chips and circuitry embedded at the top of her spine, is tied into the limbic system and the major blood vessels into the brain. Like its namesake from mechanical and electrical engineering, it maintains the levels of dopamine, noradrenaline, serotonin, and other chemicals in the brain and in her bloodstream. It filters out the chemicals when there's an excess and releases them when there's a deficit.

And it obeys her will.

The implant allows a person control over her basic emotions: fear, disgust, joy, excitement, love. It's mandatory for law enforcement officers, a way to minimize the effects of emotions on life-or-death decisions, a way to eliminate prejudice and irrationality.

"You have clearance to shoot," the voice in her headset tells her. It's the voice of her husband, Scott, the head of her department. His voice is completely calm. His Regulator is on.

She sees the head of the man bobbing up and down as he retreats with Jessica. He's heading for the van parked by the side of the road.

"He's got other hostages in there," her husband continues to speak in her ear. "If you don't shoot, you put the lives of those three other girls and who knows how many other people in danger. This is our best chance."

The sound of sirens, her backup, is still faint. Too far away.

After what seems an eternity, she manages to stand up in the shower and turn off the water. She towels herself dry and dresses slowly. She tries to think of something, anything, to take her mind off its current track. But nothing works.

She despises the raw state of her mind. Without the Regulator, she feels weak, confused, angry. Waves of despair wash over her, and everything appears in hopeless shades of gray. She wonders why she's still alive.

It will pass, she thinks. *Just a few more minutes.*

Back when she had been on the force, she had adhered to the regulation requirement not to leave the Regulator on for more than two hours at a time. There are physiological and psychological risks associated with prolonged use. Some of her fellow officers had also complained about the way the Regulator made them feel robotic, deadened. No excitement from seeing a pretty woman; no thrill at the potential for a car chase; no righteous anger when faced with an act of abuse. Everything had to be deliberate: You decided when to let the adrenaline flow, and just enough to get the job done and not too much to interfere with judgment. But sometimes, they argued, you needed emotions, instinct, intuition.

Her Regulator had been off when she came home that day and recognized the man hiding from the citywide manhunt.

Have I been working too much? she thinks. I don't know any of her friends. When did Jess meet him? Why didn't I ask her more questions when she was coming home late every night? Why did I stop for lunch instead of coming home half an hour earlier? There are a thousand things I could have done and should have done and would have done.

Fear and anger and regret are mixed up in her until she cannot tell which is which.

"Engage your Regulator," *her husband's voice tells her.* "You can make the shot."

Why do I care about the lives of the other girls? she thinks. All I care about is Jess. Even the smallest chance of hurting her is too much.

Can she trust a machine to save her daughter? Should she rely on a machine to steady her shaking hands, to clear her blurry vision, to make a shot without missing?

"Mom, he's going to let me go later. He won't hurt me. He just wants to get away from here. Put the gun down!"

Maybe Scott can make a calculus about lives saved and lives put at risk. She won't. She will not trust a machine.

"It's okay, baby," *she croaks out.* "It's all going to be okay."

She does not turn on the Regulator. She does not shoot.

Later, after she had identified the body of Jess—the bodies of all four of the girls had been badly burned when the bomb went off—after she had been disciplined and discharged, after Scott and she had split up, after she had found no solace in alcohol and pills, she did finally find the help she needed: she could leave the Regulator on all the time.

The Regulator deadened the pain, stifled grief, and numbed the ache of loss. It held down the regret, made it possible to pretend to forget. She craved the calmness it brought, the blameless, serene clarity.

She had been wrong to distrust it. That distrust had cost her Jess. She would not make the same mistake again.

Sometimes she thinks of the Regulator as a dependable lover, a comforting presence to lean on. Sometimes she thinks she's addicted. She does not probe deeply behind these thoughts.

She would have preferred to never have to turn off the Regulator, to never be in a position to repeat her mistake. But even Doctor B balked at that ("Your brain will turn into mush."). The illegal modifications he did agree to make allow the Regulator to remain on for a maximum of twenty-three hours at a stretch. Then she must take an hour-long break during which she must remain conscious.

And so there's always this hour in the morning, right as she wakes, when she's naked and alone with her memories, unshielded from the rush of red-hot hatred (for the man? for herself?) and white-cold rage, and the black, bottomless abyss that she endures as her punishment.

The alarm beeps. She concentrates like a monk in meditation and feels the hum of the Regulator starting up. Relief spreads out from the center of her mind to the very tips of her fingers, the soothing, numbing serenity of a regulated, disciplined mind. To be regulated is to be a regular person.

She stands up, limber, graceful, powerful, ready to hunt.

The Watcher has identified more of the men in the pictures. He's now in a new motel room, this one more expensive than usual because he feels like he deserves a treat after all he's been through. Hunching over all day to edit video is hard work.

He pans the cropping rectangle over the video to give it a sense of dynamism and movement. There's an artistry to this.

He's amazed how so few people seem to know about the eye implants. There's something about eyes—so vulnerable, so essential to the way people see the world and themselves—that makes people feel protective and reluctant to invade them. The laws regarding eye modifications are the most stringent, and after a while, people begin to mistake "not permitted" with "not possible."

They don't know what they don't want to know.

All his life, he's felt that he's missed some key piece of information, some secret that everyone else seemed to know. He's intelligent, diligent, but somehow things have not worked out.

He never knew his father, and when he was eleven, his mother had left him one day at home with twenty dollars and never came back. A string of foster homes had followed, and *nobody*, nobody could tell him what he was missing, why he was always at the mercy of judges and bureaucrats, why he had so little control over his life; not where he would sleep, not when he would eat, not who would have power over him next.

He made it his subject to study men, to watch and try to understand what made them tick. Much of what he learned had disappointed him. Men were vain, proud, ignorant. They let their desires carry them away, ignored risks that were obvious. They did not think, did not plan. They did not know what they really wanted. They let the TV tell them what they should have and hoped that working at their pathetic jobs would make those wishes come true.

He craved control. He wanted to see them dance to his tune the way he had been made to dance to the tune of everyone else.

So he had honed himself to be pure and purposeful, like a sharp knife in a drawer full of ridiculous, ornate, fussy kitchen gadgets. He knew what he wanted, and he worked at getting it with singular purpose.

He adjusts the colors and the dynamic range to compensate for the dim light in the video. He wants there to be no mistake in identifying the man.

He stretches his tired arms and sore neck. For a moment, he wonders if he'll be better off if he pays to have parts of his body enhanced so he can work for longer, without pain and fatigue. But the momentary fancy passes.

Most people don't like medically unnecessary enhancements and would only accept them if they're required for a job. No such sentimental considerations for bodily integrity or "naturalness" constrain the Watcher. He does not like enhancements because he views reliance on them as a sign of weakness. He would defeat his enemies with his mind, and with the aid of planning and foresight. He does not need to depend on machines.

He had learned to steal, and then rob, and eventually how to kill for money. But the money was really secondary, just a means to an end. It was control that he desired. The only man he had killed was a lawyer, someone who lied for a living. Lying had brought him money, and that gave him power, made people bow down to him and smile at him and speak in respectful voices. The Watcher had loved that moment when the man begged him for mercy, when he would have done anything the Watcher wanted. The Watcher had taken what he wanted from the man rightfully, by superiority of intellect and strength. Yet, the Watcher had been caught and gone to jail for it. A system that rewarded liars and punished the Watcher could not in any sense be called just.

He presses "save." He's done with this video.

Knowledge of the truth gave him power, and he would make others acknowledge it.

Before Ruth is about to make her next move, Daniel calls, and they meet in her office again.

"I have what you wanted."

He takes out his laptop and shows her an animation, like a movie.

"They stored videos on the adapter?"

Daniel laughs. "No. The device can't really 'see,' and that would be far too much data. No, the adapter just stored readings, numbers. I made the animation so it's easier to understand."

She's impressed. The young man knows how to give a good presentation.

"The Wi-Fi echoes aren't captured with enough resolution to give you much detail. But you can get a rough sense of people's sizes and heights and their movements. This is what I got from the day and hour you specified."

They watch as a bigger, vaguely humanoid shape appears at Mona's apartment door, precisely at six, meeting a smaller, vaguely humanoid shape.

"Seems they had an appointment," Daniel says.

They watch as the smaller shape leads the bigger shape into the bedroom, and then the two embrace. They watch the smaller shape climb into space—presumably onto the bed. They watch the bigger shape climb up after it. They watch the shooting, and then the smaller shape collapses and disappears. They watch the bigger shape lean over, and the smaller shape flickers into existence as it's moved from time to time.

So there was only one killer, Ruth thinks. And he was a client.

"How tall is he?"

"There's a scale to the side."

Ruth watches the animation over and over. The man is six foot two or six foot three, maybe 180 to 200 pounds. She notices that he has a bit of a limp as he walks.

She's now convinced that Luo was telling the truth. Not many Chinese men are six foot two, and such a man would stick out too much to be a killer for a gang. Every witness would remember him. Mona's killer had been a client, maybe even a regular. It wasn't a random robbery but carefully planned.

The man is still out there, and killers that meticulous rarely kill only once.

"Thank you," she says. "You might be saving another young woman's life."

Ruth dials the number for the police department.

"Captain Brennan, please."

She gives her name, and her call is transferred, and then she hears the gruff, weary voice of her ex-husband. "What can I do for you?"

Once again, she's glad she has the Regulator. His voice dredges up memories of his raspy morning mumbles, his stentorian laughter, his tender whispers when they were alone, the soundtrack of twenty years of a life spent together, a life that they had both thought would last until one of them died.

"I need a favor."

He doesn't answer right away. She wonders if she's too abrupt—a side effect of leaving the Regulator on all the time. Maybe she should have started with "How've you been?"

Finally, he speaks. "What is it?" The voice is restrained, but laced with exhausted, desiccated pain.

"I'd like to use your NCIC access."

Another pause. "Why?"

"I'm working on the Mona Ding case. I think this is a man who's killed before and will kill again. He's got a method. I want to see if there are related cases in other cities."

"That's out of the question, Ruth. You know that. Besides, there's no point. We've run all the searches we can, and there's nothing similar. This was a Chinese gang protecting their business, simple as that. Until we have the resources in the Gang Unit to deal with it, I'm sorry, this will have to go cold for a while."

Ruth hears the unspoken. *The Chinese gangs have always preyed on their own. Until they bother the tourists, let's just leave them alone.* She'd heard similar sentiments often enough back when she was on the force. The Regulator could do nothing about certain kinds of prejudice. It's perfectly rational. And also perfectly wrong.

"I don't think so. I have an informant who says that the Chinese gangs have nothing to do with it."

Scott snorts. "Yes, of course you can trust the word of a Chinese snakehead. But there's also the note and the phone."

"The note is most likely a forgery. And do you really think this Chinese gang member would be smart enough to realize that the phone records would give him away and then decide that the best place to hide it was around his place of business?"

"Who knows? Criminals are stupid."

"The man is far too methodical for that. It's a red herring."

"You have no evidence."

"I have a good reconstruction of the crime and a description of the suspect. He's too tall to be the kind a Chinese gang would use."

This gets his attention. "From where?"

"A neighbor had a home motion-sensing system that captured wireless echoes into Mona's apartment. I paid someone to reconstruct it."

"Will that stand up in court?"

"I doubt it. It will take expert testimony, and you'll have to get the company to admit that they capture that information. They'll fight it tooth and nail."

"Then it's not much use to me."

"If you give me a chance to look in the database, maybe I can turn it into something you *can* use." She waits a second and presses on, hoping that he'll be sentimental. "I've never asked you for much."

"This is the first time you've ever asked me for something like this."

"I don't usually take on cases like this."

"What is it about this girl?"

Ruth considers the question. There are two ways to answer it. She can try to explain the fee she's being paid and why she feels she's adding value. Or she can give what she suspects is the real reason. Sometimes the Regulator makes it hard to tell what's true. "Sometimes people think the police don't look as hard when the victim is a sex worker. I know your resources are constrained, but maybe I can help."

"It's the mother, isn't it? You feel bad for her."

Ruth does not answer. She can feel the Regulator kicking in again. Without it, perhaps she would be enraged.

"She's not Jess, Ruth. Finding her killer won't make you feel better."

"I'm asking for a favor. You can just say no."

Scott does not sigh, and he does not mumble. He's simply quiet. Then, a few seconds later: "Come to the office around eight. You can use the terminal in my office."

The Watcher thinks of himself as a good client. He makes sure he gets his money's worth, but he leaves a generous tip. He likes the clarity of money, the way it makes the flow of power obvious. The girl he just left was certainly appreciative.

He drives faster. He feels he's been too self-indulgent the last few weeks, working too slowly. He needs to make sure the last round of targets have paid. If not, he needs to carry through. Action. Reaction. It's all very simple once you understand the rules.

He rubs the bandage around his ring finger, which allows him to maintain the pale patch of skin that girls like to see. The lingering, sickly sweet perfume from the last girl—Melody, Mandy, he's already forgetting her name—reminds him of Tara, who he will never forget.

Tara may have been the only girl he's really loved. She was blonde, petite, and very expensive. But she had liked him for some reason. Perhaps because they were both broken, and the jagged pieces happened to fit.

She had stopped charging him and told him her real name. He was a kind of boyfriend. Because he was curious, she explained her business to him. How certain words and turns of phrase and tones on the phone were warning signs. What she looked for in a desired regular. What signs on a man probably meant he was safe. He enjoyed learning about this. It seemed to require careful watching by the girl, and he respected those who looked and studied and made the information useful.

He had looked into her eyes as he fucked her and then said, "Is something wrong with your right eye?"

She had stopped moving. "What?"

"I wasn't sure at first. But yes, it's like you have something behind your eye."

She wriggled under him. He was annoyed and thought about holding her down. But he decided not to. She seemed about to tell him something important. He rolled off her.

"You're very observant."

"I try. What is it?"

She told him about the implant.

"You've been recording your clients having sex with you?"

"Yes."

"I want to see the ones you have of us."

She laughed. "I'll have to go under the knife for that. Not going to happen until I retire. Having your skull opened up once was enough."

She explained how the recordings made her feel safe, gave her a sense of power, like having bank accounts whose balances only she knew and kept growing. If she were ever threatened, she would be able to call on the powerful men she knew for aid. And after retirement, if things didn't work out and she got desperate, perhaps she could use them to get her regulars to help her out a little.

He had liked the way she thought. So devious. So like him.

He had been sorry when he killed her. Removing her head was more difficult and messy than he had imagined. Figuring out what to do with the little silver half sphere had taken months. He would learn to do better over time.

But Tara had been blind to the implications of what she had done. What she had wasn't just insurance, wasn't just a rainy-day fund. She had revealed to him that she had what it took to make his dream come true, and he had to take it from her.

He pulls into the parking lot of the hotel and finds himself seized by an unfamiliar sensation: sorrow. He misses Tara, like missing a mirror you've broken.

Ruth is working with the assumption that the man she's looking for targets independent prostitutes. There's an efficiency and a method to the way Mona was killed that suggests practice.

She begins by searching the NCIC database for prostitutes who had been killed by a suspect matching the EchoSense description. As she expects, she comes up with nothing that seems remotely similar. The man hadn't left obvious trails.

The focus on Mona's eyes may be a clue. Maybe the killer has a fetish for Asian women. Ruth changes her search to concentrate on body mutilations of Asian prostitutes similar to what Mona had suffered. Again, nothing.

Ruth sits back and thinks over the situation. It's common for serial killers to concentrate on victims of a specific ethnicity. But that may be a red herring here.

She expands her search to include all independent prostitutes who had been killed in the last year or so, and now there are too many hits. Dozens and dozens of killings of prostitutes of every description pop up. Most were sexually assaulted. Some were tortured. Many had their bodies mutilated. Almost all were robbed. Gangs were suspected in several cases. She sifts through them, looking for similarities. Nothing jumps out at her.

She needs more information.

She logs on to the escort sites in the various cities and looks up the ads of the murdered women. Not all of them remain online, as some sites deactivate ads when enough patrons complain about unavailability. She prints out what she can, laying them out side by side to compare.

Then she sees it. It's in the ads.

A subset of the ads triggers a sense of familiarity in Ruth's mind. They were all carefully written, free of spelling and grammar mistakes. They were frank but not explicit, seductive without verging on parody. The johns who posted reviews described them as "classy."

It's a signal, Ruth realizes. The ads are written to give off the air of being careful, selective, *discreet*. There is in them, for lack of a better word, a sense of *taste*.

All the women in these ads were extraordinarily beautiful, with smooth skin and thick, long, flowing hair. All of them were between twenty-two and thirty—not so young as to be careless or supporting themselves through school, and not old enough to lose the ability to pass for younger. All of them were independent, with no pimp or evidence of being on drugs.

Luo's words come back to her: *The men who go to massage parlors for sixty dollars an hour and a happy ending are not the kind who'd pay for a girl like this.*

There's a certain kind of client who would be attracted to the signs given out by these girls, Ruth thinks: men who care very much about the risk of discovery and who believe that they deserve something special, suitable for their distinguished tastes.

She prints out the NCIC entries for the women.

All the women she's identified were killed in their homes. No sign of struggle—possibly because they were meeting a client. One was strangled, the others shot in the heart through the back, like Mona. In all the cases except one—the woman who was strangled—the police had found record of a suspicious call on the day of the murder from a prepaid phone that was later found somewhere in the city. The killer had taken all the women's money.

Ruth knows she's on the right track. Now, she needs to

examine the case reports in more detail to see if she can find more patterns to identify the killer.

The door to the office opens. It's Scott.

"Still here?" The scowl on his face shows that he does not have his Regulator on. "It's after midnight."

She notes, not for the first time, how the men in the department have often resisted the Regulator unless absolutely necessary, claiming that it dulled their instincts and hunches. But they had also asked her whether she had hers on whenever she dared to disagree with them. They would laugh when they asked.

"I think I'm onto something," she says calmly.

"You working with the goddamned feds now?"

"What are you talking about?"

"You haven't seen the news?"

"I've been here all evening."

He takes out his tablet, opens a bookmark, and hands it to her. It's an article in the international section of the *Globe*, which she rarely reads. "Scandal Unseats Chinese Transport Minister" says the headline.

She scans the article quickly. A video has surfaced on the Chinese microblogs showing an important official in the Transport Ministry having sex with a prostitute. Moreover, it seems that he had been paying her out of public funds. He's already been removed from his post due to the public outcry.

Accompanying the article is a grainy photo, a still capture from the video. Before the Regulator kicks in, Ruth feels her heart skip a beat. The image shows a man on top of a woman. Her head is turned to the side, directly facing the camera.

"That's your girl, isn't it?"

Ruth nods. She recognizes the bed and the nightstand with the clock and wicker basket from the crime scene photos.

"The Chinese are hopping mad. They think we had the man under surveillance when he was in Boston and released this video deliberately to mess with them. They're protesting through the back channels, threatening retaliation. The feds want us to look into it and see what we can find out about how the video was made. They don't know that she's already dead, but I recognized her as soon as I saw her. If you ask me, it's probably something the Chinese cooked up themselves to try to get rid of the guy in an internal purge. Maybe they even paid the girl to do it, and then they killed her. That, or our own spies decided to get rid of her after using her as bait, in which case I expect this investigation to be shut down pretty quickly. Either way, I'm not looking forward to this mess. And I advise you to back off as well."

Ruth feels a moment of resentment before the Regulator whisks it away. If Mona's death was part of a political plot, then Scott is right, she really is way out of her depth. The police had been wrong to conclude that it was a gang killing. But she's wrong too. Mona was an unfortunate pawn in some political game, and the trend she thought she had noticed was illusory, just a set of coincidences.

The rational thing to do is to let the police take over. She'll have to tell Sarah Ding that there's nothing she can do for her now.

"We'll have to sweep the apartment again for recording devices. And you better let me know the name of your informant. We'll need to question him thoroughly to see which gangs are involved. This could be a national security matter."

"You know I can't do that. I have no evidence he has anything to do with this."

"Ruth, we're picking this up now. If you want to find the girl's killer, help me."

"Feel free to round up all the usual suspects in Chinatown. It's what you want to do, anyway."

He stares at her, his face weary and angry, a look she's very familiar with. Then his face relaxes. He has decided to engage his Regulator, and he no longer wants to argue or talk about what couldn't be said between them.

Her Regulator kicks in automatically.

"Thank you for letting me use your office," she says placidly. "You have a good night."

The scandal had gone off exactly as the Watcher planned. He's pleased but not yet ready to celebrate. That was only the first step, a demonstration of his power. Next, he has to actually make sure it pays.

He goes through the recordings and pictures he's extracted from the dead girl and picks out a few more promising targets based on his research. Two are prominent Chinese businessmen connected with top Party bosses; one is the brother of an Indian diplomatic attaché; two more are sons of the House of Saud, studying in Boston. It's remarkable how similar the dynamics between the powerful and the people they ruled over are around the world. He also finds a prominent CEO and a justice of the Massachusetts Supreme Judicial Court, but these he sets aside. It's not that he's particularly patriotic, but he instinctively senses that if one of his victims decides to turn him in instead of paying up, he'll be in much less trouble if the victim isn't an American. Besides, American public figures also have a harder time moving money around anonymously, as evidenced by his experience with those two senators in DC, which almost unraveled his whole scheme. Finally, it never hurts to have a judge or someone famous that can be leaned on in case the Watcher is caught.

Patience, and an eye for details.

He sends off his e-mails. Each references the article about the Chinese Transport Minister ("See, this could be you!") and then includes two files. One is the full video of the minister and the girl (to show that he was the originator), and the second is a carefully curated video of the recipient coupling with her. Each e-mail contains a demand for payment and directions to make deposits to a numbered Swiss bank account or to transfer anonymous electronic cryptocurrency.

He browses the escort sites again. He's narrowed down the girls he suspects to just a few. Now, he just has to look at them more closely to pick out the right one. He grows excited at the prospect.

He glances up at the people walking past him in the streets. All these foolish men and women moving around as if dreaming. They do not understand that the world is full of secrets, accessible only to those patient enough, observant enough to locate them and dig them out of their warm, bloody hiding places, like retrieving pearls from the soft flesh inside oysters. And then, armed with those secrets, you could make men half a world away tremble and dance.

He closes his laptop and gets up to leave. He thinks about packing up the mess in his motel room, setting out the surgical kit, the baseball cap, the gun, and a few other surprises he's learned to take with him when he's hunting.

Time to dig for more treasure.

Ruth wakes up. The old nightmares have been joined by new ones. She stays curled up in bed fighting waves of despair. She wants to lie here forever.

Days of work, and she has nothing to show for it.

She'll have to call Sarah Ding later, after she turns on the Regulator. She can tell her that Mona was probably not killed by a gang, but somehow had been caught up in events bigger than she could handle. How would that make Sarah feel better?

The image from yesterday's news will not leave her mind, no matter how hard she tries to push it away.

Ruth struggles up and pulls up the article. She can't explain it, but the image just *looks* wrong. Not having the Regulator on makes it hard to think.

She finds the crime scene photo of Mona's bedroom and compares it with the image from the article. She looks back and forth.

Isn't the basket of condoms on the wrong side of the bed?

The shot is taken from the left side of the bed. So the closet doors, with the mirrors on them, should be on the far side of the shot, behind the couple. But there's only a blank wall behind them in the shot. Ruth's heart is beating so fast that she feels faint.

The alarm beeps. Ruth glances up at the red numbers and turns the Regulator on.

The clock.

She looks back at the image. The alarm clock in the shot is tiny and fuzzy, but she can just make the numbers out. They're backward.

Ruth walks steadily over to her laptop and begins to search online for the video. She finds it without much trouble and presses play.

Despite the video stabilization and the careful cropping, she can see that Mona's eyes are always looking directly into the camera.

There's only one explanation: The camera was aimed at the mirrors, and it was located in Mona's eye.

The eyes.

She goes through the NCIC entries of the other women she printed out yesterday, and now the pattern that had proven elusive seems obvious.

There was a blonde in Los Angeles whose head had been removed after death and never found; there was a brunette, also in LA, whose skull had been cracked open and her brains mashed; there was a Mexican woman and a black woman in DC, whose faces had been subjected to postmortem trauma in more restrained ways, with the cheekbones crushed and broken. Then finally, there was Mona, whose eyes had been carefully removed.

The killer has been improving his technique.

The Regulator holds her excitement in check. She needs more data.

She looks through all of Mona's photographs again. Nothing out of place shows up in the earlier pictures, but in the photo from her birthday with her parents, a flash was used, and there's an odd glint in her left eye.

Most cameras can automatically compensate for red-eye, which is caused by the light from the flash reflecting off the blood-rich choroid in the back of the eye. But the glint in Mona's picture is not red; it's bluish.

Calmly, Ruth flips through the photographs of the other girls who have been killed. And in each, she finds the telltale glint. This must be how the killer identified his targets.

She picks up the phone and dials the number for her friend. She and Gail had gone to college together, and she's now working as a researcher for an advanced medical devices company.

"Hello?"

She hears the chatter of other people in the background. "Gail, it's Ruth. Can you talk?"

"Just a minute." She hears the background conversation grow muffled and then abruptly shut off. "You never call unless you're asking about another enhancement. We're not getting any younger, you know? You have to stop at some point."

Gail had been the one to suggest the various enhancements Ruth has obtained over the years. She had even found Doctor B for her because she didn't want Ruth to end up crippled. But she had done it reluctantly, conflicted about the idea of turning Ruth into a cyborg.

"This feels wrong," she would say. "You don't need these things done to you. They're not medically necessary."

"This can save my life the next time someone is trying to choke me," Ruth would say.

"It's not the same thing," she would say. And the conversations would always end with Gail giving in, but with stern warnings about no further enhancements.

Sometimes you help a friend even when you disapprove of their decisions. It's complicated.

Ruth answers Gail on the phone, "No. I'm just fine. But I want to know if you know about a new kind of enhancement. I'm sending you some pictures now. Hold on." She sends over the images of the girls where she can see the strange glint in their eyes. "Take a look. Can you see that flash in their eyes? Do you know anything like this?" She doesn't tell Gail her suspicion so that Gail's answer would not be affected.

Gail is silent for a while. "I see what you mean. These are not great pictures. But let me talk to some people and call you back."

"Don't send the full pictures around. I'm in the middle of an investigation. Just crop out the eyes if you can."

Ruth hangs up. The Regulator is working extra hard. Something about what she said—cropping out the girls' eyes—triggered a bodily response of disgust that the Regulator is suppressing. She's not sure why. With the Regulator, sometimes it's hard for her to see the connections between things.

While waiting for Gail to call her back, she looks through the active online ads in Boston once more. The killer has a pattern of killing a few girls in each city before moving on. He must be on the hunt for a second victim here. The best way to catch him is to find her before he does.

She clicks through ad after ad, the parade of flesh a meaningless blur, focusing only on the eyes. Finally, she sees what she's looking for. The girl uses the name Carrie, and she has dirty-blonde hair and green eyes. Her ad is clean, clear, well-written, like a tasteful sign amid the parade of flashing neon. The time stamp on the ad shows that she last modified it twelve hours ago. She's likely still alive.

Ruth calls the number listed.

"This is Carrie. Please leave a message."

As expected, Carrie screens her calls.

"Hello. My name is Ruth Law, and I saw your ad. I'd like to make an appointment with you." She hesitates, and then adds, "This is not a joke. I really want to see you." She leaves her number and hangs up.

The phone rings almost immediately. Ruth picks up. But it's Gail, not Carrie.

"I asked around, and people who ought to know tell me the girls are probably wearing a new kind of retinal implant. It's not FDA approved. But of course, you can go overseas and get them installed if you pay enough."

"What do they do?"

"They're hidden cameras."

"How do you get the pictures and videos out?"

"You don't. They have no wireless connections to the outside world. In fact, they're shielded to emit as little RF emissions as possible, so that they're undetectable to camera scanners, and a wireless connection would just mean another way to hack into them. All the storage is inside the device. To retrieve them, you have to have surgery again. Not the kind of thing most people would be interested in unless you're trying to record people who *really* don't want you to be recording them."

When you're so desperate for safety that you think this provides insurance, Ruth thinks. Some future leverage.

And there's no way to get the recordings out except to cut the girl open. "Thanks."

"I don't know what you're involved in, Ruth, but you really are getting too old for this. Are you still leaving the Regulator on all the time? It's not healthy."

"Don't I know it." She changes the subject to Gail's children. The Regulator allows her to have this conversation without pain. After a suitable amount of time, she says good-bye and hangs up.

The phone rings again.

"This is Carrie. You called me."

"Yes." Ruth makes her voice sound light, carefree.

Carrie's voice is flirtatious but cautious. "Is this for you and your boyfriend or husband?"

"No, just me."

She grips the phone, counting the seconds. She tries to will Carrie not to hang up.

"I found your website. You're a private detective?"

Ruth already knew that she would. "Yes, I am."

"I can't tell you anything about any of my clients. My business depends on discretion."

"I'm not going to ask you about your clients. I just want to see you." She thinks hard about how to gain her trust. The Regulator makes this difficult, as she has become unused to the emotive quality of judgments and impressions. She thinks the truth is too abrupt and strange to convince her. So she tries something else. "I'm interested in a new experience. I guess it's something I've always wanted to try and haven't."

"Are you working for the cops? I am stating now for the record that you're paying me only for companionship, and anything that happens beyond that is a decision between consenting adults."

"Look, the cops wouldn't use a woman to trap you. It's too suspicious."

The silence tells Ruth that Carrie is intrigued. "What time are you thinking of?"

"As soon as you're free. How about now?"

"It's not even noon yet. I don't start work until six."

Ruth doesn't want to push too hard and scare her off. "Then I'd like to have you all night."

She laughs. "Why don't we start with two hours for a first date?"

"That will be fine."

"You saw my prices?"

"Yes. Of course."

"Take a picture of yourself holding your ID and text it to me first so I know you're for real. If that checks out, you can go to the corner of Victory and Beech in Back Bay at six and call me again. Put the cash in a plain envelope."

"I will."

"See you, my dear." She hangs up.

★ ★ ★ ★

165

Ruth looks into the girl's eyes. Now that she knows what to look for, she thinks she can see the barest hint of a glint in her left eye.

She hands her the cash and watches her count it. She's very pretty, and so young. The ways she leans against the wall reminds her of Jess. The Regulator kicks in.

She's in a lace nightie, black stockings, and garters. High-heeled fluffy bedroom slippers that seem more funny than erotic.

Carrie puts the money aside and smiles at her. "Do you want to take the lead or have me do it? I'm fine either way."

"I'd rather just talk for a bit first."

Carrie frowns. "I told you I can't talk about my clients."

"I know. But I want to show you something."

Carrie shrugs and leads her to the bedroom. It's a lot like Mona's room: king-size bed, cream-colored sheets, a glass bowl of condoms, a clock discreetly on the nightstand. The mirror is mounted on the ceiling.

They sit down on the bed. Ruth takes out a file and hands Carrie a stack of photographs.

"All of these girls have been killed in the last year. All of them have the same implants you do."

Carrie looks up, shocked. Her eyes blink twice, rapidly.

"I know what you have behind your eye. I know you think it makes you safer. Maybe you even think someday the information in there can be a second source of income, when you're too old to do this. But there's a man who wants to cut that out of you. He's been doing the same to the other girls."

She shows her the pictures of dead Mona, with the bloody, mutilated face.

Carrie drops the pictures. "Get out. I'm calling the police." She stands up and grabs her phone.

Ruth doesn't move. "You can. Ask to speak to Captain Scott Brennan. He knows who I am, and he'll confirm what I've told you. I think you're the next target."

She hesitates.

Ruth continues, "Or you can just look at these pictures. You know what to look for. They were all just like you."

Carrie sits down and examines the pictures. "Oh God. Oh God."

"I know you probably have a set of regulars. At your prices, you don't need and won't get many new clients. But have you taken on anyone new lately?"

"Just you and one other. He's coming at eight."

Ruth's Regulator kicks in.

"Do you know what he looks like?"

"No. But I asked him to call me when he gets to the street corner, just like you, so I can get a look at him first before having him come up."

Ruth takes out her phone. "I need to call the police."

"No! You'll get me arrested. Please!"

Ruth thinks about this. She's only guessing that this man might be the killer. If she involves the police now and he turns out to be just a customer, Carrie's life will be ruined.

"Then I'll need to see him myself, in case he's the one."

"Shouldn't I just call it off?"

Ruth hears the fear in the girl's voice, and it reminds her of Jess, too, when she used to ask her to stay in her bedroom after watching a scary movie. She can feel the Regulator kicking into action again. She cannot let her emotions get in the way. "That would probably be safer for you, but we'd lose the chance to catch him if he *is* the one. Please, I need you to go through with it so I can get a close look at him. This may be our best chance of stopping him from hurting others."

Carrie bites her bottom lip. "All right. Where will you hide?"

Ruth wishes she had thought to bring her gun, but she hadn't wanted to spook Carrie, and she didn't anticipate having to fight. She'll need to be close enough to stop the man if he turns out to be the killer, and yet not so close as to make it easy for him to discover her.

"I can't hide inside here at all. He'll look around before going into the bedroom with you." She walks into the living room, which faces the back of the building, away from the street, and lifts the window open. "I can hide out here, hanging from the ledge. If he turns out to be the killer, I have to wait till the last possible minute to come in to cut off his escape. If he's not the killer, I'll drop down and leave."

Carrie is clearly uncomfortable with this plan, but she nods, trying to be brave.

"Act as normal as you can. Don't make him think something is wrong."

Carrie's phone rings. She swallows and clicks the phone on. She walks over to the bedroom window. Ruth follows.

"This is Carrie."

Ruth looks out the window. The man standing at the corner appears to be the right height, but that's not enough to be sure. She has to catch him and interrogate him.

"I'm in the four-story building about a hundred feet behind you. Come up to apartment 303. I'm so glad you came, dear. We'll have a great time, I promise." She hangs up.

The man starts walking this way. Ruth thinks there's a limp to his walk, but again, she can't be sure.

"Is it him?" Carrie asks.

"I don't know. We have to let him in and see."

Ruth can feel the Regulator humming. She knows that the idea of using Carrie as bait frightens her, is repugnant, even. But it's the logical thing to do. She'll never get a chance like this again. She has to trust that she can protect the girl.

"I'm going outside the window. You're doing great. Just keep him talking and do what he wants. Get him relaxed and focused on you. I'll come in before he can hurt you. I promise."

Carrie smiles. "I'm good at acting."

Ruth goes to the living room window and deftly climbs out. She lets her body down, hanging on to the window ledge with her fingers so that she's invisible from inside the apartment.

"Okay, close the window. Leave just a slit open, so I can hear what happens inside."

"How long can you hang like this?"

"Long enough."

Carrie closes the window. Ruth is glad for the artificial tendons and tensors in her shoulders and arms and the reinforced fingers holding her up. The idea had been to make her more effective in close combat, but they're coming in handy now, too.

She counts off the seconds. The man should be at the building. . . . He should now be coming up the stairs. . . . He should now be at the door.

She hears the door to the apartment open.

"You're even prettier than your pictures." The voice is rich, deep, satisfied.

"Thank you."

She hears more conversation, the exchange of money. Then the sound of more walking.

They're heading toward the bedroom. She can hear the man stopping to look into the other rooms. She almost can feel his gaze pass over the top of her head, out the window.

Ruth pulls herself up slowly, quietly, and looks in. She sees the man disappear into the hallway. There's a distinct limp.

She waits a few more seconds so that the man cannot rush back past her before she can reach the hallway to block it, and then she takes a deep breath and wills the Regulator to pump her blood full of adrenaline. The world seems to grow brighter, and time slows down as she flexes her arms and pulls herself onto the window ledge.

She squats down and pulls the window up in one swift motion. She knows that the grinding noise will alert the man, and she has only a few seconds to get to him. She ducks, rolls through the open window onto the floor inside. Then she continues to roll until her feet are under her and activates the pistons in her legs to leap toward the hallway.

She lands and rolls again to not give him a clear target, and jumps again from her crouch into the bedroom.

The man shoots, and the bullet strikes her left shoulder. She tackles him as her arms, held in front of her, slam into his midsection. He falls, and the gun clatters away.

Now the pain from the bullet hits. She wills the Regulator to pump up the adrenaline and the endorphins to numb the pain. She pants and concentrates on the fight for her life.

He tries to flip her over with his superior mass, to pin her down, but she clamps her hands around his neck and squeezes hard. Men have always underestimated her at the beginning of a fight, and she has to take advantage of it. She knows that her grip feels like iron clamps around him, with all the implanted energy cells in her arms and hands activated and on full power. He winces, grabs her hands to try to pry them off. After a few seconds, realizing the futility of it, he ceases to struggle.

He's trying to talk, but can't get any air into his lungs. Ruth lets up a little, and he chokes out, "You got me."

Ruth increases the pressure again, choking off his supply of air. She turns to Carrie, who's at the foot of the bed, frozen. "Call the police. Now."

She complies. As she continues to hold the phone against her ear as the 911 dispatcher has instructed her to do, she tells Ruth, "They're on their way."

The man goes limp with his eyes closed. Ruth lets go of his neck. She doesn't want to kill him, so she clamps her hands around his wrists while she sits on his legs, holding him still on the floor.

He revives and starts to moan. "You're breaking my fucking arms!"

Ruth lets up the pressure a bit to conserve her power. The man's nose is bleeding from the fall against the floor when she tackled him. He inhales loudly, swallows, and says, "I'm going to drown if you don't let me sit up."

Ruth considers this. She lets up the pressure further and pulls him into a sitting position.

She can feel the energy cells in her arms depleting. She won't have the physical upper hand much longer if she has to keep on restraining him this way.

She calls out to Carrie. "Come over here and tie his hands together."

Carrie puts down the phone and comes over gingerly. "What do I use?"

"Don't you have any rope? You know, for your clients?"

"I don't do that kind of thing."

Ruth thinks. "You can use stockings."

As Carrie ties the man's hands and feet together in front of him, he coughs. Some of the blood has gone down the wrong pipe. Ruth is unmoved and doesn't ease up on the pressure, and he winces. "Goddamn it. You're one psycho robo bitch."

Ruth ignores him. The stockings are too stretchy and won't hold him for long. But it should last long enough for her to get the gun and point it at him.

Carrie retreats to the other side of the room. Ruth lets the man go and backs away from him toward the gun on the floor a few yards away, keeping her eyes on him. If he makes any sudden movements, she'll be back on him in a flash.

He stays limp and unmoving as she steps backward. She begins to relax. The Regulator is trying to calm her down now, to filter the adrenaline out of her system.

When she's about halfway to the gun, the man suddenly reaches into his jacket with his hands still tied together. Ruth hesitates for only a second before pushing out with her legs to jump backward to the gun.

As she lands, the man locates something inside his jacket, and suddenly Ruth feels her legs and arms go limp, and she falls to the ground, stunned.

Carrie is screaming. "My eye! Oh God, I can't see out of my left eye!"

Ruth can't seem to feel her legs at all, and her arms feel like rubber. Worst of all, she's panicking. It seems she's never been this scared or in this much pain. She tries to feel the presence of the Regulator and there's nothing, just emptiness. She can smell the sweet, sickly smell of burned electronics in the air. The clock on the nightstand is dark.

She's the one who had underestimated *him*. Despair floods through her, and there's nothing to hold it back.

Ruth can hear the man stagger up off the floor. She wills herself to turn over, to move, to reach for the gun. She crawls. One foot, another foot. She seems to be moving through molasses because she's so weak. She can feel every one of her forty-nine years. She feels every sharp stab of pain in her shoulder.

She reaches the gun, grabs it, and sits up against the wall, pointing it back into the center of the room.

The man has gotten out of Carrie's ineffective knots. He's now holding Carrie, blind in one eye, shielding his body with hers. He holds a scalpel against her throat. He's already broken the skin, and a thin stream of blood flows down her neck.

He backs toward the bedroom door, dragging Carrie with him. Ruth knows that if he gets to the bedroom door and disappears around the corner, she'll never be able to catch him. Her legs are simply useless.

Carrie sees Ruth's gun and screams, "I don't want to die! Oh God. Oh God."

"I'll let her go once I'm safe," he says, keeping his head hidden behind hers.

Ruth's hands are shaking as she holds the gun. Through the waves of nausea and the pounding of her pulse in her ears, she struggles to think through what will happen next. The police are on their way and will probably be here in five minutes. Isn't it likely that he'll let her go as soon as possible to give himself some extra time to escape?

The man backs up another two steps; Carrie is no longer kicking or struggling but trying to find purchase on the smooth floor in her stockinged feet, trying to cooperate with him. But she can't stop crying.

Mom, don't shoot! Please don't shoot!

Or is it more likely that once the man has left the room, he will slit Carrie's throat and cut out her implant? He knows there's a recording of him inside, and he can't afford to leave that behind.

Ruth's hands are shaking too much. She wants to curse at herself. She cannot get a clear shot at the man with Carrie in front of him. She cannot.

Ruth wants to evaluate the chances rationally, to make a decision, but regret and grief and rage, hidden and held down by the Regulator until they could be endured, rise now all the sharper, kept fresh by the effort at forgetting. The universe has shrunken down to the wavering spot at the end of the barrel of the gun: a young woman, a killer, and time slipping irrevocably away.

She has nothing to turn to, to trust, to lean on but herself; her angry, frightened, trembling self. She is naked and alone, as she has always known she is, as we all are.

The man is almost at the door. Carrie's cries are now incoherent sobs.

It has always been the regular state of things. There is no clarity, no relief. At the end of all rationality, there is simply the need to decide and the faith to live through, to endure.

Ruth's first shot slams into Carrie's thigh. The bullet plunges through skin, muscle, and fat, and exits out the back, shattering the man's knee.

The man screams and drops the scalpel. Carrie falls, a spray of blood blossoming from her wounded leg.

Ruth's second shot catches the man in the chest. He collapses to the floor.

Mom, Mom!

She drops the gun and crawls over to Carrie, cradling her and tending to her wound. She's crying, but she'll be fine.

A deep pain floods through her like forgiveness, like hard rain after a long drought. She does not know if she will be granted relief, but she experiences this moment fully, and she's thankful.

"It's okay," she says, stroking Carrie as she lies in her lap. "It's okay."

★ ★ ★ ★

AUTHOR'S NOTE

The EchoSense technology described in this story is a loose and liberal extrapolation of the principles behind the technology described in Qifan Pu et al, "Whole-Home Gesture Recognition Using Wireless Signals" (Nineteenth Annual International Conference on Mobile Computing and Networking, MobiCom 2013), available at wisee.cs.washington.edu/wisee_paper.pdf. There is no intent to suggest that the technology described in the paper resembles the fictional one portrayed here.

The Paper Menagerie

One of my earliest memories starts with me sobbing. I refused to be soothed no matter what Mom and Dad tried.

Dad gave up and left the bedroom, but Mom took me into the kitchen and sat me down at the breakfast table.

"*Kan, kan,*" she said, as she pulled a sheet of wrapping paper from on top of the fridge. For years, Mom carefully sliced open the wrappings around Christmas gifts and saved them on top of the fridge in a thick stack.

She set the paper down, plain side facing up, and began to fold it. I stopped crying and watched her, curious.

She turned the paper over and folded it again. She pleated, packed, tucked, rolled, and twisted until the paper disappeared between her cupped hands. Then she lifted the folded-up paper packet to her mouth and blew into it, like a balloon.

"*Kan,*" she said, "*laohu.*" She put her hands down on the table and let go.

A little paper tiger stood on the table, the size of two fists placed together. The skin of the tiger was the pattern on the wrapping paper, white background with red candy canes and green Christmas trees.

I reached out to Mom's creation. Its tail twitched, and it pounced playfully at my finger. "*Rawrr-sa,*" it growled, the sound somewhere between a cat and rustling newspapers.

I laughed, startled, and stroked its back with an index finger. The paper tiger vibrated under my finger, purring.

"*Zhe jiao zhezhi,*" Mom said. *This is called origami.*

I didn't know this at the time, but Mom's kind was special. She breathed into them so that they shared her breath, and thus moved with her life. This was her magic.

Dad had picked Mom out of a catalog.

One time, when I was in high school, I asked Dad about the details. He was trying to get me to speak to Mom again.

He had signed up for the introduction service back in the spring of 1973. Flipping through the pages steadily, he had spent no more than a few seconds on each page until he saw the picture of Mom.

I've never seen this picture. Dad described it: Mom was sitting in a chair, her side to the camera, wearing a tight green silk cheongsam. Her head was turned to the camera so that her long black hair was draped artfully over her chest and shoulder. She looked out at him with the eyes of a calm child.

"That was the last page of the catalog I saw," he said.

The catalog said she was eighteen, loved to dance, and spoke good English because she was from Hong Kong. None of these facts turned out to be true.

He wrote to her, and the company passed their messages back and forth. Finally, he flew to Hong Kong to meet her.

"The people at the company had been writing her responses. She didn't know any English other than 'hello' and 'good-bye.'"

What kind of woman puts herself into a catalog so that she can be bought? The high-school-me thought I knew so much about everything. Contempt felt good, like wine.

Instead of storming into the office to demand his money back, he paid a waitress at the hotel restaurant to translate for them.

"She would look at me, her eyes halfway between scared and hopeful, while I spoke. And when the girl began translating what I said, she'd start to smile slowly."

He flew back to Connecticut and began to apply for the papers for her to come to him. I was born a year later, in the Year of the Tiger.

At my request, Mom also made a goat, a deer, and a water buffalo out of wrapping paper. They would run around the living room while Laohu chased after them, growling. When he caught them he would press down until the air went out of them and they became just flat, folded-up pieces of paper. I would then have to blow into them to reinflate them so they could run around some more.

Sometimes, the animals got into trouble. Once, the water buffalo jumped into a dish of soy sauce on the table at dinner. (He wanted to wallow, like a real water buffalo.) I picked him out quickly but the capillary action had already pulled the dark liquid high up into his legs. The sauce-softened legs would not hold him up, and he collapsed onto the table. I dried him out in the sun, but his legs became crooked after that, and he ran around with a limp. Mom eventually wrapped his legs in Saran wrap so that he could wallow to his heart's content (just not in soy sauce).

Also, Laohu liked to pounce at sparrows when he and I played in the backyard. But one time, a cornered bird struck back in desperation and tore his ear. He whimpered and winced as I held him and Mom patched his ear together with tape. He avoided birds after that.

And then one day, I saw a TV documentary about sharks and asked Mom for one of my own. She made the shark, but he flapped about on the table unhappily. I filled the sink with water and put him in. He swam around and around happily. However, after a while he became soggy and translucent, and slowly sank to the bottom, the folds coming undone. I reached in to rescue him, and all I ended up with was a wet piece of paper.

Laohu put his front paws together at the edge of the sink and rested his head on them. Ears drooping, he made a low growl in his throat that made me feel guilty.

Mom made a new shark for me, this time out of tinfoil. The shark lived happily in a large goldfish bowl. Laohu and I liked to sit next to the bowl to watch the tinfoil shark chasing the goldfish, Laohu sticking his face up against the bowl on the other side so that I saw his eyes, magnified to the size of coffee cups, staring at me from across the bowl.

When I was ten, we moved to a new house across town. Two of the women neighbors came by to welcome us. Dad served them drinks and then apologized for having to run off to the utility company to straighten out the prior owner's bills. "Make yourselves at home. My wife doesn't speak much English, so don't think she's being rude for not talking to you."

While I read in the dining room, Mom unpacked in the kitchen. The neighbors conversed in the living room, not trying to be particularly quiet.

"He seems like a normal enough man. Why did he do that?"

"Something about the mixing never seems right. The child looks unfinished. Slanty eyes, white face. A little monster."

"Do you think *he* can speak English?"

The women hushed. After a while they came into the dining room.

"Hello there! What's your name?"

"Jack," I said.

"That doesn't sound very Chinesey."

Mom came into the dining room then. She smiled at the women. The three of them stood in a triangle around me, smiling and nodding at each other, with nothing to say, until Dad came back.

Mark, one of the neighborhood boys, came over with his Star

Wars action figures. Obi-Wan Kenobi's lightsaber lit up and he could swing his arms and say, in a tinny voice, "Use the Force!" I didn't think the figure looked much like the real Obi-Wan at all.

Together, we watched him repeat this performance five times on the coffee table. "Can he do anything else?" I asked.

Mark was annoyed by my question. "Look at all the details," he said.

I looked at the details. I wasn't sure what I was supposed to say.

Mark was disappointed by my response. "Show me your toys."

I didn't have any toys except my paper menagerie. I brought Laohu out from my bedroom. By then he was very worn, patched all over with tape and glue, evidence of the years of repairs Mom and I had done on him. He was no longer as nimble and sure-footed as before. I sat him down on the coffee table. I could hear the skittering steps of the other animals behind in the hallway, timidly peeking into the living room.

"*Xiao laohu,*" I said, and stopped. I switched to English. "This is Tiger." Cautiously, Laohu strode up and purred at Mark, sniffing his hands.

Mark examined the Christmas-wrap pattern of Laohu's skin. "That doesn't look like a tiger at all. Your mom makes toys for you from trash?"

I had never thought of Laohu as *trash*. But looking at him now, he was really just a piece of wrapping paper.

Mark pushed Obi-Wan's head again. The lightsaber flashed; he moved his arms up and down. "Use the Force!"

Laohu turned and pounced, knocking the plastic figure off the table. It hit the floor and broke, and Obi-Wan's head rolled under the couch. "*Rawwww,*" Laohu laughed. I joined him.

Mark punched me, hard. "This was very expensive! You can't even find it in the stores now. It probably cost more than what your dad paid for your mom!"

I stumbled and fell to the floor. Laohu growled and leapt at Mark's face.

Mark screamed, more out of fear and surprise than pain. Laohu was only made of paper, after all.

Mark grabbed Laohu and his snarl was choked off as Mark crumpled him in his hand and tore him in half. He balled up the two pieces of paper and threw them at me. "Here's your stupid cheap Chinese garbage."

After Mark left, I spent a long time trying, without success, to tape together the pieces, smooth out the paper, and follow the creases to refold Laohu. Slowly, the other animals came into the living room and gathered around us, me and the torn wrapping paper that used to be Laohu.

My fight with Mark didn't end there. Mark was popular at school. I never want to think again about the two weeks that followed.

I came home that Friday at the end of the two weeks. *"Xuexiao hao ma?"* Mom asked. I said nothing and went to the bathroom. I looked into the mirror. *I look nothing like her, nothing.*

At dinner I asked Dad, "Do I have a chink face?"

Dad put down his chopsticks. Even though I had never told him what happened in school, he seemed to understand. He closed his eyes and rubbed the bridge of his nose. "No, you don't."

Mom looked at Dad, not understanding. She looked back at me. *"Sha jiao* chink?"

"English," I said. "Speak English."

She tried. "What happen?"

I pushed the chopsticks and the bowl before me away: stir-fried green peppers with five-spice beef. "We should eat American food."

Dad tried to reason. "A lot of families cook Chinese sometimes."

"We are not other families." I looked at him. *Other families don't have moms who don't belong.*

He looked away. And then he put a hand on Mom's shoulder. "I'll get you a cookbook."

Mom turned to me. *"Bu haochi?"*

"English," I said, raising my voice. "Speak English."

Mom reached out to touch my forehead, feeling for my temperature. *"Fashao la?"*

I brushed her hand away. "I'm fine. Speak English!" I was shouting.

"Speak English to him," Dad said to Mom. "You knew this was going to happen someday. What did you expect?"

Mom dropped her hands to her side. She sat, looking from Dad to me, and back to Dad again. She tried to speak, stopped, and tried again, and stopped again.

"You have to," Dad said. "I've been too easy on you. Jack needs to fit in."

Mom looked at him. "If I say 'love,' I feel here." She pointed to her lips. "If I say *'ai,'* I feel here." She put her hand over her heart.

Dad shook his head. "You are in America."

Mom hunched down in her seat, looking like the water buffalo when Laohu used to pounce on him and squeeze the air of life out of him.

"And I want some real toys."

Dad bought me a full set of Star Wars action figures. I gave the Obi-Wan Kenobi to Mark.

I packed the paper menagerie in a large shoe box and put it under the bed.

The next morning, the animals had escaped and took over their old favorite spots in my room. I caught them all and put them back into the shoe box, taping the lid shut. But the animals made so much noise in the box that I finally shoved it into the corner of the attic as far away from my room as possible.

If Mom spoke to me in Chinese, I refused to answer her. After a while, she tried to use more English. But her accent and broken sentences embarrassed me. I tried to correct her. Eventually, she stopped speaking altogether if I was around.

Mom began to mime things if she needed to let me know something. She tried to hug me the way she saw American mothers did on TV. I thought her movements exaggerated, uncertain, ridiculous, graceless. She saw that I was annoyed, and stopped.

"You shouldn't treat your mother that way," Dad said. But he couldn't look me in the eyes as he said it. Deep in his heart, he must have realized that it was a mistake to have tried to take a Chinese peasant girl and expect her to fit in the suburbs of Connecticut.

Mom learned to cook American style. I played video games and studied French.

Every once in a while, I would see her at the kitchen table studying the plain side of a sheet of wrapping paper. Later a new paper animal would appear on my nightstand and try to cuddle up to me. I caught them, squeezed them until the air went out of them, and then stuffed them away in the box in the attic.

Mom finally stopped making the animals when I was in high school. By then her English was much better, but I was already at that age when I wasn't interested in what she had to say whatever language she used.

Sometimes, when I came home and saw her tiny body busily moving about in the kitchen, singing a song in Chinese to herself, it was hard for me to believe that she gave birth to me. We had nothing in common. She might as well be from the moon. I would hurry on to my room, where I could continue my all-American pursuit of happiness.

Dad and I stood, one on each side of Mom lying in her hospital bed. She was not yet even forty, but she looked much older.

For years she had refused to go to the doctor for the pain

inside her that she said was no big deal. By the time an ambulance finally carried her in, the cancer had spread far beyond the limits of surgery.

My mind was not in the room. It was the middle of the on-campus recruiting season, and I was focused on résumés, transcripts, and strategically constructed interview schedules. I schemed about how to lie to the corporate recruiters most effectively so that they'd offer to buy me. I understood intellectually that it was terrible to think about this while your mother lay dying. But that understanding didn't mean I could change how I felt.

She was conscious. Dad held her left hand with both of his own. He leaned down to kiss her forehead. He seemed weak and old in a way that startled me. I realized that I knew almost as little about Dad as I did about Mom.

Mom smiled at him. "I'm fine."

She turned to me, still smiling. "I know you have to go back to school." Her voice was very weak, and it was difficult to hear her over the hum of the machines hooked up to her. "Go. Don't worry about me. This is not a big deal. Just do well in school."

I reached out to touch her hand, because I thought that was what I was supposed to do. I was relieved. I was already thinking about the flight back, and the bright California sunshine.

She whispered something to Dad. He nodded and left the room.

"Jack, if—" She was caught up in a fit of coughing, and could not speak for some time. "If I don't make it, don't be too sad and hurt your health. Focus on your life. Just keep that box you have in the attic with you, and every year, at *Qingming*, just take it out and think about me. I'll be with you always."

Qingming was the Chinese Festival for the Dead. When I was very young, Mom used to write a letter on *Qingming* to her dead parents back in China, telling them the good news about the past year of her life in America. She would read the letter out loud to me, and if I made a comment about something, she would write it down in the letter too. Then she would fold the letter into a paper crane and release it, facing west. We would then watch as the crane flapped its crisp wings on its long journey west, toward the Pacific, toward China, toward the graves of Mom's family.

It had been many years since I last did that with her.

"I don't know anything about the Chinese calendar," I said. "Just rest, Mom."

"Just keep the box with you and open it once in a while. Just open—" She began to cough again.

"It's okay, Mom." I stroked her arm awkwardly.

"*Haizi, mama ai ni—*" Her cough took over again. An image from years ago flashed into my memory: Mom saying *ai* and then putting her hand over her heart.

"All right, Mom. Stop talking."

Dad came back, and I said that I needed to get to the airport early because I didn't want to miss my flight.

She died when my plane was somewhere over Nevada.

Dad aged rapidly after Mom died. The house was too big for him and had to be sold. My girlfriend, Susan, and I went to help him pack and clean the place.

Susan found the shoe box in the attic. The paper menagerie, hidden in the uninsulated darkness of the attic for so long, had become brittle, and the bright wrapping paper patterns had faded.

"I've never seen origami like this," Susan said. "Your mom was an amazing artist."

The paper animals did not move. Perhaps whatever magic had animated them stopped when Mom died. Or perhaps I had only imagined that these paper constructions were once alive. The memory of children could not be trusted.

It was the first weekend in April, two years after Mom's death. Susan was out of town on one of her endless trips as a management consultant, and I was home, lazily flipping through the TV channels.

I paused at a documentary about sharks. Suddenly I saw, in my mind, Mom's hands, as they folded and refolded tinfoil to make a shark for me while Laohu and I watched.

A rustle. I looked up and saw that a ball of wrapping paper and torn tape was on the floor next to the bookshelf. I walked over to pick it up for the trash.

The ball of paper shifted, unfurled itself, and I saw that it was Laohu, who I hadn't thought about in a very long time. *"Rawrr-sa."* Mom must have put him back together after I had given up.

He was smaller than I remembered. Or maybe it was just that back then my fists were smaller.

Susan had put the paper animals around our apartment as decoration. She probably left Laohu in a pretty hidden corner because he looked so shabby.

I sat down on the floor and reached out a finger. Laohu's tail twitched, and he pounced playfully. I laughed, stroking his back. Laohu purred under my hand.

"How've you been, old buddy?"

Laohu stopped playing. He got up, jumped with feline grace into my lap, and proceeded to unfold himself.

In my lap was a square of creased wrapping paper, the plain side up. It was filled with dense Chinese characters. I had never learned to read Chinese, but I knew the characters for "son," and they were at the top, where you'd expect them in a letter addressed to you, written in Mom's awkward, childish handwriting.

I went to the computer to check the Internet. Today was *Qingming*.

I took the letter with me downtown, where I knew the Chinese tour buses stopped. I stopped every tourist, asking, *"Nin hui du zhongwen ma?"* Can you read Chinese? I hadn't spoken Chinese in so long that I wasn't sure if they understood.

A young woman agreed to help. We sat down on a bench together, and she read the letter to me aloud. The language that I had tried to forget for years came back, and I felt the words sinking into me, through my skin, through my bones, until they squeezed tight around my heart.

SON,

We haven't talked in a long time. You are so angry when I try to touch you that I'm afraid. And I think maybe this pain I feel all the time now is something serious.

So I decided to write to you. I'm going to write in the paper animals I made for you that you used to like so much.

The animals will stop moving when I stop breathing. But if I write to you with all my heart, I'll leave a little of myself behind on this paper, in these words. Then, if you think of me on Qingming, *when the spirits of the departed are allowed to visit their families, you'll make the parts of myself I leave behind come alive too. The creatures I made for you will again leap and run and pounce, and maybe you'll get to see these words then.*

Because I have to write with all my heart, I need to write to you in Chinese.

All this time I still haven't told you the story of my life. When you were little, I always thought I'd tell you the story when you were older, so you could understand. But somehow that chance never came up.

I was born in 1957, in Sigulu Village, Hebei Province. Your grandparents were both from very poor peasant families with few relatives. Only a few years after I was born, the Great Famines struck China, during which thirty million people died. The first memory I have was waking up to see my mother eating dirt so that she could fill her belly and leave the last bit of flour for me.

Things got better after that. Sigulu is famous for its zhezhi *papercraft, and my mother taught me how to make paper animals and give them life. This was practical magic in the life of the village. We made paper birds to chase grasshoppers away from the fields, and paper tigers to keep away the mice. For Chinese New Year my friends and I made red paper dragons. I'll never forget the sight of all those little dragons zooming across the sky overhead, holding up strings of exploding firecrackers to scare away all the bad memories of the past year. You would have loved it.*

Then came the Cultural Revolution in 1966. Neighbor turned on neighbor, and brother against brother. Someone remembered that my mother's brother, my uncle, had left for Hong Kong back in 1946 and became a merchant there. Having a relative in Hong Kong meant we were spies and enemies of the people, and we had to be struggled against in every way. Your poor grandmother—she couldn't take the abuse and threw herself down a well. Then some boys with hunting muskets dragged your grandfather away one day into the woods, and he never came back.

There I was, a ten-year-old orphan. The only relative I had in the world was my uncle in Hong Kong. I snuck away one night and climbed onto a freight train going south.

Down in Guangdong Province a few days later, some men caught me stealing food from a field. When they heard that I was trying to get to Hong Kong, they laughed. "It's your lucky day. Our trade is to bring girls to Hong Kong."

They hid me in the bottom of a truck along with other girls and smuggled us across the border.

We were taken to a basement and told to stand up and look healthy and intelligent for the buyers. Families paid the warehouse a fee and came by to look us over and select one of us to "adopt."

The Chin family picked me to take care of their two boys. I got up every morning at four to prepare breakfast. I fed and bathed the boys. I shopped for food. I did the laundry and swept the floors. I followed the boys around and did their bidding. At night I was locked into a cupboard in the kitchen to sleep. If I was slow or did anything wrong I was beaten. If the boys did anything wrong I was beaten. If I was caught trying to learn English I was beaten.

"Why do you want to learn English?" Mr. Chin asked. "You want to go to the police? We'll tell the police that you are a mainlander illegally in Hong Kong. They'd love to have you in their prison."

Six years I lived like this. One day, an old woman who sold fish to me in the morning market pulled me aside.

"I know girls like you. How old are you now, sixteen? One day, the man who owns you will get drunk, and he'll look at you and pull you to him and you can't stop him. The wife will find out, and then you will think you really have gone to hell. You have to get out of this life. I know someone who can help."

She told me about American men who wanted Asian wives. If I can cook, clean, and take care of my American husband, he'll give me a good life. It was the only hope I had. And that was how I got into the catalog with all those lies and met your father. It is not a very romantic story, but it is my story.

In the suburbs of Connecticut, I was lonely. Your father was kind and gentle with me, and I was very grateful to him. But no one understood me, and I understood nothing.

But then you were born! I was so happy when I looked into your face and saw shades of my mother, my father, and myself. I had lost my entire family, all of Sigulu, everything I ever knew and loved. But there you were, and your face was proof that they were real. I hadn't made them up.

Now I had someone to talk to. I would teach you my language, and we could together remake a small piece of everything that I loved and lost. When you said your first *words to me, in Chinese that had the same accent as my mother and me, I cried for hours. When I made the first zhezhi animals for you, and you laughed, I felt there were no worries in the world.*

You grew up a little, and now you could even help your father and I talk to each other. I was really at home now. I finally found a good life. I wished my parents could be here, so that I could cook for them and give them a good life too. But my parents were no longer around. You know what the Chinese think is the saddest feeling in the world? It's for a child to finally grow the desire to take care of his parents, only to realize that they were long gone.

Son, I know that you do not like your Chinese eyes, which are my eyes. I know that you do not like your Chinese hair, which is my hair. But can you understand how much joy your very existence brought to me? And can you understand how it felt when you stopped talking to me and won't let me talk to you in Chinese? I felt I was losing everything all over again.

Why won't you talk to me, son? The pain makes it hard to write.

The young woman handed the paper back to me. I could not bear to look into her face.

Without looking up, I asked for her help in tracing out the character for *ai* on the paper below Mom's letter. I wrote the character again and again on the paper, intertwining my pen strokes with her words.

The young woman reached out and put a hand on my shoulder. Then she got up and left, leaving me alone with my mother.

Following the creases, I refolded the paper back into Laohu. I cradled him in the crook of my arm, and as he purred, we began the walk home.

An Advanced Readers'

Picture Book Of Comparative Cognition

My darling, my child, my connoisseur of sesquipedalian words and convoluted ideas and meandering sentences and baroque images, while the sun is asleep and the moon somnambulant, while the stars bathe us in their glow from eons ago and light-years away, while you are comfortably nestled in your blankets and I am hunched over in my chair by your bed, while we are warm and safe and still for the moment in this bubble of incandescent light cast by the pearl held up by the mermaid lamp, you and I, on this planet spinning and hurtling through the frigid darkness of space at dozens of miles per second, let's read.

The brains of Telosians record all the stimuli from their senses: every tingling along their hairy spine, every sound wave striking their membranous body, every image perceived by their simple-compound-refractive light-field eyes, every molecular gustatory and olfactory sensation captured by their waving stalk-feet, every ebb and flow in the magnetic field of their irregular, potato-shaped planet.

When they wish, they can recall every experience with absolute fidelity. They can freeze a scene and zoom in to focus on any detail; they can parse and reparse each conversation to extract every nuance. A joyful memory may be relived countless times, each replay introducing new discoveries. A painful memory may be replayed countless times as well, each time creating a fresh outrage. Eidetic reminiscence is a fact of existence.

Infinity pressing down upon the finite is clearly untenable.

The Telosian organ of cognition is housed inside a segmented body that buds and grows at one end while withering and shedding at the other. Every year, a fresh segment is added at the head to record the future; every year, an old segment is discarded from the tail, consigning the past to oblivion.

Thus, while the Telosians do not forget, they also do not remember. They are said to never die, but it is arguable whether they ever live.

It has been argued that thinking is a form of compression.

Remember the first time you tasted chocolate? It was a summer afternoon; your mother had just come back from shopping. She broke off a piece from a candy bar and put it in your mouth while you sat in the high chair.

As the stearate in the cocoa butter absorbed the heat from your mouth and melted over your tongue, complex alkaloids were released and seeped into your taste buds: twitchy caffeine, giddy phenethylamine, serotonic theobromine.

"Theobromine," your mother said, "means the food of the gods."

We laughed as we watched your eyes widen in surprise at the texture, your face scrunch up at the biting bitterness, and then your whole body relax as the sweetness overwhelmed your taste buds, aided by the dance of a thousand disparate organic compounds.

Then she broke the rest of the chocolate bar in halves and fed a piece to me and ate the other herself. "We have children because we can't remember our own first taste of ambrosia."

I can't remember the dress she wore or what she had bought; I can't remember what we did for the rest of that afternoon;

I can't re-create the exact timbre of her voice or the precise shapes of her features, the lines at the corners of her mouth or the name of her perfume. I only remember the way sunlight through the kitchen window glinted from her forearm, an arc as lovely as her smile.

A lit forearm, laughter, food of the gods. Thus are our memories compressed, integrated into sparkling jewels to be embedded in the limited space of our minds. A scene is turned into a mnemonic, a conversation reduced to a single phrase, a day distilled to a fleeting feeling of joy.

Time's arrow is the loss of fidelity in compression. A sketch, not a photograph. A memory is a re-creation, precious because it is both more and less than the original.

Living in a warm, endless sea rich with light and clumps of organic molecules, the Esoptrons resemble magnified cells, some as large as our whales. Undulating their translucent bodies, they drift, rising and falling, tumbling and twisting, like phosphorescent jellyfish riding on the current.

The thoughts of Esoptrons are encoded as complex chains of proteins that fold upon themselves like serpents coiling in the snake charmer's basket, seeking the lowest energy level so that they may fit into the smallest space. Most of the time, they lie dormant.

When two Esoptrons encounter each other, they may merge temporarily, a tunnel forming between their membranes. This kissing union can last hours, days, or years, as their memories are awakened and exchanged with energy contributions from both members. The pleasurable ones are selectively duplicated in a process much like protein expression—the serpentine proteins unfold and dance mesmerizingly in the electric music of coding sequences as they're first read and then re-expressed— while the unpleasant ones are diluted by being spread among the two bodies. For the Esoptrons, a shared joy truly is doubled, while a shared sorrow is indeed halved.

By the time they part, they each have absorbed the experiences of the other. It is the truest form of empathy, for the very qualia of experience are shared and expressed without alteration. There is no translation, no medium of exchange. They come to know each other in a deeper sense than any other creatures in the universe.

But being the mirrors for each other's souls has a cost: by the time they part from each other, the individuals in the mating pair have become indistinguishable. Before their merger, they each yearned for the other; as they part, they part from the self. The very quality that attracted them to each other is also, inevitably, destroyed in their union.

Whether this is a blessing or a curse is much debated.

Your mother has never hidden her desire to leave.

We met on a summer night, in a campground high up in the Rockies. We were from opposite coasts, two random particles on separate trajectories: I was headed for a new job, driving across the country and camping to save money; she was returning to Boston after having moved a friend and her truckful of possessions to San Francisco, camping because she wanted to look at the stars.

We drank cheap wine and ate even cheaper grilled hot dogs. Then we walked together under the dark velvet dome studded with crystalline stars like the inside of a geode, brighter than I'd ever seen them, while she explained to me their beauty: each as unique as a diamond, with a different-colored light. I could not remember the last time I'd looked up at the stars.

"I'm going there," she said.

"You mean Mars?" That was the big news back then, the announcement of a mission to Mars. Everyone knew it was a propaganda effort to make America seem great again, a new space race to go along with the new nuclear arms race and the stockpiling of rare Earth elements and zero-day cyber vulnerabilities. The other side had already promised their own Martian base, and we had to mirror their move in this new Great Game.

She shook her head. "What's the point of jumping onto a reef just a few steps from shore? I mean out there."

It was not the kind of statement one questioned, so instead of why and how and what are you talking about, I asked her what she hoped to find out there among the stars.

other Suns perhaps
With thir attendant Moons thou wilt descrie
Communicating Male and Femal Light,
Which two great Sexes animate the World,
Stor'd in each Orb perhaps with some that live.
For such vast room in Nature unpossest
By living Soule, desert and desolate,
Onely to shine, yet scarce to contribute
Each Orb a glimps of Light, conveyd so farr
Down to this habitable, which returnes
Light back to them, is obvious to dispute.

"What do they think about? How do they experience the world? I've been imagining such stories all my life, but the truth will be stranger and more wonderful than any fairy tale."

She spoke to me of gravitational lenses and nuclear pulse propulsion, of the Fermi Paradox and the Drake Equation, of Arecibo and Yevpatoria, of Blue Origin and SpaceX.

"Aren't you afraid?" I asked.

"I almost died before I could begin to remember."

She told me about her childhood. Her parents were avid sailors who had been lucky enough to retire early. They bought a boat and lived on it, and the boat was her first home. When she was three, her parents decided to sail across the Pacific. Halfway across the ocean, somewhere near the Marshall Islands, the boat sprung a leak. The family tried everything they could to save the vessel, but in the end had to activate the emergency beacon to call for help.

"That was my very first memory. I wobbled on this immense

bridge between the sea and the sky, and as it sank into the water and we had to jump off, Mom had me say good-bye."

By the time they were rescued by a Coast Guard plane, they had been adrift in the water in life vests for almost a full day and night. Sunburned and sickened by the salt water she swallowed, she spent a month in the hospital afterward.

"A lot of people were angry at my parents, saying they were reckless and irresponsible to endanger a child like that. But I'm forever grateful to them. They gave me the greatest gift parents could give to a child: fearlessness. They worked and saved and bought another boat, and we went out to the sea again."

It was such an alien way of thinking that I didn't know what to say. She seemed to detect my unease, and, turning to me, smiled.

"I like to think we were carrying on the tradition of the Polynesians who set out across the endless Pacific in their canoes or the Vikings who sailed for America. We have always lived on a boat, you know? That's what Earth is, a boat in space."

For a moment, as I listened to her, I felt as if I could step through the distance between us and hear an echo of the world through her ears, see the stars through her eyes: an austere clarity that made my heart leap.

Cheap wine and burned hot dogs, other Suns perhaps, the diamonds in the sky seen from a boat adrift at sea, the fiery clarity of falling in love.

The Tick-Tocks are the only uranium-based life forms known in the universe.

The surface of their planet is an endless vista of bare rock. To human eyes it seems a wasteland, but etched into this surface are elaborate, colorful patterns at an immense scale, each as large as an airport or stadium: curlicues like calligraphy strokes; spirals like the tips of fiddlehead ferns; hyperbolas like the shadows of flashlights against a cave wall; dense, radiating clusters like glowing cities seen from space. From time to time, a plume of superheated steam erupts from the ground like the blow of a whale or the explosion of an ice volcano on Enceladus.

Where are the creatures who left these monumental sketches? These tributes to lives lived and lost, these recordings of joys and sorrows known and forgotten?

You dig beneath the surface. Tunneling into the sandstone deposits over granite bedrock, you find pockets of uranium steeped in water.

In the darkness, the nucleus of a uranium atom spontaneously breaks apart, releasing a few neutrons. The neutrons travel through the vast emptiness of internuclear space like ships bound for strange stars (this is not really an accurate picture, but it's a romantic image and easy to illustrate). The water molecules, nebula-like, slow down the neutrons until they touch down on another uranium nucleus, a new world.

But the addition of this new neutron makes the nucleus unstable. It oscillates like a ringing alarm clock, breaks apart into two new elemental nuclei and two or three neutrons, new starships bound for distant worlds, to begin the cycle again.

To have a self-sustaining nuclear chain reaction with uranium, you need enough concentration of the right kind of uranium, uranium-235, which breaks apart when it absorbs the free neutrons, and something to slow down the speeding neutrons so that they can be absorbed, and water works well enough. Creation has blessed the world of the Tick-Tocks with both.

The by-products of fission, those fragments split from the uranium atom, fall along a bimodal distribution. Cesium, iodine, xenon, zirconium, molybdenum, technetium . . . like new stars formed from the remnants of a supernova, some last a few hours, others millions of years.

The thoughts and memories of the Tick-Tocks are formed from these glowing jewels in the dark sea. The atoms take the place of neurons, and the neutrons act as neurotransmitters. The moderating medium and neutron poisons act as inhibitors and deflect the flight of neutrons, forming neural pathways through the void. The computation process emerges at the subatomic level, and is manifested in the flight paths of messenger neutrons; the topology, composition, and arrangement of atoms; and the brilliant flashes of fissile explosion and decay.

As the thoughts of the Tick-Tocks grow ever more lively, excited, the water in the pockets of uranium heats up. When the pressure is great enough, a stream of superheated water flows up a crack in the sandstone cap and explodes at the surface in a plume of steam. The grand, intricate, fractal patterns made by the varicolored salt deposits they leave on the surface resemble the ionization trails left by subatomic particles in a bubble chamber.

Eventually, enough of the water will have been boiled away that the fast neutrons can no longer be captured by the uranium atoms to sustain the reaction. The universe sinks into quiescence, and thoughts disappear from this galaxy of atoms. This is how the Tick-Tocks die: with the heat of their own vitality.

Gradually, water seeps back into the mines, trickling through seams in the sandstone and cracks in the granite. When enough water has filled the husk of the past, a random decaying atom will release the neutron that will start the chain reaction again, ushering forth a florescence of new ideas and new beliefs, a new generation of life lit from the embers of the old.

Some have disputed the notion that the Tick-Tocks can think. How can they be said to be thinking, the skeptics ask, when the flight of neutrons are determined by the laws of physics with a soupçon of quantum randomness? Where is their free will? Where is their self-determination? Meanwhile, the electrochemical reactor piles in the skeptics' brains hum along, following the laws of physics with an indistinguishable rigor.

Like tides, the Tick-Tock nuclear reactions operate in pulses. Cycle after cycle, each generation discovers the world anew. The ancients leave no wisdom for the future, and the young do not look to the past. They live for one season and one season alone.

Yet, on the surface of the planet, in those etched, fantastic rock paintings, is a palimpsest of their rise and fall, the exhalations of empires. The chronicles of the Tick-Tocks are left for other intelligences in the cosmos to interpret.

As the Tick-Tocks flourish, they also deplete the concentration of uranium-235. Each generation consumes some of the nonrenewable resources of their universe, leaving less for future generations and beckoning closer the day when a sustained chain reaction will no longer be possible. Like a clock winding down inexorably, the world of the Tick-Tocks will then sink into an eternal, cold silence.

Your mother's excitement was palpable.

"Can you call a Realtor?" she asked. "I'll get started on liquidating our stocks. We don't need to save anymore. Your mother is going to go on that cruise she's always wanted."

"When did we win the lottery?" I asked.

She handed me a stack of paper. *LENS Program Orientation.*

I flipped through it. . . . *Your application essay is among the most extraordinary entries we've received . . . pending a physical examination and psychological evaluation . . . limited to the immediate family . . .*

"What is this?"

Her face fell as she realized that I truly did not understand.

Radio waves attenuated rapidly in the vastness of space, she explained. If anyone is shouting into the void in the orbs around those distant stars, they would not be heard except by their closest neighbors. A civilization would have to harness the energy of an entire star to broadcast a message that could traverse interstellar distances—and how often would that happen? Look at Earth: we'd barely managed to survive one Cold War before another started. Long before we get to the point of harnessing the energy of the Sun, our children will be either wading through a postapocalyptic flooded landscape or shivering in a nuclear winter, back in another Stone Age.

"But there is a way to cheat, a way for even a primitive civilization like ours to catch faint whispers from across the galaxy and perhaps even answer back."

The Sun's gravity bends the light and radio waves from distant stars around it. This is one of the most important results from general relativity.

Suppose some other world out there in our galaxy, not much more advanced than ours, sent out a message with the most powerful antenna they could construct. By the time those emissions reached us, the electromagnetic waves would be so faint as to be undetectable. We'd have to turn the entire Solar System into a parabolic dish to capture it.

But as those radio waves grazed the surface of the Sun, the gravity of the star would bend them slightly, much as a lens bends rays of light. Those slightly bent beams from around the rim of the sun would converge at some distance beyond.

"Just as rays of sunlight could be focused by a magnifying glass into a spot on the ground."

The gain of an antenna placed at the focal point of the sun's gravitational lens would be enormous, close to ten billion times in certain frequency ranges, and orders of magnitude more in others. Even a twelve-meter inflatable dish would be able to detect transmissions from the other end of the galaxy. And if others in the galaxy were also clever enough to harness the gravitational lenses of their own suns, we would be able to talk to them as well—though the exchange would more resemble monologues delivered across the lifetimes of stars than a conversation, messages set adrift in bottles bound for distant shores, from one long-dead generation to generations yet unborn.

This spot, as it turns out, is about 550 AU from the Sun, almost fourteen times the distance of Pluto. The Sun's light would take just over three days to reach it, but at our present level of technology, it would take more than a century for a spacecraft.

Why send people? Why now?

"Because by the time an automated probe reached the focal point, we don't know if anyone will still be here. Will the human race survive even another century? No, we must send people so that they can be there to listen, and perhaps talk back.

"I'm going, and I'd like you to come with me."

The Thereals live within the hulls of great starships.

Their species, sensing the catastrophe of a world-ending disaster, commissioned the construction of escape arks for a small percentage of their world's population. Almost all of the refugees were children, for the Thereals loved their young as much as any other species.

Years before their star went supernova, the arks were launched in various directions at possible new home worlds. The ships began to accelerate, and the children settled down to learning from machine tutors and the few adults on board, trying to carry on the traditions of a dying world.

Only when the last of the adults were about to die aboard each ship did they reveal the truth to the children: the ships were not equipped with means for deceleration. They would accelerate forever, asymptotically approaching the speed of light, until the ships ran out of fuel and coasted along at the final cruising speed, toward the end of the universe.

Within their frame of reference, time would pass normally. But outside the ship, the rest of the universe would be hurtling along to its ultimate doom against the tide of entropy. To an outside observer, time seemed to stop in the ships.

Plucked out of the stream of time, the children would grow a few years older, but not much more. They would die only when the universe ended. This was the only way to ensure their safety, the adults explained, an asymptotic approach to triumphing over death. They would never have their own children; they would never have to mourn; they would never have to fear, to plan, to make impossible choices in sacrifice. They would be the last Thereals alive and possibly the last intelligent beings in the universe.

All parents make choices for their children. Almost always they think it's for the best.

All along, I had thought I could change her. I had thought she would want to stay because of me, because of our child. I had loved her because she was different; I also thought she would transform out of love.

"Love has many forms," she said. "This is mine."

Many are the stories we tell ourselves of the inevitable parting of lovers when they're from different worlds: selkies, *gu huo niao*, *Hagoromo*, swan maidens . . . What they have in common is the belief by one half of a couple that the other half could be changed, when in fact it was the difference, the resistance to change, that formed the foundation of their love. And then the day would come when the old sealskin or feather cape would be found, and it would be time to return to the sea or the sky, the ethereal realm that was the beloved's true home.

The crew of *Focal Point* would spend part of the voyage in hibernation; but once they reached their first target point, 550 AU from the Sun, away from the galactic center, they would have to stay awake and listen for as long as they could. They would guide the ship along a helical path away from the Sun, sweeping out a larger slice of the galaxy from which they might detect signals. The farther they drifted from the Sun, the better the Sun's magnification effect would be due to the reduction of interference from the solar corona on the deflected radio waves. The crew was expected to last as long as a few centuries, growing up, growing old, having children to carry on their work, dying in the void, an outpost of austere hope.

"You can't make a choice like that for our daughter," I said.

"You're making a choice for her too. How do you know if

she'll be safer or happier here? This is a chance for transcendence, the best gift we can give her."

And then came the lawyers and the reporters and the pundits armed with sound bites taking sides.

Then the night that you tell me you still remember. It was your birthday, and we were together again, just the three of us, for your sake because you said that was what you wished.

We had chocolate cake (you requested "teo-broom"). Then we went outside onto the deck to look up at the stars. Your mother and I were careful to make no mention of the fight in the courts or the approaching date for her departure.

"Is it true you grew up on a boat, Mommy?" you asked.

"Yes."

"Was it scary?"

"Not at all. We're all living on a boat, sweetheart. Earth is just a big raft in the sea of stars."

"Did you like living on a boat?"

"I loved that boat—well, I don't really remember. We don't remember much about what happened when we were really young; it's a quirk of being human. But I do remember being very sad when I had to say good-bye to it. I didn't want to. It was home."

"I don't want to say good-bye to my boat, either."

She cried. And so did I. So did you.

She gave you a kiss before she left. "There are many ways to say I love you."

The universe is full of echoes and shadows, the afterimages and last words of dead civilizations that have lost the struggle against entropy. Fading ripples in the cosmic background radiation, it is doubtful if most, or any, of these messages will ever be deciphered.

Likewise, most of our thoughts and memories are destined to fade, to disappear, to be consumed by the very act of choosing and living.

That is not a cause for sorrow, sweetheart. It is the fate of every species to disappear into the void that is the heat death of the universe. But long before then, the thoughts of any intelligent species worthy of the name will become as grand as the universe itself.

Your mother is asleep now on *Focal Point*. She will not wake up until you're a very old woman, possibly not even until after you're gone.

After she wakes up, she and her crewmates will begin to listen, and they'll also broadcast, hoping that somewhere else in the universe, another species is also harnessing the energy of their star to focus the faint rays across light-years and eons. They'll play a message designed to introduce us to strangers, written in a language based on mathematics and logic. I've always found it funny that we think the best way to communicate with extraterrestrials is to speak in a way that we never do in life.

But at the end, as a closing, there will be a recording of compressed memories that will not be very logical: the graceful arc of whales breaching, the flicker of campfire and wild dancing, the formulas of chemicals making up the smell of a thousand foods, including cheap wine and burned hot dogs, the laughter of a child eating the food of the gods for the first time. Glittering jewels whose meanings are not transparent, and for that reason, are alive.

And so we read this, my darling, this book she wrote for you before she left, its ornate words and elaborate illustrations telling fairy tales that will grow as you grow, an apologia, a bundle of letters home, and a map of the uncharted waters of our souls.

There are many ways to say I love you in this cold, dark, silent universe, as many as the twinkling stars.

★ ★ ★ ★

For more on consciousness as compression, see:
Maguire, Phil, et al. "Is Consciousness Computable? Quantifying Integrated Information Using Algorithmic Information Theory." *arXiv preprint arXiv:1405.0126* (2014) (available at arxiv.org/pdf/ 1405.0126).

For more on natural nuclear reactor piles, see:
Teper, Igor. "Inconstants of Nature," *Nautilus*, January 23, 2014 (available at nautil.us/issue/9/time/inconstants-of-nature).
Davis, E. D., C. R. Gould, and E. I. Sharapov. "Oklo reactors and implications for nuclear science." *International Journal of Modern Physics E* 23.04 (2014) (available at arxiv.org/pdf/1404.4948).

For more on SETI and the Sun's gravitational lens, see:
Maccone, Claudio. "Interstellar radio links enhanced by exploiting the Sun as a gravitational lens." *Acta Astronautica* 68.1 (2011): 76–84 (available at snolab.ca/public/JournalClub/alex1.pdf).

The Waves

Long ago, just after Heaven was separated from Earth, Nü Wa wandered along the bank of the Yellow River, savoring the feel of the rich loess against the bottom of her feet.

All around her, flowers bloomed in all the colors of the rainbow, as pretty as the eastern edge of the sky, where Nü Wa had to patch a leak made by petty warring gods with a paste made of melted gemstones. Deer and buffalo dashed across the plains, and golden carp and silvery crocodiles frolicked in the water.

But she was all alone. There was no one to converse with her, no one to share all this beauty.

She sat down next to the water, and scooping up a handful of mud, began to sculpt. Before long, she had created a miniature version of herself: a round head, a long torso, arms and legs and tiny hands and fingers that she carefully carved out with a sharp bamboo skewer.

She cupped the tiny, muddy figure in her hands, brought it up to her mouth, and breathed the breath of life into it. The figure gasped, wriggled in Nü Wa's hands, and began to babble.

Nü Wa laughed. Now she would be alone no longer. She sat the little figure down on the bank of the Yellow River, scooped up another handful of mud, and began to sculpt again.

Man was thus created from earth, and to earth he would return, always.

★★★★

"What happened next?" a sleepy voice asked.

"I'll tell you tomorrow night," Maggie Chao said. "It's time to sleep now."

She tucked in Bobby, five, and Lydia, six, turned off the bedroom light, and closed the door behind her.

She stood still for a moment, listening, as if she could hear the flow of photons streaming past the smooth, spinning hull of the ship.

The great solar sail strained silently in the vacuum of space as the *Sea Foam* spiraled away from the sun, accelerating year after year until the sun had shifted into a dull red, a perpetual, diminishing sunset.

There's something you should see, João, Maggie's husband and the first officer, whispered in her mind. They were able to speak to each other through a tiny optical-neural interface chip implanted in each of their brains. The chips stimulated genetically modified neurons in the language-processing regions of the cortex with pulses of light, activating them in the same way that actual speech would have.

Maggie sometimes thought of the implant as a kind of miniature solar sail, where photons strained to generate thought.

João thought of the technology in much less romantic terms. Even a decade after the operation, he still didn't like the way they could be in each other's heads. He understood the advantages of the communication system, which allowed them to stay constantly in touch, but it felt clumsy and alienating, as though they were slowly turning into cyborgs, machines. He never used it unless it was urgent.

I'll be there, Maggie said, and quickly made her way up to the research deck, closer to the center of the ship. Here, the gravity simulated by the spinning hull was lighter, and the colonists joked that the location of the labs helped people think better because more oxygenated blood flowed to the brain.

Maggie Chao had been chosen for the mission because she was an expert on self-contained ecosystems and also because she was young and fertile. With the ship traveling at a low fraction of the speed of light, it would take close to four hundred years (by the ship's frame of reference) to reach 61 Virginis, even taking into account the modest time-dilation effects. That required planning for children and grandchildren so that, one day, the colonists' descendants might carry the memory of the three hundred original explorers onto the surface of an alien world.

She met João in the lab. He handed her a display pad without saying anything. He always gave her time to come to her own conclusions about something new without his editorial comment. That was one of the first things she liked about him when they started dating years ago.

"Extraordinary," she said as she glanced at the abstract. "First time Earth has tried to contact us in a decade."

Many on Earth had thought the *Sea Foam* a folly, a propaganda effort from a government unable to solve real problems. How could sending a centuries-long mission to the stars be justified when there were still people dying of hunger and diseases on Earth? After launch, communication with Earth had been kept to a minimum and then cut. The new administration did not want to keep paying for those expensive ground-based antennas. Perhaps they preferred to forget about this ship of fools.

But now, they had reached out across the emptiness of space to say something.

As she read the rest of the message, her expression gradually shifted from excitement to disbelief.

"They believe the gift of immortality should be shared by all of humanity," João said. "Even the farthest wanderers."

The transmission described a new medical procedure. A small, modified virus—a molecular nano-computer, for those who liked to think in those terms—replicated itself in somatic cells and roamed up and down the double helices of DNA strands, repairing damage, suppressing certain segments and overexpressing others, and the net effect was to halt cellular senescence and stop aging.

Humans would no longer have to die.

Maggie looked into João's eyes. "Can we replicate the procedure here?" *We will live to walk on another world, to breathe unrecycled air.*

"Yes," he said. "It will take some time, but I'm sure we can." Then he hesitated. "But the children . . ."

Bobby and Lydia were not the result of chance but the interplay of a set of careful algorithms involving population planning, embryo selection, genetic health, life expectancy, and rates of resource renewal and consumption.

Every gram of matter aboard the *Sea Foam* was accounted for. There was enough to support a stable population but little room for error. The children's births had to be timed so that they would have enough time to learn what they needed to learn from their parents, and then take their place as their elders died a peaceful death, cared for by the machines.

". . . would be the last children to be born until we land," Maggie finished João's thought. The *Sea Foam* had been designed for a precise population mix of adults and children. Supplies, energy, and thousands of other parameters were all tied to that mix. There was some margin of safety, but the ship could not support a population composed entirely of vigorous, immortal adults at the height of their caloric needs.

"We could either die and let our children grow," João said, "or we could live forever and keep them always as children."

Maggie imagined it: the virus could be used to stop the process of growth and maturation in the very young. The children would stay children for centuries, childless themselves.

Something finally clicked in Maggie's mind.

"That's why Earth is suddenly interested in us again," she said. "Earth is just a very big ship. If no one is going to die, they'll run out of room eventually too. Now there is no other problem on Earth more pressing. They'll have to follow us and move into space."

★ ★ ★ ★

You wonder why there are so many stories about how people came to be? It's because all true stories have many tellings.

Tonight, let me tell you another one.

There was a time when the world was ruled by the Titans, who lived on Mount Othrys. The greatest and bravest of the Titans was Cronus, who once led them in a rebellion against Uranus, his father and a tyrant. After Cronus killed Uranus, he became the king of the gods.

But as time went on, Cronus himself became a tyrant. Perhaps out of fear that what he had done to his own father would happen to him, Cronus swallowed all his children as soon as they were born.

Rhea, the wife of Cronus, gave birth to a new son, Zeus. To save the boy, she wrapped a stone in a blanket like a baby and fooled Cronus into swallowing that. The real baby Zeus she sent away to Crete, where he grew up drinking goat milk.

Don't make that face. I hear goat milk is quite tasty.

When Zeus was finally ready to face his father, Rhea fed Cronus a bitter wine that caused him to vomit up the children he had swallowed, Zeus's brothers and sisters. For ten years, Zeus led the Olympians, for that was the name by which Zeus and his siblings would come to be known, in a bloody war against his father and the Titans. In the end, the new gods won against the old, and Cronus and the Titans were cast into lightless Tartarus.

And the Olympians went on to have children of their own, for that was the way of the world. Zeus himself had many children, some mortal, some not. One of his favorites was Athena, the goddess who was born from his head, from his thoughts alone. There are many stories about them as well, which I will tell you another time.

But some of the Titans who did not fight by the side of Cronus were spared. One of these, Prometheus, molded a race of beings out of clay, and it is said that he then leaned down to whisper to them the words of wisdom that gave them life.

We don't know what he taught the new creatures, us. But this was a god who had lived to see sons rise up against fathers, each new generation replacing the old, remaking the world afresh each time. We can guess what he might have said.

Rebel. Change is the only constant.

"Death is the easy choice," Maggie said.

"It is the right choice," João said.

Maggie wanted to keep the argument in their heads, but João refused. He wanted to speak with lips, tongue, bursts of air, the old way.

Every gram of unnecessary mass had been shaved off the *Sea Foam*'s construction. The walls were thin and the rooms closely packed. Maggie and João's voices echoed through the decks and halls.

All over the ship, other families, who were having the same argument in their heads, stopped to listen.

"The old must die to make way for the new," João said. "You knew that we would not live to see the *Sea Foam* land when you signed up for this. Our children's children, generations down the line, are meant to inherit the new world."

"We can land on the new world ourselves. We don't have to leave all the hard work to our unborn descendants."

"We need to pass on a viable human culture for the new colony. We have no idea what the long-term consequences of this treatment will be on our mental health—"

"Then let's do the job we signed up for: exploration. Let's figure it out—"

"If we give in to this temptation, we'll land as a bunch of four-hundred-year-olds who were afraid to die and whose ideas were ossified from old Earth. How can we teach our children the value of sacrifice, the meaning of heroism, of beginning afresh? We'll barely be human."

"We stopped being human the moment we agreed to this

mission!" Maggie paused to get her voice under control. "Face it, the birth allocation algorithms don't care about us, or our children. We're nothing more than vessels for the delivery of a planned, optimal mix of genes to our destination. Do you really want generations to grow and die in here, knowing nothing but this narrow metal tube? I worry about *their* mental health."

"Death is essential to the growth of our species." His voice was filled with faith, and she heard in it his hope that it was enough for both of them.

"It's a myth that we must die to retain our humanity." Maggie looked at her husband, her heart in pain. There was a divide between them, as inexorable as the dilation of time.

She spoke to him now inside his head. She imagined her thoughts, now transformed into photons, pushing against his brain, trying to illuminate the gap. *We stop being human at the moment we give in to death.*

João looked back at her. He said nothing, either in her mind or aloud, which was his way of saying all that he needed to say.

They stayed like that for a long time.

God first created mankind to be immortal, much like the angels.

Before Adam and Eve chose to eat from the Tree of the Knowledge of Good and Evil, they did not grow old and they never became sick. During the day, they cultivated the Garden, and at night, they enjoyed each other's company.

Yes, I suppose the Garden was a bit like the hydroponics deck.

Sometimes the angels visited them, and—according to Milton, who was born too late to get into the regular Bible—they conversed and speculated about everything: Did Earth revolve around the Sun or was it the other way around? Was there life on other planets? Did angels also have sex?

Oh no, I'm not joking. You can look it up in the computer.

So Adam and Eve were forever young and perpetually

curious. They did not need death to give their life purpose, to be motivated to learn, to work, to love, to give existence meaning.

If that story is true, then we were never meant to die. And the knowledge of good and evil was really the knowledge of regret.

"You know some very strange stories, Gran-Gran," six-year-old Sara said.

"They're old stories," Maggie said. "When I was a little girl, my grandmother told me many stories, and I did a lot of reading."

"Do you want me to live forever like you, and not grow old and die someday like my mother?"

"I can't tell you what to do, sweetheart. You'll have to figure that out when you're older."

"Like the knowledge of good and evil?"

"Something like that."

She leaned down and kissed her great-great-great-great—she had long lost count—granddaughter as gently as she could. Like all children born in the low gravity of the *Sea Foam*, her bones were thin and delicate, like a bird's. Maggie turned off the night-light and left.

Though she would pass her four hundredth birthday in another month, Maggie didn't look a day older than thirty-five. The recipe for the fountain of youth, Earth's last gift to the colonists before they lost all communications, worked well.

She stopped and gasped. A small boy, about ten years in age, waited in front of the door to her room.

Bobby, she said. Except for the very young, who did not yet have the implants, all the colonists now conversed through thoughts rather than speech. It was faster and more private.

The boy looked at her, saying nothing and thinking nothing at her. She was struck by how like his father he was. He had the same expressions, the same mannerisms, even the same ways to speak by not speaking.

She sighed, opened the door, and walked in after him.

One more month, he said, sitting on the edge of the couch so that his feet didn't dangle.

Everybody on the ship was counting down the days. In one more month they'd be in orbit around the fourth planet of 61 Virginis, their destination, a new Earth.

After we land, will you change your mind about—she hesitated, but went on after a moment—*your appearance?*

Bobby shook his head, and a hint of boyish petulance crossed his face. *Mom, I've made my decision a long time ago. Let it go. I like the way I am.*

In the end, the men and women of the *Sea Foam* had decided to leave the choice of eternal youth to each individual.

The cold mathematics of the ship's enclosed ecosystem meant that when someone chose immortality, a child would have to remain a child until someone else on the ship decided to grow old and die, opening up a new slot for an adult.

João chose to age and die. Maggie chose to stay young. They sat together as a family, and it felt a bit like a divorce.

"One of you will get to grow up," João said.

"Which one?" Lydia asked.

"We think you should decide," João said, glancing at Maggie, who nodded reluctantly.

Maggie had thought it was unfair and cruel of her husband to put such a choice before their children. How could children decide if they wanted to grow up when they had no real idea what that meant?

"It's no more unfair than you and I deciding whether we want to be immortal," João had said. "We have no real idea what that means either. It is terrible to put such a choice before them, but to decide *for* them would be even more cruel." Maggie had to agree that he had a point.

It seemed like they were asking the children to take sides. But maybe that was the point.

Lydia and Bobby looked at each other, and they seemed to reach a silent understanding. Lydia got up, walked to João, and hugged him. At the same time, Bobby came and hugged Maggie.

"Dad," Lydia said, "when my time comes, I will choose the same as you." João tightened his arms around her and nodded.

Then Lydia and Bobby switched places and hugged their parents again, pretending that everything was fine.

For those who refused the treatment, life went on as planned. As João grew old, Lydia grew up: first an awkward teenager, then a beautiful young woman. She went into engineering, as predicted by her aptitude tests, and decided that she *did* like Catherine, the shy young doctor that the computers suggested would be a good mate for her.

"Will you grow old and die with me?" Lydia asked the blushing Catherine one day.

They married and had two daughters of their own—to replace them, when their time came.

"Do you ever regret choosing this path?" João asked her one time. He was very old and ill by then, and in another two weeks the computers would administer the drugs to allow him to fall asleep and not wake up.

"No," Lydia said, holding his hand with both of hers. "I'm not afraid to step out of the way when something new comes to take my place."

But who's to say that we aren't the "something new"? Maggie thought.

In a way, her side was winning the argument. Over the years, more and more colonists had decided to join the ranks of the immortals. But Lydia's descendants had always stubbornly refused. Sara was the last untreated child on the ship. Maggie knew Sara would miss the nightly story times when she grew up.

Bobby was frozen at the physical age of ten. He and the other perpetual children integrated only uneasily into the life of the colonists. They had decades—sometimes centuries— of experience, but retained juvenile bodies and brains. They possessed adult knowledge, but kept the emotional range and mental flexibility of children. They could be both old and young in the same moment.

There was a great deal of tension and conflict about what roles they should play on the ship, and occasionally, parents who once thought they wanted to live forever would give up their spots when their children demanded it of them.

But Bobby never asked to grow up.

My brain has the plasticity of a ten-year-old's. Why would I want to give that up? Bobby said.

Maggie had to admit that she always felt more comfortable with Lydia and her descendants. Even though they had all chosen to die, as João did, which could be seen as a kind of rebuke of her decision, she found herself better able to understand their lives and play a role in them.

With Bobby, on the other hand, she couldn't imagine what went on in his head. She sometimes found him a little creepy, which she agreed was a bit hypocritical, considering he only made the same choice she did.

But you won't experience what it's like to be grown, she said. *To love as a man and not a boy.*

He shrugged, unable to miss what he never had. *I can pick up new languages quickly. It's easy for me to absorb a new worldview. I'll always like new things.*

Bobby switched to speech, and his boyish voice rose as it filled with excitement and longing. "If we meet new life and new civilization down there, we'll need people like me, the forever children, to learn about them and understand them without fear."

It had been a long time since Maggie had really listened to her son. She was moved. She nodded, accepting his choice.

Bobby's face opened in a beautiful smile, the smile of a ten-year-old boy who had seen more than almost every human who had ever lived.

"Mom, I'll get that chance. I came to tell you that we've received the results of the first close-up scans of 61 Virginis e. It's inhabited."

Under the *Sea Foam*, the planet spun slowly. Its surface was covered by a grid of hexagonal and pentagonal patches, each a thousand miles across. About half of the patches were black as obsidian, while the rest were a grainy tan. 61 Virginis e reminded Maggie of a soccer ball.

Maggie stared at the three aliens standing in front of her in the shuttle bay, each about six feet tall. The metallic bodies, barrel-shaped and segmented, rested on four stick-thin, multi-jointed legs.

When the vehicles first approached the *Sea Foam*, the colonists had thought they were tiny scout ships until scans confirmed the absence of any organic matter. Then the colonists had thought they were autonomous probes until they came right up to the ship's camera, displayed their hands, and lightly tapped the lens.

Yes, *hands*. Midway up each of the metallic bodies, two long, sinuous arms emerged and terminated in soft, supple hands made of a fine alloy mesh. Maggie looked down at her own hands. The alien hands looked just like hers: four slender fingers, an opposable thumb, flexible joints.

On the whole, the aliens reminded Maggie of robotic centaurs.

At the very top of each alien body was a spherical protuberance studded with clusters of glass lenses, like compound eyes. Other than the eyes, this "head" was also covered by a dense array of pins attached to actuators that moved in synchrony like the tentacles of a sea anemone.

The pins shimmered as though a wave moved through them. Gradually, they took on the appearance of pixellated eyebrows, lips, eyelids—a face, a human face.

The alien began to speak. It sounded like English but Maggie couldn't make it out. The phonemes, like the shifting patterns of the pins, seemed elusive, just beyond coherence.

It is English, Bobby said to Maggie, *after centuries of pronunciation drift. He's saying, "Welcome back to humanity."*

The fine pins on the alien face shifted, unveiling a smile. Bobby continued to translate. *We left Earth long after your departure, but we were faster and passed you in transit centuries ago. We've been waiting for you.*

Maggie felt the world shift around her. She looked around, and many of the older colonists, the immortals, looked stunned.

But Bobby, the eternal child, stepped forward. "Thank you," he said aloud, and smiled back.

Let me tell you a story, Sara. We humans have always relied on stories to keep the fear of the unknown at bay.

I've told you how the Mayan gods created people out of maize, but did you know that before that, there were several other attempts at creation?

First came the animals: brave jaguar and beautiful macaw, flat fish and long serpent, the great whale and the lazy sloth, the iridescent iguana and the nimble bat. (We can look up pictures for all of these on the computer later.) But the animals only squawked and growled, and could not speak their creators' names.

So the gods kneaded a race of beings out of mud. But the mud men could not hold their shape. Their faces drooped, softened by water, yearning to rejoin the earth whence they were taken. They could not speak but only gurgled incoherently. They grew lopsided and were unable to procreate, to perpetuate their own existence.

The gods' next effort is the one of most interest to us. They created a race of wooden manikins, like dolls. The articulated joints allowed their limbs to move freely. The carved faces allowed their lips to flap and eyes to open. The stringless puppets lived in houses and villages, and went busily about their lives.

But the gods found that the wooden men had neither souls nor minds, and so they could not praise their makers properly. They sent a great flood to destroy the wooden men and asked the animals of the jungle to attack them. When the anger of the gods was over, the wooden men had become monkeys.

And only then did the gods turn to maize.

Many have wondered if the wooden men were really content to lose to the children of the maize. Perhaps they're still waiting in the shadows for an opportunity to come back, for creation to reverse its course.

The black hexagonal patches were solar panels, Atax, the leader of the three envoys from 61 Virginis e, explained. Together, they provided the power needed to support human habitation on the planet. The tan patches were cities, giant computing arrays where trillions of humans lived as virtual patterns of computation.

When Atax and the others colonists had first arrived, 61 Virginis e was not particularly hospitable to life from Earth. It was too hot, the air was too poisonous, and the existing alien life, mostly primitive microbes, was quite deadly.

But Atax and the others who had stepped onto the surface were not human, not in the sense Maggie would have understood the term. They were composed of more metal than water, and they were no longer trapped by the limits of organic chemistry. The colonists quickly constructed forges and foundries, and their descendants soon spread out across the globe.

Most of the time they chose to merge into the Singularity, the overall World-Mind that was both artificial and organic, where eons passed in a second as thought was processed at the speed of quantum computation. In the world of bits and qubits, they lived as gods.

But sometimes, when they felt the ancestral longing for physicality, they could choose to become individuals and be embodied in machines, as Atax and his companions were. Here, they lived in the slow-time, the time of atoms and stars.

There was no more line between the ghost and the machine.

"This is what humanity looks like now," Atax said, spinning around slowly to display his metal body for the benefit of the colonists on the *Sea Foam*. "Our bodies are made of steel and titanium, and our brains graphene and silicon. We are practically indestructible. Look, we can even move through space without the need for ships, suits, layers of protection. We have left corruptible flesh behind."

Atax and the others gazed intently at the ancient humans around them. Maggie stared back into their dark lenses, trying to fathom how the machines felt. Curiosity? Nostalgia? Pity?

Maggie shuddered at the shifting, metallic faces, a crude imitation of flesh and blood. She looked over at Bobby, who appeared ecstatic.

"You may join us, if you wish, or continue as you are. It is of course difficult to decide when you have no experience of our mode of existence. Yet you must choose. We cannot choose for you."

Something new, Maggie thought.

Even eternal youth and eternal life did not appear so wonderful compared to the freedom of being a machine, a thinking machine endowed with the austere beauty of crystalline matrices instead of the messy imperfections of living cells.

At last, humanity has advanced beyond evolution into the realm of intelligent design.

"I'm not afraid," Sara said.

She had asked to stay behind for a few minutes with Maggie after all the others had left. Maggie gave her a long hug, and the little girl squeezed her back.

"Do you think Gran-Gran João would have been disappointed in me?" Sara asked. "I'm not making the choice he would have made."

"I know he would have wanted you to decide for yourself," Maggie said. "People change, as a species and as individuals. We don't know what he would have chosen if he had been offered your choice. But no matter what, never let the past pick your life for you."

She kissed Sara on the cheek and let go. A machine came to take Sara away by the hand so that she could be transformed.

She's the last of the untreated children, Maggie thought. *And now she'll be the first to become a machine.*

Though Maggie refused to watch the transformation of the others, at Bobby's request, she watched as her son was replaced piece by piece.

"You'll never have children," she said.

"On the contrary," he said, as he flexed his new metal hands, so much larger and stronger than his old hands, the hands of a child, "I will have countless children, born of my mind." His voice was a pleasant electronic hum, like a patient teaching program's. "They'll inherit from my thoughts as surely as I have inherited your genes. And someday, if they wish, I will construct bodies for them, as beautiful and functional as the ones I'm being fitted with."

He reached out to touch her arm, and the cold metal fingertips slid smoothly over her skin, gliding on nanostructures that flexed like living tissue. She gasped.

Bobby smiled as his face, a fine mesh of thousands of pins, rippled in amusement.

She recoiled from him involuntarily.

Bobby's rippling face turned serious, froze, and then showed no expression at all.

She understood the unspoken accusation. What right did she have to feel revulsion? She treated her body as a machine too, just a machine of lipids and proteins, of cells and muscles. Her mind was maintained in a shell too, a shell of flesh that

had long outlasted its designed-for life. She was as "unnatural" as he.

Still, she cried as she watched her son disappear into a frame of animated metal.

He can't cry anymore, she kept on thinking, as if that was the only thing that divided her from him.

Bobby was right. Those who were frozen as children were quicker to decide to upload. Their minds were flexible, and to them, to change from flesh to metal was merely a hardware upgrade.

The older immortals, on the other hand, lingered, unwilling to leave their past behind, their last vestiges of humanity. But one by one, they succumbed as well.

For years, Maggie remained the only organic human on 61 Virginis e, and perhaps the entire universe. The machines built a special house for her, one insulated from the heat and poison and ceaseless noise of the planet, and Maggie occupied herself by browsing through the *Sea Foam*'s archives, the records of humanity's long, dead past. The machines left her pretty much alone.

One day, a small machine, about two feet tall, came into her house and approached her hesitantly. It reminded her of a puppy.

"Who are you?" Maggie asked.

"I'm your grandchild," the little machine said.

"So Bobby has finally decided to have a child," Maggie said. "It took him long enough."

"I'm the 5,032,322th child of my parent."

Maggie felt dizzy. Soon after his transformation into a machine, Bobby had decided to go all the way and join the Singularity. They had not spoken to each other for a long time.

"What's your name?"

"I don't have a name in the sense you think of it. But why don't you call me Athena?"

"Why?"

"It's a name from a story my parent used to tell me when I was little."

Maggie looked at the little machine, and her expression softened.

"How old are you?"

"That's a hard question to answer," Athena said. "We're born virtual and each second of our existence as part of the Singularity is composed of trillions of computation cycles. In that state, I have more thoughts in a second than you have had in your entire life."

Maggie looked at her granddaughter, a miniature mechanical centaur, freshly made and gleaming, and also a being much older and wiser than she by most measures.

"So why have you put on this disguise to make me think of you as a child?"

"Because I want to hear your stories," Athena said. "The ancient stories."

There are still young people, Maggie thought. *Still something new.*

Why can't the old become new again?

And so Maggie decided to upload as well, to rejoin her family.

In the beginning, the world was a great void crisscrossed by icy rivers full of venom. The venom congealed, dripped, and formed into Ymir, the first giant, and Auðumbla, a great ice cow.

Ymir fed on Auðumbla's milk and grew strong.

Of course you have never seen a cow. Well, it is a creature that gives milk, which you would have drunk if you were still . . .

I suppose it is a bit like how you absorbed electricity, at first in trickles, when you were still young, and then in greater measure as you grew older, to give you strength.

Ymir grew and grew until finally, three gods, the brothers

Vili, and Vé, and Odin, slew him. Out of his carcass the gods created the world: his blood became the warm, salty sea, his flesh the rich, fertile earth, his bones the hard, plow-breaking hills, and his hair, the swaying, dark forests. Out of his wide brows the gods carved Midgard, the realm in which humans lived.

After the death of Ymir, the three brother gods walked along a beach. At the end of the beach, they came upon two trees leaning against each other. The gods fashioned two human figures out of their wood. One of the brother gods breathed life into the wooden figures, another endowed them with intelligence, and the third gave them sense and speech. And this was how Ask and Embla, the first man and the first woman, came to be.

You are skeptical that men and women were once made from trees? But you're made of metal. Who's to say trees wouldn't do just as well?

Now let me tell you the story behind the names. "Ask" comes from "ash," a hard tree that is used to make a drill for fire. "Embla" comes from "vine," a softer sort of wood that is easy to set on fire. The motion of twirling a fire drill until the kindling is inflamed reminded the people who told this story of an analogy with sex, and that may be the real story they wanted to tell.

Once your ancestors would have been scandalized that I speak to you of sex so frankly. The word is still a mystery to you, but without the allure that it once held. Before we found how to live forever, sex and children were the closest we came to immortality.

Like a thriving hive, the Singularity began to send a constant stream of colonists away from 61 Virginis e.

One day, Athena came to Maggie and told her that she was ready to be embodied and lead her own colony.

At the thought of not seeing Athena again, Maggie felt an emptiness. *So it is possible to love again, even as a machine.*

Why don't I come with you? she asked. *It will be good for your children to have some connection with the past.*

And Athena's joy at her request was electric and contagious.

Sara came to say good-bye to her, but Bobby did not show up. He had never forgiven her for her rejection of him the moment he became a machine.

Even the immortals have regrets, she thought.

And so a million consciousnesses embodied themselves in metal shells shaped like robot centaurs, and like a swarm of bees leaving to found a new hive, they lifted into the air, tucked their limbs together so that they were shaped like graceful tear-drops, and launched themselves straight up.

Up and up they went, through the acrid air, through the crimson sky, out of the gravity well of the heavy planet, and steering by the shifting flow of the solar wind and the dizzying spin of the galaxy, they set out across the sea of stars.

Light-year after light-year, they crossed the void between the stars. They passed the planets that had already been settled by earlier colonies, worlds now thriving with their own hexagonal arrays of solar panels and their own humming Singularities.

Onward they flew, searching for the perfect planet, the new world that would be their new home.

While they flew, they huddled together against the cold emptiness that was space. Intelligence, complexity, life, computation—everything seemed so small and insignificant against the great and eternal void. They felt the longing of distant black holes and the majestic glow of exploding novas. And they pulled closer to each other, seeking comfort in their common humanity.

As they flew on, half dreaming, half awake, Maggie told the colonists stories, weaving her radio waves among the constellation of colonists like strands of spider silk.

★ ★ ★ ★

There are many stories of the Dreamtime, most secret and sacred. But a few have been told to outsiders, and this is one of them.

In the beginning there was the sky and the earth, and the earth was as flat and featureless as the gleaming titanium alloy surface of our bodies.

But under the earth, the spirits lived and dreamed.

And time began to flow, and the spirits woke from their slumber.

They broke through the surface, where they took on the forms of animals: Emu, Koala, Platypus, Dingo, Kangaroo, Shark . . . Some even took the shapes of humans. Their forms were not fixed but could be changed at will.

They roamed over the earth and shaped it, stamping out valleys and pushing up hills, scraping the ground to make deserts, digging through it to make rivers.

And they gave birth to children, children who could not change forms: animals, plants, humans. These children were born from the Dreamtime but not of it.

When the spirits were tired, they sank back into the earth whence they came. And the children were left behind with only vague memories of the Dreamtime, the time before there was time.

But who is to say that they will not return to that state, to a time when they could change form at will, to a time where time had no meaning?

And they woke from her words into another dream.

One moment, they were suspended in the void of space, still light-years from their destination. The next, they were surrounded by shimmering light.

No, not exactly *light*. Though the lenses mounted on their chassis could see far beyond the spectrum visible to primitive human eyes, this energy field around them vibrated at frequencies far above and below even their limits.

The energy field slowed down to match the subluminal flight of Maggie and the other colonists.

Not too far now.

The thought pushed against their consciousness like a wave, as though all their logic gates were vibrating in sympathy. The thought felt both alien and familiar.

Maggie looked at Athena, who was flying next to her.

Did you hear that? they said at the same time. Their thought strands tapped each other lightly, a caress with radio waves.

Maggie reached out into space with a thought strand, *You're human?*

A pause that lasted a billionth of a second, which seemed like an eternity at the speed they were moving.

We haven't thought of ourselves in that way in a long time.

And Maggie felt a wave of thoughts, images, feelings push into her from every direction. It was overwhelming.

In a nanosecond she experienced the joy of floating along the surface of a gas giant, part of a storm that could swallow Earth. She learned what it would be like to swim through the chromosphere of a star, riding white-hot plumes and flares that rose hundreds of thousands of miles. She felt the loneliness of making the entire universe your playground, yet having no home.

We came after you, and we passed you.

Welcome, ancient ones. Not too far now.

There was a time when we knew many stories of the creation of the world. Each continent was large and there were many peoples, each told their own story.

Then many peoples disappeared, and their stories forgotten.

This is one that survived. Twisted, mangled, retold to fit what strangers want to hear, there is nonetheless some truth left in it.

In the beginning the world was void and without light, and the spirits lived in the darkness.

The Sun woke up first, and he caused the water vapors to rise into the sky and baked the land dry. The other spirits—Man, Leopard, Crane, Lion, Zebra, Wildebeest, and even Hippopotamus—rose up next. They wandered across the plains, talking excitedly with each other.

But then the Sun set, and the animals and Man sat in darkness, too afraid to move. Only when morning came again did everyone start going again.

But Man was not content to wait every night. One night, Man invented fire to have his own sun, heat and light that obeyed his will, and that divided him from the animals that night and forever after.

So Man was always yearning for the light, the light that gives him life and the light to which he will return.

And at night, around the fire, they told each other the true stories, again and again.

Maggie chose to become part of the light.

She shed her chassis, her home and her body for such a long time. Had it been centuries? Millennia? Eons? Such measures of time no longer had any meaning.

Patterns of energy now, Maggie and the others learned to coalesce, stretch, shimmer, and radiate. She learned how to suspend herself between stars, her consciousness a ribbon across both time and space.

She careened from one edge of the galaxy to the other.

One time, she passed right through the pattern that was now Athena. Maggie felt the child as a light tingling, like laughter.

Isn't this lovely, Gran-Gran? Come visit Sara and me sometime!

But it was too late for Maggie to respond. Athena was already too far away.

I miss my chassis.

That was Bobby, whom she met hovering next to a black hole.

For a few thousand years, they gazed at the black hole tog-ether from beyond the event horizon.

This is very lovely, he said. *But sometimes I think I prefer my old shell.*

You're getting old, she said. *Just like me.*

They pressed against each other, and that region of the uni-verse lit up briefly like an ion storm laughing.

And they said good-bye to each other.

This is a nice planet, Maggie thought.

It was a small planet, rather rocky, mostly covered by water.

She landed on a large island near the mouth of a river.

The sun hovered overhead, warm enough that she could see steam rising from the muddy riverbanks. Lightly, she glided over the alluvial plains.

The mud was too tempting. She stopped, condensed herself until her energy patterns were strong enough. Churning the water, she scooped a mound of the rich, fertile mud onto the bank. Then she sculpted the mound until it resembled a man: arms akimbo, legs splayed, a round head with vague indenta-tions and protrusions for eyes, nose, mouth.

She looked at the sculpture of João for a while, caressed it, and left it to dry in the sun.

Looking about herself, she saw blades of grass covered with bright silicon beads and black flowers that tried to absorb every bit of sunlight. She saw silver shapes darting through the brown water and golden shadows gliding through the indigo sky. She saw great scale-covered bodies lumbering and bellowing in the distance, and close by a great geyser erupted near the river, and rainbows appeared in the warm mist.

She was all alone. There was no one to converse with her, no one to share all this beauty.

She heard a nervous rustling and looked for the source of the sound. A little ways from the river, tiny creatures with eyes studded all over their heads like diamonds peered out of the dense forests, made of trees with triangular trunks and pentagonal leaves.

Closer and closer, she drifted to those creatures. Effortlessly, she reached inside them and took ahold of the long chains of a particular molecule, their instructions for the next generation. She made a small tweak, and then let go.

The creatures yelped, and skittered away at the strange sensation of having their insides adjusted.

She had done nothing drastic, just a small adjustment, a nudge in the right direction. The change would continue to mutate, and the mutations would accumulate long after she left. In another few hundred generations, the changes would be enough to cause a spark, a spark that would feed itself until the creatures would start to think of keeping a piece of the sun alive at night, of naming things, of telling stories to each other about how everything came to be. They would be able to choose.

Something new in the universe. Someone new to the family.

But for now, it was time to return to the stars.

Maggie began to rise from the island. Below her, the sea sent wave after wave to crash against the shore, each wave catching and surpassing the one before it, reaching a little farther up the beach. Bits of sea foam floated up and rode the wind to parts unknown.

Mono No Aware

The world is shaped like the kanji for "umbrella," only written so poorly, like my handwriting, that all the parts are out of proportion.

My father would be greatly ashamed at the childish way I still form my characters. Indeed, I can barely write many of them anymore. My formal schooling back in Japan ceased when I was only eight.

Yet for present purposes, this badly drawn character will do.

The canopy up there is the solar sail. Even that distorted kanji can only give you a hint of its vast size. A hundred times thinner than rice paper, the spinning disk fans out a thousand kilometers into space like a giant kite intent on catching every passing photon. It literally blocks out the sky.

Beneath it dangles a long cable of carbon nanotubes a hundred kilometers long: strong, light, and flexible. At the end of the cable hangs the heart of the *Hopeful*, the habitat module, a five-hundred-meter-tall cylinder into which all the 1,021 inhabitants of the world are packed.

The light from the sun pushes against the sail, propelling

us on an ever widening, ever accelerating, spiraling orbit away from it. The acceleration pins all of us against the decks, gives everything weight.

Our trajectory takes us toward a star called 61 Virginis. You can't see it now because it is behind the canopy of the solar sail. The *Hopeful* will get there in about three hundred years, more or less. With luck, my great-great-great—I calculated how many "greats" I needed once, but I don't remember now—grandchildren will see it.

There are no windows in the habitat module, no casual view of the stars streaming past. Most people don't care, having grown bored of seeing the stars long ago. But I like looking through the cameras mounted on the bottom of the ship so that I can gaze at this view of the receding, reddish glow of our sun, our past.

"Hiroto," Dad said as he shook me awake. "Pack up your things. It's time."

My small suitcase was ready. I just had to put my Go set into it. Dad gave this to me when I was five, and the times we played were my favorite hours of the day.

The sun had not yet risen when Mom and Dad and I made our way outside. All the neighbors were standing outside their houses with their bags as well, and we greeted one another politely under the summer stars. As usual, I looked for the Hammer. It was easy. Ever since I could remember, the asteroid had been the brightest thing in the sky except for the moon, and every year it grew brighter.

A truck with loudspeakers mounted on top drove slowly down the middle of the street.

"Attention, citizens of Kurume! Please make your way in an orderly fashion to the bus stop. There will be plenty of buses to take you to the train station, where you can board the train for Kagoshima. Do not drive. You must leave the roads open for the evacuation buses and official vehicles!"

Every family walked slowly down the sidewalk.

"Mrs. Maeda," Dad said to our neighbor. "Why don't I carry your luggage for you?"

"I'm very grateful," the old woman said.

After ten minutes of walking, Mrs. Maeda stopped and leaned against a lamppost.

"It's just a little longer, Granny," I said. She nodded but was too out of breath to speak. I tried to cheer her. "Are you looking forward to seeing your grandson in Kagoshima? I miss Michi too. You will be able to sit with him and rest on the spaceships. They say there will be enough seats for everyone."

Mom smiled at me approvingly.

"How fortunate we are to be here," Dad said. He gestured at the orderly rows of people moving toward the bus stop, at the young men in clean shirts and shoes looking solemn, the middle-aged women helping their elderly parents, the clean, empty streets, and the quietness—despite the crowd, no one spoke above a whisper. The very air seemed to shimmer with the dense connections between all the people—families, neighbors, friends, colleagues—as invisible and strong as threads of silk.

I had seen on TV what was happening in other places around the world: looters screaming, dancing through the streets, soldiers and policemen shooting into the air and sometimes into crowds, burning buildings, teetering piles of dead bodies, generals shouting before frenzied crowds, vowing vengeance for ancient grievances even as the world was ending.

"Hiroto, I want you to remember this," Dad said. He looked around, overcome by emotion. "It is in the face of disasters that we show our strength as a people. Understand that we are not defined by our individual loneliness, but by the web of relationships in which we're enmeshed. A person must rise above his selfish needs so that all of us can live in harmony. The individual is small and powerless, but bound tightly together, as a whole, the Japanese nation is invincible."

★ ★ ★ ★

"Mr. Shimizu," eight-year-old Bobby says, "I don't like this game."

The school is located in the very center of the cylindrical habitat module, where it can have the benefit of the most shielding from radiation. In front of the classroom hangs a large American flag to which the children say their pledge every morning. To the sides of the American flag are two rows of smaller flags belonging to other nations with survivors on the *Hopeful*. At the very end of the left side is a child's rendition of the Hinomaru, the corners of the white paper now curled and the once bright red rising sun faded to the orange of sunset. I drew it the day I came aboard the *Hopeful*.

I pull up a chair next to the table where Bobby and his friend Eric are sitting. "Why don't you like it?"

Between the two boys is a nineteen-by-nineteen grid of straight lines. A handful of black and white stones have been placed on the intersections.

Once every two weeks, I have the day off from my regular duties monitoring the status of the solar sail and come here to teach the children a little bit about Japan. I feel silly doing it sometimes. How can I be their teacher when I have only a boy's hazy memories of Japan?

But there is no other choice. All the non-American technicians like me feel it is our duty to participate in the cultural-enrichment program at the school and pass on what we can.

"All the stones look the same," Bobby says, "and they don't move. They're boring."

"What game do you like?" I ask.

"*Asteroid Defender*!" Eric says. "Now *that* is a good game. You get to save the world."

"I mean a game you do not play on the computer."

Bobby shrugs. "Chess, I guess. I like the queen. She's powerful and different from everyone else. She's a hero."

"Chess is a game of skirmishes," I say. "The perspective of Go is bigger. It encompasses entire battles."

233

"There are no heroes in Go," Bobby says stubbornly.

I don't know how to answer him.

There was no place to stay in Kagoshima, so everyone slept outside along the road to the spaceport. On the horizon we could see the great silver escape ships gleaming in the sun.

Dad had explained to me that fragments that had broken off the Hammer were headed for Mars and the moon, so the ships would have to take us farther, into deep space, to be safe.

"I would like a window seat," I said, imagining the stars steaming by.

"You should yield the window seat to those younger than you," Dad said. "Remember, we must all make sacrifices to live together."

We piled our suitcases into walls and draped sheets over them to form shelters from the wind and the sun. Every day inspectors from the government came by to distribute supplies and to make sure everything was all right.

"Be patient!" the government inspectors said. "We know things are moving slowly, but we're doing everything we can. There will be seats for everyone."

We were patient. Some of the mothers organized lessons for the children during the day, and the fathers set up a priority system so that families with aged parents and babies could board first when the ships were finally ready.

After four days of waiting, the reassurances from the government inspectors did not sound quite as reassuring. Rumors spread through the crowd.

"It's the ships. Something's wrong with them."

"The builders lied to the government and said they were ready when they weren't, and now the prime minister is too embarrassed to admit the truth."

"I hear that there's only one ship, and only a few hundred of the most important people will have seats. The other ships are only hollow shells, for show."

"They're hoping that the Americans will change their mind and build more ships for allies like us."

Mom came to Dad and whispered in his ear.

Dad shook his head and stopped her. "Do not repeat such things."

"But for Hiroto's sake—"

"No!" I'd never heard Dad sound so angry. He paused, swallowed. "We must trust each other, trust the prime minister and the Self-Defense Forces."

Mom looked unhappy. I reached out and held her hand. "I'm not afraid," I said.

"That's right," Dad said, relief in his voice. "There's nothing to be afraid of."

He picked me up in his arms—I was slightly embarrassed, for he had not done such a thing since I was very little—and pointed at the densely packed crowd of thousands and thousands spread around us as far as the eye could see.

"Look at how many of us there are: grandmothers, young fathers, big sisters, little brothers. For anyone to panic and begin to spread rumors in such a crowd would be selfish and wrong, and many people could be hurt. We must keep to our places and always remember the bigger picture."

Mindy and I make love slowly. I like to breathe in the smell of her dark curly hair, lush, warm, tickling the nose like the sea, like fresh salt.

Afterward we lie next to each other, gazing up at my ceiling monitor.

I keep looping on it a view of the receding star field. Mindy works in navigation, and she records the high-resolution cockpit video feed for me.

I like to pretend that it's a big skylight, and we're lying under the stars. I know some others like to keep their monitors showing photographs and videos of old Earth, but that makes me too sad.

"How do you say 'star' in Japanese?" Mindy asks.

"*Hoshi,*" I tell her.

"And how do you say 'guest'?"

"*Okyakusan.*"

"So we are *hoshi okyakusan*? Star guests?"

"It doesn't work like that," I say. Mindy is a singer, and she likes the sound of languages other than English. "It's hard to hear the music behind the words when their meanings get in the way," she told me once.

Spanish is Mindy's first language, but she remembers even less of it than I do of Japanese. Often, she asks me for Japanese words and weaves them into her songs.

I try to phrase it poetically for her, but I'm not sure if I'm successful. "*Wareware ha, hoshi no aida ni kyaku ni kite.*" *We have come to be guests among the stars.*

"There are a thousand ways of phrasing everything," Dad used to say, "each appropriate to an occasion." He taught me that our language is full of nuances and supple grace, each sentence a poem. The language folds in on itself, the unspoken words as meaningful as the spoken, context within context, layer upon layer, like the steel in samurai swords.

I wish Dad were around so that I could ask him: How do you say "I miss you" in a way that is appropriate to the occasion of your twenty-fifth birthday, as the last survivor of your race?

"My sister was really into Japanese picture books. Manga."

Like me, Mindy is an orphan. It's part of what draws us together.

"Do you remember much about her?"

"Not really. I was only five or so when I came on board the ship. Before that, I only remember a lot of guns firing and all of us hiding in the dark and running and crying and stealing food. She was always there to keep me quiet by reading from the manga books. And then . . ."

I had watched the video only once. From our high orbit, the blue-and-white marble that was Earth seemed to wobble for a moment as the asteroid struck, and then, the silent, roiling waves of spreading destruction that slowly engulfed the globe.

I pull her to me and kiss her forehead, lightly, a kiss of comfort. "Let us not speak of sad things."

She wraps her arms around me tightly, as though she will never let go.

"The manga, do you remember anything about them?" I ask.

"I remember they were full of giant robots. I thought: *Japan is so powerful.*"

I try to imagine it: heroic giant robots all over Japan, working desperately to save the people.

The prime minister's apology was broadcast through the loudspeakers. Some also watched it on their phones.

I remember very little of it except that his voice was thin and he looked very frail and old. He looked genuinely sorry. "I've let the people down."

The rumors turned out to be true. The shipbuilders had taken the money from the government but did not build ships that were strong enough or capable of what they promised. They kept up the charade until the very end. We found out the truth only when it was too late.

Japan was not the only nation that failed her people. The other nations of the world had squabbled over who should contribute how much to a joint evacuation effort when the Hammer was first discovered on its collision course with Earth. And then, when that plan had collapsed, most decided that it was better to gamble that the Hammer would miss and spend the money and lives on fighting with one another instead.

After the prime minister finished speaking, the crowd remained silent. A few angry voices shouted but soon quieted down as well. Gradually, in an orderly fashion, people began to pack up and leave the temporary campsites.

★ ★ ★ ★

"The people just went home?" Mindy asks, incredulous.

"Yes."

"There was no looting, no panicked runs, no soldiers mutinying in the streets?"

"This was Japan," I tell her. And I can hear the pride in my voice, an echo of my father's.

"I guess the people were resigned," Mindy says. "They had given up. Maybe it's a culture thing."

"No!" I fight to keep the heat out of my voice. Her words irk me, like Bobby's remark about Go being boring. "That is not how it was."

"Who is Dad speaking to?" I asked.

"That is Dr. Hamilton," Mom said. "We—he and your father and I—went to college together in America."

I watched Dad speak English on the phone. He seemed like a completely different person: it wasn't just the cadences and pitch of his voice; his face was more animated, his hand gestured more wildly. He looked like a foreigner.

He shouted into the phone.

"What is Dad saying?"

Mom shushed me. She watched Dad intently, hanging on every word.

"No," Dad said into the phone. "No!" I did not need that translated.

Afterward Mom said, "He is trying to do the right thing, in his own way."

"He is as selfish as ever," Dad snapped.

"That's not fair," Mom said. "He did not call me in secret. He called you instead because he believed that if your positions were reversed, he would gladly give the woman he loved a chance to survive, even if it's with another man."

Dad looked at her. I had never heard my parents say "I love you" to each other, but some words did not need to be said to be true.

"I would never have said yes to him," Mom said, smiling. Then she went to the kitchen to make our lunch. Dad's gaze followed her.

"It's a fine day," Dad said to me. "Let us go on a walk."

We passed other neighbors walking along the sidewalks. We greeted one another, inquired after one another's health. Everything seemed normal. The Hammer glowed even brighter in the dusk overhead.

"You must be very frightened, Hiroto," he said.

"They won't try to build more escape ships?"

Dad did not answer. The late summer wind carried the sound of cicadas to us: *chirr, chirr, chirrrrrr.*

> *"Nothing in the cry*
> *Of cicadas suggests they*
> *Are about to die."*

"Dad?"

"That is a poem by Bashō. Do you understand it?"

I shook my head. I did not like poems much.

Dad sighed and smiled at me. He looked at the setting sun and spoke again:

> *"The fading sunlight holds infinite beauty*
> *Though it is so close to the day's end."*

I recited the lines to myself. Something in them moved me. I tried to put the feeling into words: "It is like a gentle kitten is licking the inside of my heart."

Instead of laughing at me, Dad nodded solemnly.

"That is a poem by the classical Tang poet Li Shangyin. Though he was Chinese, the sentiment is very much Japanese."

We walked on, and I stopped by the yellow flower of a dandelion. The angle at which the flower was tilted struck me as very beautiful. I got the kitten-tongue-tickling sensation in my heart again.

"The flower . . ." I hesitated. I could not find the right words. Dad spoke,

> *"The drooping flower*
> *As yellow as the moonbeam*
> *So slender tonight."*

I nodded. The image seemed to me at once so fleeting and so permanent, like the way I had experienced time as a young child. It made me a little sad and glad at the same time.

"Everything passes, Hiroto," Dad said. "That feeling in your heart: it's called *mono no aware*. It is a sense of the transience of all things in life. The sun, the dandelion, the cicada, the Hammer, and all of us: we are all subject to the equations of James Clerk Maxwell, and we are all ephemeral patterns destined to eventually fade, whether in a second or an eon."

I looked around at the clean streets, the slow-moving people, the grass, and the evening light, and I knew that everything had its place; everything was all right. Dad and I went on walking, our shadows touching.

Even though the Hammer hung right overhead, I was not afraid.

My job involves staring at the grid of indicator lights in front of me. It is a bit like a giant Go board.

It is very boring most of the time. The lights, indicating tension on various spots of the solar sail, course through the same pattern every few minutes as the sail gently flexes in the fading light of the distant sun. The cycling pattern of the lights is as familiar to me as Mindy's breathing when she's asleep.

We're already moving at a good fraction of the speed of light. Some years hence, when we're moving fast enough, we'll change our course for 61 Virginis and its pristine planets, and we'll leave the sun that gave birth to us behind like a forgotten memory.

But today, the pattern of the lights feels off. One of the lights in the southwest corner seems to be blinking a fraction of a second too fast.

"Navigation," I say into the microphone, "this is Sail Monitor Station Alpha, can you confirm that we're on course?"

A minute later Mindy's voice comes through my earpiece, tinged slightly with surprise. "I hadn't noticed, but there was a slight drift off course. What happened?"

"I'm not sure yet." I stare at the grid before me, at the one stubborn light that is out of sync, out of harmony.

Mom took me to Fukuoka without Dad. "We'll be shopping for Christmas," she said. "We want to surprise you." Dad smiled and shook his head.

We made our way through the busy streets. Since this might be the last Christmas on Earth, there was an extra sense of gaiety in the air.

On the subway I glanced at the newspaper held up by the man sitting next to us. USA STRIKES BACK! was the headline. The big photograph showed the American president smiling triumphantly. Below that was a series of other pictures, some I had seen before: the first experimental American evacuation ship from years ago exploding on its test flight; the leader of some rogue nation claiming responsibility on TV; American soldiers marching into a foreign capital.

Below the fold was a smaller article: AMERICAN SCIEN- TISTS SKEPTICAL OF DOOMSDAY SCENARIO. Dad had said that some people preferred to believe that a disaster was unreal rather than accept that nothing could be done.

I looked forward to picking out a present for Dad. But instead of going to the electronics district, where I had expected Mom to take me to buy him a gift, we went to a section of the city I had never been to before. Mom took out her phone and made a brief call, speaking in English. I looked up at her, surprised.

Then we were standing in front of a building with a great American flag flying over it. We went inside and sat down in an office. An American man came in. His face was sad, but he was working hard not to look sad.

"Rin." The man called my mother's name and stopped. In that one syllable I heard regret and longing and a complicated story.

"This is Dr. Hamilton," Mom said to me. I nodded and offered to shake his hand, as I had seen Americans do on TV.

Dr. Hamilton and Mom spoke for a while. She began to cry, and Dr. Hamilton stood awkwardly, as though he wanted to hug her but dared not.

"You'll be staying with Dr. Hamilton," Mom said to me.

"What?"

She held my shoulders, bent down, and looked into my eyes. "The Americans have a secret ship in orbit. It is the only ship they managed to launch into space before they got into this war. Dr. Hamilton designed the ship. He's my . . . old friend, and he can bring one person aboard with him. It's your only chance."

"No, I'm not leaving."

Eventually, Mom opened the door to leave. Dr. Hamilton held me tightly as I kicked and screamed.

We were all surprised to see Dad standing there.

Mom burst into tears.

Dad hugged her, which I'd never seen him do. It seemed a very American gesture.

"I'm sorry," Mom said. She kept saying "I'm sorry" as she cried.

"It's okay," Dad said. "I understand."

Dr. Hamilton let me go, and I ran up to my parents, holding on to both of them tightly.

Mom looked at Dad, and in that look she said nothing and everything.

Dad's face softened like a wax figure coming to life. He sighed and looked at me.

"You're not afraid, are you?" Dad asked.

I shook my head.

"Then it is okay for you to go," he said. He looked into Dr. Hamilton's eyes. "Thank you for taking care of my son."

Mom and I both looked at him, surprised.

> *"A dandelion*
> *In late autumn's cooling breeze*
> *Spreads seeds far and wide."*

I nodded, pretending to understand.

Dad hugged me, fiercely, quickly.

"Remember that you're Japanese."

And they were gone.

"Something has punctured the sail," Dr. Hamilton says.

The tiny room holds only the most senior command staff—plus Mindy and me because we already know. There is no reason to cause a panic among the people.

"The hole is causing the ship to list to the side, veering off course. If the hole is not patched, the tear will grow bigger, the sail will soon collapse, and the *Hopeful* will be adrift in space."

"Is there any way to fix it?" the captain asks.

Dr. Hamilton, who has been like a father to me, shakes his headful of white hair. I have never seen him so despondent.

"The tear is several hundred kilometers from the hub of the sail. It will take many days to get someone out there because you can't move too fast along the surface of the sail—the risk of another tear is too great. And by the time we do get anyone out there, the tear will have grown too large to patch."

And so it goes. Everything passes.

I close my eyes and picture the sail. The film is so thin that if it is touched carelessly, it will be punctured. But the membrane is supported by a complex system of folds and struts that give the sail rigidity and tension. As a child, I had watched them unfold in space like one of my mother's origami creations.

I imagine hooking and unhooking a tether cable to the scaffolding of struts as I skim along the surface of the sail, like a dragonfly dipping across the surface of a pond.

"I can make it out there in seventy-two hours," I say. Everyone turns to look at me. I explain my idea. "I know the patterns of the struts well because I have monitored them from afar for most of my life. I can find the quickest path."

Dr. Hamilton is dubious. "Those struts were never designed for a maneuver like that. I never planned for this scenario."

"Then we'll improvise," Mindy says. "We're Americans, damn it. We never just give up."

Dr. Hamilton looks up. "Thank you, Mindy."

We plan, we debate, we shout at each other, we work throughout the night.

The climb up the cable from the habitat module to the solar sail is long and arduous. It takes me almost twelve hours.

Let me illustrate for you what I look like with the second character in my name:

It means "to soar." See that radical on the left? That's me, tethered to the cable with a pair of antennae coming out of my helmet. On my back are the wings—or, in this case, booster rockets and extra fuel tanks that push me up and up toward the great reflective dome that blocks out the whole sky, the gossamer mirror of the solar sail.

Mindy chats with me on the radio link. We tell each other jokes, share secrets, speak of things we want to do in the future. When we run out of things to say, she sings to me. The goal is to keep me awake.

"Wareware ha, hoshi no aida ni kyaku ni kite."

But the climb up is really the easy part. The journey across the sail along the network of struts to the point of puncture is far more difficult.

It has been thirty-six hours since I left the ship. Mindy's voice is now tired, flagging. She yawns.

"Sleep, baby," I whisper into the microphone. I'm so tired that I want to close my eyes just for a moment.

I'm walking along the road on a summer evening, my father next to me.

"We live in a land of volcanoes and earthquakes, typhoons and tsunamis, Hiroto. We have always faced a precarious existence, suspended in a thin strip on the surface of this planet between the fire underneath and the icy vacuum above."

And I'm back in my suit again, alone. My momentary loss of concentration causes me to bang my backpack against one of the beams of the sail, almost knocking one of the fuel tanks loose. I grab it just in time. The mass of my equipment has been lightened down to the last gram so that I can move fast, and there is no margin for error. I can't afford to lose anything.

I try to shake the dream and keep on moving.

"Yet it is this awareness of the closeness of death, of the beauty inherent in each moment, that allows us to endure. Mono no aware, my son, is an empathy with the universe. It is the soul of our nation. It has allowed us to endure Hiroshima,

to endure the occupation, to endure deprivation and the prospect of annihilation without despair."

"Hiroto, wake up!" Mindy's voice is desperate, pleading. I jerk awake. I have not been able to sleep for how long now? Two days, three, four?

For the final fifty or so kilometers of the journey, I must let go of the sail struts and rely on my rockets alone to travel untethered, skimming over the surface of the sail while everything is moving at a fraction of the speed of light. The very idea is enough to make me dizzy.

And suddenly my father is next to me again, suspended in space below the sail. We're playing a game of Go.

"Look in the southwest corner. Do you see how your army has been divided in half? My white stones will soon surround and capture this entire group."

I look where he's pointing and I see the crisis. There is a gap that I missed. What I thought was my one army is in reality two separate groups with a hole in the middle. I have to plug the gap with my next stone.

I shake away the hallucination. I have to finish this, and then I can sleep.

There is a hole in the torn sail before me. At the speed we're traveling, even a tiny speck of dust that escaped the ion shields can cause havoc. The jagged edge of the hole flaps gently in space, propelled by solar wind and radiation pressure. While an individual photon is tiny, insignificant, without even mass, all of them together can propel a sail as big as the sky and push a thousand people along.

The universe is wondrous.

I lift a black stone and prepare to fill in the gap, to connect my armies into one.

The stone turns back into the patching kit from my backpack. I maneuver my thrusters until I'm hovering right over the gash in the sail. Through the hole I can see the stars beyond, the stars that no one on the ship has seen for many years. I look at them and imagine that around one of them, one day, the human race, fused into a new nation, will recover from near extinction, will start afresh and flourish again.

Carefully, I apply the bandage over the gash, and I turn on the heat torch. I run the torch over the gash, and I can feel the bandage melting to spread out and fuse with the hydrocarbon chains in the sail film. When that's done I'll vaporize and deposit silver atoms over it to form a shiny, reflective layer.

"It's working," I say into the microphone. And I hear the muffled sounds of celebration in the background.

"You're a hero," Mindy says.

I think of myself as a giant Japanese robot in a manga and smile.

The torch sputters and goes out.

"Look carefully," Dad says. "You want to play your next stone there to plug that hole. But is that what you really want?"

I shake the fuel tank attached to the torch. Nothing. This was the tank that I banged against one of the sail beams. The collision must have caused a leak and there isn't enough fuel left to finish the patch. The bandage flaps gently, only half attached to the gash.

"Come back now," Dr. Hamilton says. "We'll replenish your supplies and try again."

I'm exhausted. No matter how hard I push, I will not be able to make it back out here as fast. And by then who knows how big the gash will have grown? Dr. Hamilton knows this as well as I do. He just wants to get me back to the warm safety of the ship.

I still have fuel in my tank, the fuel that is meant for my return trip.

My father's face is expectant.

"I see," I speak slowly. "If I play my next stone in this hole, I will not have a chance to get back to the small group up in the northeast. You'll capture them."

"One stone cannot be in both places. You have to choose, son."

"Tell me what to do."

I look into my father's face for an answer.

"Look around you," Dad says. And I see Mom, Mrs. Maeda, the prime minister, all our neighbors from Kurume, and all the people who waited with us in Kagoshima, in Kyushu, in all the Four Islands, all over Earth, and on the *Hopeful*. They look expectantly at me, for me to do something.

Dad's voice is quiet:

> *"The stars shine and blink.*
> *We are all guests passing through,*
> *A smile and a name."*

"I have a solution," I tell Dr. Hamilton over the radio.

"I knew you'd come up with something," Mindy says, her voice proud and happy.

Dr. Hamilton is silent for a while. He knows what I'm thinking. And then: "Hiroto, thank you."

I unhook the torch from its useless fuel tank and connect it to the tank on my back. I turn it on. The flame is bright, sharp, a blade of light. I marshal photons and atoms before me, transforming them into a web of strength and light.

The stars on the other side have been sealed away again. The mirrored surface of the sail is perfect.

"Correct your course," I speak into the microphone. "It's done."

"Acknowledged," Dr. Hamilton says. His voice is that of a sad man trying not to sound sad.

"You have to come back first," Mindy says. "If we correct course now, you'll have nowhere to tether yourself."

"It's okay, baby," I whisper into the microphone. "I'm not coming back. There's not enough fuel left."

"We'll come for you!"

"You can't navigate the struts as quickly as I did," I tell her gently. "No one knows their patterns as well as I do. By the time you get here, I will have run out of air."

I wait until she's quiet again. "Let us not speak of sad things. I love you."

Then I turn off the radio and push off into space so that they aren't tempted to mount a useless rescue mission. And I fall down, far, far below the canopy of the sail.

I watch as the sail turns away, unveiling the stars in their full glory. The sun, so faint now, is only one star among many, neither rising nor setting. I am cast adrift among them, alone and also at one with them.

A kitten's tongue tickles the inside of my heart.

I play the next stone in the gap.

Dad plays as I thought he would, and my stones in the northeast corner are gone, cast adrift.

But my main group is safe. They may even flourish in the future.

"Maybe there are heroes in Go," Bobby's voice says.

Mindy called me a hero. But I was simply a man in the right place at the right time. Dr. Hamilton is also a hero because he designed the *Hopeful*. Mindy is also a hero because she kept me awake. My mother is also a hero because she was willing to give me up so that I could survive. My father is also a hero because he showed me the right thing to do.

We are defined by the places we hold in the web of others' lives.

I pull my gaze back from the Go board until the stones fuse into larger patterns of shifting life and pulsing breath. "Individual stones are not heroes, but all the stones together are heroic."

"It is a beautiful day for a walk, isn't it?" Dad says.

And we walk together down the street, so that we can remember every passing blade of grass, every dewdrop, every fading ray of the dying sun, infinitely beautiful.

All The Flavors

A Tale of Guan Yu, the Chinese God of War,
in America

All life is an experiment.
—RALPH WALDO EMERSON

For an American, one's entire life is spent as a game
of chance, a time of revolution, a day of battle.
—ALEXIS DE TOCQUEVILLE

IDAHO CITY

The Missouri Boys snuck into Idaho City around four thirty a.m., when everything was still dark and Isabelle's Joy Club was the only house with a lit window.

Obee and Crick made straight for the Thirsty Fish. Earlier in the day, J. J. Kelly, the proprietor, had invited Obee and Crick out of his saloon with his Smith & Wesson revolver. With little effort and making no sound, Obee and Crick broke the latch on the door of the Thirsty Fish and quickly disappeared inside.

"I'll show that little Irishman some manners," Crick hissed. Through the alcoholic mist, his eyes could focus on only one image: the diminutive Kelly walking toward him, gun at the ready, and the jeering crowd behind him. *We might just bury you under the new outhouse next time you show yourselves in Idaho City.*

Though he was a little unsteady on his feet, he successfully tiptoed his way up the stairs to the family's living quarters, an iron crowbar in hand.

Obee, less drunk, set about rectifying that situation promptly by jumping behind the bar and helping himself to the supplies. Carelessly, he took down bottles of various sizes and colors from the shelves around him, and having taken a sip from each, smashed the bottles against the counters or dashed them to the ground. Alcohol flowed freely everywhere, soaking into the floors and the furniture.

A woman's scream tore out of the darkness upstairs. Obee jumped up and drew his revolver. Not sure whether to run upstairs to help his friend or out the door, down the street, and into the woods before he could be caught, he hesitated at the bottom of the stairs. Overhead came the sound of boots that no longer cared about silence, followed by the crash of something heavy and soft onto the floor. Obee cursed and jumped back, his big, dirty hands trying to rub out the coat of dust that just fell from the ceiling into his eyes. More muffled screams and cursing, and then, complete silence.

"Woo!" Crick appeared at the top of the stairs, the gleeful grin on his face limned by the light of the oil lamp he held aloft. "Grab some rags. Let's burn this dump down."

By the time the seven thousand people of Idaho City had tallied up the damage of the Great Fire of May 18, 1865, the Missouri Boys were miles away on the Wells Fargo trail, sleeping off the headache from hard drinking and fast riding. Idaho City lost a newspaper, two theaters, two photograph galleries, three express offices, four restaurants, four breweries, four drugstores, five groceries, six blacksmith shops, seven meat markets, seven bakeries, eight hotels, twelve doctor's offices, twenty-two law offices, twenty-four saloons, and thirty-six general merchandise stores.

This was why, when the band of weary and gaunt Chinamen showed up a few weeks later with their funny bamboo carrying poles over their shoulders and their pockets heavy with cold, hard cash sewn into the lining, the people of Idaho City almost held a welcome party for them. Everyone promptly set about the task of separating the Chinamen from their money.

Elsie Seaver, Lily's mother, complained to Lily's father about the Chinamen almost every evening.

"Thaddeus, will you please tell the heathens to keep their noise down? I can't hear myself think."

"For fourteen dollars a week in rent, Elsie, I think the China-men are entitled to a few hours of their own music."

The Seavers' store had been one of those burned down a few weeks earlier. Lily's father, Thad (though he preferred to be called Jack) Seaver, was still in the middle of rebuilding it. Elsie knew as well as her husband that they needed the Chinamen's rent. She sighed, stuffed some cotton balls in her ears, and took her sewing into the kitchen.

Lily rather liked the music of the Chinamen. It was indeed loud. The gongs, cymbals, wooden clappers, and drums made such a racket that her heart wanted to beat in time to their rhythm. The high-pitched fiddle with only two strings wailed so high and pure that Lily thought she could float on air just listening to it. And then in the fading light of the dusk, the big, red-faced Chinaman would pluck out a sad quiet tune on the three-stringed lute and sing his songs in the street, his compan-ions squatting in a circle around him, quiet as they listened to him, and their faces by turns smiling and grave. He was more than six feet tall and had a dark, bushy beard that covered his chest. Lily thought his thin, long eyes looked like the eyes of a great eagle as he turned his head, looking at each of his companions. Once in a while they burst into loud guffaws, and they slapped the big, red-faced Chinaman on his back as he smiled and kept on singing.

"What do you think he's singing about?" Lily asked her mother from the porch.

"No doubt some unspeakably vile vice of their barbaric homeland. Opium dens and sing-song girls and such. Come back in here and close the door. Have you finished your sewing?"

Lily continued to watch them from her window, wishing she could understand what his songs were about. She was glad that the music made her mother unable to think. It meant that she couldn't think of more chores for Lily to do.

Lily's father was more intrigued by the Chinamen's cooking. Even their cooking was loud, the splattering and sizzling of hot oil and the *suh-suh-suh* beating of cleaver against chopping board making another kind of music. The cooking also smelled loud, the smoke drifting from the open door carrying the peppery smell of unknown spices and unknown vegetables across the street and making Lily's stomach growl.

"What in the world are they making over there? There's no way cucumbers can smell like that," Lily's father asked no one in particular. Lily saw him lick his lips.

"We could ask them," Lily suggested.

"Ha! Don't get any ideas. I'm sure the Chinamen would love to chop up a little Christian girl like you and fry you in those big saucepans of theirs. Stay away from them, you hear?"

Lily didn't believe that the Chinamen would eat her. They seemed friendly enough. And if they were going to supplement their diet with little girls, why would they bother spending all day working on that vegetable garden they'd planted behind their house?

There were many mysteries about the Chinamen, not the least of which was how they managed to all fit inside those tiny houses they had rented. The band of twenty-seven Chinamen rented five saltbox houses along Placer Street, two of them owned by Jack Seaver, and bought three others from Mr. Kenan, whose bank had been burned down and who was moving his family back East. The saltbox houses were simple, one-story affairs with a living room in the front that doubled as the kitchen, and a bedroom in the back. Twelve feet deep and thirty feet across, the small houses were made of thin planks of wood, and their front porches were squeezed so tightly together that they formed a covered sidewalk.

The white miners who had rented these houses from Jack Seaver in the past lived in them alone or at most shared a house with one roommate. The Chinamen, on the other hand, lived five or six to a house. This frugality rather disappointed some of the people in Idaho City, who had been hoping the Chinamen would be more free with their money. They broke down the tables and chairs left by the previous tenants of the houses and used the lumber to build bunks along the walls of the bedrooms and laid out mattresses on the floors of the living rooms. The previous occupants also left pictures of Lincoln and Lee on the walls. These the Chinamen left alone.

"Logan said he likes the pictures," Jack Seaver said at dinner.

"Who's Logan?"

"The big, red-faced Chinaman. He asked me who Lee was, and I told him he was a great general who picked the losing side but was still admired for his bravery and loyalty. He was impressed by that. Oh, and he also liked Lee's beard."

Lily had heard the conversation between her father and the Chinaman by hiding herself behind the piano. She didn't think the big Chinaman's name sounded anything like "Logan." She had listened to the other Chinamen calling out to him, and it sounded to her like they were saying "Lao Guan."

"Such a strange people, these Celestials," Elsie said. "That Logan scares me. The size of his hands! He has killed. I'm sure of it. I wish you could find some other tenants, Thaddeus."

No one except Lily's mother ever called her husband "Thaddeus." To everyone else he was either "Mr. Seaver" or "Jack." Lily was used to the fact that people had many names out here in the West. After all, everyone called the banker "Mr. Kenan" when they were at the bank, but when he wasn't around they called him "Shylock." And while Lily's mother always addressed her as "Liliane," Lily's father always called her "Nugget." And it seemed that the big Chinaman already got a new name in this house, "Logan."

"You are my nugget of gold, sweetie," Lily's father told her every morning, before he left for the store.

"You're going to puff her up full of vanity," Lily's mother said from the kitchen.

It was the height of the mining season, and the Chinamen began to head out to look for gold the moment they were settled in. They left as soon as it was light, dressed in their loose blouses and baggy trousers, their queues snaking out from under their big straw hats. A few of the older men stayed behind to work in the vegetable garden or to do the laundry and the cooking.

Lily was largely left alone during the day. While her mother went shopping or busied herself around the house, her father was away working at the site for the new store. Jack was thinking of setting aside a section in the new store for preserved duck eggs, pickled vegetables, dried tofu, spices, soy sauce, and bitter melons imported from San Francisco to sell to the Chinese miners.

"These Chinamen are going to be carting around a lot of gold dust soon, Elsie. I'll be ready to take it from them when they do."

Elsie didn't like this plan. The thought of the Chinamen's strange food making everything smell funny in her husband's store made her queasy. But she knew it was pointless to argue with Thad once he got a notion in his head. After all, he had packed up everything and dragged her and Lily all the way out here from Hartford, where he had been doing perfectly well as a tutor, just because he got it in his head that they'd be much happier on their own out West, where nobody knew them and they knew nobody.

Not even Elsie's father could persuade her husband to change his mind then. He had asked Thad to come to Boston and work for him in his law office. Business was good, he said, he could use his help. Elsie beamed at the thought of all the shops and the fashion of Beacon Hill.

"I appreciate the offer," Thad had said to her father. "But I don't think I'm cut out to be a lawyer."

Elsie had to placate her father for hours afterward with tea and a fresh batch of oatmeal cookies. And even then he refused to say good-bye to Thad the next day, when he left to go back to Boston. "Damned the day that I became friends with his father," he muttered, too loud for Elsie to pretend that she hadn't heard him.

"I'm sick of this," Thad said to her later. "We don't know anybody who's ever *done* anything. Everyone in Hartford just carries on what his father had started. Aren't we supposed to be a nation where every generation picks up and goes somewhere new? I think we should go and start our own life. You can even pick a new name for yourself. Wouldn't that be fun?"

Elsie was happy with her own name. But Thad wasn't. This was how he ended up as "Jack."

"I've always wanted to be a 'Jack,'" he told her, as if names were like shirts that you could just put on and take off. She refused to call him by his new name.

Once when Lily was alone with her mother she had told Lily that this was all because of the War.

"That Rebel bullet put him on his back in less than a day from when he got onto the field. This is what happens to a man when he has to lie on his back for eight months. He gets all sorts of strange notions into his head and not even an angelic manifestation can get those ideas out of him."

If the Rebels were responsible for getting her family out here to Idaho, Lily wasn't sure they were such evil people.

Lily had learned the hard way that if she stayed in the house her mother would always find something for her to do. Until school started again, the best thing for Lily was to get out of the house the first chance she had in the morning and not return until it was dinnertime.

Lily liked to be in the hills outside the town. The forest of Douglas firs, mountain maples, and ponderosa pines shaded her from the noon sun. She could take some bread and cheese with her for lunch, and there were plenty of streams to drink from. She spent some time picking out leaves that had been chewed by worms into shapes that reminded her of different animals. When she was bored with that she waded in a stream to cool off. Before she went into the water, she took the back hem of her dress, pulled it forward and up from between her legs, and tucked the hem into the sash at her waist. She was glad that her mother was not around to see her turning her skirt into pants. But it was much easier to wade in the mud and the water with her skirt out of the way.

Lily waded downstream along the shallow edge of the stream. The day was starting to get more hot than warm, and she splashed some water on her neck and forehead. Lily looked for bird nests in the trees and raccoon prints in the mud. She thought she could walk on like this forever, alone and not trying to get anything done in particular, her feet cool in the water, the sun warm on her back, and knowing that she had a good, filling lunch with her that she could have any time she wanted and would have an even better dinner waiting for her later.

Faint sounds of men singing came to her from around the bend in the river. Lily stopped. Maybe there was a camp of placer miners just downstream from where she was. That would be fun to watch.

She walked onto the bank of the river and into the woods. The singing became louder. Although she couldn't make out any of the words, the melody told her it wasn't any song that she recognized.

She carefully made her way among the trees. She was deep in the shadows now, and a light breeze quickly dried the sweat and water on her face. Her heart began to beat faster. She could hear the singing voices more clearly now. A lone deep, male voice sang in words that she could not make out, the strange shape of the melody reminding her of the way the Chinamen's music had sounded. Then a chorus of other male voices answered, the slow, steady rhythm letting her know that it was a working men's song, whose words and music came from the cycle of labored breath and heartbeat.

She came to the edge of the woods, and hiding herself behind the thick trunk of a maple, she peeked out at the singing men by the stream.

Except the stream was nowhere to be found.

After they found this bend to be a good placer spot, the Chinese miners had built a dam to divert the stream. Where the stream used to be, there were now five or six miners using picks and shovels to dig down to the bedrock. Others were digging out bits of gold-laden sand and gravel from between the crevices in areas where the digging had already been done. The men wore their straw hats to keep the sun off their heads. The solo singer, Lily now saw, was Logan. The red-faced Chinaman had wrapped a rolled-up handkerchief around his thick beard and tucked the ends of the handkerchief into his shirt to keep it out of his way as he worked. Every time he bellowed out another verse of the song, he stood still and leaned on his shovel, and his beard pouch moved with his singing like the neck of a rooster. Lily almost giggled out loud.

A loud bang cut through the noise and activity and echoed around the banks of the dry streambed. The singing stopped and all the miners stopped where they were. The mountain air suddenly became quiet and still, and only the sound of panicked birds taking flight into the air broke the silence.

Crick, slowly waving above his head the pistol that fired the shot, swaggered out of the woods across the streambed from where Lily was hiding. Obee came behind him, his shotgun's barrel shifting from pointing at one miner to the next with each step he took.

"Well, well, well," Crick said. "Lookee here. A singing circus of Chinee monkeys."

Logan stared at him. "What do you boys want?"

"*Boys?*" Crick let out a holler. "Obee, listen to this. The Chinaman just called us 'boys.'"

"He won't be saying much after I blow his head off," Obee said.

Logan began to walk toward them. The heavy shovel trailed from his large hand and long arm.

"Stop right where you are, you filthy yellow monkey." Crick pointed the pistol at him.

"What do you want?"

"Why, to collect what's ours, of course. We know you've been keeping our gold safe, and we've come to ask for it back."

"We don't have any of your gold."

"Jesus," Crick said, shaking his head. "I've always heard that Chinamen are thieves and liars, on account of them growing up eating rats and maggots, but I've always kept an open mind about the Celestials. But now I'm seeing it with my own eyes."

"Filthy liars," Obee affirmed.

"Obee and me, we found this spot last spring and claimed it. We've been a little busy lately, and so we thought we'd take pity on you and let you work the deposit and pay you a fair wage for your work. We thought we were doing our Christian duty."

"We were being nice," Obee added.

"Very generous of us," Crick agreed. "But look where that's gotten us? Being kind doesn't work with these heathens. On our way here I was still inclined to let you keep a little gold dust for your work these last few weeks, but now I think we are going to take it all."

"Ingrates," Obee said.

A young Chinaman, barely more than a boy, really, angrily

shouted something in his own language at Logan. Logan waved his hand at the youth to keep him back, his gaze never leaving Crick's face.

"I don't think you have your facts straight," Logan said. Even though he didn't shout, his voice reverberated and echoed around the valley of the river and the woods in a way that made Lily tremble with its force and strength. "We found this deposit and we put the claim on it. You can go check at the courthouse."

"Are you deaf?" Crick asked. "What makes you think I need to check at the courthouse? I just told you the facts, and after conferring with the law"—he waved his pistol impatiently—"I'm told that the claim is indeed mine and you are the claim jumpers. By law I'm entitled to shoot you dead like so many rats right where you are. But as I am unwilling to shed blood needlessly, I'll let you hand over the gold and spare your worthless lives. I may even let you keep on working this deposit for me if you agree not to pull a stunt like this and deny us our gold in the future."

Without any warning that he was going to do it, Obee fired his gun. The shot shattered the rocks at the feet of the boy who had angrily shouted at Logan earlier. Obee and Crick doubled over in laughter as the boy jumped back and dropped his pickax, giving out a startled yelp. A piece of shattered rock had cut his hand, and he slowly sat down on the ground, staring incredulously as the blood from the wound in his palm quickly soaked the tan sleeves of his shirt. A few of the other Chinamen gathered around to tend to him. Lily barely managed to stifle her own scream. She wanted to turn around and run back into town, but her legs would not hold her up if she didn't hug tightly the tree she was hiding behind.

Logan turned his attention back to Crick. His face had turned an even darker shade of red, so that Lily was afraid that blood would pour from his eyes.

"Don't," he said.

"Hand over the gold," Crick said, "or I'll make him stop breathing instead of just getting him dancing."

Logan casually threw the shovel, which had been dangling from his hand until now, behind him. "Why don't you put down your gun, and we'll have a fair fight?"

Crick hesitated for a moment. If it came to that, he thought he could take care of himself in a fight, having survived enough brawls in New Orleans to know exactly how it felt to have your ribs stop a knife. But Logan was taller by about a foot and heavier by about fifty pounds, and though that beard made him look ancient, Crick wasn't sure whether Logan really was old enough to have his reflexes slow down. And in any case Crick was a little scared of the red-faced Chinaman: He looked angry enough to fight like a crazy man, and Crick knew enough about fights to know that you didn't come out of fights with crazy men without at least a few broken bones.

The plan was going all wrong! Crick and Obee knew all about Chinamen, having spent years in San Francisco. They had all been scrawny midgets, giving him and Obee barely more trouble than a bunch of women, which was not surprising considering all they did was women's work: cooking and laundry, and not one of them had ever put up a real fight. This band of Chinamen was supposed to fall down on their knees and beg for mercy as soon as he and Obee slowly walked out of the woods, and hand over all their gold. The red-faced giant was ruining their plan!

"I think we have a pretty fair fight right now," Crick said. He pointed his revolver at Logan. "Almighty God created men, but Colonel Colt made them equal."

Logan untied the handkerchief around his beard, unrolled it, and tied it around the top of his head like a bandanna. He took off his jacket and rolled up the sleeves of his shirt. The leathery, brown skin covering the wiry muscles on his arms was full of scars. He took a few steps toward Crick. Though his face was redder than ever, his walk was calm, like he was taking a stroll at night, singing his songs back in front of Lily's house back in Idaho City.

"Don't think I won't shoot," Crick said. "The Missouri Boys don't have a lot of patience."

Logan bent down and picked up a rock the size of an egg. He wrapped his fingers around it tightly. "Get out of here. We don't have any of your gold." He took another few calm steps toward Crick.

And in another moment he was running, his legs closing up the distance between him and the gunmen. He cocked his right arm back as he ran, looking steadily into Crick's face.

Obee fired. He didn't have the time to brace himself, and the force of the shot threw him on his back.

Logan's left shoulder exploded. A bright red shower of blood sprayed behind him. In the sunlight it looked to Lily like a rose was blossoming behind him.

None of the other Chinamen said anything. They looked on, stunned.

Lily's breath stopped. Time seemed frozen to her. The mist of blood hung in the air, refusing to fall or dissipate.

Then she sucked in a great gulp of air and screamed as loud as she could ever remember, louder even than the time she was stung on the lips by that wasp she hadn't seen hiding in her lemonade cup. Her scream echoed around the woods, startling more birds into the air. *Is that really me?* Lily thought. It didn't sound like her. It didn't even sound human.

Crick was looking into her eyes from across the river. His face was so filled with cold rage and hatred that Lily's heart stopped beating.

Oh God, please, please, I promise I'll pray every night from now on. I promise I won't disobey Mother ever again.

She tried to turn around and run, but her legs wouldn't listen to her. She stumbled back, tripped over an exposed root, and fell heavily to the ground. The fall knocked the air out of her and finally cut off her scream. She struggled to sit up, expecting to see Crick's gun pointed at her.

Logan was looking at her. Incredibly, he was still standing.

Half of his body was soaked with blood. He was looking at her, and she thought he didn't look like someone who had just been shot, someone who was about to die. Though blood had splattered half of his face, the other half had lost its deep, crimson color. Still, Lily thought he looked calm, like he wasn't in any pain, though he was a little sad.

Lily felt a calmness come over her. She didn't know why, but she *knew* everything was going to be all right.

Logan turned away from her. He began to walk toward Crick again. His walk was slow, deliberate. His left arm was hanging limply at his side.

Crick aimed his pistol at Logan.

Logan stumbled. Then he stopped. The blood had soaked into his beard, and as the wind lifted it, droplets of blood flew into the air. He took a step back and let fly the rock in his hand. The rock made a graceful arc in the air. Crick stood frozen where he was. The rock smashed into his face, and the thud as the rock cracked open his skull was as loud as Obee's gunshot.

His body stayed up for a few seconds before collapsing into a lifeless heap on the ground. Obee scrambled to his feet, took a look at Crick's motionless body, and without looking back at the Chinamen began to run as fast as he could deep into the woods.

Logan fell to his knees. For a moment he swayed uncertainly in place as his left arm swung at his side, useless for stopping his fall. Then he toppled over. The other Chinamen ran to him.

It all seemed so unreal to Lily, like a play on a stage. She thought she should have been terrified. She should have been screaming, or maybe even fainted. That's what her mother would have done, she thought. But everything had slowed down in the last few seconds, and she felt safe, calm, like nothing could hurt her.

She came out from behind her tree and walked toward the crowd of Chinamen.

★ ★ ★ ★

Lily wasn't sure if she would ever understand this game.

"I can't move the seeds at all? Ever?"

They were sitting in the vegetable garden behind Logan's house, where her mother wouldn't be able to see her if she happened to look out the living room window as she finished her needlework. They were both sitting with their legs folded under them, and Lily liked the way the cool, moist soil felt under her legs. ("This was how the Buddha sat," Logan had told her.) On the ground between them Logan had drawn a grid of nine horizontal lines intersected with nine vertical lines with the tip of his knife.

"No, you can't." Logan shifted his left arm to make it easier for Ah Yan, the young Chinaman who had been the target of Obee's first shot, to run the wet rag in his hand over the wound in Logan's shoulder. Lily gingerly touched the bandage on her leg. Her fall against the tree root had scraped off a large patch of skin on the back of her left calf. Ah Yan had cleaned it for her and wrapped it up in a plain cotton bandage that was coated in some black paste that smelled strongly of medicine and spices. The cool paste had stung at first against the wound, but Lily bit her lip and didn't cry out. Ah Yan's touch had been gentle, and Lily asked him if he was a doctor.

"No," the young Chinaman had said. Then he had smiled at her and given her a piece of dried plum coated in sugar for her to suck on. Lily thought it was the sweetest thing she had ever tasted.

Ah Yan rinsed the rag out in the basin next to Logan. The water was again bright red and this was already the third basin of hot water.

Logan paid no attention to Ah Yan's ministrations. "We'll play on a smaller board than usual since you are just learning. This game is called *wei qi*, which means 'the game of surrounding.'

Think of laying down each seed as driving a post into the field as you build a fence to surround the land you are claiming. The posts don't move, do they?"

Lily was playing with lotus seeds while Logan's pieces were watermelon seeds. The white and black pieces made a pretty pattern on the grid between them.

"So it's kind of like the way they get land in Kansas," Lily said.

"Yes," Logan said. "I guess it's a little like that, though I've never been to Kansas. You want to surround the largest territory possible, and defend your land well so that my posts can't carve out another homestead in your land."

He took a long drink from the gourd in his hand. The gourd looked a little like a snowman, a small sphere on top of a larger one, with a piece of red silk tied around the narrow waist to provide a good grip. The golden surface of the gourd was shiny from constant use in Logan's rough, leathery palm. Logan had told her that the gourd grew on a vine. When the gourd was ripe it was cut down and the top sawn off so that the seeds inside could be taken out to make the shell into a good bottle for wine.

Logan smacked his lips and sighed. "Whiskey, it's almost as good as sorghum mead." He offered Lily a sip. Lily, shocked, shook her head. No wonder her mother thought these Chinamen barbaric. To drink whiskey out of a gourd was bad enough, but to offer a drink to a young Christian girl?

"There's no whiskey in China?"

Logan took another drink and wiped the whiskey from his beard. "When I was a boy I was taught that there were only five flavors in the world, and all the world's joys and sorrows came from different mixtures of the five. I've learned since then that's not true. Every place has a taste that's new to it, and whiskey is the taste of America."

"Lao Guan," Ah Yan called out. Logan turned toward him. Ah Yan spoke to him in Chinese, gesturing at the basin. After looking at the water in the basin, Logan nodded. Ah Yan got up with the basin and poured out the water in a far corner of the field before going into the house.

"He's gotten as much of the poisoned blood and dirt and torn rags out as possible," Logan explained. "Time to sew me up."

"My dad thinks your name is Logan," Lily said. "I knew he was wrong."

Logan laughed. His laugh was loud and careless, the same as the way he sang and told his stories. "All my friends call me *Lao Guan*, which just means 'Old Guan,' *Guan* being my family name. I guess it sounds like 'Logan' to your dad. I kind of like the ring of it. Maybe I'll just use it as my American name."

"He also picked out a new name for himself when we came here," Lily said. "Mother doesn't think he should do that."

"I don't know why she should be so against it. This is a country full of new names. Didn't she change her name when she married your father? Everyone gets a new name when they come here."

Lily thought about this. It was true. Her father didn't call her "Nugget" until they lived here.

Ah Yan came back with a needle and some thread. He proceeded to stitch up the wound on Logan's shoulder. Lily looked closely at Logan's face to see if he would wince with the pain.

"It's still your turn," Logan said. "And I'm going to capture all your seeds in that corner if you don't do something about it."

"Doesn't it hurt?"

"This?" The way he pointed at his shoulder by wagging his beard made Lily laugh. "This is nothing compared to the time I had to have my bones scraped."

"You had to have your bones scraped?"

"Once I was shot with a poisoned arrow, and the tip of the arrow was buried into the bones in my arm. I was going to die unless I got the poison out. Hua Tuo, the most skilled doctor in the world, came to help me. He had to cut into my arm, peel back the flesh and skin, and scrape off the poisoned bits of bone with his scalpel. Let me tell you, that hurt a lot more than this. It helped that Hua Tuo had me drink the strongest rice wine he could find, and I was playing *wei qi* against my first lieutenant, a very good player himself. It took my mind off the pain."

"Where was this? Back in China?"

"Yes, a long time ago back in China."

Ah Yan finished his sutures. Logan said something to him, and Ah Yan handed a small silk bundle to him. Lily was about to ask Ah Yan about the bundle, but he just smiled at her and held a finger to his lips. He pointed at Logan and mouthed "watch" at her.

Logan laid the bundle on the ground and unrolled the silk wrap. Inside was a set of long, silver needles. Logan picked up one of the needles in his right hand, and before Lily could even yell "Stop," he stuck the needle into his left shoulder, right above the wound.

"What did you do that for?" Lily squeaked. For some reason the sight of the long needle sticking out of Logan's shoulder made her more queasy than when Logan's shoulder had exploded with Obee's shot.

"It stops the pain," Logan said. He took another needle and stuck it into his shoulder about an inch above the other one. He twisted the end of the needle a little to make sure it settled in the right spot.

"I don't believe you."

Logan laughed. "There are many things little American girls don't understand, and many things old Chinamen don't understand. I can show you how it works. Does your leg still hurt?"

"Yes."

"Here, hold still." Logan leaned forward and held out his left palm low to the ground. "Put your foot in my hand."

"Hey, you can move your left arm again."

"Oh, this is nothing. The time I had to have my bones scraped, I was back on the battlefield within two hours."

Lily was sure that Logan was joking with her. "My father was shot in the leg and chest in the War, and it took him eight months before he could walk again. He still has a limp." She lifted her foot, wincing at the pain. Logan cupped her ankle with his palm.

His palm felt warm, hot actually, on Lily's ankle. Logan closed his eyes and began to breathe slowly and evenly. Lily felt the heat on her ankle increase. It felt nice, like having a very hot towel pressed around her injured calf. The pain gradually melted into the heat. Lily felt so relaxed and comfortable that she could fall asleep. She closed her eyes.

"Okay, you are all set."

Logan released her ankle and gently deposited her foot on the ground. Lily opened her eyes and saw a great silver needle sticking out from her leg just below her kneecap.

Lily was going to cry out in pain until she realized that she didn't feel any. There was a slight numbness around where the needle went into her skin, and heat continued to radiate from it, blocking any pain from her wound.

"That feels weird," Lily said. She experimentally flexed her leg a few times.

"As good as new."

"Mother is going to faint when she sees this."

"I'll take it out before you go home. Your skin won't heal for a few more days, but most of the poison in your blood should be gone with the medicine Ah Yan put on the bandage, and the acupuncture should have taken out the rest. Just get the bandage changed to a clean one tomorrow and you shouldn't even have a scar when this is over."

Lily wanted to thank him, but she suddenly felt shy. Talking with Logan was strange. He was unlike anyone she had ever met. One moment he was killing a man with his bare hands, and the next he was holding her ankle as gently as she would a kitten. One moment he was singing songs that seemed as old as the earth itself, and the next he was laughing with her over a game played with watermelon and lotus seeds. He was interesting but also more than a little scary.

"I like playing with the black seeds," Logan said as he placed another seed on the grid, capturing a block of Lily's seeds. He picked them up and popped the handful of lotus seeds into his mouth. "Lotus seeds are much better to eat."

Lily laughed. How could she be scared of an old man who talked with his mouth full?

"Logan, that story about the poisoned arrow and the doctor scraping your bones, that didn't really happen to you, did it?"

Logan tilted his head and looked at Lily thoughtfully. Slowly, he chewed the lotus seeds in his mouth, swallowed, and grinned. "That happened to Guan Yu, the Chinese God of War."

"I knew it! You're just like my father's friends, always telling me tall tales just because I'm a child."

Logan laughed his deep, booming laugh. "Not all stories are made up."

Lily had never heard of the Chinese God of War, and she was sure that her father hadn't either. It was now twilight, and the sounds and the smell of the loud and oily cooking of the Chinamen filled the garden.

"I should go home," Lily said, even though she desperately wanted to try some of the food that she was smelling and hear more about Guan Yu. "Can I come and visit you tomorrow, and you can tell me more stories about Guan Yu?"

Logan stroked his beard with his hand. His face was serious. "It would be an honor." Then his face broke into a smile. "Even though I'll have to eat all the seeds myself now."

The God of War

Before Guan Yu became a god, he was just a boy.

Actually, before that, he was almost just a ghost. His mother carried him in her belly for twelve months, and still he refused to be born. The midwife gave her some herbs and

269

then told her husband to hold her down while she kicked and screamed. The baby finally came out and didn't breathe. Its face was bright red. *Either from choking or too much barbaric blood in the father,* the midwife thought.

"It would have been a huge baby," the midwife whispered to the father. The mother was asleep. "Too big to have a long life, anyway." She began to wrap up the body with what would have been his swaddling clothes. "Did you have a name picked out?"

"No."

"Just as well. You don't want to give the demons a name to hang on to on his way down below."

The baby let out an earsplitting cry. The midwife almost dropped him.

"He's too big to have a long life," the midwife insisted as she unwrapped the body, a little peeved that the baby dared to defy her authority on these matters. "And that face. So red!"

"Then I'll call him Chang Sheng, Long Life."

The dry summer sun and the dusty spring winds of Shanxi carved lines and sprinkled salt into the chapped, ruddy faces of the Chinese who tried to make a living here in the heart of northern China. When the barbarians climbed over the Great Wall and rode down from the north on their raids on the backs of their towering steeds, it was these men who took up their hoes and melted their plows to fight them to the death. It was these women who fought alongside the men with their kitchen knives, and, when they failed, ended up as the slaves and then the wives of the barbarians, learning their language and bearing their children, until the barbarians began to think of themselves as Chinese, and they, in turn, fought against the next wave of barbarians.

While weak men and delicate women who were afraid to die fled south so that they could row around on their flower boats and sing their drunken verses, those who stayed behind, matching the music of their lives to the rhythm of the howling rage of the desert, grew tall with the barbaric blood mixed into their veins and became full of pride at their life of toil.

"This is why," Chang Sheng's father said to him, "the Qin and Han Emperors all came out of the Great Northwest, our land. From us come the generals and the poets, the ministers and the scholars of the Empire. We are the only ones who value pride."

In addition to helping his father in the fields, it was Chang Sheng's job to gather the firewood and kindling for the kitchen. Chang Sheng's favorite time of the day was the hour or so before the sun set. That was when he took the rusty ax and the even rustier machete from behind the kitchen door and climbed the mountain behind the village.

Crack, the ax split the rotting trunk of a tree. *Zang*, the blade swung through the dry grass. It was hard work, but Chang Sheng pretended that he was a great hero cutting down his enemies like weeds.

Back home, dinner was stir-fried bitter melon and pickled cabbage to go with scallions dipped in soy sauce and wrapped in flat sorghum pancakes. Sometimes, when his father was in a particular good mood, Chang Sheng would even get a sip of plum wine, sweet on the tip of the tongue, burning hot down the throat. His face grew to an even darker shade of red.

"There you are, little one," his father said, smiling as Chang Sheng's eyes teared up from the alcohol burn while his hand reached out for another sip. "Sweet, sour, bitter, hot, and salty, all the flavors in balance."

Chang Sheng grew up to be a tall boy. His mother was forever sewing new robes for him as he outgrew the old ones. The drought that had already lasted five years showed no signs of letting up, and even though the men labored harder than ever in the fields, the harvest seemed to grew smaller year after year. There was no money to send him to school, so his father took up the task of teaching him.

History was his favorite subject, but there was always

something sad in his father's eyes when they discussed history. Chang Sheng learned to not ask too many questions. Instead, he spent more time reading the history books. Then, when he was out gathering firewood, he acted out the great battles with his ax and machete against the endless hordes of the barbaric woods.

"You like to fight?" his father asked him one day.

He nodded.

"I'll teach you to play *wei qi*, then."

"Did Chang Sheng's father use lotus seeds and watermelon seeds too?"

"No, he used real stones."

"I prefer your way of playing wei qi. *Using seeds is more fun."*

"I think so too. And I like eating too much. Now, where was I?"

Within a day Chang Sheng was able to win one game out of three against his father. In a week he was losing only one out of five. In a month he was winning every game even when he gave his father the advantage of a five-stone handicap.

Wei qi was even better than plum wine. There was sweetness in the simplicity of the rules, bitterness in defeat, and burning-hot joy in victory. The patterns made by the stones were meant to be chewed over, savored.

While out walking, he got lost staring at the patterns made by black streaks of mud thrown up by passing oxcarts against the whitewashed house walls. Instead of chopping firewood, he carved the nineteen-by-nineteen playing grid into the floor of the kitchen with his ax. During dinner, Chang Sheng forgot to eat while he laid out formations on the table with grains of wild rice and black watermelon seeds. His mother wanted to scold him.

"Let him alone," his father said. "That boy has the makings of a great general."

"Maybe he does," his mother said. "But your family hasn't been in the Emperor's service for generations. What is he going to be a general of? A flock of geese?"

"He's still the son of queens and poets, generals and ministers," his father insisted.

"Playing a game is not going to put rice in the pot, nor wood into the stove. We are going to need to borrow money again this year."

The neighboring villages sent their best players to challenge him. He defeated them all. Eventually, Hua Xiong, the son of the county's wealthiest man, heard about Chang Sheng, the *wei qi* prodigy.

Hua Xiong's family made its fortune by acquiring a coveted license to sell salt. There was a large lake in the county, its waters made salty by the blood of Chi Yu after he was defeated by the Yellow Emperor and his body chopped into pieces. The Han Emperors taxed the salt trade as their principal source of revenue, and the imperial salt monopoly was strictly enforced. Hua Xiong's grandfather placed some strategic bribes, and the family had been growing fat from the salt fortune ever since.

Hua Xiong was the same age as Chang Sheng. He was the sort of boy who tortured cats and delighted in galloping his horse through the fields of his father's tenants, trampling down the sorghum and wheat so that the tracks formed his name. That was how he showed up at the door of the Guan house when he came to play a game of *wei qi* with Chang Sheng, high on his horse, a swath of trampled sorghum behind him.

He brought his *wei qi* set with him: the board made from the pine trees of Mount Tai; the black stones were green jade while the white stones were polished pieces of coral. Chang Sheng made the game last as long as he could so he could finger the cool, smooth stones a little longer.

"The game is getting boring," Hua Xiong said. "I haven't lost to anyone in years."

Chang Sheng's father smiled as he thought, *Doesn't he know that people who have to borrow money from his father would make sure he wins the game?*

Hua Xiong was actually a pretty good *wei qi* player, but not as good as Chang Sheng.

"Very impressive," Hua Xiong said to Chang Sheng's father. "Brother Chang Sheng has a gift. I am ashamed to say that I am not his match."

Chang Sheng's father was surprised. He was too proud to ever tell his son to deliberately throw the game to Hua Xiong. He had expected Hau Xiong to throw a tantrum. But not this.

He's not so bad, he thought. *He's graceful in defeat. That's a quality that belongs to a phoenix among men.*

"What's so impressive about that? I never get mad when my father beats me at checkers. I know I just have to get better."

"Those are wise words. Not everyone sees a loss as an opportunity."

"So is this Hua Xiong really a good man?"

"If you don't interrupt me, you'll soon find out."

"I'll have more watermelon seeds. I won't be able to talk if my mouth is full."

The harvests grew even worse in the next five years. Locusts hit the province. A plague sealed off the next county. There were rumors of cannibalism. The Emperor raised the taxes.

Now eighteen years of age, Hua Xiong was the head of the family after his father choked to death on the leg bone of a pheasant cooked in rice wine. He took advantage of depressed property prices to buy up as much land as possible in the county. Chang Sheng's father went to see him on New Year's Eve.

"Don't worry, Master Guan," Hua Xiong said as they both signed the deed. "I have fond memories of the games

Chang Sheng and I used to play as children. I will take care of you and your family."

In exchange for selling his land to Hua Xiong, Chang Sheng's father got enough money to pay off the family's mounting debt. He was then supposed to lease back the land from Hua Xiong and pay a share of the proceeds from the harvest each year as rent.

"He gave us a good deal," he told Chang Sheng's mother. "I always knew he would grow up to be a good man."

That year, they worked especially hard in the fields. The locusts came again to the county but missed their village. The sorghum stalks shot up tall and straight, bobbing in the dry winds of late summer. It was the best harvest they had had in years.

On New Year's Eve, Hua Xiong arrived with a retinue of burly servants.

"May the new year bring you good fortune, Master Guan." They bowed to each other at the door.

Chang Sheng's father invited him in for some tea and plum wine. They knelt down on the clean, new straw mats, across from each other, the small table with the pot of warm wine between them.

They toasted each other's health and had the customary three cups each. Hua Xiong gave a little awkward laugh. "Well, Master Guan, I came for the little matter of the rent."

"Of course," Chang Sheng's father said. He called for Chang Sheng to bring out the five taels of silver. "Here you are, Master Hua. Five percent of my year's proceeds."

Hua Xiong gave a little cough. "Of course I understand how things have been rather hard on you and your family for the last few years. If you'd like some time to prepare the rest of the payment, that is perfectly acceptable." He got up and bowed deeply.

"But I have all the money here. I can show you the books. I had a good year and took in ninety-three taels of silver at the market. Five percent of that is four taels and eight coins. But since you were generous to me in the original sale, I thought I would pay you five full taels to thank you."

Hua Xiong bowed even deeper. "Surely Master Guan is having a joke at lowly Hua Xiong's expense. Some evil persons have been saying that Master Guan is going to try to get out of paying the full amount of the rent this year, but lowly Hua Xiong did not believe them. Lowly Hua Xiong was sure that everything would be cleared up as soon as he came to see Master Guan in person."

"What are you talking about?"

Hua Xiong looked as if a spider were crawling up his spine. He spread out his hands helplessly. "Is Master Guan asking lowly Hua Xiong to produce the deed and the lease?"

Chang Sheng's father's face became an iron mask. "Show me."

Hua Xiong made a great show of searching for the documents. He patted down his sleeves and the breast pockets of his robe. He shouted at his burly servants to look in the wagon. Finally, one of them, a big man with gigantic, misshapen knuckles, came up to Hua Xiong and presented the rolled-up document to him, giving Chang Sheng's father a hard, long sneer.

"Whew." Hua Xiong wiped his forehead with his sleeve. "I thought we almost lost it. I had not thought it would be necessary."

They knelt down again, and Hua Xiong spread out the lease on the table between them. "The rent is to be eighty-five percent of the proceeds from the year's sale of crops," he read, pointing to the characters with his delicate, long fingers.

"Perhaps you could explain to me why the 'eighty' is written in such narrow characters as compared with the rest of the document," Chang Sheng's father said after examining the lease.

"The clerk who drafted the lease was indeed a poor writer,"

Hua Xiong said. He gave an ingratiating smile. "No doubt Master Guan is a much more cultivated calligrapher. But for a lease you will agree that it does not matter that his hand was poor?"

Chang Sheng's father stood up. Chang Sheng could see that the hem of his sleeves trembled. "Do you think I would have placed my seal on a lease like that? Eighty-five percent? I might as well go join a band of bandits if I want to live on that." He took a step toward Hua Xiong.

Hua Xiong backed up a few steps. Two of the big, burly men stepped up and formed a screen between him and the older man. "Please," Hua Xiong said, his face twisted in a show of regret. "Don't make me take this to the magistrate."

Chang Sheng looked at the ax leaning behind the door. He began to walk toward it.

"Oh no. Don't do it!"

"Go to the kitchen and see if your mother needs more wood," his father said.

Chang Sheng hesitated.

"Go!" his father said.

Chang Sheng walked away and the burly men relaxed.

"Sorry I interrupted."

"No, it's fine. You were trying to save Chang Sheng, like his father."

Later, after Hua Xiong left, the family ate the New Year's Eve dinner in silence.

"A phoenix among men indeed," his father finally said after the meal. He laughed long and hard. Chang Sheng stayed up the whole night with him, drinking the last of their plum wine.

The father wrote a long petition to the magistrate's court, detailing Hua Xiong's treachery.

"It is a sad thing that the bureaucrats must be involved," he said to Chang Sheng, "but sometimes we have no choice."

The soldiers showed up at their house a week later. They broke down the door and hauled Chang Sheng and his mother into the yard and proceeded to overturn every piece of furniture in the house and break every plate, cup, bowl, and dish.

"What is the charge against me?"

"Crafty peasant," the captain said as his soldiers locked the cangue around the neck and arms of Chang Sheng's father, "you are plotting to raise a band of bandits to join the Yellow Turbans. Now confess the names of your coconspirators."

Four soldiers had to hold Chang Sheng back, eventually wrestling him to the ground and sitting on him, as he struggled and cursed the soldiers.

"I think your son also has a rebellious spine," the captain said. "I think we'll bring him in too."

"Chang Sheng, stop fighting. This is not the time. I'll go see the magistrate. This will be cleared up."

His father did not come back the next day, or the day after that. Runners from the town came to the village to tell the family that he had been thrown into jail by the magistrate, pending his trial for treasonous rebellion. Horrified, mother and son made the trip into town to appeal to the magistrate at the *yamen*.

The magistrate refused to see them, or to let them see Chang Sheng's father.

"Crafty peasants, out, out!" The magistrate threw the scholar's rock that he used as a paperweight at Chang Sheng, missing him by a foot. Swinging their bamboo poles, the guards drove Chang Sheng and his mother out of the halls of the *yamen*.

Spring came but mother and son let the fields go fallow. Hua Xiong's henchmen came to cart away anything of value left in the house that hadn't been broken by the soldiers.

His mother held him back as Chang Sheng clenched his teeth and ground them together until he felt the saltiness of blood on his tongue. His face grew redder and redder so that Hua Xiong's servants were frightened and left before they could take everything.

He took his ax and machete and spent the days in the mountains. He cleared out entire hillsides with his swinging blade. *Crack!* Boys playing in the mountains ran back to their mothers and spoke of how they had seen a great eagle swooping among the trees, breaking down the branches with its iron beak. *Zang!* Girls doing the washing by the river ran back to the village and told one another how they had heard an angry tiger crashing through the woods, tearing down saplings with its great paws.

The bundles of firewood and kindling were exchanged for sorghum meal and pickled vegetables from the neighbors. The son waited while the mother swallowed the food in silence, flavoring it with her tears. He seemed to survive on sorghum mead and plum wine alone. With each drink, his face grew darker and redder. The blood hue of sorghum and plum would not fade from his face.

THE MEAL

"Chila, chila!" Ah Yan called out, interrupting Logan's story.

"It's time for dinner," Logan said to Lily. He set down his bowl of watermelon seeds. "Will you join us? Ah Yan is making *Mala* Wife's Tofu and Duke of Wei's Meat, his best dishes."

Lily didn't want Logan to stop. She wanted Hua Xiong to get what he deserved. She wished she could see Chang Sheng angry in the forest, flying and dancing like an eagle or a tiger. But the Chinamen were bustling about, arranging empty crates and benches around the garden in a circle, talking loudly and laughing amongst themselves. The smell emanating from the open kitchen door made Lily's stomach growl. She had been so absorbed in Logan's tale that she didn't even know she was hungry.

"I promise we'll finish the story some other time."

The miners were in high spirits. Logan had told her that the spot that they had been working on turned out to be a rich deposit, yielding gold by the panful. Ah Yan had checked on her leg as soon as he came back with the other Chinamen and pronounced himself satisfied with her healing process so long as she kept up with plenty of good food and exercise to keep up her strength.

"I have a good story for you," Ah Yan said.

During the day the Chinese miners were visited by the sheriff, Davey Gaskins. The territorial legislature had passed a Foreign Miner's Tax a few years earlier at the rate of five dollars per person per month, and he was there to collect it. The tax was meant to drive out the Chinamen, who were pouring into the territory like so many locusts. But the towns had a lot of trouble collecting it. Gaskins hated the monthly rounds to the Chinese mining camps. They made him feel like he was losing his mind.

First of all, the camps were so far apart that he could never hit all of them in a single day. And somehow they always knew when he was coming to collect the tax. There he would be, standing in a middle of a camp with enough picks, pans, and shovels strewn about for twenty or thirty men at least, and only five or six Chinamen would greet him, insisting that the extra tools were there because they worked so hard that the tools "wore out quickie quickie."

And even worse, they seemed to constantly move about.

"Howdy, Sheriff," Ah Yan greeted him that afternoon. "Good to see you again."

"What's your name again?" Gaskins could never tell the Chinamen apart.

"I'm Loh Yip," Ah Yan said. "You came for our taxes on Monday, remember?"

Gaskins was sure that he had not come to this camp on Monday. He was on the other side of the town, collecting the taxes from three claims that were each supposedly just being worked on by five men.

"I was over near Pioneerville on Monday."

"Sure, so were we. We just moved here yesterday."

Ah Yan showed the sheriff the tax receipts. Sure enough, there was the name "Loh Yip" and four others, followed by Gaskin's own signature.

"Sorry I didn't recognize you," Gaskins said. He felt for sure that he was being tricked, but he had no proof. There were the receipts, written out in his own hand.

"No problem," Ah Yan said, giving him a huge grin. "All Chinamen look alike. Easy mistake to make."

Lily laughed along with the miners as Ah Yan finished his story. She couldn't believe how silly Sheriff Gaskins was. How could he not recognize Ah Yan? It was absurd.

As they worked to set up the makeshift table and chairs in the vegetable garden, the Chinamen talked and joked with one another loudly and easily. Lily found it amusing to try to pick out the English words in their conversation. She was getting used to their accent, which she thought was like their music, brassy, percussive, and punctuated by a rhythm like the beating of a joyous heart.

I have to tell Dad about this later, she thought. *He always told me that the Irish accent of his uncles and aunts reminded him of his favorite drinking songs.*

Lily hadn't been able to go out to see the miners during the day while they were working. Her mother was adamant about keeping her inside the house after her "accident" yesterday.

"I just tripped, that's all. I promise to be more careful."

Her mother just told her to write out more verses in her copybook.

Lily knew that her mother suspected that there was more to the accident than she was telling. She had been dying to tell her dad about everything that happened to her yesterday, but her mother became so alarmed at the sight and smell of her bandaged leg that she insisted Lily wash off all the "Chinamen's poison" immediately. After that it was simply impossible to tell them the truth.

It was only after Jack Seaver got home that Lily managed to get out of the house.

"Elsie, she's a child, not a houseplant. You can't keep her in the house all day. She's got to get some skin scraped off now and then. Someday maybe you can put a corset on her and wrap her up for her husband, but not for a while. For now she needs to be out in the sun, running around."

Elsie Seaver was not happy with this, but she let Lily out. "Dinner is going to be late tonight," she said. "Your father and I need to talk."

Lily slipped out of the house before she could change her mind. The sun was low in the west, casting long shadows on the street, where a cool breeze carried the voices of the returning miners far among the houses of Idaho City. The two Chinamen at the door of the house across the street told her that Logan was in the vegetable garden. She had gone there directly, and, when Lily lost their *wei qi* game from yesterday, Logan began to tell her the story of Guan Yu, the God of War, to console her.

The results of Ah Yan's cooking were carried out of the kitchen into the garden on large plates and set on a makeshift table made out of overturned crates in the middle of the circle. The Chinamen, each holding a large bowl of steamed white rice, milled around the table to pile food on top of the rice. Ah Yan emerged from the crowd and handed Lily a small blue porcelain bowl decorated with pink birds and flowers. The rice in the bowl was covered with small cubes of tofu and pork coated in red sauce and dark pieces of roasted meat with scallions and slices of bitter melon. The smell from the unfamiliar hot spice made Lily's eyes and mouth water at the same time.

Ah Yan handed her a pair of chopsticks and headed back

into the crowd to get his own food. He was so small and thin that he nimbly ducked under the shoulders and arms of the other men like a rabbit running under a hedgerow. Before long he ducked back out with his own large bowl of rice piled high with tofu and meat. He saw that Lily was watching him, anxious that he got his fair share. Lifting his bowl from his seat on a stool across the circle from Logan, he told Lily, "Eat, eat!"

Lily sort of got the hang of using chopsticks, after Logan showed her how. It amazed Lily to see his big clumsy hands manipulating his chopsticks so skillfully that he could pick up the delicate pieces of tofu and carry them to his mouth without crushing any of the pieces, causing them to fall, as Lily did the first few times she tried to eat the tofu.

Lily finally managed to get a piece of tofu into her mouth, and she gratefully bit down on it. Flavors until then unknown filled her mouth. Her whole tongue delighted in the richness of the taste: the saltiness, a hint of hot peppers, the almost-sweet base of the sauce, and something else that tickled her tongue. She tried to chew the tofu a little, to bring the flavor out so she could identify that new component more clearly. The taste of hot peppers became stronger, and the tickling grew into a tingling that covered her tongue from tip to base. She chewed yet a little more. . . .

"Awww!" Lily cried out. The tingling suddenly exploded into a thousand hot little needles all over her tongue. The back of her nose felt full of water and her vision became blurry with tears. The Chinamen, stunned into silence by her yelp, burst into laughter when they saw what caused it.

"Eat some white rice," Logan said to her. "Quick."

Lily gulped down several mouthfuls of rice as fast as she could, letting the soft grains massage her tongue and sooth the back of her throat. Her tongue felt numb, paralyzed, and the tingling, now subdued, continued to tickle the inside of her cheeks.

"Welcome to a new taste," Logan said to her, a mischievous joy in his eyes. "That was *mala*, the tingling hotness that made the Kingdom of Shu famous throughout China. You have to be careful with it, as the taste lures you in and then hits you like a mouthful of flame. But once you get used to it, it will make your tongue dance and nothing less will do."

Following Logan's suggestions, Lily tried a few pieces of bitter melon and scallions to rest her tongue a little between pieces of tofu. The bitterness of the melons contrasted nicely with the *mala* of the tofu.

"I bet you've never liked anything bitter before," Logan said.

Lily nodded. She couldn't think of a single dish her mother made that tasted bitter.

"It's all about the balance of the flavors. The Chinese know that you cannot avoid having things be sweet, sour, bitter, hot, salty, *mala*, and whiskey-smooth all at the same time—well, actually the Chinese don't know about whiskey, but you understand my point."

"Lily, it's time for dinner."

Lily looked up. Her father was standing beyond the edge of the vegetable garden, beckoning for her to come over.

"Jack," Logan called out. "Why don't you join us for some of Ah Yan's cooking?"

Taken aback by the suggestion, Jack Seaver nodded after a short pause. He could barely hide his grin as he strode between the rows of cucumbers and cabbages, coming up next to Logan.

"Thank you," he said. "I've been wanting to try this since the first time I smelled it back when you first moved in." He turned to the rest of the circle. "How's the mining been so far, boys?"

"Wonderful, Mr. Seaver." "The gold is everywhere." "Logan has the touch."

"That's just what I want to hear," Jack said. "I'm about to put in an order to San Francisco for my store. Tell me what you want from Chinatown, and I'll work on getting some of that gold out of your hands into mine."

While the circle laughed and shouted out suggestions, which Jack scribbled down on a piece of scrap paper, occasionally pausing so that one of the Chinamen could write down the suggestion in Chinese characters for his agent in San Francisco if the men didn't know the English name for something, Ah Yan ran back into the kitchen to retrieve a new bowl of rice for Jack.

Jack stared at the dishes in the middle of the circle, licking his lips appreciatively. "What are we having today?"

"*Mala* Wife's Tofu," Lily told him. "You have to be careful with it. It has a new taste. And Duke Wei's Meat."

"What kind of meat is it?"

"Dog meat roasted with scallions and bitter melon," Logan said.

Lily, who was about to eat a piece of the roasted meat, dropped her bowl. Rice and tofu and meat and red sauce spilled everywhere. She felt sick.

Jack picked her up and hugged her closely. "How can you do such a thing?" he demanded. "Whose dog did you kill? There's going to be trouble from this." His frown grew more pronounced. "Elsie is going to be hysterical if she hears about this."

"Nobody's. It was a wild dog running in the woods. It looked like a dog that's been abandoned out in the woods since it was a pup. I killed it when it tried to bite me," said Ah Yan, who had come out of the kitchen holding the new bowl of rice for Jack.

"But don't you have dogs as pets? Eating a dog is like . . . like eating a child," Jack said.

"We also have dogs as pets. We do not eat them if they are pets. But this dog was wild, and Ah Yan had to kill it to defend himself. Why would you let a wild dog's meat go to waste when it is delicious?" Logan said. The rest of the Chinamen had stopped eating, intent on the conversation.

"Whether it was wild or not, eating a dog is barbaric."

"You do not eat dogs because you like them too much." Logan thought about this. "I thought you also do not eat rats."

"Of course not! What a disgusting thought. Rats are dirty creatures full of disease." Jack's stomach turned at the very idea.

"We don't eat rats, as a rule," said Logan. "But if we are starving and there's no other meat, it could be cooked to be palatable."

Was there no end to the depravity of the Chinamen? "I can't imagine when I would willingly eat a rat."

"I see," said Logan. "You only eat animals you like a little, but not too much."

There really wasn't anything to say in response to that. Cradling Lily, who was trying hard not to throw up, Jack Seaver walked out of the vegetable garden back to his own house. Elsie had made a chicken pot pie, but neither he nor Lily was any longer in the mood for eating.

Feather, Long Clouds

The eastern sky was still as gray as the belly of a fish when Chang Sheng climbed over the wall. By the time he had finished, the rooster had yet to crow for the first time. The old house, its beams and walls hollowed out by termites and rats over the years, burned easily. By the time the villagers raised the alarm, he was already twenty *li* away.

The rising sun burned the clouds that were draped across the mountains on the eastern horizon in an unbroken chain to a hue red enough to match his face. *Bloodred long clouds,* he thought. *Even the Heavens are celebrating with me.* He laughed long and loud at the joy of vengeance. He felt light as a feather, like he could run forever toward the east, until he ran into the long clouds or into the ocean.

I will need a new name now, thought Chang Sheng. *I shall henceforth be known as* Guan Yu, *the Feather, also styled* Yun Chang, *Long Clouds.*

A month ago, the Autumn Assizes had taken place. Because the penalty for rebellion was death, the Circuit Intendant had overseen the trial himself. The Elder Guan had been hauled into the hall of the *yamen* in chains and made to kneel on the hard, stone floor while Chang Sheng and his mother watched from among the crowd that had gathered for the trial.

Hua Xiong, now fatter than ever and shaking like a leaf in the wind in front of the Intendant, a young scholar judge fresh out of Luo Yang and filled with the arrogance of the Emperor's favor, produced the lease for the Intendant's inspection. He recounted how he had tried to help out the Guan family during their time of need and was dumbfounded when the Elder Guan insisted on setting the lease at 85 percent.

"I asked him, 'How could you live on that?' And Your Reverence, he told me, 'Everyone is going to starve if that'— and here he disrespected the Son of Heaven's name—'is going to rule the country by the advice of his eunuchs and the flattering courtiers that pass for scholars these days. I might as well give all the harvest to you as to lose it all in taxes. It doesn't matter. I'll have a better chance joining the Yellow Turbans and living as a bandit." He bowed his head before the Intendant and continued to tremble.

The Intendant glanced at the kneeling figure of the Elder Guan below the dais of the *yamen*, the corners of his mouth turned down in displeasure. "Humph. 'Flattering courtiers that pass for scholars these days.' Indeed, peasant, is there no respect for the Emperor and the majesty of the law in your eyes? Have you lost all sense of piety? What do you have to say in answer to these accusations?"

The Elder Guan straightened his back as much as he could in his shackles. He looked up at the severe, young face of the Intendant. "It is true that I believe the Emperor has been misled by unscrupulous advisers who view the people as so much fish and meat to be squeezed for their last drop of wealth without regard for their suffering. But I have not forgotten my duty toward the Emperor or my family's many generations of service in the Imperial Army, and I would never raise my arm in rebellion to him. My accuser has fabricated these lies in order to impoverish my family and disgrace me, simply because my son had humiliated him in a game. The Emperor has entrusted you with the power of life and death no doubt because you have wisdom despite your youth, and I have no doubt that your wisdom will reveal the truth of my innocence to you."

Even though he was kneeling, the air that he spoke with made him seem to tower over everyone in the hall of the *yamen*. Even the Intendant seemed impressed.

Noting the change in the Intendant's mien, Hua Xiong fell to his knees and kowtowed three times in rapid succession. "Your Reverence, I should never have dared to accuse Master Guan unless I had solid evidence, seeing as how his son and I have been childhood friends. I am merely a lowly merchant, while Master Guan is descended from a distinguished family of generals and scholars in the Emperor's service. But I was motivated by love and zeal for the Emperor, so much so that I dared to accuse such a man. It was my fear that he would use his family's glorious record as a shield to cover up all his impious vices. I pray that you would uphold justice." He kept on kowtowing after this speech.

"Stop that," the Intendant said impatiently. "You need not fear his family's history of glory. The Emperor's law is to be administered blindly and impartially. Even were he the son of a Duke or a Prince, if he plotted against the Emperor, you need not fear accusing him." He took another look at the Elder Guan, his face hardening. "I have known many evil men like him: puffed up with the honors heaped upon their families by the Emperor for their ancestors' loyal service, they think they are beyond the law. Well, I will be sure to punish them extra harshly. What other evidence do you have?"

Hua Xiong nodded toward three young girls cowering in the corner behind him. "These young women have seen and heard Master Guan practicing with his ax and machete in the woods. They saw him leaping about, pretending to . . . to . . ."

"To do what?"

"To be visiting those blows upon the Son of Heaven."

Hua Xiong went back to his incessant kowtowing, drawing blood on his forehead.

"That is a lie," Chang Sheng cried out from the crowd. He was livid at those young girls for agreeing to back up such a blatant falsehood. But then he saw that they were all from families who owed a great deal of money to Hua Xiong. He felt as if the veins in his neck would burst if he didn't speak. "I was the one—"

"Chang Sheng, whatever happens, do not speak," the Elder Guan shouted. "You must take care of your mother."

"Come," the Intendant called out to his soldiers, "drive that lawless child and his unchaste mother from the *yamen*. I will not have them make a spectacle of my court."

To keep himself from striking back, Chang Sheng bit down on his tongue until he drew blood. He tried to shield his mother from the blows of the soldiers as they stumbled away from the *yamen*.

The Elder Guan was sentenced to death that afternoon for plotting treason, and his head soon afterward was hung on the flagpole outside the *yamen*. That evening, Chang Sheng's mother put her head in a loop of rope tied to the beam in the middle of the kitchen and kicked the stool out from under herself.

Chang Sheng had left Hua Xiong alive until the end. After he had dispatched the rest of the Hua household (some twenty people), he woke Hua Xiong from his slumber (pausing first to slit the throats of the two concubines in bed with him with quick flicks of his wrist). In the dim light of the torch that Chang Sheng was carrying with him, Hua Xiong thought he looked like a red-faced demon, a soldier from hell coming for his soul.

"I'm sorry, I'm sorry," he blabbered, and lost control of his bowels.

Chang Sheng used his knife to cut the ligaments in Hua

Xiong's shoulders and hips, completely paralyzing him. He laid the drooping, heavy body back down on the bed, cuddled between the lifeless bodies of the two concubines.

"I will not give you a clean death. You said my father was a bandit. I will now show you how a bandit deals with people like you."

He proceeded to set fire throughout the house. Soon the smoke was so heavy that Hua Xiong could no longer scream for help. His coughing grew spasmodic and panicked; he was choking on his own spit.

Guan Yu continued to run to the east, where the bloodred long clouds beckoned to him. His heart was light as a feather, and it seemed as if love of the fight and joy in vengeance would never leave him. He felt like a god.

IMPRESSIONS

There was a clearing in the middle of the woods on the side of the hill opposite the river from the Chinamen's mining camp. Now that it was late June, the syringa bushes were in full bloom in the rocky soil along the edge of the clearing, filling the air with their fresh, orangelike scent. The yellow of the blooming arrowleaf balsamroot carpeted the middle of the clearing, with a touch here and there of the purple-blue of the chicory to break the monotony.

Lily loved to sit in the shade of the trees at the edge of the clearing and stare at the colors in front of her. If she sat still long enough, the gentle breeze and the slanting rays of the sun would conspire to blend the individual flowers into an undulating field of light. The world seemed then made afresh to her, full of tomorrows and undiscovered delights. And singing seemed the only thing worth doing.

A plume of smoke rose at the edge of the clearing, breaking her reverie.

She walked across the clearing toward the smoke. The dark figure of a man crouched by it. He was cooking something that smelled delicious to Lily. But there was also a hint of something unpleasant in that smell, like burning hair.

Lily was close enough now to see that the man was large, even larger than Logan. Just as Lily realized that the man was roasting the whole carcass of a large dog whose hide was red as blood, he turned around and grinned at Lily, revealing a mouth full of sharp, daggerlike teeth.

It was Crick.

Lily screamed.

Jack told Elsie to go back to sleep.

"It's all right. I'll make some tea for her."

The sound of water boiling and the comforting warmth of her father's arms dissipated the last traces of the nightmare from Lily's mind. Sipping tea and whispering lest they be overheard by her mother, Lily told Jack what she had seen of the fight between Logan and Crick.

"What happened to Obee?"

"I don't know, he ran off."

"And what did they do with Crick's body?"

Lily wasn't sure about that either.

"And you definitely saw Obee shoot first? And the bullet hit Logan in the shoulder?"

Lily nodded vigorously. The image of Logan's shoulder exploding was carved indelibly into her brain. And she marveled again at how calm she felt when Logan looked at her, as if he had some power to pass his strength onto her, letting her know that she would be safe.

Jack pondered this. If Lily was right, the wound to Logan was serious, yet he had been back at work with his companions less than twelve hours later. Either the Chinaman was the toughest human being he had ever known, or Lily was exaggerating.

But he knew his daughter. She was an imaginative child, but not one who lied.

Obee and Crick were notorious outlaws, and lots of people in town suspected that they were behind the fire that had ruined so many people in town and killed the Kellys. But there were no witnesses to the fire and the murders, and no charges had been brought. Now if Obee decided to accuse Logan of murder, he might indeed have a chance of getting Logan hanged since he and Lily and all the Chinamen actually saw it happen. The Chinamen weren't well liked by the whites, on account of their taking claims away from the white miners—never mind that most of these claims had been abandoned by the whites since they didn't have the Chinese rice farmers' skill and patience with water management or their willingness to survive on rice and vegetables and to squeeze as many people as possible into the tiny saltbox houses in order to save money. There was no telling what a jury might do even if it sounded like Logan killed Crick to protect himself and the others.

"Dad, are you angry with me?"

Startled from his reverie, Jack collected himself. "No. Why should I be?"

"Because you said Logan looked like a killer and you told me to stay away from the Chinamen, and . . . and I almost ate a dog last week."

Jack laughed. "I can't be angry with you for that. The Chinamen's cooking smelled so good that I was interested in the dog myself—and still am, a little. You didn't do anything wrong. Although it was dangerous for you to get mixed up in their fight, it wasn't by any means your fault. And I guess it turned out all right. You weren't hurt."

"I was, a little."

"Luckily, the Chinamen's medicine seemed to have fixed it. That Logan is quite a character."

"He tells good stories," Lily said. She wanted to tell him about the battles of Guan Yu, the God of War, or the songs of Jie You, the Princess Who Became a Barbarian. She wanted to describe to him how she felt, listening to Logan recite those stories in the rhythm of his clanging, whiskey-sharpened accent so that they sounded at the same time so fantastic and so familiar while the long, gnarled fingers of his large hands made the scene come alive with comic and solemn gestures. But it was all still so new and confusing, and she didn't think she knew the right words yet to paint a proper picture of those moments for her father.

"I'm sure he does. This is why we are out here, where the country belongs to nobody and everyone is a stranger with a tale of his own. The Celestials are filling up California and soon, Idaho Territory. Soon everyone here will know their stories."

Lily finished her tea. She was comfortable, but the lingering excitement from the nightmare kept her from being sleepy.

"Dad, will you sing me a song? I can't sleep now."

"Sure thing, Nugget. But let's go outside and take a walk, or else we'll wake your mother."

Lily and Jack threw jackets over their nightclothes and slipped outside the house. The summer evening was warm, and the sky, cloudless and moonless, glowed with the light of a million stars.

Some of the Chinamen were still up on the porch. They played a game with dice by the weak light of an oil lamp. Jack and Lily waved at them as the two of them strode down the street.

"Guess they can't sleep either," Jack said. "Don't blame them. Can't imagine how you'd sleep with five other guys packed in like sardines with you, all of them snoring and with smelly feet."

Before long they had left the weak light of the Chinamen's oil lamp behind them, and then they were beyond the edge of the town. Jack sat down on a rock by the side of the road into the hills and lifted Lily to sit beside him, his arm wrapped around her.

"What song would you like to hear?"

"How about the one that Mom would never let you sing, the one about the funeral?"

"That's a good one."

Jack took out his pipe and lit it to keep the insects away from them, and he began to sing:

> *Tim Finnegan lived in Walkin' Street,*
> *A gentle Irishman mighty odd;*
> *He had a brogue both rich and sweet,*
> *And to rise in the world he carried a hod.*
> *Now Tim had a sort of a tipplin' way,*
> *With a love of the whiskey he was born,*
> *And to help him on with his work each day,*
> *He'd a drop of the craythur every morn.*

Lily looked up into her father's face. Lit by the flame from the pipe, it took on a red glow that brought a sudden rush of love and comfort to her heart. Smiling at each other, father and daughter belted out the chorus:

> *Whack fol the dah O, dance to your partner,*
> *Welt the floor, your trotters shake;*
> *Wasn't it the truth I told you,*
> *Lots of fun at Finnegan's wake!*

Jack continued with the rest of the song:

> *One mornin' Tim was feelin' full,*
> *His head was heavy which made him shake;*
> *He fell from the ladder and broke his skull,*
> *And they carried him home his corpse to wake.*
> *They rolled him up in a nice clean sheet,*
> *And laid him out upon the bed,*
> *A gallon of whiskey at his feet,*
> *And a barrel of porter at his head.*

> *His friends assembled at the wake,*
> *And Mrs. Finnegan called for lunch,*

First they brought in tay and cake,
Then pipes, tobacco and whiskey punch.
Biddy O'Brien began to bawl,
"Such a nice clean corpse, did you ever see?
O Tim, mavourneen, why did you die?"
"Arragh, hold your gob," said Paddy McGhee!

Then Maggie O'Connor took up the job,
"O Biddy," says she. "You're wrong, I'm sure."
Biddy she gave her a belt in the gob,
And left her sprawlin' on the floor.
And then the war did soon engage,
'Twas woman to woman and man to man,
Shillelagh law was all the rage,
And a row and a ruction soon began.

Then Mickey Maloney ducked his head,
When a noggin of whiskey flew at him,
It missed, and falling on the bed,
The liquor scattered over Tim!
The corpse revives! See how he raises!
Timothy rising from the bed,
Says, "Whirl your whiskey around like blazes,
Thanum an Dhoul! Do you think I'm dead?"

"Feeling sleepy yet?"
"No."
"All right, we'll sing another one."
They stayed out under the stars for a long, long time.

The Apotheosis

It was whispered among the soldiers of all the Three
Kingdoms that Guan Yu could not be killed. The generals

of the deceitful Cao Cao and the arrogant Sun Quan tried to laugh at this rumor and executed those who spread it. All the same, when it came time to face Guan Yu on the battlefield, even the invincible Lü Bu hesitated.

But I have gotten ahead of myself. How did the Han Dynasty fall? How did the Three Kingdoms rise? Who were the heroes among whom Guan Yu made his way?

The Yellow Turbans ravaged the land, their rallying rebel cry that the Emperor was a child who had never set foot outside the Palace while his eunuchs preyed upon the blood and flesh of the peasants. Taking up arms against the rebels, the dreaded warlord Cao Cao made the Emperor a hostage in his own capital and ruled in his name from the plains and deserts of the North.

In the South, the rich rice fields and winding rivers propelled Sun Quan, the Little Tyrant, to hold sway over ships, and hunger for the title of Emperor.

Everywhere there was sickness and starvation, and armies marched over fields empty of cultivation.

Liu Bei, a man so full of charm that his earlobes reached his shoulders, was merely a peddler of straw shoes and straw mats when he met Zhang Fei, the butcher, and Guan Yu, the outlaw who was still running. Guan Yu now had the beginning of his famous beard, a bushy and vibrant beard that made him look old and young at the same time. It made a nice addition to a handsome face, whose smooth features looked like they were carved out of the red stone of the Crimson Cliffs of the Yangtze River.

"If I had men who could fight like tigers with me, I would restore the glory of the Han Dynasty," Liu Bei said to the two strangers who shared a bowl of sorghum mead with him in the peach orchard.

"And what good is that to me?" asked Zhang Fei, whose face was black as coal and whose arms daily wrestled oxen to the ground for the slaughter.

Liu Bei shrugged. "Maybe you do not care. But if I were Emperor, the magistrates would again mete out justice, the fields would be cultivated with industry and virtue, and the teahouses would again be filled with the songs and laughter of scholars and dancing women." His eyes lingered a moment longer on Guan Yu's face, which was familiar to him from the many posters putting a price on his head that he had seen around the city. "There are many men who are outlaws in this day and age, but many of them are outside the law only because the laws have not been administered with virtue. Were I Emperor, I would make them the judges, not the criminals."

"And what makes you think you will succeed?" asked Guan Yu. His face darkened to the color of blood, but he stroked his beard carelessly, like a scholar stroking his brush as he was about to pen a poem about girls collecting flowers in May.

"I don't know I will succeed," Liu Bei said. "All life is an experiment. But when I die I will know that I once tried to fly as high as a dragon."

In the peach orchard then, they became sworn brothers.

"Though we were not born on the same day of the same month of the same year, we ask that Fate give us the satisfaction of dying on the same second of the same minute of the same hour."

They headed West, and there, in the mountainous Province of Shu, where Guan Yu first tasted *mala*, they founded the Kingdom of Shu Han.

All-Under-Heaven was thus split into the Three Kingdoms of Cao Cao, Sun Quan, and Liu Bei. Of the three, Cao Cao had the valor and wildness of the Northern Skies while Sun Quan had the wealth and resilience of the Southern Earth, but only Liu Bei had the virtue and love of the People.

Guan Yu was his greatest warrior. He had the strength of a thousand men and the love of even more.

"He is not made of flesh and blood." Cao Cao sighed when he heard the report of how Guan Yu slew six of his best generals and broke through five passes to rejoin Liu Bei on his Long March of a Thousand Li.

"He is a phoenix among swallows and sparrows." Sun Quan shook his head when he heard how Guan Yu laughed and played *wei qi* while his bones were scraped free of poison. Guan Yu was back on his horse and swinging his sword the next day.

War raged between the Three Kingdoms for years, neither one able to subdue the other two. Guan Yu's face never lost its bloodred color, and his dark beard grew longer and longer until he wore it in a silk pouch to keep it clean and out of the way in battle.

Though Liu Bei was virtuous, the Mandate of Heaven was not with him. His armies fought and lost, lost and fought, in battle after battle. During a retreat on one of their campaigns to the North, Guan Yu and Zhang Fei were separated from the main army, and their detachment of one hundred scouts became surrounded by the army of Cao Cao, numbering more than ten thousand. Cao Cao asked for parley with the two.

"Surrender and swear fealty to me, and I shall make you into Dukes who do not have to kneel even in the presence of the Son of Heaven," Cao Cao said.

Guan Yu laughed. "You do not understand why men like me fight. There is the joy of battle, of course, but that is not all." He opened up his old, faded battle cape to show Cao Cao the holes in the fabric, the frayed edges and patches upon more patches. "This was given to me by my sworn brother Liu Bei. Before I put on the cape, I was nobody, a murderer running from the law. But after I put on the cape, every swing of my sword was in the name of virtue. What can you offer me better than that?"

Cao Cao turned around and rode back to his camp. He ordered his army to begin attack immediately. The generals gave the orders, but the soldiers, thousands upon thousands of them lined up in rank after rank, refused to advance against Guan Yu and Zhang Fei and their small circle of one hundred men.

Cao Cao ordered the soldiers standing in the back killed on the spot. The panicked soldiers pushed against their comrades in front. The tide of men surged slowly forward, closing in on Guan Yu and Zhang Fei.

The battle lasted from morning till night and then throughout the night till the next morning.

"Remember the Oath of the Peach Orchard," Guan Yu yelled to Zhang Fei. He was riding through Cao Cao's men on his war stallion, the great Red Hare, whose skin matched the hue of Guan Yu's face and who sweated blood as he trampled men beneath his giant hooves. "If Fate will have us succumb this day, then we will have at least fulfilled our oath."

"But then our brother Liu Bei will be late," replied Zhang Fei as he impaled two men at once on his iron-shafted spear.

"We will forgive him," Guan Yu said. The Brothers laughed and separated once again for the battle.

Wherever Guan Yu rode, swinging his moon-shaped sword, the soldiers of Cao Cao fell over one another to get away from the rider and his horse, parting before them like a flock of sheep before a tiger or a brood of chickens before an eagle. Guan Yu mowed them down mercilessly, and Red Hare frothed at the mouth, the bloodlust overcoming his exhaustion.

"When I am fighting next to you," Zhang Fei said, wiping streams of blood from his black face, "I do not know what fear is. My mind is harder, my heart keener, my spirit the greater as our might lessens."

The one hundred men with Guan Yu and Zhang Fei gradually became fifty men, and then fifteen, and finally, only Guan Yu and Zhang Fei were left, charging back and forth through the sea of swords and spears that was Cao Cao's army.

It was evening again. Cao Cao called for a halt to the battle, pulling his troops back. Rivers of blood ran across the field, and hacked-off limbs and heads littered the ground like sea shells on the beach at low tide. The evening sun cast long, scarlet shadows over everything so that one could no longer be sure whether the redness was from the light or blood.

"Surrender," Cao Cao called out to them. "You have proven your courage and loyalty to Liu Bei. No god or man would ask more of you."

"I would," Guan Yu said.

Though Cao Cao was a man with a cold heart and a narrow mind, he was overwhelmed with admiration for Guan Yu.

"Will you drink with me," he said, "before you die?"

"Of course," said Guan Yu. "I never say no to sorghum mead."

"No sorghum mead here, I'm afraid. But I have some barrels of a new drink the barbarians of the West have given to me as tribute."

The drink was made from grapes, a new fruit brought over the desert by the barbarian emissaries of the West.

You mean wine?
Yes, but that was the first time Guan Yu had seen it.

Guan Yu and Cao Cao drank it in jade cups, whose cold stony surface complemented the warmth of the wine excellently. It was getting dark, but the jade from which the cups were made had an inner glow to them that lit up the faces of the two men. The pretty barbarian girls who were part of the tribute to Cao Cao played a mournful tune on their strange pear-shaped lutes, which they called *pi pa*.

Guan Yu listened to the music, lost in his own thoughts. Suddenly he stood up and began to sing to the tune of the barbarian lute:

> *Give me grape wine overflowing night-glowing cups,*
> *I would drink it all but the* pi pa *calls me to my*
> *horse.*

If I should fall down drunk on the battlefield, do not
*   laugh at me,*
For how many have ever returned from war, how
*   many?*

He tossed the cup away. "Lord Cao Cao, I thank you for the wine, but I think it is now time to get back to what we have to do."

"So, that banjo-thing you were playing, that's a *pi pa*, isn't it?" The mournful song Logan had been singing was still in Lily's head. She wanted to ask Logan to teach it to her.

"Yes, it is." He shifted the *pi pa* around on his knees, cradling its pear-shaped body lovingly, like a baby. "This one is pretty old, and it sounds better with every year that passes."

"But it's not really Chinese, is it?"

Logan was thoughtful for a moment. "I don't know. I guess you'd say it's really not, not if you look back thousands of years. But I don't think that way. Lots of things start out not Chinese and end up that way."

"That's not what I would have expected to hear from a Celestial," Jack said. He was still trying to get used to the taste of the sorghum liquor that Logan assured him was what every Chinese boy drank along with mother's milk. Swallowing it was like swallowing a mouthful of razors. Lily saw his furrowed brows as he took another drink and laughed.

"Why not?"

"I thought you Celestials were supposed to be mighty jealous of your long history, Confucius being from before Christ and everything. I didn't think I'd hear one of you admit that you learned anything from the barbarians."

Logan laughed at this. "I myself have some blood of the northern barbarians flowing in my veins. What is Chinese? What is barbarian? These questions will not put rice into bellies

301

or smiles onto the faces of my companions. I'd much rather sing about pretty girls with green eyes from west of the Gobi Desert and play my *pi pa*."

"If I didn't know better, Logan, I'd say you sound like a Chinese American."

Jack and Logan laughed at this. *"Gan bei, gan bei,"* they said, and tossed back cups of whiskey and sorghum liquor.

"I want to learn 'Finnegan's Wake' from you. Ever since I heard the two of you singing that night, I can't get it out of my head."

"You have to finish the story first!" Lily said.

"All right. But I have to warn you. I've told this story so many times, and each time I tell it, it's different. I'm not sure I know how the story ends anymore."

How long did the battle last? Was it still against the treacherous Cao Cao or the deceitful Sun Quan? Guan Yu could not remember.

He did remember telling Zhang Fei to leave and get back to Liu Bei.

"I am in charge of the men, and because of my carelessness, I have led them into death. I cannot show my face back in Cheng Du, where the wives and fathers of those men will ask me why I have returned when their husbands and sons have not. Fight your way out, Brother, and seek revenge for me."

Zhang Fei halted his horse and gave a long cry. At the piercing sound of that cry, full of sorrow and regret, the ten thousand men around them shook in their boots and stumbled back three steps each.

"Good-bye, Brother." Zhang Fei spurred his horse to the west, and the soldiers parted to make way for his spear and horse, fought with one another to get out of his path.

"On, on!" Cao Cao shouted angrily. "The man who captures Guan Yu shall be made a Duke."

Red Hare stumbled. He had lost too much blood. Guan Yu

deftly leapt off the back of the war stallion just as he fell to the ground.

"I'm sorry, old friend. I wish I could have protected you." Blood and sweat dripped from his beard, and tears carved out clear channels through the dried blood and dirt on his face.

He threw down his sword and put his hands behind him, looking for all the world like a scholar-poet about to recite from the *Book of Poetry* in front of the Emperor at his court. He stared at the approaching soldiers with contempt.

"They cut off his head at the next sunrise," Logan said.

"Oh," said Lily. This wasn't the ending she had wanted to hear.

The three of them were silent for a bit, while the smoke from Ah Yan's cooking in the kitchen drifted into the clear sky. The sound of spatula on wok sounded like the din of sword on shield to Lily's ears.

"You are not going to ask me what happened next?" Logan said.

"What do you mean?" Jack and Lily said at the same time.

"What do you mean?" Cao Cao shouted, and stood up in a hurry, overturning the writing desk in the process. The ink stone and brushes flew everywhere. "What do you mean you can't find it?"

"Lord Cao Cao, I am telling you what I saw with my own eyes. One minute his head was rolling on the ground, and the next his head and body were simply nowhere to be found. He . . . he disappeared into thin air."

"What kind of fool do you take me for? Come!" Cao Cao gestured to the guards. "Tie him up and have him executed. We'll hang his head outside my tent since he lost Guan Yu's head."

"Of course he's not dead," the grizzled veteran said to the pink-faced new recruits. "I was there the day Lord Guan Yu was captured. Among the one hundred thousand men of the Army of Wei, he fought as if they were nothing more than motes of dust. A man like that, do you think he would succumb to an executioner's ax?"

"Of course he's not dead," Liu Bei said to Zhang Fei. They were both covered in the white armor of mourning, and they had raised an army of every last able-bodied man of the Kingdom of Shu for vengeance. "Our brother would not die when he still has the Oath of the Peach Orchard to fulfill."

"Of course he's not dead," Sun Quan said as he lay on his deathbed. "Guan Yu had no fear of death, and my only regret is that I will not have his company where I am going. I had hoped we might one day be friends."

"Of course he's not dead," said Cao Cao to Liu Chan, Liu Bei's son, as he gave the order to break the Seal of the Kingdom of Shu, now that he had finally united the Three Kingdoms. "I have never thought much of your father or you, but if Guan Yu was willing to serve your father, then he must have seen something that I couldn't. As Lord Guan Yu may still be watching over you, I would show him that I am not without virtue. I will not harm you and you will always live in my house as an honored guest."

"Of course he's not dead," said the mother to the child. "Lord Guan Yu was the greatest man the Middle Kingdom has ever produced. If you have even one hundredth of his strength and courage, I will never need to fear thieves and bandits."

"Let us pray to Lord Guan Yu," said the scholar to his students. "He was a poet and a warrior, and he lived each day as a test of his honor."

"Let us pray to Lord Guan Yu," said the Emperor as he dedicated the Temple to the God of War. "May he grant us victory over the barbarians."

"Let us pray to Lord Guan Yu," said the player with the black stones. "All of us *wei qi* players wish we could play a game against him. If we play well today, perhaps he will deign to come and give us lessons."

"Let us pray to Lord Guan Yu," said the merchants as they prepared to set out across the ocean for the fabled ports of Ceylon and Singapore. "He will watch over us and subdue the pirates and typhoons."

"Let us pray to Lord Guan Yu," said the laborers as they boarded the sailing ships headed for the Sandalwood Mountains of Hawaii and the Old Gold Mountain of California. "He will help us endure the journey, and he will break apart mountains before us. He will keep us safe until we have made our fortune, and then he will guide us home."

THE CHINESE RESTAURANT

By late summer, the stream that fed the Chinamen's claim had dried to a trickle. Though Logan and his men were good at managing water, the onset of the dry season meant that it was no longer possible to mine the placer deposit effectively. They had to settle in and wait until next spring.

Though they had done well with the mining season during spring and summer, the Chinamen had by no means accumulated a large fortune. As they settled into the life of Idaho City and waited out the rest of the year, they tried to figure out other ways to make ends meet.

Ah Yan and some of the younger men looked for work around the town and talked amongst themselves. They noticed that there were plenty of single men in town who simply refused to or couldn't wash their own shirts, and there simply weren't enough laundresses taking in the washing for all the men.

"But that's women's work! Have these men no sense of decency?" Elsie was incredulous when Jack told her the Chinamen's plan.

"Well, what of it? Why do you seem to hate everything the Chinamen do?" Jack said, amusement and annoyance struggling in his voice.

"Thaddeus Seaver." Elsie looked sternly at her husband. She knew better than to expect that her husband would show any proper sense of shock at the antics of these outrageous Chinamen when Thad was the one who encouraged them to become bolder and bolder every day. But then she hit upon an argument that even Thad had to acknowledge.

"Why, think about it, Thad," she said. "I've seen the way these heathen Chinamen go about their work. When they set up their laundry shops, they'll work seven days a week, sixteen hours a day. They'll do it since their hearts are filled with greed for gold and pumped full of sinful opium so that they never stop for a moment to think about the Glory of God, not even on Sundays. And I've seen the way they eat. The Chinamen are like locusts: they survive on nothing but cheap rice and vegetables when honest Christian men and women need to eat meat to keep up their strength. And they do not spend money on honest wholesome entertainment and camaraderie that keep the town's shops and taverns afloat as our men do, but rather waste their evenings away wailing their cacophonous songs and telling their secretive stories. Finally, when night rolls around and every Christian family withdraws around the privacy of the familial hearth"—and here she paused to give Jack a meaningful stare—"the Chinamen squeeze as many bodies into as few beds as possible to save on rent."

"Why, Elsie," Jack laughed uproariously. "I've heard of faint praise before, but I do believe this is the first time I've ever heard of faint damnation. The way you go on, I'd think you are a lover of the Chinese if I didn't know better. You claim to be showing me their faults, but all you've said simply show that they are industrious, frugal, clever, happy with each other's company, and willing to bear hardships. If this is the worst you can say about the Chinamen, then it is all but certain that the Civilization of Confucius is going to triumph over the Civilization of Christ."

"You are not thinking," Elsie said coldly. "What do you think the inevitable result of the cheap labor of these Chinamen will be? These Chinamen are going to undercharge Mrs. O'Scannlain and Mrs. Day and all the other widows. These women have a hard enough time as it is, working day and night, their fingers all red and raw from the constant washing, and they barely make enough to feed themselves and their children. Naturally, the weak men of this town, uncertain of their Christian duty, will give their work to the Chinamen, who'll charge them less than the honest widows who must keep God and their virtue close to their hearts. What will you have these widows do when their work has been stolen from them by the Chinamen? Will you have them throwing themselves at the mercy of Madam Isabelle and her house of sin?"

For once, Jack Seaver didn't know what to say in reply to his wife.

"How about carpentry? Furniture finishing? I could hire you to come and work in my store as clerks," Jack said to Ah Yan.

"You can't afford me," Ah Yan said. "We charge twenty-five cents a shirt, and that means almost ten dollars a day from the bachelors alone. I'm not even counting the money from the blankets and sheets from the hotels. I've been told that we do a better job ironing than the women used to." Ah Yan gave a rueful smile and flexed out his wiry right arm to look at the distended thumb at the end. "Even my thumb is getting bigger from pushing that iron all day. My wife back home will be tickled pink to hear that I'm a master of the iron now."

To hear Ah Yan talk of his family was jarring to Jack, reminding him that Ah Yan, who looked so young to Jack's eyes, wasn't just some clever young man who knew how to cook and wash, but rather a husband and probably a father who was forced to learn how to do these things because his wife couldn't be with him.

Lily had told Jack a few days earlier that the Chinamen were coming up with some new ideas that they wanted to ask his advice on. Finally, this morning, he could leave the store for a few hours to come over with Lily, who ran into the backyard to be with Logan as soon as they arrived. Jack thoughtfully bit into the steamed bun that Ah Yan had given him for breakfast; the bun burst open in his mouth, filling his tongue with the juice and flavor of sweet pork and hot and salty vegetables.

"Wait." Jack swallowed quickly, regretting that he couldn't enjoy the taste as long as he would have liked. "I have an idea. Before tasting your cooking, I would never have believed that cabbage and beans could taste better than beef and sausage, or that bitterness that lingered could be something that you liked. But you've been able to prove me wrong. Why not show the other people in Idaho City? You and the others could open up a restaurant and make a lot more money."

Ah Yan shook his head. "Won't work, Mr. Seaver. My friends in Old Gold Mountain tried it. Most Americans aren't like you. They can't stand the taste of Chinese food. It makes them sick."

"I've heard of Chinese restaurants in San Francisco."

"Those aren't Chinese restaurants. Well, they are, but not the kind you are thinking of. They are owned by Chinese people, but all they serve is Western food: roast beef, chocolate cake, French toast. I don't know how to make any of that stuff, not even well enough to the point where I'd want to eat it myself."

"But I'm telling you, you are good, really good." Jack looked around and lowered his voice. "You cook a lot better than Elsie, and I know she cooks as well as most of the wives out here. If you open your restaurant and I pass the word to the men discreetly, you'll have filled tables every night."

"Mr. Seaver, you are too generous with your praise. I know that in the eyes of a husband, there's no way for anyone's cooking to best his wife's." He paused for a moment, as if his thoughts were momentarily somewhere far away. "Besides, we are not chefs. All the stuff I make is just homestyle cooking, the kind of thing the real chefs in Canton would not even feed to their dogs. There can't be a Chinese restaurant in America until there are enough Chinese people in America—and rich enough to want to eat at one."

"That just means more Chinese will have to become Americans," said Jack.

"Or lots more Americans will have to learn to be more Chinese," said Ah Yan.

A few of the other Chinamen had gathered around to listen to the conversation. One of them offered a comment in Chinese at this point, and the group exploded in laughter. Tears came out of Ah Yan's eyes.

"What did he say?" Although Jack was making an earnest effort to learn the language by singing drinking songs with Logan, he was nowhere good enough to follow a conversation yet, though Lily seemed to have picked it up much more easily and now often conversed with Logan half in Chinese and half in English.

Ah Yan wiped his eyes. "San Long said that we should name the restaurant 'Dog Won't Eat Here and You Won't Eat Dog.'"

"I don't get it."

"There's this really famous kind of steamed buns in China that's called 'Dog Won't Eat Here,' and you know how you Americans have this thing about eating dog meat"—Ah Yan gave up when he saw the expression on Jack's face. "Never mind. This humor is too Chinese for you."

San Long now picked up some twigs from the ground and mimed doing something with them and looked to Jack as if he were drunkenly throwing darts at some target a few inches in front of his face. Ah Yan and the others laughed even harder.

"He's saying that a Chinese restaurant will never work in America since every customer will have to learn to use chopsticks," Ah Yan explained to Jack.

"Yeah, yeah, very funny. Fine, no restaurant for you. And while we are on the subject of dogs and compliments that don't sound like compliments, you did manage to make me curious about eating a dog for the first time in my life that evening."

"Dad is worried about the laundresses who are now out of work," Lily told Logan.

They were walking down the middle of Chicory Lane together, side by side. Logan had a bamboo pole over his shoulder. At each end of the pole hung giant woven baskets filled with cucumbers, green onions, carrots, squash, tomatoes, string beans, and sugar beets.

"He's not sure what to do. He says Ah Yan and the others are charging too little for the washing and the ironing, but if the women don't charge less, the white men won't give them any work."

"Two dollars for a dozen cucumbers, a dollar for a dozen green onions!" Logan called out in his booming voice, which reverberated in all directions until the echoes disappeared into the alleyways between the tightly packed houses. "Fresh carrots, beans, and beets! Come and have a look for yourself. Girls, fresh vegetables make your skin soft and smooth. Boys, fresh vegetables get rid of sailor's lips!"

He called out his prices and offerings in a steady, rolling chant, not unlike the way he led the others in their work songs.

Doors opened on all sides of them. The curious wives and bachelors came out into the street to see what Logan was singing about.

"You should bring some of this up to Owyhee Creek, where

Davey's crew is still working their claim on account of that spring the Indians helped them find," said one of the men. "I know they haven't had any greens for a week now, and they'd pay you five dollars for a dozen of those cucumbers."

"Thanks for the tip."

"Where did you get the produce?" one of the wives wanted to know. "It looks a lot fresher than what you find in Seaver's store, though I know he ships them in quick as he can."

"It's all grown right in our backyard, ma'am. Plucked those carrots from the ground myself this morning not even a hour ago."

"In your backyard? How do you manage it? I can't even get a bit of sage and rosemary to grow properly."

"Well," said Logan, "I started in China as a dirt-poor farmer. I guess I just have the knack for getting food to come out of dirt, one way or another."

"Sure wish I had these fresh green onions and cucumbers to eat back in the spring instead of having to chew on potatoes soaked in vinegar every other day," one of the older miners said, handling the giant cucumbers and tomatoes from Logan's basket lovingly. "You are right that scurvy is a terrible thing, and fresh vegetables are the only thing for it. Too bad none of the young men believe it till it's too late. I'll have a dozen of these."

"I don't think we are going to let you leave today without emptying out your baskets," another one of the younger wives said, to the sound of approval of the other women. "Did you save any for yourself and your friends?"

"Don't worry about us," Logan said. "I think we can get five or six harvests out of the garden this year. Buy as much as you want. I'll be back again in a few weeks."

Soon Logan sold all the vegetables he had with him. He counted out twenty dollars and handed the bills to Lily. "Give ten dollars to Mrs. O'Scannlain; I know she doesn't have much saved up, and she's got two growing boys to feed. Ask your father who should have the rest."

The old man and the young girl turned around and began

the long, leisurely walk back to the Chinaman's house on the other side of the town. In the empty street bathed in the bright, shimmering sunlight of high noon, the loping gait of the tall Chinaman and the baskets swinging lazily at the end of the bamboo pole over his shoulder made him look like some graceful water strider gliding across the still surface of a sunlit pond.

And in a moment, the man and the girl disappeared around the street corner and all was still again in the street.

CHINESE NEW YEAR

It had been snowing nonstop for a whole week. The whole of Idaho City seemed asleep in the middle of February, resigned to wait for the spring that was still months away.

Well, almost the whole of Idaho City. The Chinamen were busy preparing for Chinese New Year.

For the whole week the Chinamen talked about nothing except the coming New Year celebration. Strings of bright red firecrackers shipped from San Francisco were unpacked and laid out on shelves so that they would be kept dry. A few of the more nimble-fingered were set to the task of folding and cutting the paper animals that would be offered along with bundles of incense to the ancestors. Everyone worked to wrap pieces of candy and dried lotus seeds in red paper to be handed out to the children as sweet beginnings to a new year. Two days before New Year's Eve, Ah Yan directed all the men in the preparation of the thousands of dumplings that would be consumed on New Year's Day. The living room was turned into an assembly line for a dumpling factory, with some men rolling out the dough at one end, others preparing the stuffing of diced pork and shrimp and chopped vegetables mixed with sesame oil, and the rest wrapping scoops of stuffing into dumplings shaped like closed clams. The finished dumplings were then packed into buckets covered with dried sheets of lotus leaves and left outside, frozen in the ice, until they could be cooked in boiling water on New Year's Eve.

Lily helped out wherever she could. She sorted the strings of firecrackers by size until her fingers smelled of gunpowder. She learned to cut pieces of colorful paper into the shapes of chickens and goats and sheep so that they could be burned in the presence of the gods and the ancestors and allow them to share in the feast of the people.

"Will Lord Guan Yu be there to appreciate the paper sheep?" Lily asked Logan.

Logan looked amused for a moment before his face, made even ruddier than usual because of the cold, turned serious. "I'm sure he will be there."

In the end, Lily proved most valuable as the final step in the dumpling assembly line. She was an expert at sculpting the edges of the dumplings with a fork to create the wavy scallop shell pattern that signified the unbroken line of prosperity.

"You are really good at that," Logan said. "If you didn't have red hair and green eyes, I'd think you were a Chinese girl."

"It's just like shaping a pie crust," Lily said. "Mom taught me."

"You'll have to show me how to make a proper pie crust after New Year's," Ah Yan said. "I've always wanted to learn that American trick."

The activity of the Chinamen stirred up all kinds of excitement in the rest of Idaho City.

"Everybody gets a red packet filled with money and sweets," the children whispered to one another. "All you have to do is to show up at their door and wish them to come into their fortune in the new year."

"Jack Seaver has been raving about the cooking of the Chinamen for months now," the women said to one another in the shops and streets. "Here's our only chance to try it out. They say the Chinamen will serve anyone who comes to their door with pork dumplings that combine all the flavors in the world."

"Are you going to be at the Chinamen's when they celebrate their New Year?" the men asked one another. "They say that the heathens will put on a parade to honor their ancestors, with lots of loud music and colorful costumes. At the end, they'll even serve up a feast such as never before seen in all of Boise Basin."

"What was Logan like back in China? Does he have a large family there?" Lily asked Ah Yan as she helped the young man carry large jars of sweet bamboo shoots into the house. She was tired from all the work she had done that day and couldn't wait until the feast tomorrow. Truth be told, she felt a little guilty. She was never this eager when her own mother asked her to help around the house. She resolved to do better after tomorrow.

"Don't know," Ah Yan said. "Logan wasn't from our village. He wasn't even a Southerner. He just showed up on the docks on the day we were supposed to ship out for San Francisco."

"So he was a stranger even in his own land."

"Yup. You should ask him to tell you the story of our trip here."

It is hardly the happy and the powerful
who go into exile.
— ALEXIS DE TOCQUEVILLE

When in America

On a good day the captain allowed a small number of his cargo to come up on deck from steerage for some air. The rest of the time each man made do with a six-foot bunk that was narrower than a coffin. In the complete darkness of the locked hold they tried to sleep away the hours, their dreams mixtures of unfounded hopes and cryptic dangers. Their constant companion was the smell of sixty men and their vomit and excrement and their food and unwashed bodies crammed into a space meant for bales of cotton and drums of rum. That, and the constant motion of the sailing ship as it made the six-week journey across the Pacific Ocean.

They asked for water. Sometimes that request was even granted. Other times they waited for it to rain and listened for leaks into the hold. They learned very quickly to cut salted fish out of their diet. It made them thirsty.

To keep the darkness from making them crazy, they told one another stories that they all knew by heart.

They took turns to recite the story of Lord Guan Yu, the God of War, and how he once made it through six forts and slew five of Treacherous Cao Cao's generals with the help of only Red Hare, his war steed, and Green Dragon Moon, his trusty sword.

"Lord Guan Yu would laugh at us as mere children if he heard us complaining about a little thirst and hunger and taking a trip in a boat," said the Chinaman whom the others called Lao Guan. He was so tall that he had to sleep with his knees curled up to his chest to fit into his bunk. "What are we afraid of? We are not going there to fight a war but to build a railroad. America is not a land of wolves and tigers. It is a land of men. Men who must work and eat, just as we do."

The others laughed in the darkness. They imagined the red face of Lord Guan Yu, fearless in any battle and full of witty stratagems to get himself out of any trap. What was a little hunger and thirst and darkness when Lord Guan Yu faced down dangers ten thousand times worse?

They sucked and nursed on the turnips and cabbages they had carried with them from the fields of their villages. The men held them up to their noses and inhaled deeply the smell of the soil that still clung to the roots. It would be the last time they would smell home for years.

Some of the men became sick and coughed all night, and the noise kept everyone awake for hours. Their foreheads felt like irons left for too long on the stove. The men had no medicine with them, no cubes of ice sugar or slices of goose pear. All they could do was to wait in the darkness silently.

"Let us sing the songs that our mothers sang to us as children," said Lao Guan. He was so tall he had to stoop as he felt his way around the dark hold, clasping the hand of each comrade, sick and healthy alike. "Since our families are not with us, we should do as Lord Guan Yu did with Lord Liu Bei and Lord Zhang Fei in the Peach Orchard. We must become as brothers to each other."

The men sang the nonsense songs of their childhood in the stifling air of the hold, and their voices washed over the bodies of sick men like a cool breeze, lulling them to sleep.

In the morning the coughing did not resume. A few of the men were found in their coffin-wide bunks, their unmoving legs curled close to their still bodies like sleeping babies.

"Throw them overboard," said the captain. "The rest of you will now have to pay back the price of their tickets."

Lao Guan's face was redder than the fever-flushed faces of the sick. He stooped next to the bodies and cut off locks of hair from each of them, carefully sealing each lock into an envelope. "I'll bring these back to their ancestral villages so that their spirits will not wander the oceans without being able to return home."

Wrapped up in dirty sheets, the bodies were cast over the side of the ship.

At last they made it to San Francisco, the Old Gold Mountain. Although sixty men boarded the ship, only fifty walked down the planks onto the quays. The men squinted in the bright sunlight at the rows of small houses running up and down the steep, rolling hills. The streets, they found, were not paved with gold, and some of the white men on the quays looked as hungry and dirty as they felt.

They were taken by a Chinaman who was dressed like the white men to a dank basement in Chinatown. He didn't have a queue, and his hair was parted and slicked down with oil whose strange smell made the other Chinamen sneeze.

"Here are your employment contracts," the white Chinaman said. He gave them pieces of paper filled with characters smaller than flies' heads to sign.

"According to this," said Lao Guan, "we still owe you interest for the price of the passage from China. But the families of these men have already sold everything they could in order to raise money to buy the tickets that got us here."

"If you don't like it," said the white Chinaman, picking between his teeth with the long, manicured nail of his right pinkie, "you can try to find a way to go back on your own. What can I say? Shipping Chinamen is expensive."

"But it would take us three years of work to pay back the amount you say we owe you here, even longer since you have now made us responsible for the debts of the men who died on the sea."

"Then you should have taken care that they didn't get sick." The white Chinaman checked his pocket watch. "Hurry up and sign the contracts. I don't have all day."

The next day they were packed into wagons and taken inland. The camp in the mountains where they were finally dropped off was a city of tents. On one side of the camp the railroad stretched into the distance as far as they could see. On the other side was a mountain over which the Chinamen with spades and pickaxes swarmed like ants.

Night fell, and the Chinamen at the camp welcomed the new arrivals with a feast by the campfires.

"Eat, eat," they told the new arrivals. "Eat as much as you like." The Chinamen had trouble deciding which was sweeter: the food that went into their bellies, or the sound of those words in their ears.

They passed around bottles of a liquor that the old-timers

said was called "whiskey." It was strong and there was enough for everyone to get drunk. When they ran out of drink the old-timers asked the new group whether they wanted to visit the large tent at the edge of the camp with them. A red silk scarf and a pair of women's shoes dangled from a pole outside the tent.

"You lucky bastards," grumbled one of the older man, whose name was San Long. "I gave all my money to Annie on Monday. I'll have to wait another week."

"She'll run a tab for you," said one of the others. "Though you might have to be with Sally instead of her tonight."

San Long cracked a huge smile and got up to join his companions.

"This must be heaven," said Ah Yan, who was barely more than a boy. "Look how free they are with money! They must be making so much that they paid off their debt early and can save up a fortune for their families while having all this fun."

Lao Guan shook his head and stroked his beard. He sat next to the dying embers of the fire and smoked his pipe, staring at the big tent with the silk scarf and the pair of women's shoes. The light in that tent stayed lit until late into the night.

The work was hard. They had to carve a path through the mountain in front of them for the railroad. The mountain yielded to their pickaxes and chisels reluctantly, and only after repeated hammering that made the men's shoulders and arms sore down to the bones. There was so much mountain to move that it was like trying to gouge through the steel doors of the Emperor's palace with wooden spoons. All the while, the white foremen screamed at the Chinamen to move faster and set upon anyone who tried to sit down for a minute with whips and fists.

They were making so little progress day after day that the men were tired each morning before they had even begun their work. Their spirit sagged. One by one they laid down their tools. The mountain had defeated them. The white foremen jumped around, whipping at the Chinamen to get them to go back to work, but the Chinamen simply ducked away.

Lao Guan jumped onto a rock on the side of the mountain so that he was higher than everyone. "Tu-ne-mah!" he shouted, and spit at the mountain. "Tu-ne-mah!" He look at the white foremen and smiled at them.

The mountain pass was filled with the laughter of Chinamen. One by one they took up the chant. "Tu-ne-mah! Tu-ne-mah!" They smiled at the white foremen as they sang and gestured at them. The white foremen, not sure what was wanted, joined in the chanting. This seemed to make the Chinamen even happier. They picked up their tools and went back to hacking at the mountain with a fury and vengeance directed by the rhythm of their chant. They made more progress in that afternoon than they had all week.

"Goddamn these monkeys," said the site overseer. "But they certainly can work when they want to. What is that song they are singing?"

"Who knows?" The foremen shook their heads. "We can't ever make heads or tails of their pidgin. It sounds like a work song."

"Tell them that we'll name this pass Tunemah," said the overseer. "Maybe these monkeys will work even harder when they know that their song will be forever remembered every time a train passes this place."

The Chinamen continued their chant even after they were done with their work for the day. "Tu-ne-mah!" they shouted at the white foremen, their smiles as wide as they'd ever smiled. "Fuck your mother!"

At the end of the week the Chinamen were paid.

"This is not what I was promised," said Lao Guan to the clerk. "This is not even as much as half of what my wages should be."

"You are deducted for the food you eat and for your space

in the tents. I'd show you the math if you could count that high." The clerk gestured for Lao Guan to move away from the table. "Next!"

"Have they always done this?" Lao Guan asked San Long.

"Oh, yeah. It's always been that way. The amount they charge for food and sleep has already gone up three times this year."

"But this means you'll never be able to pay back your debt and save up a fortune to take home with you."

"What else can you do?" San Long shrugged. "There's no place to buy food within fifty miles of here. We'll never be able to pay back the debt we owe them, anyway, since they just raise the interest whenever it seems like someone is about to pay it all back. All we can do is to take the money that we do get and drink and gamble and spend it all on Annie and the other girls. When you are drunk and asleep, you won't be thinking about it."

"They are playing a trick on us, then," said Lao Guan. "This is all a trap."

"Hey," said San Long, "it's too late to cry about that now. This is what you get for believing those stories told about the Old Gold Mountain. Serves us right."

Lao Guan went around and asked men to come and join him. He had a plan. They would run away into the mountains and go into hiding, and then make their way back to San Francisco.

"We'll need to learn English and understand the ways of this land if we want to make our fortune. Staying here will only make us into slaves with nothing to call our own excepting mounting debts in the white men's books." Lao Guan looked at each man in the eyes, and he was so tall and imposing that the other men avoided looking back.

"But we'll be breaking our contract and leaving our debts unpaid," said Ah Yan. "We will be burdening our families

320

and ancestors with shame. It is not Chinese to break one's word."

"We've already paid back the debt we owe these people twenty times and more. Why should we be faithful when they have not been honest with us? This is a land of trickery, and we must learn to become as tricky as the Americans."

The men were still not convinced. Lao Guan decided to tell them the story of of Jie You, the Han Princess whose name meant "Dissolver of Sorrows."

She was given away in marriage by the Martial Emperor to a barbarian king out in the Western Steppes, a thousand *li* from China, so that the barbarians would sell the Chinese the strong warhorses that the Chinese army needed to defend the Empire.

"I hear that you are homesick," wrote the Martial Emperor, "my precious daughter, and that you cannot swallow the rough uncooked meat of the foreigners, nor fall asleep on their beds made from the hairy hides of yaks and bears. I hear that the sandstorms have scarred your skin that was once as flawless as silk, and the deadly chill of the winters has darkened your eyes that were once bright as the moon. I hear that you call for home and cry yourself to sleep. If any of this is true, then write to me and I shall send the whole army to bring you home. I cannot bear to think that you are suffering, my child, for you are the light of my old age, the solace of my soul."

"Father and Emperor," wrote the Princess. "What you have heard is true. But I know my duty, and you know yours. The Empire needs horses for the defense of the frontier against the Xiong Nu raids. How can you let the unhappiness of your daughter cause you to risk the death and suffering of your people at the hands of the invading barbarian hordes? You have named me wisely, and I will dissolve my sorrow to learn the happiness of my new home. I will learn to mix the rough meat with milk, and I will learn to sleep with a nightshirt. I will learn to cover my face with a veil, and I will learn to keep warm by riding with my husband. Since I am in a foreign land, I will learn the foreigners' ways. By becoming one of the barbarians I will become truly Chinese. Though I will never return to China, I will bring glory to you."

"How can we be less wise or less manly than a young girl, even if she was a daughter of the Martial Emperor?" said Lao Guan. "If you truly want to bring glory to your ancestors and your families, then you must first become Americans."

"What will the gods think of this?" asked San Long. "We will become outlaws. Aren't we struggling against our fate? Some of us are not meant to have great fortunes, but only to work and starve—we are lucky to have what we have even now."

"Wasn't Lord Guan Yu once an outlaw? Didn't he teach us that the gods only smile upon those who take fate into their own hands? Why should we settle for having nothing for the rest of our lives when we know that we have enough strength in our arms to blast a path through mountains and enough wit in our heads to survive an ocean with only our stories and laughter?"

"But how do you know we'll find anything better if we run away?" asked Ah Yan. "What if we are caught? What if we are set upon by bandits? What if we find only more suffering and danger in the darkness out there, beyond the firelight of this camp?"

"I don't know what will happen to us out there," Lao Guan said. "All life is an experiment. But at the end of our lives we'd know that no man could do with our lives as he pleased except ourselves, and our triumphs and mistakes alike were our own."

He stretched out his arms and described the circle of the horizon around them. Long clouds piled low in the sky to the west. "Though the land here does not smell of home, the sky here is wider and higher than I have ever known. Every day I learn names for things I did not know existed and perform feats that I did not know that I could do. Why should we fear to rise as high as we can and make new names for ourselves?"

In the dim firelight Lao Guan looked to the others to be as tall as a tree, and his long, slim eyes glinted like jewels set in his flame-colored face. The hearts of the Chinamen were suddenly filled with resolve and a yearning for something that they did not yet know the name for.

"You feel it?" asked Lao Guan. "You feel that lift in your heart? That lightness in your head? That is the taste of whiskey, the essence of America. We have been wrong to be drunk and asleep. We should be drunk and fighting."

> *To exchange the pure and tranquil pleasures that the native country offers even to the poor for the sterile enjoyments that well-being provides under a foreign sky; to flee the paternal hearth and the fields where one's ancestors rest; to abandon the living and the dead to run after fortune—there is nothing that merits more praise in their eyes.*
> — ALEXIS DE TOCQUEVILLE

CHICKEN BLOOD

The Idaho City Brass Band played "Finnegan's Wake" at the insistence of Logan.

"There's not enough noise," he told them. "In China we'd have all the children of the village setting off firecrackers and fireworks for the whole day to chase off the greedy evil spirits. Here we have only enough firecrackers to last a few hours. We'll need all the help you boys can give us to scare the evil spirits off."

The men of the brass band, their bellies now full of sweet sticky rice buns filled with bean paste and hot and spicy dumplings, set to their appointed task with gusto. They had not played with as much spirit even for Independence Day.

All the rumors about the Chinese New Year celebration were true. The children's pockets were filled with sweets and jangling coins, and the men and women were laughing as they enjoyed the feast that had been laid out before them. They had to shout to make one another heard amid the unending explosions of the firecrackers and the music blasting from the brass band.

Jack found Elsie among the other women in the vegetable garden. An open bonfire had been lit there so that the guests would be warm as they mingled and ate.

"I'm surprised at you," Jack said to her. "I'd swear that I saw you take three servings of the dumplings. I thought you said you'd never touch the food of the Chinamen."

"Thaddeus Seaver," Elsie said severely. "I don't know where you get such strange notions. It's positively unchristian to behave as you suggest when your neighbors have opened up their houses to you and invited you to break bread with them in their feast. If I didn't know better, I'd think you were the heathen here."

"That's my girl," said Jack. "Though isn't it time for you to start calling me Jack? Everyone else does now."

"I'll think about it after I've tried a piece of that sweet ginger," Elsie said. She laughed, and Jack realized how much he missed hearing that sound since they moved here to Idaho City. "Did you know that the first boy I liked was named Jack?"

The other women laughed, and Jack laughed along with them.

Abruptly the brass band stopped playing. One by one the men stopped talking and turned to the door of the house. There, in the door, stood Sheriff Gaskins, who was looking apologetic and a little ashamed.

"Sorry, folks," he said. "This isn't my idea."

He saw Ah Yan in the corner and waved to him. "Don't think I won't recognize you next time I come for your taxes."

"Time enough for that later, sheriff. This is a day of feasting and joy."

"You might want to wait on that. I'm here on official business."

Logan walked into the room, and the crowd parted before him. He was face-to-face with the sheriff before another man darted into view behind the sheriff and just as quickly skulked out of sight.

"Obee has accused you with murder," said the sheriff. "And I'm here to arrest you."

As a child growing up in Mock Turtle, Pennsylvania, the last thing Emmett Hayworth thought he would end up doing one day was to be a judge out in the middle of the Rocky Mountains.

Emmett was a big man, the same as his father, a banker who had retired from Philadelphia to live quietly out in the country. Before he was twenty, Emmett's greatest claim to fame was that he had won the all-county pie-eating contest three years in a row. It was assumed that Emmett would never amount to much, since he would have enough money to not have to work very hard, and not enough money to really get into much mischief. Everyone liked him, for he was always willing to buy you a drink if you called him "Sir."

And then came the War, and back then everyone still thought the Rebels would fold like a house of cards in three months. Emmett said to himself, "Why the heck not? This will probably be my only chance in life to see New Orleans." With his father's money he raised a regiment, and overnight he was Colonel Emmett Hayworth of the Union Army.

He took surprisingly well to being a soldier, and while his body slimmed down with riding and getting less than enough to eat, his good cheer never flagged. Somehow his regiment managed to stay out of the meat grinders that were the great battles that made newspaper headlines, and they lost fewer men than most. The men were grateful for Emmett's luck. "Oh, if I were a woman as I am a man," they sang, "Colonel Hayworth is the man I'd marry. His hands are steady, and his words are always merry. He'll bring us to New Orleans." Emmett laughed when he heard the song.

They did get to New Orleans eventually, but by then it wasn't much of a party town anymore. The War was over, and Emmett had scraped through with no bullet holes in him and no medals. "That's not so bad," he said to himself. "I can live with that."

But then he got the order that President Lincoln wanted to see him in DC.

Emmett did not remember much about the meeting, save that Lincoln was a lot taller than he had imagined. They shook hands, and Lincoln began to explain to him about the situation in Idaho Territory.

"The Confederate Democratic refugees from Missouri are filling up the mines of Idaho. I'll need men like you there, men who have proven their bravery, integrity, and dedication to the cause."

The only thing Emmett could think of was that they had the wrong man.

The trouble, as it turned out, had entirely been the fault of that song his men made up as a joke. It grew to be popular with the other regiments, and spread its way wherever the Union marched. New verses were added as it passed from man to man, and the soldiers, having no idea who Emmett Hayworth was, attributed great acts of courage and sacrifice to him. Colonel Hayworth became famous, almost as famous as John Brown.

Be that as it may, Emmett Hayworth packed up everything he owned and left for Boise, and only when he arrived did he find out that the Territorial Governor had just appointed him to be a district judge for the Idaho Territory.

★ ★ ★ ★

326

Jack Seaver looked across the desk at the plump form of the Honorable Emmett Hayworth. The judge was still working on a plate of fried chicken that served as his lunch. Life out here in the booming territory of Idaho had been good to him, and he showed it in his barrel-like chest, his sacklike belly, his glistening forehead dripping with sweat from the effort of licking strips of juicy meat from the chicken bones.

The man was supposed to be some kind of war hero. Jack Seaver knew the type: a man accustomed to living off the money of his father who probably bought himself a cushy commission managing the supply lines and then puffed up his every accomplishment in the name of Union and Glory until he weaseled his way to a sinecure here while men like Jack Seaver dodged bullets in the mud and froze their toes off in winter. Jack clenched his teeth. This was neither the time nor the place to show his contempt. He did reflect upon the irony that despite what he had told Elsie's father back East, he now wished that he had studied to be a lawyer.

"What is this I hear about chicken blood?" Emmett asked.

"That's outrageous," said Obee. "I won't do it. Why are you even letting the Chinaman talk? This is not the way it works in California."

"You are going to have to," Judge Hayworth said to him. He hadn't been very enamored of the idea of the Chinamen's ceremony at first, but that Jack Seaver had been very persuasive. If he ever decided to become a lawyer, he'd eat the other guys in town for lunch. "Maybe in California they'll just take a white man's word for it since the Chinamen can't testify in court, but this isn't California. The accused has the right to a fair trial, and since he has agreed to swear with his hand on the Bible as is our custom, it's only fair that you agree to swear the way that his people have always sworn in witnesses."

"It's barbaric!"

"That may be. But if you won't do it, I'll have to direct the jury to acquit."

Obee swore under his breath.

"Fine," he said. He stared at Logan, who was across the courthouse from him. Obee's eyes were so filled with hate that he looked even more like a rat than usual.

Ah Yan was called for, and he came up to the witness box. In his left hand was a struggling hen dangling by her legs while in his right hand was a small bowl.

He set the bowl down in front of Obee. Taking a knife from his belt, he slit the hen's throat efficiently. The blood of the hen dripped into the bowl until the hen stopped kicking in Ah Yan's hands.

"Dip your hand into the blood and make sure it covers your whole hand," Ah Yan said. Obee reluctantly did as he was told. His hand shook so much that the bowl clattered against the wooden surface on which it was set.

"Now you have to clasp Logan's hand and look into his eyes, and swear that you'll tell the truth."

Logan was escorted over to the witness box by Sheriff Gaskins. Since his legs and arms were shackled together, this took some time.

Logan looked down at Obee, contempt written in every wrinkle in his bloodred face. He dipped both of his shackled hands into the bowl of chicken blood, soaking them thoroughly. Lifting his hands out of the bowl, he shook off the excess blood and stretched the open palm of his right hand toward Obee. The color of his hands now matched his face.

Obee hesitated.

"Well," Judge Hayworth said impatiently. "Get on with it. Shake the man's hand."

"Your honor." Obee turned toward him. "This is a trick. He's going to crush my hand if I give it to him."

Laughter shook the courtroom.

"No, he won't," said the judge, trying to control his smirk. "If he does, I'll personally thrash him."

Obee gingerly stretched his hand toward Logan's hand. He eyes were focused on the shrinking distance between their palms as if his life depended on it. He wasn't breathing, and his hand shook violently.

Logan stepped forward and made a grab for Obee's hand, and he gave a low growl from his throat.

Obee screamed as if he had been stabbed with a hot poker. He stumbled back frantically, pulling his hand out of Logan's grasp. A spreading, wet patch appeared at the crotch of his pants. A moment later the sheriff and the judge were hit with the unpleasant smell of excrement.

"I didn't even get to touch him," Logan said, holding up his hands. The pattern of chicken blood on his right palm was undisturbed with the print from Obee's hand.

"Order, order!" Judge Hayworth banged the gavel. Then he gave up and shook his head in disbelief. "Get him out of here and cleaned up," he said to Sheriff Gaskins, trying to keep himself from smiling. "Stop laughing. It's, uh, unbecoming for officers of the law. And hand me that chicken, will you? No sense in letting perfectly good poultry go to waste."

"All you have to do is to tell the truth," Lily said to Logan. "That's what Dad told me to do. It's easy."

"The law is a funny thing," said Logan. "You've heard my stories."

"It won't be like that here. I promise."

Earlier that day, she had told the jury what she saw on that day by the Chinamen's camp.

Mrs. O'Scannlain, who was in the front row of the court-room, had smiled at her as she walked up to sit in the witness box next to the judge. It had made her feel very brave.

The faces of the men in the jury box were severe and expressionless, and she had been terrified. But then she told herself that it was just like telling a story, the way Logan told her his stories.

The only thing was that it was all true so she didn't even have to make any of it up.

Afterward, she couldn't tell if they believed her. But Mrs. O'Scannlain and the others in the courtroom clapped after her testimony and that made her happy, even after the judge banged his gavel several times to get the crowd to settle down.

But now was not the time to tell Logan that. "Of course they will believe you," she said to Logan. "You have all these people who saw what happened."

"But except for you, they are all just worthless Chinamen."

"Why do you say that?" Lily became angry. "I'd rather be a Chinaman than someone who'd believe Obee's lies."

Logan laughed, but he was quickly serious again. "I'm sorry, Lily. Even men who have lived as long as I have sometimes get cynical."

They were silent for a while, each lost in their own thoughts.

Lily broke the silence after a while. "When you are freed, will you stay here instead of going back to China?"

"I'm going home."

"Oh," Lily said.

"Though I'd like to have my own house instead of always renting. Maybe your father will consider helping me build one?"

Lily looked at him, not understanding.

"This is home," Logan said, smiling at her. "This is where I have finally found all the flavors of the world, all the sweetness and bitterness, all the whiskey and sorghum mead, all the excitement and agitation of a wilderness of untamed, beautiful men and women, all the peace and solitude of a barely settled land—in a word, the exhilarating lift to the spirit that is the taste of America."

Lily wanted to shout for joy, but she didn't want to get her hopes up, not just yet. Logan had yet to tell his story to the jury tomorrow.

But meanwhile, there was a still a night of storytelling ahead.

"Will you tell me another story?" Lily asked.

"Sure, but I think from now on I won't tell you any more stories about my life as a Chinaman. I'll tell you the story of how I became an American."

When the band of weary and gaunt Chinamen showed up in Idaho City with their funny bamboo carrying poles over their shoulders . . .

EPILOGUE

The Chinese made up a large percentage of the population of Idaho Territory in the late 1800s.[1] They formed a vibrant community of miners, cooks, laundry operators, and gardeners that integrated well with the white communities of the mining towns. Almost all the Chinese were men seeking to make their fortune in America.[2]

By the time many of them decided to settle in America and become Americans, anti-Chinese sentiment had swept the western half of the United States. Beginning with the passage of the Chinese Exclusion Act of 1882, a series of national laws, state laws, and court decisions forbade these men from bringing their wives into America from China and stemmed the flow of any more Chinese, men or women, from entering America. Intermarriage between whites and Chinese was not permitted by law. As a result, the bachelor communities of Chinese in the Idaho mining towns gradually dwindled until all the Chinese had died before the repeal of the Exclusion Acts during World War II.

To this day, some of the mining towns of Idaho still celebrate Chinese New Year in memory of the presence of the Chinese among them.

1 The Chinese were 28.5 percent of the population of Idaho in 1870.
2 For more on the history of the Chinese in gold-rush Idaho, see Zhu, Liping. *A Chinaman's Chance: The Chinese on the Rocky Mountain Mining Frontier.* Boulder: University Press of Colorado, 1997.

A Brief History of
The Trans-Pacific Tunnel

At the noodle shop, I wave the other waitress away, waiting for the American woman: skin pale and freckled as the moon; swelling breasts that fill the bodice of her dress; long chestnut curls spilling past her shoulders, held back with a flowery bandanna. Her eyes, green like fresh tea leaves, radiate a bold and fearless smile that is rarely seen among Asians. And I like the wrinkles around them, fitting for a woman in her thirties.

"Hai." She finally stops at my table, her lips pursed impatiently. *"Hoka no okyakusan ga imasu yo. Nani wo chuumon shimasu ka?"* Her Japanese is quite good, the pronunciation maybe even better than mine—though she is not using the honorific. It is still rare to see Americans here in the Japanese half of Midpoint City, but things are changing now, in the thirty-sixth year of the Shōwa Era (she, being an American, would think of it as 1961).

"A large bowl of *tonkotsu* ramen," I say, mostly in English. Then I realize how loud and rude I sound. Old Diggers like me always forget that not everyone is practically deaf. "Please," I add, a whisper.

Her eyes widen as she finally recognizes me. I've cut my hair and put on a clean shirt, and that's not how I looked the past few times I've come here. I haven't paid much attention to my appearance in a decade. There hasn't been any need to. Almost all my time is spent alone and at home. But the sight of her has quickened my pulse in a way I haven't felt in years, and I wanted to make an effort.

"Always the same thing," she says, and smiles.

I like hearing her English. It sounds more like her natural voice, not so high-pitched.

"You don't really like the noodles," she says, when she brings me my ramen. It isn't a question.

I laugh, but I don't deny it. The ramen in this place is terrible. If the owner were any good he wouldn't have left Japan to set up shop here at Midpoint City, where the tourists stopping for a break on their way through the Trans-Pacific Tunnel don't know any better. But I keep on coming, just to see her.

"You are not Japanese."

"No," I say. "I'm Formosan. Please call me Charlie." Back when I coordinated work with the American crew during the construction of Midpoint City, they called me Charlie because they couldn't pronounce my Hokkien name correctly. And I liked the way it sounded, so I kept using it.

"Okay, Charlie. I'm Betty." She turns to leave.

"Wait," I say. I do not know from where I get this sudden burst of courage. It is the boldest thing I've done in a long time. "Can I see you when you are free?"

She considers this, biting her lip. "Come back in two hours."

From *The Novice Traveler's Guide to the Trans-Pacific Tunnel*, published by the TPT Transit Authority, 1963:

> *Welcome, traveler! This year marks the twenty-fifth anniversary of the completion of the Trans-Pacific Tunnel. We are excited to see that this is your first time through the Tunnel.*
>
> *The Trans-Pacific Tunnel follows a Great Circle path just below the seafloor to connect Asia to North America, with three surface terminus stations in Shanghai, Tokyo, and*

Seattle. The Tunnel takes the shortest path between the cities, arcing north to follow the Pacific Rim mountain ranges. Although this course increased the construction cost of the Tunnel due to the need for earthquake-proofing, it also allows the Tunnel to tap into geothermal vents and hot spots along the way, which generate the electrical power needed for the Tunnel and its support infrastructure, such as the air-compression stations, oxygen generators, and sub-seafloor maintenance posts.

The Tunnel is in principle a larger—gigantic—version of the pneumatic tubes or capsule lines familiar to all of us for delivering interoffice mail in modern buildings. Two parallel concrete-enclosed steel transportation tubes, one each for westbound and eastbound traffic, 60 feet in diameter, are installed in the Tunnel. The transportation tubes are divided into numerous shorter self-sealing sections, each with multiple air-compression stations. The cylindrical capsules, containing passengers and goods, are propelled through the tubes by a partial vacuum pulling in front and by compressed air pushing from behind. The capsules ride on a monorail for reduced friction. Current maximum speed is about a 120 miles per hour, and a trip from Shanghai to Seattle takes a little more than two full days. Plans are under way to eventually increase maximum speed to two hundred MPH.

The Tunnel's combination of capacity, speed, and safety makes it superior to zeppelins, aeroplanes, and surface shipping for almost all trans-Pacific transportation needs. It is immune to storms, icebergs, and typhoons, and very cheap to operate, as it is powered by the boundless heat of the Earth itself. Today, it is the chief means by which passengers and manufactured goods flow between Asia and America. More than 30% of global container shipping each year goes through the Tunnel.

We hope you enjoy your travel along the Trans-Pacific Tunnel, and wish you a safe journey to your final destination.

I was born in the second year of the Taishō Era (1913), in a small village in Shinchiku Prefecture, in Formosa. My family were simple peasants who never participated in any of the uprisings against Japan. The way my father saw it, whether the Manchus on the mainland or the Japanese were in charge didn't much matter, since they all left us alone except when it came time for taxes. The lot of the Hoklo peasant was to toil and suffer in silence.

Politics were for those who had too much to eat. Besides, I always liked the Japanese workers from the lumber company, who would hand me candy during their lunch break. The Japanese colonist families we saw were polite, well-dressed, and very lettered. My father once said, "If I got to choose, in my next life I'd come back as a Japanese."

During my boyhood, a new prime minister in Japan announced a change in policy: natives in the colonies should be turned into good subjects of the Emperor. The Japanese governor-general set up village schools that everyone had to attend. The more clever boys could even expect to attend high schools formerly reserved for the Japanese and then go on to study in Japan, where they would have bright futures.

I was not a good student, however, and never learned Japanese very well. I was content to know how to read a few characters and go back to the fields, the same as my father and his father before him.

All this changed in the year I turned seventeen (the fifth year of the Shōwa Era, or 1930), when a Japanese man in a Western suit came to our village, promising riches for the families of young men who knew how to work hard and didn't complain.

We stroll through Friendship Square, the heart of Midpoint City. A few pedestrians, both American and Japanese, stare and whisper as they see us walking together. But Betty does not care, and her carelessness is infectious.

Here, kilometers under the Pacific Ocean and the seafloor, it's late afternoon by the City's clock, and the arc lamps around us are turned up as bright as can be.

"I always feel like I'm at a night baseball game when I go through here," Betty says. "When my husband was alive, we went to many baseball games together as a family."

I nod. Betty usually keeps her reminiscences of her husband light. She mentioned once that he was a lawyer, and he had left their home in California to work in South Africa, where he died because some people didn't like who he was defending. "They called him a race traitor," she said. I didn't press for details.

Now that her children are old enough to be on their own, she's traveling the world for enlightenment and wisdom. Her capsule train to Japan had stopped at Midpoint Station for a standard one-hour break for passengers to get off and take some pictures, but she had wandered too far into the City and missed the train. She took it as a sign and stayed in the City, waiting to see what lessons the world had to teach her.

Only an American could lead such a life. Among Americans, there are many free spirits like hers.

We've been seeing each other for four weeks, usually on Betty's days off. We take walks around Midpoint City, and we talk. I prefer that we converse in English, mostly because I do not have to think much about how formal and polite to be.

As we pass by the bronze plaque in the middle of the Square, I point out to her my Japanese-style name on the plaque: Takumi Hayashi. The Japanese teacher in my village school had helped me pick the first name, and I had liked the characters: "open up, sea." The choice turned out to be prescient.

She is impressed. "That must have been something. You should tell me more about what it was like to work on the Tunnel."

There are not many of us old Diggers left now. The years of hard labor spent breathing hot and humid dust that stung our lungs had done invisible damage to our insides and joints. At forty-eight, I've said good-bye to all my friends as they succumbed to illnesses. I am the last keeper of what we had done together.

When we finally blasted through the thin rock wall dividing our side from the American side and completed the Tunnel in the thirteenth year of the Shōwa Era (1938), I had the honor of being one of the shift supervisors invited to attend the ceremony. I explain to Betty that the blast-through spot is in the main tunnel due north of where we are standing, just beyond Midpoint Station.

We arrive at my apartment building, on the edge of the section of the City where most Formosans live. I invite her to come up. She accepts.

My apartment is a single room eight mats in size, but there is a window. Back when I bought it, it was considered a very luxurious place for Midpoint City, where space was and is at a premium. I mortgaged most of my pension on it, since I had no desire ever to move. Most men made do with coffinlike one-mat rooms. But to her American eyes, it probably seems very cramped and shabby. Americans like things to be open and big.

I make her tea. It is very relaxing to talk to her. She does not care that I am not Japanese, and assumes nothing about me. She takes out a joint, as is the custom for Americans, and we share it.

Outside the window, the arc lights have been dimmed. It's evening in Midpoint City. Betty does not get up and say that she has to leave. We stop talking. The air feels tense, but in a good way, expectant. I reach out for her hand, and she lets me. The touch is electric.

From *Splendid America*, AP ed., 1995:

> *In 1929, the fledging and weak Republic of China, in order to focus on the domestic Communist rebellion, appeased Japan by signing the Sino-Japanese Mutual Cooperation*

Treaty. The treaty formally ceded all Chinese territories in Manchuria to Japan, which averted the prospect of all-out war between China and Japan and halted Soviet ambitions in Manchuria. This was the capstone on Japan's thirty-five-year drive for imperial expansion. Now, with Formosa, Korea, and Manchuria incorporated into the Empire and a collaborationist China within its orbit, Japan had access to vast reserves of natural resources, cheap labor, and a potential market of hundreds of millions for its manufactured goods.

Internationally, Japan announced that it would continue its rise as a Great Power henceforth by peaceful means. Western powers, however, led by Britain and the United States, were suspicious. They were especially alarmed by Japan's colonial ideology of a "Greater East Asia Co-Prosperity Sphere," which seemed to be a Japanese version of the Monroe Doctrine and suggested a desire to drive European and American influence from Asia.

Before the Western powers could decide on a plan to contain and encircle Japan's "Peaceful Ascent," however, the Great Depression struck. The brilliant Emperor Hirohito seized the opportunity and suggested to President Herbert Hoover his vision of the Trans-Pacific Tunnel as the solution to the worldwide economic crisis.

The work was hard and dangerous. Every day men were injured and sometimes killed. It was also very hot. In the finished sections, they installed machines to cool the air. But in the most forward parts of the Tunnel, where the actual digging happened, we were exposed to the heat of the Earth, and we worked in nothing but our undershorts, sweating nonstop. The work crews were segregated by race—there were Koreans, Formosans, Okinawans, Filipinos, Chinese (separated again by topolect)—but after a while we all looked the same, covered in sweat and dust and mud, only little white circles of skin showing around our eyes.

It didn't take me long to get used to living underground, to the constant noise of dynamite, hydraulic drills, the bellows cycling cooling air, and to the flickering faint yellow light of arc lamps. Even when you were sleeping, the next shift was already at it. Everyone grew hard of hearing after a while, and we stopped talking to each other. There was nothing to say, anyway; just more digging.

But the pay was good, and I saved up and sent money home. However, visiting home was out of the question. By the time I started, the head of the tunnel was already halfway between Shanghai and Tokyo. They charged you a month's wages to ride the steam train carrying the excavated waste back to Shanghai and up to the surface. I couldn't afford such luxuries. As we made progress, the trip back only grew longer and more expensive.

It was best not to think too much about what we were doing, about the miles of water over our heads, and the fact that we were digging a tunnel through the Earth's crust to get to America. Some men did go crazy under those conditions and had to be restrained before they could hurt themselves or others.

From *A Brief History of the Trans-Pacific Tunnel*, published by the TPT Transit Authority, 1960:

Osachi Hamaguchi, prime minister of Japan during the Great Depression, claimed that Emperor Hirohito was inspired by the American effort to build the Panama Canal to conceive of the Trans-Pacific Tunnel. "America has knit together two oceans," the Emperor supposedly said. "Now let us chain together two continents." President Hoover, trained as an engineer, enthusiastically promoted and backed the project as an antidote to the global economic contraction.

The Tunnel is, without a doubt, the greatest engineering project ever conceived by Man. Its sheer scale makes the Great Pyramids and the Great Wall of China seem like mere

toys, and many critics at the time described it as hubristic
lunacy, a modern Tower of Babel.

Although tubes and pressurized air have been used for
passing around documents and small parcels since Victorian
times, before the Tunnel, pneumatic tube transport of
heavy goods and passengers had only been tried on a few
intracity subway demonstration programs. The extraordi-
nary engineering demands of the Tunnel thus drove many
technological advances, often beyond the core technologies
involved, such as fast-tunneling directed explosives. As one
illustration, thousands of young women with abacuses and
notepads were employed as computers for engineering calcu-
lations at the start of the project, but by the end of the project
electronic computers had taken their place.

In all, construction of the 5,880-mile tunnel took ten years
between 1929 and 1938. Some seven million men worked on
it, with Japan and the United States providing the bulk of the
workers. At its height, one in ten working men in the United
States was employed in building the Tunnel. More than thir-
teen billion cubic yards of material were excavated, almost
fifty times the amount removed during the construction of
the Panama Canal, and the fill was used to extend the shore-
lines of China, the Japanese home islands, and Puget Sound.

Afterward we lie still on the futon, our limbs entwined. In
the darkness I can hear her heart beating, and the smell of sex
and our sweat, unfamiliar in this apartment, is comforting.

She tells me about her son, who is still going to school in
America. She says that he is traveling with his friends in the
southern states of America, riding the buses together.

"Some of the friends are Negroes," she says.

I know some Negroes. They have their own section in the
American half of the City, where they mostly keep to themselves.
Some Japanese families hire the women to cook Western meals.

"I hope he's having a good time," I say.

My reaction surprises Betty. She turns to stare at me and then laughs. "I forget that you cannot understand what this is about."

She sits up in bed. "In America, the Negroes and whites are separated: where they live, where they work, where they go to school."

I nod. That sounds familiar. Here in the Japanese half of the City, the races also keep to themselves. There are superior and inferior races. For example, there are many restaurants and clubs reserved only for the Japanese.

"The law says that whites and Negroes can ride the bus together, but the secret of America is that law is not followed by large swaths of the country. My son and his friends want to change that. They ride the buses together to make a statement, to make people pay attention to the secret. They ride in places where people do not want to see Negroes sitting in seats that belong only to whites. Things can become violent and dangerous when people get angry and form a mob."

This seems very foolish: to make statements that no one wants to hear, to speak when it is better to be quiet. What difference will a few boys riding a bus make?

"I don't know if it's going to make any difference, change anyone's mind. But it doesn't matter. It's good enough for me that he is speaking, that he is not silent. He's making the secret a little bit harder to keep, and that counts for something." Her voice is full of pride, and she is beautiful when she is proud.

I consider Betty's words. It is the obsession of Americans to speak, to express opinions on things that they are ignorant about. They believe in drawing attention to things that other people may prefer to keep quiet, to ignore and forget.

But I can't dismiss the image Betty has put into my head: a boy stands in darkness and silence. He speaks; his words float up like a bubble. It explodes, and the world is a little brighter, and a little less stiflingly silent.

I have read in the papers that back in Japan, they are

debating about granting Formosans and Manchurians seats in the Imperial Diet. Britain is still fighting the native guerrillas in Africa and India, but may be forced soon to grant the colonies independence. The world is indeed changing.

"What's wrong?" Betty asks. She wipes the sweat from my forehead. She shifts to give me more of the flow from the air conditioner. I shiver. Outside, the great arc lights are still off, not yet dawn. "Another bad dream?"

We've been spending many of our nights together since that first time. Betty has upset my routine, but I don't mind at all. That was the routine of a man with one foot in the grave. Betty has made me feel alive after so many years under the ocean, alone in darkness and silence.

But being with Betty has also unblocked something within me, and memories are tumbling out.

If you really couldn't stand it, they provided comfort women from Korea for the men. But you had to pay a day's wages.

I tried it only once. We were both so dirty, and the girl stayed still like a dead fish. I never used the comfort women again.

A friend told me that some of the girls were not there willingly but had been sold to the Imperial Army, and maybe the one I had was like that. I didn't really feel sorry for her. I was too tired.

From *The Ignoramus's Guide to American History*, 1995:

So just when everyone was losing jobs and lining up for soup and bread, Japan came along and said, "Hey, America, let's build this big-ass tunnel and spend a whole lot of money and hire lots of workers and get the economy going again.

Whaddya say?" And the idea basically worked, so everyone was like: "Dōmo arigatō, Japan!"

Now, when you come up with a good idea like that, you get some chips you can cash in. So that's what Japan did the next year, in 1930. At the London Naval Conference, where the Big Bullies—oops, I meant "Great Powers"—figured out how many battleships and aircraft carriers each country got to build, Japan demanded to be allowed to build the same number of ships as the United States and Britain. And the US and Britain said fine.[3]

This concession to Japan turned out to be a big deal. Remember Hamaguchi, the Japanese prime minister, and the way he kept on talking about how Japan was going to "ascend peacefully" from then on? This had really annoyed the militarists and nationalists in Japan because they thought Hamaguchi was selling out the country. But when Hamaguchi came home with such an impressive diplomatic victory, he was hailed as a hero, and people began to believe that his "Peaceful Ascent" policy was going to make Japan strong. People thought maybe he really could get the Western powers to treat Japan as an equal without turning Japan into a giant army camp. The militarists and nationalists got less support after that.

At that fun party, the London Naval Conference, the Big Bullies also scrapped all those humiliating provisions of the Treaty of Versailles that made Germany toothless. Britain and Japan both had their own reasons for supporting this: They each thought Germany liked them better than the other and would join up as an ally if a global brawl for Asian colonies broke out one day. Everyone was wary about the Soviets, too, and wanted to set up Germany as a guard dog of sorts for the polar bear.[4]

---

3 The Washington Naval Treaty of 1922 had set the ratio of capital ships among the US, Britain, and Japan at 5:5:3. This was the ratio Japan got adjusted in 1930.

4 Allowing Germany to re-arm also let the German government heave a big sigh of relief. The harsh Treaty of Versailles, especially those articles about neutering

Things to Think About in the Shower

1. *Many economists describe the Tunnel as the first real Keynesian stimulus project, which shortened the Great Depression.*
2. *The Tunnel's biggest fan was probably President Hoover: He won an unprecedented four terms in office because of its success.*
3. *We now know that the Japanese military abused the rights of many of the workers during the Tunnel's construction, but it took decades for the facts to emerge. The bibliography points to some more books on this subject.*
4. *The Tunnel ended up taking a lot of business away from surface shipping, and many Pacific ports went bust. The most famous example of this occurred in 1949, when Britain sold Hong Kong to Japan because it didn't think the harbor city was all that important anymore.*
5. *The Great War (1914–1918) turned out to be the last global "hot war" of the twentieth century (so far). Are we turning into wimps? Who wants to start a new world war?*

After the main work on the Tunnel was completed in the thirteenth year of the Shōwa Era (1938), I returned home for the first and only time since I left eight years earlier. I bought a window seat on the westbound capsule train from Midpoint Station, coach class. The ride was smooth and comfortable, the capsule quiet save for the low voices of my fellow passengers and a faint *whoosh* as we were pushed along by air. Young female attendants pushed carts of drinks and food up and down the aisles.

Some clever companies had bought advertising space along

Germany, made a lot of Germans very angry and some of them joined a group of goose-stepping thugs called the German Nationalist Socialist Party, which scared everyone, including the government. After those provisions of the treaty were scrapped, the thugs got no electoral support at the next election in 1930, and faded away. Heck, they are literally now a footnote of history, like this one.

the inside of the tube and painted pictures at window height. As the capsule moved along, the pictures rushing by centimeters from the windows blurred together and became animated, like a silent film. My fellow passengers and I were mesmerized by the novel effect.

The elevator ride up to the surface in Shanghai filled me with trepidation, my ears popping with the changes in pressure. And then it was time to get on a boat bound for Formosa.

I hardly recognized my home. With the money I sent, my parents had built a new house and bought more land. My family was now rich, and my village a bustling town. I found it hard to speak to my siblings and my parents. I had been away so long that I did not understand much about their lives, and I could not explain to them how I felt. I did not realize how much I had been hardened and numbed by my experience, and there were things I had seen that I could not speak of. In some sense I felt that I had become like a turtle, with a shell around me that kept me from feeling anything.

My father had written to me to come home because it was long past time for me to find a wife. Since I had worked hard, stayed healthy, and kept my mouth shut—it also helped that as a Formosan I was considered superior to the other races except the Japanese and Koreans—I had been steadily promoted to crew chief and then to shift supervisor. I had money, and if I settled in my hometown, I would provide a good home.

But I could no longer imagine a life on the surface. It had been so long since I had seen the blinding light of the sun that I felt like a newborn when out in the open. Things were so quiet. Everyone was startled when I spoke because I was used to shouting. And the sky and tall buildings made me dizzy—I was so used to being underground, under the sea, in tight, confined spaces, that I had trouble breathing if I looked up.

I expressed my desire to stay underground and work in one of the station cities strung like pearls along the Tunnel. The faces of the fathers of all the girls tightened at this thought.

I didn't blame them: Who would want their daughter to spend the rest of her life underground, never seeing the light of day? The fathers whispered to one another that I was deranged.

I said good-bye to my family for the last time, and I did not feel I was home until I was back at Midpoint Station, the warmth and the noise of the heart of the Earth around me, a safe shell. When I saw the soldiers on the platform at the station, I knew that the world was finally back to normal. More work still had to be done to complete the side tunnels that would be expanded into Midpoint City.

"Soldiers," Betty says, "why were there soldiers at Midpoint City?"

I stand in darkness and silence. I cannot hear or see. Words churn in my throat, like a rising flood waiting to burst the dam. I have been holding my tongue for a long, long time.

"They were there to keep the reporters from snooping around," I say.

I tell Betty about my secret, the secret of my nightmares, something I've never spoken of all these years.

As the economy recovered, labor costs rose. There were fewer and fewer young men desperate enough to take jobs as Diggers in the Tunnel. Progress on the American side had slowed for a few years, and Japan was not doing much better. Even China seemed to run out of poor peasants who wanted this work.

Hideki Tōjō, Army Minister, came up with a solution. The Imperial Army's pacification of the Communist rebellions supported by the Soviet Union in Manchuria and China resulted in many prisoners. They could be put to work, for free.

The prisoners were brought into the Tunnel to take the place of regular work crews. As shift supervisor, I managed them with the aid of a squad of soldiers. The prisoners were a sorry sight, chained together, naked, thin like scarecrows. They did not look like dangerous and crafty Communist bandits. I wondered sometimes how there could be so many prisoners, since the news always said that the pacification of the Communists was going well and the Communists were not much of a threat.

They usually didn't last long. When a prisoner was discovered to have expired from the work, his body was released from the shackles and a soldier would shoot it a few times. We would then report the death as the result of an escape attempt.

To hide the involvement of the slave laborers, we kept visiting reporters away from work on the main Tunnel. They were used mainly on the side excavations, for station cities or power stations, in places that were not well surveyed and more dangerous.

One time, while making a side tunnel for a power station, my crew blasted through to a pocket of undetected slush and water, and the side tunnel began to flood. We had to seal the breach quickly before the flood got into the main Tunnel. I woke up the crews of the two other shifts and sent a second chained crew into the side tunnel with sandbags to help with plugging up the break.

The corporal in charge of the squad of soldiers guarding the prisoners asked me, "What if they can't plug it?"

His meaning was obvious. We had to make sure that the water did not get into the main Tunnel, even if the repair crews we sent in failed. There was only one way to make sure, and as water was flowing back up the side tunnel, time was running out.

I directed the chained crew I'd kept behind as a reserve to begin placing dynamite around the side tunnel, behind the men we had sent in earlier. I did not much like this, but I told myself that these were hardened Communist terrorists, and they were probably sentenced to death already, anyway.

The prisoners hesitated. They understood what we were trying to do, and they did not want to do it. Some worked slowly. Others just stood.

The corporal ordered one of the prisoners shot. This motivated the remaining ones to hurry.

I set off the charges. The side tunnel collapsed, and the pile of debris and falling rocks filled most of the entrance, but there was still some space at the top. I directed the remaining prisoners to climb up and seal the opening. Even I climbed up to help them.

The sound of the explosion told the prisoners we sent in earlier what was happening. The chained men lumbered back, sloshing through the rising water and the darkness, trying to get to us. The corporal ordered the soldiers to shoot a few of the men, but the rest kept on coming, dragging the dead bodies with their chains, begging us to let them through. They climbed up the pile of debris toward us.

The man at the front of the chain was only a few meters from us, and in the remaining cone of light cast by the small opening that was left I could see his face, contorted with fright.

"Please," he said. "Please let me through. I just stole some money. I don't deserve to die."

He spoke to me in Hokkien, my mother tongue. This shocked me. Was he a common criminal from back home in Formosa, and not a Chinese Communist from Manchuria?

He reached the opening and began to push away the rocks, to enlarge the opening and climb through. The corporal shouted at me to stop him. The water level was rising. Behind the man, the other chained prisoners were climbing to help him.

I lifted a heavy rock near me and smashed it down on the hands of the man grabbing onto the opening. He howled and fell back, dragging the other prisoners down with him. I heard the splash of water.

"Faster, faster!" I ordered the prisoners on our side of the collapsed tunnel. We sealed the opening, then retreated to set up more dynamite and blast down more rocks to solidify the seal.

When the work was finally done, the corporal ordered all the remaining prisoners shot, and we buried their bodies under yet more blast debris.

There was a massive prisoner uprising. They attempted to sabotage the project, but failed and instead killed themselves.

This was the corporal's report of the incident, and I signed my name to it as well. Everyone understood that was the way to write up such reports.

I remember the face of the man begging me to stop very well. That was the face I saw in the dream last night.

The Square is deserted right before dawn. Overhead, neon advertising signs hang from the City's ceiling, a few hundred meters up. They take the place of long-forgotten constellations and the moon.

Betty keeps an eye out for unlikely pedestrians while I swing the hammer against the chisel. Bronze is a hard material, but I have not lost the old skills I learned as a Digger. Soon the characters of my name are gone from the plaque, leaving behind a smooth rectangle.

I switch to a smaller chisel and begin to carve. The design is simple: three ovals interlinked, a chain. These are the links that bound two continents and three great cities together, and these are the shackles that bound men whose voices were forever silenced, whose names were forgotten. There is beauty and wonder here, and also horror and death.

With each strike of the hammer, I feel as though I am chipping away the shell around me, the numbness, the silence.

Make the secret a bit harder to keep. That counts for something.

"Hurry," Betty says.

My eyes are blurry. And suddenly the lights around the Square come on. It is morning under the Pacific Ocean.

The Litigation Master And
The Monkey King

The tiny cottage at the edge of Sanli Village—away from the villagers' noisy houses and busy clan shrines and next to the cool pond filled with lily pads, pink lotus flowers, and playful carp—would have made an ideal romantic summer hideaway for some dissolute poet and his silk-robed mistress from nearby bustling Yangzhou.

Indeed, having such a country lodge was the fashion among the literati in the lower Yangtze region in this second decade of the glorious reign of the Qianlong Emperor. Everyone agreed—as they visited one another in their vacation homes and sipped tea—that he was the best Emperor of the Qing Dynasty: so wise, so vigorous, and so solicitous of his subjects! And as the Qing Dynasty, founded by Manchu sages, was without a doubt the best dynasty ever to rule China, the scholars competed to compose poems that best showed their gratitude for having the luck to bear witness to this golden age, gift of the greatest Emperor who ever lived.

Alas, any scholar interested in *this* cottage must be disappointed, for it was decrepit. The bamboo grove around it was wild and unkempt; the wooden walls crooked, rotting, and full of holes; the thatching over the roof uneven, with older layers peeking out through holes in the newer layers—

—not unlike the owner and sole inhabitant of the cottage,

actually. Tian Haoli was in his fifties but looked ten years older. He was gaunt, sallow, his queue as thin as a pig's tail, and his breath often smelled of the cheapest rice wine and even cheaper tea. An accident in youth lamed his right leg, but he preferred to shuffle slowly rather than use a cane. His robe was patched all over, though his under-robe still showed through innumerable holes.

Unlike most in the village, Tian knew how to read and write, but as far as anyone knew, he never passed any level of the Imperial Examinations. From time to time, he would write a letter for some family or read an official notice in the teahouse in exchange for half a chicken or a bowl of dumplings.

But that was not how he really made his living.

The morning began like any other. As the sun rose lazily, the fog hanging over the pond dissipated like dissolving ink. Bit by bit, the pink lotus blossoms, the jade-green bamboo stalks, and the golden-yellow cottage roof emerged from the fog.

Knock, knock.

Tian stirred but did not wake up. The Monkey King was hosting a banquet, and Tian was going to eat his fill.

Ever since Tian was a little boy, he had been obsessed with the exploits of the Monkey King, the trickster demon who had seventy-two transformations and defeated hundreds of monsters, who had shaken the throne of the Jade Emperor with a troop of monkeys.

And Monkey liked good food and loved good wine, a must in a good host.

Knock, knock.

Tian ignored the knocking. He was about to bite into a piece of drunken chicken dipped in four different exquisite sauces—

You going to answer that? Monkey said.

As Tian grew older, Monkey would visit him in his dreams, or, if he was awake, speak to him in his head. While others prayed to the Goddess of Mercy or the Buddha, Tian enjoyed conversing with Monkey, who he felt was a demon after his own heart.

Whatever it is, it can wait, said Tian.

I think you have a client, said Monkey.

Knock-knock-knock—

The insistent knocking whisked away Tian's chicken and abruptly ended his dream. His stomach growled, and he cursed as he rubbed his eyes.

"Just a moment!" Tian fumbled out of bed and struggled to put on his robe, muttering to himself all the while. "Why can't they wait till I've woken up properly and pissed and eaten? These unlettered fools are getting more and more unreasonable. . . . I must demand a whole chicken this time. . . . It was such a nice dream. . . ."

I'll save some plum wine for you, said Monkey.

You better.

Tian opened the door. Li Xiaoyi, a woman so timid that she apologized even when some rambunctious child ran into *her*, stood there in a dark green dress, her hair pinned up in the manner prescribed for widows. Her fist was lifted and almost smashed into Tian's nose.

"Aiya!" Tian said. "You owe me the best drunk chicken in Yangzhou!" But Li's expression, a combination of desperation and fright, altered his tone. "Come on in."

He closed the door behind the woman and poured a cup of tea for her.

Men and women came to Tian as a last resort, for he helped them when they had nowhere else to turn, when they ran into trouble with the law.

The Qianlong Emperor might be all-wise and all-seeing, but he still needed the thousands of *yamen* courts to actually govern. Presided over by a magistrate, a judge-administrator who held the power of life and death over the local citizens in his charge, a *yamen* court was a mysterious, opaque place full of terror for the average man and woman.

Who knew the secrets of the Great Qing Code? Who understood how to plead and prove and defend and argue? When the magistrate spent his evenings at parties hosted by the local gentry, who could predict how a case brought by the poor against the rich would fare? Who could intuit the right clerk to bribe to avoid torture? Who could fathom the correct excuse to give to procure a prison visit?

No, one did not go near the *yamen* courts unless one had no other choice. When you sought justice, you gambled everything.

And you needed the help of a man like Tian Haoli.

Calmed by the warmth of the tea, Li Xiaoyi told Tian her story in halting sentences.

She had been struggling to feed herself and her two daughters on the produce from a tiny plot of land. To survive a bad harvest, she had mortgaged her land to Jie, a wealthy distant cousin of her dead husband, who promised that she could redeem her land at any time, interest free. As Li could not read, she had gratefully inked her thumbprint to the contract her cousin handed her.

"He said it was just to make it official for the tax collector," Li said.

Ah, a familiar story, said the Monkey King.

Tian sighed and nodded.

"I paid him back at the beginning of this year, but yesterday Jie came to my door with two bailiffs from the *yamen*. He said that my daughters and I had to leave our house immediately because we had not been making the payments on the loan. I was shocked, but he took out the contract and said that I had promised to pay him back double the amount loaned in one year or else the land would become his forever. 'It's all here in black characters on white paper,' he said, and waved the contract in my face. The bailiffs said that if I don't leave by tomorrow, they'll arrest me and sell me and my daughters to a blue house to satisfy the debt." She clenched her fists. "I don't know what to do!"

Tian refilled her teacup and said, "We'll have to go to court and defeat him."

You sure about this? said the Monkey King. *You haven't even seen the contract.*

You worry about the banquets, and I'll worry about the law.

"How?" Li asked. "Maybe the contract does say what he said."

"I'm sure it does. But don't worry, I'll think of something."

To those who came to Tian for help, he was a *songshi*, a litigation master. But to the *yamen* magistrate and the local gentry, to the men who wielded money and power, Tian was a *songgun*, a "litigating hooligan."

The scholars who sipped tea and the merchants who caressed their silver taels despised Tian for daring to help the illiterate peasants draft complaints, devise legal strategies, and prepare for testimony and interrogation. After all, according to Confucius, neighbors should not sue neighbors. A conflict was nothing more than a misunderstanding that needed to be harmonized by a learned Confucian gentleman. But men like Tian Haoli dared to make the crafty peasants think that they could haul their superiors into court and could violate the proper hierarchies of respect! The Great Qing Code made it clear that champerty, maintenance, barratry, pettifoggery—whatever name you used to describe what Tian did—were crimes.

But Tian understood the *yamen* courts were parts of a complex machine. Like the watermills that dotted the Yangtze River, complicated machines had patterns, gears, and levers. They could be nudged and pushed to do things, provided you were clever. As much as the scholars and merchants hated Tian, sometimes they also sought his help and paid him handsomely for it too.

"I can't pay you much."

Tian chuckled. "The rich pay my fee when they use my services but hate me for it. In your case, it's payment enough to see this moneyed cousin of yours foiled."

★ ★ ★ ★

354

Tian accompanied Li to the *yamen* court. Along the way, they passed the town square, where a few soldiers were putting up posters of wanted men.

Li glanced at the posters and slowed down. "Wait, I think I may know—"

"Shush!" Tian pulled her along. "Are you crazy? Those aren't the magistrate's bailiffs, but real Imperial soldiers. How can you possibly recognize a man wanted by the Emperor?"

"But—"

"I'm sure you're mistaken. If one of them hears you, even the greatest litigation master in China won't be able to help you. You have trouble enough. When it comes to politics, it's best to see no evil, hear no evil, speak no evil."

That's a philosophy a lot of my monkeys used to share, said the Monkey King. *But I disagree with it.*

You would, you perpetual rebel, thought Tian Haoli. *But you can grow a new head when it's cut off, a luxury most of us don't share.*

Outside the *yamen* court, Tian picked up the drumstick and began to beat the Drum of Justice, petitioning the court to hear his complaint.

Half an hour later, an angry Magistrate Yi stared at the two people kneeling on the paved-stone floor below the dais: the widow trembling in fear, and that troublemaker, Tian, his back straight with a false look of respect on his face. Magistrate Yi had hoped to take the day off to enjoy the company of a pretty girl at one of the blue houses, but here he was, forced to work. He had a good mind to order both of them flogged right away, but he had to at least keep up the appearance of being a caring magistrate lest one of his disloyal underlings make a report to the judicial inspector.

"What is your complaint, guileful peasant?" asked the magistrate, gritting his teeth.

Tian shuffled forward on his knees and kowtowed. "Oh, Most Honored Magistrate," he began—Magistrate Yi wondered how Tian managed to make the phrase sound almost like an insult—"Widow Li cries out for justice, justice, justice!"

"And why are *you* here?"

"I'm Li Xiaoyi's cousin, here to help her speak, for she is distraught over how she's been treated."

Magistrate Yi fumed. This Tian Haoli always claimed to be related to the litigant to justify his presence in court and avoid the charge of being a litigating hooligan. He slammed his hardwood ruler, the symbol of his authority, against the table. "You lie! How many cousins can you possibly have?"

"I lie not."

"I warn you, if you can't prove this relation in the records of the Li clan shrine, I'll have you given forty strokes of the cane." Magistrate Yi was pleased with himself, thinking that he had finally come up with a way to best the crafty litigation master. He gave a meaningful look to the bailiffs standing to the sides of the court, and they pounded their staffs against the ground rhythmically, emphasizing the threat.

But Tian seemed not worried at all. "Most Sagacious Magistrate, it was Confucius who said that 'Within the Four Seas, all men are brothers.' If all men were brothers at the time of Confucius, then it stands to reason that being descended from them, Li Xiaoyi and I are related. With all due respect, surely, Your Honor isn't suggesting that the genealogical records of the Li family are more authoritative than the words of the Great Sage?"

Magistrate Yi's face turned red, but he could not think of an answer. Oh, how he wished he could find some excuse to punish this sharp-tongued *songgun*, who always seemed to turn black into white and right into wrong. The Emperor needed better laws to deal with men like him.

"Let's move on." The magistrate took a deep breath to calm himself. "What is this injustice she claims? Her cousin Jie read me the contract. It's perfectly clear what happened."

"I'm afraid there's been a mistake," Tian said. "I ask that the contract be brought so it can be examined again."

Magistrate Yi sent one of the bailiffs to bring back the wealthy cousin with the contract. Everyone in court, including Widow Li, looked at Tian in puzzlement, unsure what he planned. But Tian simply stroked his beard, appearing to be without a care in the world.

You do have a plan, yes? said the Monkey King.

Not really. I'm just playing for time.

Well, said Monkey, *I always like to turn my enemies' weapons against them. Did I tell you about the time I burned Nezha with his own fire-wheels?*

Tian dipped his hand inside his robe, where he kept his writing kit.

The bailiff brought back a confused, sweating Jie, who had been interrupted during a luxurious meal of swallow-nest soup. His face was still greasy as he hadn't even gotten a chance to wipe himself. Jie knelt before the magistrate next to Tian and Li and lifted the contract above his head for the bailiff.

"Show it to Tian," the magistrate ordered.

Tian accepted the contract and began to read it. He nodded his head from time to time, as though the contract was the most fascinating poetry.

Though the legalese was long and intricate, the key phrase was only eight characters long:

上賣莊稼,下賣田地

The mortgage was structured as a sale with a right of redemption, and this part provided that the widow sold her cousin "the crops above, and the field below."

"Interesting, most interesting," said Tian as he held the contract and continued to move his head about rhythmically.

Magistrate Yi knew he was being baited, yet he couldn't help but ask, "*What* is so interesting?"

"Oh Great, Glorious Magistrate, you who reflect the truth like a perfect mirror, you must read the contract yourself."

Confused, Magistrate Yi had the bailiff bring him the contract. After a few moments, his eyes bulged out. Right there, in clear black characters, was the key phrase describing the sale:

上賣莊稼, 不賣田地

"The crops above, but *not* the field," muttered the magistrate.

Well, the case was clear. The contract did not say what Jie claimed. All that Jie had a right to were the crops, but not the field itself. Magistrate Yi had no idea how this could have happened, but his embarrassed fury needed an outlet. The sweaty, greasy-faced Jie was the first thing he laid his eyes on.

"How dare you lie to me?" Yi shouted, slamming his ruler down on the table. "Are you trying to make me look like a fool?"

It was now Jie's turn to shake like a leaf in the wind, unable to speak.

"Oh, now you have nothing to say? You're convicted of obstruction of justice, lying to an Imperial official, and attempting to defraud another of her property. I sentence you to a hundred and twenty strokes of the cane and confiscation of half of your property."

"Mercy, mercy! I don't know what happened—" The piteous cries of Jie faded as the bailiffs dragged him out of the *yamen* to jail.

Litigation Master Tian's face was impassive, but inside he smiled and thanked Monkey. Discreetly, he rubbed the tip of his finger against his robe to eliminate the evidence of his trick.

A week later, Tian Haoli was awakened from another banquet-dream with the Monkey King by persistent knocking. He opened the door to find Li Xiaoyi standing there, her pale face drained of blood.

"What's the matter? Is your cousin again—"

"Master Tian, I need your help." Her voice was barely more than a whisper. "It's my brother."

"Is it a gambling debt? A fight with a rich man? Did he make a bad deal? Was he—"

"Please! You have to come with me!"

Tian Haoli was going to say no because a clever *songshi* never got involved in cases he didn't understand—a quick way to end a career. But the look on Li's face softened his resolve. "All right. Lead the way."

Tian made sure that there was no one watching before he slipped inside Li Xiaoyi's hut. Though he didn't have much of a reputation to worry about, Xiaoyi didn't need the village gossips wagging their tongues.

Inside, a long, crimson streak could be seen across the packed-earth floor, leading from the doorway to the bed against the far wall. A man lay asleep on the bed, bloody bandages around his legs and left shoulder. Xiaoyi's two children, both girls, huddled in a shadowy corner of the hut, their mistrustful eyes peeking out at Tian.

One glance at the man's face told Tian all he needed to know: It was the same face on those posters the soldiers were putting up.

Tian Haoli sighed. "Xiaoyi, what kind of trouble have you brought me now?"

Gently, Xiaoyi shook her brother, Xiaojing, awake. He became alert almost immediately, a man used to light sleep and danger on the road.

"Xiaoyi tells me that you can help me," the man said, gazing at Tian intently.

Tian rubbed his chin as he appraised Xiaojing. "I don't know."

"I can pay." Xiaojing struggled to turn on the bed and lifted a corner of a cloth bundle. Tian could see the glint of silver underneath.

"I make no promises. Not every disease has a cure, and not every fugitive can find a loophole. It depends on who's after you and why." Tian walked closer and bent down to examine the promised payment, but the tattoos on Xiaojing's scarred face, signs that he was a convicted criminal, caught his attention. "You were sentenced to exile."

"Yes, ten years ago, right after Xiaoyi's marriage."

"If you have enough money, there are doctors that can do something about those tattoos, though you won't look very handsome afterward."

"I'm not very worried about looks right now."

"What was it for?"

Xiaojing laughed and nodded at the table next to the window, upon which a thin book lay open. The wind fluttered its pages. "If you're as good as my sister says, you can probably figure it out."

Tian glanced at the book and then turned back to Xiaojing.

"You were exiled to the border near Vietnam," Tian said to himself as he deciphered the tattoos. "Eleven years ago . . . the breeze fluttering the pages . . . ah, you must have been a servant of Xu Jun, the Hanlin Academy scholar."

Eleven years ago, during the reign of the Yongzheng Emperor, someone had whispered in the Emperor's ear that the great scholar Xu Jun was plotting rebellion against the Manchu rulers. But when the Imperial guards seized Xu's house and ransacked it, they could find nothing incriminating.

However, the Emperor could never be wrong, and so his legal advisers had to devise a way to convict Xu. Their solution was to point at one of Xu's seemingly innocuous lyric poems:

清風不識字，何故亂翻書
Breeze, you know not how to read,
So why do you mess with my book?

The first character in the word for "breeze," *qing*, was the same as the name of the dynasty. The clever legalists serving the Emperor—and Tian did have a begrudging professional admiration for their skill—construed it as a treasonous composition mocking the Manchu rulers as uncultured and illiterate. Xu and his family were sentenced to death, his servants exiled.

"Xu's crime was great, but it has been more than ten years." Tian paced beside the bed. "If you simply broke the terms of your exile, it might not be too difficult to bribe the right officials and commanders to look the other way."

"The men after me cannot be bribed."

"Oh?" Tian looked at the bandaged wounds covering the man's body. "You mean . . . the Blood Drops."

Xiaojing nodded.

The Blood Drops were the Emperor's eyes and talons. They moved through the dark alleys of cities like ghosts and melted into the streaming caravans on roads and canals, hunting for signs of treason. They were the reason that teahouses posted signs for patrons to avoid talk of politics and neighbors looked around and whispered when they complained about taxes. They listened, watched, and sometimes came to people's doors in the middle of the night, and those they visited were never seen again.

Tian waved his arms impatiently. "You and Xiaoyi are wasting my time. If the Blood Drops are after you, I can do nothing. Not if I want to keep my head attached to my neck." Tian headed for the door of the hut.

"I'm not asking you to save me," said Xiaojing.

Tian paused.

"Eleven years ago, when they came to arrest Master Xu, he gave me a book and told me it was more important than his life, than his family. I kept the book hidden and took it into exile with me.

"A month ago, two men came to my house, asking me to turn over everything I had from my dead master. Their accents told me they were from Beijing, and I saw in their eyes the cold stare of the Emperor's falcons. I let them in and told them to look around, but while they were distracted with my chests and drawers, I escaped with the book.

"I've been on the run ever since, and a few times they almost caught me, leaving me with these wounds. The book they're after is over there on the table. *That*'s what I want you to save."

Tian hesitated by the door. He was used to bribing *yamen* clerks and prison guards and debating Magistrate Yi. He liked playing games with words and drinking cheap wine and bitter tea. What business did a lowly *songgun* have with the Emperor and the intrigue of the Court?

I was once happy in Fruit-and-Flower Mountain, spending all day in play with my fellow monkeys, said the Monkey King. *Sometimes I wish I hadn't been so curious about what lay in the wider world.*

But Tian was curious, and he walked over to the table and picked up the book. *An Account of Ten Days at Yangzhou*, it said, by Wang Xiuchu.

A hundred years earlier, in 1645, after claiming the Ming Chinese capital of Beijing, the Manchu Army was intent on completing its conquest of China.

Prince Dodo and his forces came to Yangzhou, a wealthy city of salt merchants and painted pavilions, at the meeting point of the Yangtze River and the Grand Canal. The Chinese commander, Grand Secretary Shi Kefa, vowed to resist to the utmost. He rallied the city's residents to reinforce the walls and tried to unite the remaining Ming warlords and militias.

His efforts came to naught on May 20, 1645, when the Manchu forces broke through the city walls after a seven-day siege. Shi Kefa was executed after refusing to surrender. To punish the residents of Yangzhou and to teach the rest of China a lesson about the price of resisting the Manchu Army, Prince Dodo gave the order to slaughter the entire population of the city.

One of the residents, Wang Xiuchu, survived by moving from hiding place to hiding place and bribing the soldiers with whatever he had. He also recorded what he saw:

One Manchu soldier with a sword was in the lead, another with a lance was in the back, and a third roamed in the middle to prevent the captives from escaping. The three of them herded dozens of captives like dogs and sheep. If any captive walked too slow, they would beat him immediately or else kill him on the spot.

The women were strung together with ropes, like a strand of pearls. They stumbled as they walked through the mud, and filth covered their bodies and clothes. Babies were everywhere on the ground, and as horses and people trampled over them, their brains and organs mixed into the earth, and the howling of the dying filled the air.

Every gutter or pond we passed was filled with corpses, their arms and legs entangled. The blood mixing with the green water turned into a painter's palette. So many bodies filled the canal that it turned into flat ground.

The mass massacre, raping, pillaging, and burning of the city lasted six days.

On the second day of the lunar month, the new government ordered all the temples to cremate the bodies. The temples had sheltered many women, though many had also died from hunger and fright. The final records of the cremations included hundreds of thousands of bodies, though this figure does not include all those who had committed suicide by jumping into wells or canals or through self-immolation and hanging to avoid a worse fate. . . .

On the fourth day of the lunar month, the weather finally turned sunny. The bodies piled by the roadside, having soaked in rainwater, had inflated and the skin on them was a bluish black and stretched taut like the surface of a drum. The flesh inside rotted and the stench was overwhelming. As the sun baked the bodies, the smell grew worse. Everywhere in Yangzhou, the survivors were cremating bodies. The smoke permeated inside all the houses and formed a miasma. The smell of rotting bodies could be detected a hundred li away.

Tian's hands trembled as he turned over the last page.

"Now you see why the Blood Drops are after me," said Xiao-jing, his voice weary. "The Manchus have insisted that the Yangzhou Massacre is a myth, and anyone speaking of it is guilty of treason. But here is an eyewitness account that will reveal their throne as built on a foundation of blood and skulls."

Tian closed his eyes and thought about Yangzhou, with its teahouses full of indolent scholars arguing with singing girls about rhyme schemes, with its palatial mansions full of richly robed merchants celebrating another good trading season, with its hundreds of thousands of inhabitants happily praying for the Manchu Emperor's health. Did they know that each day, as they went to the markets and laughed and sang and praised this golden age they lived in, they were treading on the bones of the dead, they were mocking the dying cries of the departed, they were denying the memories of ghosts? He himself had not even believed the stories whispered in his childhood about Yangzhou's past, and he was quite sure that most young men in Yangzhou now had never even heard of them.

Now that he knew the truth, could he allow the ghosts to continue to be silenced?

But then he also thought about the special prisons the Blood Drops maintained, the devious tortures designed to prolong the journey from life to death, the ways that the Manchu Emperors always got what they wanted in the end. The Emperor's noble Banners had succeeded in forcing all the Chinese to shave their heads and wear queues to show submission to the Manchus, and to abandon their *hanfu* for Manchu clothing on pain of death. They had cut the Chinese off from their past, made them a people adrift without the anchor of their memories. They were more powerful than the Jade Emperor and ten thousand heavenly soldiers.

It would be so easy for them to erase this book, to erase him, a lowly *songgun*, from the world, like a momentary ripple across a placid pond.

Let others have their fill of daring deeds; he was a survivor.

"I'm sorry," Tian said to Xiaojing, his voice low and hoarse. "I can't help you."

Tian Haoli sat down at his table to eat a bowl of noodles. He had flavored it with fresh lotus seeds and bamboo shoots, and the fragrance was usually refreshing, perfect for a late lunch.

The Monkey King appeared in the seat opposite him: fierce eyes, wide mouth, a purple cape that declared him to be the Sage Equal to Heaven, rebel against the Jade Emperor.

This didn't happen often. Usually Monkey spoke to Tian only in his mind.

"You think you're not a hero," the Monkey King said.

"That's right," replied Tian. He tried to keep the defensiveness out of his voice. "I'm just an ordinary man making a living by scrounging for crumbs in the cracks of the law, happy to have enough to eat and a few coppers left for drink. I just want to live."

"I'm not a hero either," the Monkey King said. "I just did my job when needed."

"Ha!" said Tian. "I know what you're trying to do, but it's not going to work. Your job was to protect the holiest monk on a perilous journey, and your qualifications consisted of peerless strength and boundless magic. You could call on the aid of the Buddha and Guanyin, the Goddess of Mercy, whenever you needed to. Don't you compare yourself to me."

"Fine. Do you know of *any* heroes?"

Tian slurped some noodles and pondered the question. What he had read that morning was fresh in his mind. "I guess Grand Secretary Shi Kefa was a hero."

"How? He promised the people of Yangzhou that as long as

he lived, he would not let harm come to them, and yet when the city fell, he tried to escape on his own. He seems to me more a coward than a hero."

Tian put down his bowl. "That's not fair. He held the city when he had no reinforcements or aid. He pacified the warlords harassing the people in Yangzhou and rallied them to their defense. In the end, despite a moment of weakness, he willingly gave his life for the city, and you can't ask for more than that."

The Monkey King snorted contemptuously. "Of course you can. He should have seen that fighting was futile. If he hadn't resisted the Manchu invaders and instead surrendered the city, maybe not so many would have died. If he hadn't refused to bow down to the Manchus, maybe he wouldn't have been killed." The Monkey King smirked. "Maybe he wasn't very smart and didn't know how to survive."

Blood rushed to Tian's face. He stood up and pointed a finger at the Monkey King. "Don't you talk about him that way. Who's to say that had he surrendered, the Manchus wouldn't have slaughtered the city, anyway? You think lying down before a conquering army bent on rape and pillage is the right thing to do? To turn your argument around, the heavy resistance in Yangzhou slowed the Manchu Army and might have allowed many people to escape to safety in the south, and the city's defiance might have made the Manchus willing to give better terms to those who did surrender later. Grand Secretary Shi was a real hero!"

The Monkey King laughed. "Listen to you, arguing like you are in Magistrate Yi's *yamen*. You're awfully worked up about a man dead for a hundred years."

"I won't let you denigrate his memory that way, even if you're the Sage Equal to Heaven."

The Monkey King's face turned serious. "You speak of memory. What do you think about Wang Xiuchu, who wrote the book you read?"

"He was just an ordinary man like me, surviving by bribes and hiding from danger."

"Yet he recorded what he saw, so that a hundred years later the men and women who died in those ten days can be remembered. Writing that book was a brave thing to do—look at how the Manchus are hunting down someone today just for *reading* it. I think he was a hero too."

After a moment, Tian nodded. "I hadn't thought about it that way, but you're right."

"There are no heroes, Tian Haoli. Grand Secretary Shi was both courageous and cowardly, capable and foolish. Wang Xiuchu was both an opportunistic survivor and a man of greatness of spirit. I'm mostly selfish and vain, but sometimes even I surprise myself. We're all just ordinary men—well, I'm an ordinary demon—faced with extraordinary choices. In those moments, sometimes heroic ideals demand that we become their avatars."

Tian sat down and closed his eyes. "I'm just an old and frightened man, Monkey. I don't know what to do."

"Sure you do. You just have to accept it."

"Why me? What if I don't want to?"

The Monkey King's face turned somber, and his voice grew faint. "Those men and women of Yangzhou died a hundred years ago, Tian Haoli, and nothing can be done to change that. But the past lives on in the form of memories, and those in power are always going to want to erase and silence the past, to bury the ghosts. Now that you know about that past, you're no longer an innocent bystander. If you do not act, you're complicit with the Emperor and his Blood Drops in this new act of violence, this deed of erasure. Like Wang Xiuchu, you're now a witness. Like him, you must choose what to do. You must decide if, on the day you die, you will regret your choice."

The figure of the Monkey King faded away, and Tian was left alone in his hut, remembering.

"I have written a letter to an old friend in Ningbo," said Tian. "Bring it with you to the address on the envelope. He's a good surgeon and will erase these tattoos from your face as a favor to me."

"Thank you," said Li Xiaojing. "I will destroy the letter as soon as I can, knowing how much danger this brings you. Please accept this as payment." He turned to his bundle and retrieved five taels of silver.

Tian held up a hand. "No, you'll need all the money you can get." He handed over a small bundle. "It's not much, but it's all I have saved."

Li Xiaojing and Li Xiaoyi both looked at the litigation master, not understanding.

Tian continued. "Xiaoyi and the children can't stay here in Sanli because someone will surely report that she harbored a fugitive when the Blood Drops start asking questions. No, all of you must leave immediately and go to Ningbo, where you will hire a ship to take you to Japan. Since the Manchus have sealed the coast, you will need to pay a great deal to a smuggler."

"To Japan!?"

"So long as that book is with you, there is nowhere in China where you'll be safe. Of all the states around, only Japan would dare to defy the Manchu Emperor. Only there will you and the book be safe."

Xiaojing and Xiaoyi nodded. "You will come with us, then?"

Tian gestured at his lame leg and laughed. "Having me along will only slow you down. No, I'll stay here and take my chances."

"The Blood Drops will not let you go if they suspect you helped us."

Tian smiled. "I'll come up with something. I always do."

A few days later, when Tian Haoli was just about to sit down and have his lunch, soldiers from the town garrison came to his door. They arrested him without explanation and brought him to the *yamen*.

Tian saw that Magistrate Yi wasn't the only one sitting behind the judging table on the dais this time. With him was another official, whose hat indicated that he came directly from Beijing. His cold eyes and lean build reminded Tian of a falcon.

May my wits defend me again, Tian whispered to the Monkey King in his mind.

Magistrate Yi slammed his ruler on the table. "Deceitful Tian Haoli, you're hereby accused of aiding the escape of dangerous fugitives and of plotting acts of treason against the Great Qing. Confess your crimes immediately so that you may die quickly."

Tian nodded as the magistrate finished his speech. "Most Merciful and Farsighted Magistrate, I have absolutely no idea what you're talking about."

"You presumptuous fool! Your usual tricks will not work this time. I have ironclad proof that you gave comfort and aid to the traitor Li Xiaojing and read a forbidden, treasonous, false text."

"I have indeed read a book recently, but there was nothing treasonous in it."

"What?"

"It was a book about sheepherding and pearl stringing. Plus some discussions about filling ponds and starting fires."

The other man behind the table narrowed his eyes, but Tian went on as if he had nothing to hide. "It was very technical and very boring."

"You lie!" The veins on Magistrate Yi's neck seemed about to burst.

"Most Brilliant and Perspicacious Magistrate, how can you say that I lie? Can you tell me the contents of this forbidden book, so that I may verify if I have read it?"

"You . . . you . . ." The magistrate's mouth opened and closed like the lips of a fish.

Of course Magistrate Yi wouldn't have been told what was in the book—that was the point of it being forbidden—but

Tian was also counting on the fact that the man from the Blood Drops wouldn't be able to say anything either. To accuse Tian of lying about the contents of the book was to admit that the accuser had read the book, and Tian knew that no member of the Blood Drops would admit such a crime to the suspicious Manchu Emperor.

"There has been a misunderstanding," said Tian. "The book I read contained nothing that was false, which means that it can't possibly be the book that has been banned. Certainly, Your Honor can see the plain and simple logic." He smiled. Surely, he had found the loophole that would allow him to escape.

"Enough of this charade." The man from the Blood Drops spoke for the first time. "There's no need to bother with the law with traitors like you. On the Emperor's authority, I hereby declare you guilty without appeal and sentence you to death. If you do not wish to suffer much longer, immediately confess the whereabouts of the book and the fugitives."

Tian felt his legs go rubbery and, for a moment, he saw only darkness and heard only an echo of the Blood Drop's pronouncement: *sentence you to death.*

I guess I've finally run out of tricks, he thought.

You've already made your choice, said the Monkey King. *Now you just have to accept it.*

Besides being great spies and assassins, the Blood Drops were experts at the art of torture.

Tian screamed as they doused his limbs in boiling water.

Tell me a story, said Tian to the Monkey King. *Distract me so I don't give in.*

Let me tell you about the time they cooked me in the alchemical furnace of the Jade Emperor, said the Monkey King. *I survived by hiding among smoke and ashes.*

And Tian told his torturers a tale about how he had helped Li Xiaojing burn his useless book and saw it turn into smoke and ashes. But he had forgotten where the fire was set. Perhaps the Blood Drops could search the nearby hills thoroughly?

They burned him with iron pokers heated until they glowed white.

Tell me a story, Tian screamed as he breathed in the smell of charred flesh.

Let me tell you about the time I fought the Iron Fan Princess in the Fire Mountains, said the Monkey King. *I tricked her by pretending to run away in fear.*

And Tian told his torturers a tale about how he had told Li Xiaojing to escape to Suzhou, famed for its many alleys and canals, as well as refined lacquer fans.

They cut his fingers off one by one.

Tell me a story, Tian croaked. He was weak from loss of blood.

Let me tell you about the time they put that magical head-band on me, said the Monkey King. *I almost passed out from the pain but still I wouldn't stop cursing.*

And Tian spat in the faces of his torturers.

Tian woke up in the dim cell. It smelled of mildew and shit and piss. Rats squeaked in the corners.

He was finally going to be put to death tomorrow, as his torturers had given up. It would be death by a thousand cuts. A skilled executioner could make the victim suffer for hours before taking his final breath.

I didn't give in, did I? he asked the Monkey King. *I can't remember everything I told them.*

You told them many tales, none true.

Tian thought he should be content. Death would be a release. But he worried that he hadn't done enough. What if Li Xiaojing didn't make it to Japan? What if the book was destroyed at sea? If only there were some way to save the book so that it could *not* be lost.

Have I told you about the time I fought Lord Erlang and confused him by transforming my shape? I turned into a sparrow, a fish, a snake, and finally a temple. My mouth was the door, my eyes the windows, my tongue the buddha, and my tail a flagpole. Ha, that was fun. None of Lord Erlang's demons could see through my disguises.

I am clever with words, thought Tian. *I am, after all, a* songgun.

The voices of children singing outside the jail cell came to him faintly. He struggled and crawled to the wall with the tiny barred window at the top and called out, "Hey, can you hear me?"

The singing stopped abruptly. After a while, a timid voice said, "We're not supposed to talk to condemned criminals. My mother says that you're dangerous and crazy."

Tian laughed. "I *am* crazy. But I know some good songs. Would you like to learn them? They're about sheep and pearls and all sorts of other fun things."

The children conferred among themselves, and one of them said, "Why not? A crazy man must have some good songs."

Tian Haoli mustered up every last bit of his strength and concentration. He thought about the words from the book:

The three of them herded dozens of captives like dogs and sheep. If any captive walked too slow, they would beat him immediately, or else kill him on the spot. The women were strung together with ropes, like a strand of pearls.

He thought about disguises. He thought about the way the tones differed between Mandarin and the local topolect, the way he could make puns and approximations and rhymes and shift the words and transform them until they were no longer recognizable. And he began to sing:

> *The Tree of Dem herded dozens of Cap Tea*
> *Like dogs and sheep.*
> *If any Cap Tea walked too slow, the Wood Beet*
> *Hmm'd immediately.*

Or else a quill, slim on the dot.
The Why-Men were strong to gather wits & loupes
Like a strand of pearls.

And the children, delighted by the nonsense, picked up the songs quickly.

They tied him to the pole on the execution platform and stripped him naked.

Tian watched the crowd. In the eyes of some, he saw pity, in others, he saw fear, and in still others, like Li Xiaoyi's cousin Jie, he saw delight at seeing the hooligan *songgun* meet this fate. But most were expectant. This execution, this horror, was entertainment.

"One last chance," the Blood Drop said. "If you confess the truth now, we will slit your throat cleanly. Otherwise, you can enjoy the next few hours."

Whispers passed through the crowd. Some tittered. Tian gazed at the bloodlust in some of the men. *You have become a slavish people*, he thought. *You have forgotten the past and become docile captives of the Emperor. You have learned to take delight in his barbarity, to believe that you live in a golden age, never bothering to look beneath the gilded surface of the Empire at its rotten, bloody foundation. You desecrate the very memory of those who died to keep you free.*

His heart was filled with despair. *Have I endured all this and thrown away my life for nothing?*

Some children in the crowd began to sing:

The Tree of Dem herded dozens of Cap Tea
Like dogs and sheep.
If any Cap Tea walked too slow, the Wood Beet
Hmm'd immediately.
Or else a quill, slim on the dot.

The Why-Men were strong to gather wits & loupes
Like a strand of pearls.

The Blood Drop's expression did not change. He heard nothing but the nonsense of children. True, this way, the children would not be endangered by knowing the song. But Tian also wondered if anyone would ever see through the nonsense. Had he hidden the truth too deep?

"Stubborn till the last, eh?" The Blood Drop turned to the executioner, who was sharpening his knives on the grindstone. "Make it last as long as possible."

What have I done? thought Tian. *They're laughing at the way I'm dying, the way I've been a fool. I've accomplished nothing except fighting for a hopeless cause.*

Not at all, said the Monkey King. *Li Xiaojing is safe in Japan, and the children's songs will be passed on until the whole county, the whole province, the whole country fills with their voices. Someday, perhaps not now, perhaps not in another hundred years, but someday the book will come back from Japan, or a clever scholar will finally see through the disguise in your songs as Lord Erlang finally saw through mine. And then the spark of truth will set this country aflame, and this people will awaken from their torpor. You have preserved the memories of the men and women of Yangzhou.*

The executioner began with a long, slow cut across Tian's thighs, removing chunks of flesh. Tian's scream was like that of an animal's, raw, pitiful, incoherent.

Not much of a hero, am I? thought Tian. *I wish I were truly brave.*

You're an ordinary man who was given an extraordinary choice, said the Monkey King. *Do you regret your choice?*

No, thought Tian. And as the pain made him delirious and reason began to desert him, he shook his head firmly. *Not at all.*

You can't ask for more than that, said the Monkey King.

And he bowed before Tian Haoli, not the way you kowtowed to an Emperor, but the way you would bow to a great hero.

* * * *

AUTHOR'S NOTES

For more about the historical profession of *songshi* (or *songgun*), please contact the author for an unpublished paper. Some of Tian Haoli's exploits are based on folktales about the great Litigation Master Xie Fangzun collected by the anthologist Ping Heng in *Zhongguo da zhuangshi* ("Great Plaintmasters of China"), published in 1922.

For more than 250 years, *An Account of Ten Days at Yangzhou* was suppressed in China by the Manchu emperors, and the Yangzhou Massacre, along with numerous other atrocities during the Manchu Conquest, was forgotten. It wasn't until the decade before the Revolution of 1911 that copies of the book were brought back from Japan and republished in China. The text played a small, but important, role in the fall of the Qing and the end of Imperial rule in China. I translated the excerpts used in this story.

Due to the long suppression, which continues to some degree to this day, the true number of victims who died in Yangzhou may never be known. This story is dedicated to their memory.

The Man Who Ended History:

A Documentary

Akemi Kirino, Chief Scientist,
Feynman Laboratories:

[*Dr. Kirino is in her early forties. She has the kind of beauty that doesn't require much makeup. If you look closely, you can see bits of white in her otherwise black hair.*]

Every night, when you stand outside and gaze upon the stars, you are bathing in time as well as light.

For example, when you look at this star in the constellation Libra called Gliese 581, you are really seeing it as it was just over two decades ago because it's about twenty light-years from us. And conversely, if someone around Gliese 581 had a powerful enough telescope pointed to around *here* right now, they'd be able to see Evan and me walking around Harvard Yard, back when we were graduate students.

[*She points to Massachusetts on the globe on her desk, as the camera pans to zoom in on it. She pauses, thinking over her words. The camera pulls back, moving us farther and farther away from the globe, as though we are flying away from it.*]

The best telescopes we have today can see as far back as about thirteen billion years ago. If you strap one of those to a rocket moving away from the Earth at a speed that's faster than light—a detail that I'll get to in a minute—and point the telescope back at the Earth, you'll see the history of humanity unfold before you in reverse. The view of everything that has happened on Earth leaves here in an ever-expanding sphere of light. And you only have to control how far away you travel in space to determine how far back you'll go in time.

[*The camera keeps on pulling back, through the door of her office, down the hall, as the globe and Dr. Kirino become smaller and smaller in our view. The long hallway we are backing down is dark, and in that sea of darkness, the open door of the office becomes a rectangle of bright light framing the globe and the woman.*]

Somewhere about here you'll witness Prince Charles's sad face as Hong Kong is finally returned to China. Somewhere about here you'll see Japan's surrender aboard the USS *Missouri*. Somewhere about here you'll see Hideyoshi's troops set foot on the soil of Korea for the first time. And somewhere about here you'll see Lady Murasaki completing the first chapter of the *Tale of Genji*. If you keep on going, you can go back to the beginning of civilization and beyond.

But the past is consumed even as it is seen. The photons enter the lens, and from there they strike an imaging surface, be it your retina or a sheet of film or a digital sensor, and then they are gone, stopped dead in their paths. If you look but don't pay attention and miss a moment, you cannot travel farther out to catch it again. That moment is erased from the universe, forever.

[*From the shadows next to the door to the office an arm reaches out to slam the door shut. Darkness swallows Dr. Kirino, the globe, and the bright rectangle of light. The screen stays black for a few seconds before the opening credits roll.*]

Remembrance Films HK Ltd.
in association with
Yurushi Studios
presents
a Heraclitus Twice Production
THE MAN WHO ENDED HISTORY
This film has been banned by the Ministry of Culture of the
People's Republic of China and is released under strong protest
from the government of Japan

Akemi Kirino:

[*We are back in the warm glow of her office.*]
Because we have not yet solved the problem of how to travel faster than light, there is no real way for us to actually get a telescope out there to see the past. But we've found a way to cheat.

Theorists long suspected that at each moment, the world around us is literally exploding with newly created subatomic particles of a certain type, now known as Bohm-Kirino particles. My modest contribution to physics was to confirm their existence and to discover that these particles always come in pairs. One member of the pair shoots away from the Earth, riding the photon that gave it birth and traveling at the speed of light. The other remains behind, oscillating in the vicinity of its creation.

The pairs of Bohm-Kirino particles are under quantum entanglement. This means that they are bound together in such a way that no matter how far apart they are from each other physically, their properties are linked together as though they are but aspects of a single system. If you take a measurement on one member of the pair, thereby collapsing the wave function, you would immediately know the state of the other member of the pair, even if it is light-years away.

Since the energy levels of Bohm-Kirino particles decay at a known rate, by tuning the sensitivity of the detection field, we can attempt to capture and measure Bohm-Kirino particles of a precise age created in a specific place.

When a measurement is taken on the local Bohm-Kirino particle in an entangled pair, it is equivalent to taking a measurement on that particle's entangled twin, which, along with its host photon, may be trillions of miles away, and thus, decades in the past. Through some complex but standard mathematics, the measurement allows us to calculate and infer the state of the host photon. But, like any measurement performed on entangled pairs, the measurement can be taken only once, and the information is then gone forever.

In other words, it is as though we have found a way to place a telescope as far away from the Earth, and as far back in time, as we like. If you want, you can look back on the day you were married, your first kiss, the moment you were born. But for each moment in the past, we get only one chance to look.

Archival Footage: September 18, 20XX.
Courtesy of APAC Broadcasting Corporation

[*The camera shows an idle factory on the outskirts of the city of Harbin, Heilongjiang Province, China. It looks just like any other factory in the industrial heartland of China in the grip of another downturn in the country's merciless boom-and-bust cycles: ramshackle, silent, dusty, the windows and doors shuttered and boarded up. Samantha Paine, the correspondent, wears a wool cap and scarf. Her cheeks are bright red with the cold, and her eyes are tired. As she speaks in her calm voice, the condensation from her breath curls and lingers before her face.*]

★ ★ ★ ★

Samantha:

On this day, back in 1931, the first shots in the Second Sino-Japanese War were fired near Shenyang, here in Manchuria. For the Chinese, that was the beginning of World War Two, more than a decade before the United States would be involved.

We are in Pingfang District, on the outskirts of Harbin. Although the name "Pingfang" means nothing to most people in the West, some have called Pingfang the Asian Auschwitz. Here, Unit 731 of the Japanese Imperial Army performed gruesome experiments on thousands of Chinese and Allied prisoners throughout the war as part of Japan's effort to develop biological weapons and to conduct research into the limits of human endurance.

On these premises, Japanese army doctors directly killed thousands of Chinese and Allied prisoners through medical and weapons experiments, vivisections, amputations, and other systematic methods of torture. At the end of the War, the retreating Japanese army killed all remaining prisoners and burned the complex to the ground, leaving behind only the shell of the administrative building and some pits used to breed disease-carrying rats. There were no survivors.

Historians estimate that between two hundred thousand and half a million Chinese persons, almost all civilians, were killed by the biological and chemical weapons researched and developed in this place and other satellite labs: anthrax, cholera, the bubonic plague. At the end of the War, General MacArthur, supreme commander of the Allied forces, granted all members of Unit 731 immunity from war crimes prosecution in order to get the data from their experiments and to keep the data away from the Soviet Union.

Today, except for a small museum nearby with few visitors, little evidence of those atrocities is visible. Over there, at the edge of an empty field, a pile of rubble stands where the incinerator for destroying the bodies of the victims used to be. This factory behind me is built on the foundation of a storage depot used by

Unit 731 for germ-breeding supplies. Until the recent economic downturn, which shuttered its doors, the factory built moped engines for a Sino-Japanese joint venture in Harbin. And in a gruesome echo of the past, several pharmaceutical companies have quietly settled in around the site of Unit 731's former headquarters.

Perhaps the Chinese are content to leave behind this part of their past and move on. And if they do, the rest of the world will probably move on as well.

But not if Evan Wei has anything to say about it.

[*Samantha speaks over a montage of images of Evan Wei lecturing in front of a classroom and posing before complex machinery with Dr. Kirino. In the photographs they look to be in their twenties.*]

Dr. Evan Wei, a Chinese-American historian specializing in Classical Japan, is determined to make the world focus on the suffering of the victims of Unit 731. He and his wife, Dr. Akemi Kirino, a noted Japanese-American experimental physicist, have developed a controversial technique that they claim will allow people to travel back in time and experience history as it occurred. Today, he will publicly demonstrate his technique by traveling back to the year 1940, at the height of Unit 731's activities, and personally bear witness to the atrocities of Unit 731.

The Japanese government claims that China is engaged in a propaganda stunt, and it has filed a strongly worded protest with Beijing for allowing this demonstration. Citing principles of international law, Japan argues that China does not have the right to sponsor an expedition into World War Two–era Harbin because Harbin was then under the control of Manchukuo, a puppet regime of the Japanese Empire. China has rejected the Japanese claim, and responded by declaring Dr. Wei's demonstration an "excavation of national heritage" and now claims ownership rights over any visual or audio record of Dr. Wei's proposed journey to the past under Chinese antiquities-export laws.

Dr. Wei has insisted that he and his wife are conducting this experiment in their capacities as individual American citizens, with no connection to any government. They have asked the American Consul General in nearby Shenyang, as well as representatives of the United Nations, to intervene and protect their effort from any governmental interference. It's unclear how this legal mess will be resolved.

Meanwhile, numerous groups from China and overseas, some in support of Dr. Wei, some against, have gathered to hold protests. China has mobilized thousands of riot police to keep these demonstrators from approaching Pingfang.

Stay tuned, and we will bring you up-to-date reports on this historic occasion. This is Samantha Paine, for APAC.

Akemi Kirino:

To truly travel back in time, we still had to jump over one more hurdle.

The Bohm-Kirino particles allow us to reconstruct, in detail, all types of information about the moment of their creation: sight, sound, microwaves, ultrasound, the smell of antiseptic and blood, and the sting of cordite and gunpowder in the back of the nose.

But this is a staggering amount of information, even for a single second. We had no realistic way to store it, let alone process it in real time. The amount of data gathered for a few minutes would have overwhelmed all the storage servers at Harvard. We could open up a door to the past, but would see nothing in the tsunami of bits that flooded forth.

[*Behind Dr. Kirino is a machine that looks like a large clinical MRI scanner. She steps to the side so that the camera can zoom slowly inside the tube of the scanner where the volunteer's body would go during the process. As the camera moves through the tube, continuing toward the light at the end of the tunnel, her voice continues off camera.*]

Perhaps given enough time, we could have come up with a solution that would have allowed the data to be recorded. But Evan believed that we could not afford to wait. The surviving relatives of the victims were aging, dying, and the War was about to fade out of living memory. There was a duty, he felt, to offer the surviving relatives whatever answers we could get.

So I came up with the idea of using the human brain to process the information gathered by the Bohm-Kirino detectors. The brain's massively parallel processing capabilities, the bedrock of consciousness, proved quite effective at filtering and making sense of the torrent of data from the detectors. The brain could be given the raw electrical signals, throw 99.999 percent of it away, and turn the rest into sight, sound, smell, and make sense of it all and record them as memories.

This really shouldn't surprise us. After all, this is what our brains do, every second of our lives. The raw signals from our eyes, ears, skin, and tongue would overwhelm any supercomputer, but from second to second, our brain manages to construct the consciousness of our existence from all that noise.

"For our volunteer subjects, the process creates the illusion of experiencing the past, as though they were in that place, at that time," I wrote in *Nature*.

How I regret using the word "illusion" now. So much weight ended up being placed on my poor word choice. History is like that: The truly important decisions never seemed important at the time.

Yes, the brain takes the signals and makes a story out of them, but there's nothing illusory about it, whether in the past or now.

★ ★ ★ ★

Archibald Ezary, Radhabinod Pal Professor of Law,
Codirector of East Asian Studies,
Harvard Law School:

[*Ezary has a placid face that is belied by the intensity of his gaze. He enjoys giving lectures, not because he likes hearing himself talk, but because he thinks he will learn something new each time he tries to explain.*]

The legal debate between China and Japan about Wei's work, almost twenty years ago, was not really new. Who should have control over the past is a question that has troubled all of us, in various forms, for many years. But the invention of the Kirino Process made this struggle to control the past a literal, rather than merely a metaphorical, issue.

A state has a temporal dimension as well as a spatial one. It grows and shrinks over time, subjugating new peoples and sometimes freeing their descendants. Japan today may be thought of as just the home islands, but back in 1942, at its height, the Japanese Empire ruled Korea, most of China, Taiwan, Sakhalin, the Philippines, Vietnam, Thailand, Laos, Burma, Malaysia, and large parts of Indonesia, as well as large swaths of the islands in the Pacific. The legacy of that time shapes Asia to this day.

One of the most vexing problems created by the violent and unstable process by which states expand and contract over time is this: As control over a territory shifts between sovereigns over time, which sovereign should have jurisdiction over that territory's past?

Before Evan Wei's demonstration, the most that the issue of jurisdiction over the past intruded on real life was an argument over whether Spain or America would have the right to the sovereign's share of treasure from sunken sixteenth-century Spanish galleons recovered in contemporary American waters, or whether Greece or England should keep the Elgin Marbles. But now the stakes are much higher.

So, is Harbin during the years between 1931 and 1945 Japanese territory, as the Japanese government contends? Or is it Chinese, as the People's Republic argues? Or perhaps we should treat the past as something held in trust for all of humanity by the United Nations?

The Chinese view would have had the support of most of the Western world—the Japanese position is akin to Germany arguing that attempts to travel to Auschwitz-Birkenau between 1939 and 1945 should be subject to its approval—but for the fact that it is the People's Republic of China, a Western pariah, which is now making the claim. And so you see how the present and the past will strangle each other to death.

Moreover, behind both the Japanese and the Chinese positions is the unquestioned assumption that if we can resolve whether *China* or *Japan* has sovereignty over World War Two-era Harbin, then either the People's Republic or the present Japanese government would be the right authority to exercise that sovereignty. But this is far from clear. Both sides have problems making the legal case.

First, Japan has always argued, when it comes to Chinese claims for compensation for wartime atrocities, that the present Japan, founded on the Constitution drafted by America, cannot be the responsible party. Japan believes that those claims are against its predecessor government, the Empire of Japan, and all such claims have been resolved by the Treaty of San Francisco and other bilateral treaties. But if that is so, for Japan now to assert sovereignty over that era in Manchuria, when it has previously disavowed all responsibility for it, is more than a little inconsistent.

But the People's Republic is not home free either. At the time Japanese forces took control of Manchuria in 1932, it was only nominally under the control of the Republic of China, the entity that we think of as the "official" China during the Second World War, and the People's Republic of China did not even exist. It is true that during the War, armed resistance in Manchuria to the Japanese occupation came almost entirely from the Han Chinese, Manchu, and Korean guerrillas led by Chinese and Korean Communists. But these guerrillas were not under the real direction of the Chinese Communist Party led by Mao Zedong and so had little to do with the eventual founding of the People's Republic.

So why should we think that either the present government of Japan or China has any claim to Harbin during that era? Wouldn't the Republic of China, which now resides in Taipei and calls itself Taiwan, have a more legitimate claim? Or perhaps we should conjure up a "Provisional Historical Manchurian Authority" to assume jurisdiction over it?

Our doctrines concerning the succession of states, developed under the Westphalian framework, simply cannot deal with these questions raised by Dr. Wei's experiments.

If these debates have a clinical and evasive air to them, that is intentional. "Sovereignty," "jurisdiction," and similar words have always been mere conveniences to allow people to evade responsibility or to sever inconvenient bonds. "Independence" is declared, and suddenly the past is forgotten; a "revolution" occurs, and suddenly memories and blood debts are wiped clean; a treaty is signed, and suddenly the past is buried and gone. Real life does not work like that.

However you want to parse the robber's logic that we dignify under the name "international law," the fact remains that the people who call themselves Japanese today are connected to those who called themselves Japanese in Manchuria in 1937, and the people who call themselves Chinese today are connected to those who called themselves Chinese there and then. These are the messy realities, and we make do with what we are given.

All along, we have made international law work only by assuming that the past would remain silent. But Dr. Wei has given the past a voice and made dead memories come alive. What role, if any, we wish to give the voices of the past in the present is up to us.

★ ★ ★ ★

Akemi Kirino:

Evan always called me *Tóngyě Míngměi*, or just *Míngměi*, which are the Mandarin readings for the kanji that are used to write my name (桐野明美). Although this is the customary way to pronounce Japanese names in Chinese, he's the only Chinese I've ever permitted that liberty.

Saying my name like that, he told me, allowed him to picture it in those old characters that are the common heritage of China and Japan, and thus keep in mind their meaning. The way he saw it, "the sound of a name doesn't tell you anything about the person, only the characters do."

My name was the first thing he loved about me.

"A paulownia tree alone in the field, bright and beautiful," he said to me, the first time we met at a Graduate School of Arts and Sciences mixer.

That was also how my grandfather explained my name to me, years earlier, when he taught me how to write the characters in my name as a little girl. A paulownia is a pretty, deciduous tree, and in old Japan it was the custom to plant one when a baby girl was born and make a dresser out of the wood for her trousseau when she got married. I remember the first time my grandfather showed me the paulownia that he had planted for me the day I was born, and I told him that I didn't think it looked very special.

"But a paulownia is the only tree on which a phoenix would land and rest," my grandfather then said, stroking my hair in that slow, gentle way that he had that I loved. I nodded, and I was glad that I had such a special tree for my name.

Until Evan spoke to me, I hadn't thought about that day with my grandfather in years.

"Have you found your phoenix yet?" Evan asked, and then he asked me out.

Evan wasn't shy, not like most Chinese men I knew. I felt at ease listening to him. And he seemed genuinely happy about his life, which was rare among the grad students and made it fun to be around him.

In a way it was natural that we would be drawn to each other. We had both come to America as young children and knew something about the meaning of growing up as outsiders trying hard to become Americans. It made it easy for us to appreciate each other's foibles, the little corners of our personalities that remained defiantly fresh-off-the-boat.

He wasn't intimidated by the fact that I had a much better sense about numbers, statistics, the "hard" qualities in life. Some of my old boyfriends used to tell me that my focus on the quantifiable and the logic of mathematics made me seem cold and unfeminine. It didn't help that I knew my way around power tools better than most of them—a necessary skill for a lab physicist. Evan was the only man I knew who was perfectly happy to defer to me when I told him that I could do something requiring mechanical skills better than he could.

Memories of our courtship have grown hazy with time and are now coated with the smooth, golden glow of sentiment— but they are all that I have left. If ever I am allowed to run my machine again, I would like to go back to those times.

I liked driving with him to bed-and-breakfasts up in New Hampshire in the fall to pick apples. I liked making simple dishes from a book of recipes and seeing that silly grin on his face. I liked waking up next to him in the mornings and feeling happy that I was a woman. I liked that he could argue passionately with me and hold his ground when he was right and back down gracefully when he was wrong. I liked that he always took my side whenever I was in an argument with others and backed me up to the hilt, even when he thought I was wrong.

But the best part was when he talked to me about the history of Japan.

Actually, he gave me an interest in Japan that I never had. Growing up, whenever people found out that I was Japanese, they assumed that I would be interested in anime, love karaoke, and giggle into my cupped hands, and the boys, in particular, thought I would act out their Oriental sex fantasies. It was tiring. As a teenager, I rebelled by refusing to do anything that seemed "Japanese," including speaking Japanese at home. Just imagine how my poor parents felt.

Evan told the history of Japan to me not as a recitation of dates or myths, but as an illustration of scientific principles embedded in humanity. He showed me that the history of Japan is not a story about emperors and generals, poets and monks. Rather, the history of Japan is a model demonstrating the way all human societies grow and adapt to the natural world as the environment, in turn, adapts to their presence.

As hunter-gatherers, the ancient Jōmon Japanese were the top predators in their environment; as self-sufficient agriculturalists, the Japanese of the Nara and Heian periods began to shape and cultivate the ecology of Japan into a human-centric symbiotic biota, a process that wasn't completed until the intensive agriculture and population growth that came with feudal Japan; finally, as industrialists and entrepreneurs, the people of Imperial Japan began to exploit not merely the living biota, but also the dead biota of the past: the drive for reliable sources of fossil fuels would dominate the history of modern Japan, as it has the rest of the modern world. We are all now exploiters of the dead.

Clearing away the superficial structure of the reigns of emperors and the dates of battles, there was the deeper rhythm of history's ebb and flow not as the deeds of great men, but as lives lived by ordinary men and women wading through the currents of the natural world around them: its geology, its seasons, its climate and ecology, the abundance and scarcity of the raw material for life. It was the kind of history that a physicist could love.

Japan was at once universal and unique. Evan made me aware of the connection between me and the people who have called themselves Japanese for millennia.

Yet, history was not merely deep patterns and the long now. There was also a time and a place where individuals could leave an extraordinary impact. Evan's specialty was the Heian Period, he told me, because that was when Japan first became *Japan*.

A courtly elite of at most a few thousand people transformed continental influences into a uniquely native, Japanese aesthetic ideal that would reverberate throughout the centuries and define what it meant to be Japanese until the present day. Unique among the world's ancient cultures, the high culture of Heian Japan was made as much by women as by men. It was a golden age as lovely as it was implausible, unrepeatable. That was the kind of surprise that made Evan love history.

Inspired, I took a Japanese history class and asked my father to teach me calligraphy. I took a new interest in advanced Japanese language classes, and I learned to write *tanka*, the clean, minimalist Japanese poems that follow strict, mathematical metrical requirements. When I was finally satisfied with my first attempt, I was so happy, and I'm certain that I did, for a moment, feel what Murasaki Shikibu felt when she completed her first *tanka*. More than a millennium in time and more than ten thousand miles in space separated us, but there, in that moment, we would surely have understood each other.

Evan made me proud to be Japanese, and so he made me love myself. That was how I knew I was really in love with him.

Li Jianjian, Manager, Tianjin Sony Store:

The War has been over for a long time, and at some point you have to move on. What is the point of digging up memories like this now? Japanese investment in China has been very important for jobs, and all the young people in China like Japanese culture. I don't like it that Japan does not want to apologize, but what can we do? If we dwell on it, then only we will be angry and sad.

Song Yuanwu, waitress:

I read about it in the newspapers. That Dr. Wei is not Chinese; he's an American. The Chinese all know about Unit 731, so it's not news to us.

I don't want to think about it much. Some stupid young people shout about how we should boycott Japanese goods, but then they can't wait to buy the next issue of manga. Why should I listen to them? This just upsets people without accomplishing anything.

Name withheld, executive:

Truth be told, the people who were killed there in Harbin were mostly peasants, and they died like weeds during that time all over China. Bad things happen in wars, that's all.

What I'm going to say will make everyone hate me, but many people also died during the Three Years of Natural Disasters under the Chairman and then during the Cultural Revolution. The War is sad, but it is just one sadness among many for the Chinese. The bulk of China's sorrow lies unmourned. That Dr. Wei is a stupid troublemaker. You can't eat, drink, or wear memories.

Nie Liang and Fang Rui, college students:

Nie: I'm glad that Wei did his work. Japan has never faced up to its history. Every Chinese knows that these things happened, but Westerners don't, and they don't care. Maybe now that they know the truth they'll put pressure on Japan to apologize.

Fang: Be careful, Nie. When Westerners see this, they are going to call you a *fenqing* and a brainwashed nationalist. They like Japan in the West. China, not so much. The Westerners don't want to understand China. Maybe they just can't. We have nothing to say to these journalists. They won't believe us, anyway.

Sun Maying, office worker:

I don't know who Wei is, and I don't care.

Akemi Kirino:

Evan and I wanted to go see a movie that night. The romantic comedy we wanted was sold out, and so we chose the movie with the next earliest start time. It was called *Philosophy of a Knife*. Neither of us had heard of it. We just wanted to spend some time together.

Our lives are ruled by these small, seemingly ordinary moments that turn out to have improbably large effects. Such randomness is much more common in human affairs than in nature, and there was no way that I, as a physicist, could have foreseen what happened next.

Scenes from Andrey Iskanov's
Philosophy of a Knife are shown as
Dr. Kirino speaks.

The movie was a graphical portrayal of the activities of Unit 731, with many of the experiments reenacted. "God created heaven, men created hell" was the tagline.

Neither of us could get up at the end of it. "I didn't know," Evan murmured to me. "I'm sorry. I didn't know."

He was not apologizing for taking me to the movie. Instead, he was consumed by guilt because he had not known about the horrors committed by Unit 731. He had never encountered it in his classes or in his research. Because his grandparents had taken refuge in Shanghai during the War, no one in his family was directly affected.

But due to their employment with the puppet government in Japanese-occupied Shanghai, his grandparents were later labeled collaborationists after the War, and their harsh treatment at the hands of the government of the People's Republic eventually caused his family to flee for the United States. And so the War shaped Evan's life, as it has shaped the lives of all Chinese, even if he was not aware of all its ramifications.

For Evan, ignorance of history, a history that determined who he was in many ways, was a sin in itself.

"It's just a film," our friends told him. "Fiction."

But in that moment, history as he understood it ended for Evan. The distance he had once maintained, the abstractions of history at a grand scale, which had so delighted him before, lost meaning to him in the bloody scenes on the screen.

He began to dig into the truth behind the film, and it soon consumed all his waking moments. He became obsessed with the activities of Unit 731. It became his waking life and his nightmare. For him, his ignorance of those horrors was simultaneously a rebuke and a call to arms. He could not let the victims' suffering be forgotten. He would not allow their torturers to get away.

That was when I explained to him the possibilities presented by Bohm-Kirino particles.

Evan believed that time travel would make people care.

When Darfur was merely a name on a distant continent, it was possible to ignore the deaths and atrocities. But what if your neighbors came to you and told you of what they had seen in their travels to Darfur? What if the victims' relatives showed up at the door to recount their memories in that land? Could you still ignore it?

Evan believed that something similar would happen with time travel. If people could see and hear the past, then it would no longer be possible to remain apathetic.

Excerpts from the televised hearing before the
Subcommittee on Asia, the Pacific, and the Global
Environment of the Committee on Foreign Affairs,
House of Representatives, 11Xth Congress,
courtesy of C–SPAN

Mr. Chairman and Members of the Subcommittee, thank you for giving me the opportunity to testify here today. I would also like to thank Dr. Wei and Dr. Kirino, whose work has made my presence here today possible.

I was born on January 5, 1962, in Hong Kong. My father, Jaiyi "Jimmy" Chang, had come to Hong Kong from mainland China after World War Two. There, he became a successful merchant of men's shirts and married my mother. Each year we celebrated my birthday one day early. When I asked my mother why we did this, she said that it had something to do with the War.

As a little girl, I didn't know much about my father's life before I was born. I knew that he had grown up in Japanese-occupied Manchuria, that his whole family was killed by the Japanese, and that he was rescued by Communist guerrillas. But he did not tell me any details.

Only once did Father talk to me directly about his life during the War. It was the summer before I went to college, in 1980. A traditionalist, he held a *jíjĭlĭ* ceremony for me where I would pick my *biǎozì*, or courtesy name. That is the name young Chinese people traditionally chose for themselves when they came of age and by which they would be known by their peers. It wasn't something that most Chinese, even the Hong Kong Chinese, did anymore.

We prayed together, bowing before the shrine to our ancestors, and I lit my joss sticks and placed them in the bronze incense brazier in the courtyard. For the first time in my life, instead of me pouring tea for him, my father poured tea for *me*. We lifted our cups and drank tea together, and my father told me how proud he was of me.

I put down the teacup and asked him which of my older female relatives he most admired so that I might choose a name that would honor her memory. That was when he showed me the only photograph he had of his family. I have brought it here today and would like to enter it into the record.

This picture was taken in 1940 on the occasion of my father's tenth birthday. The family lived in Sanjiajiao, a village about twenty kilometers from Harbin, where they went to take this portrait in a studio. In this picture you can see my grandparents sitting together in the center. My father is standing next to my grandfather, and here, next to my grandmother, is my aunt, Changyi (暢怡). Her name means "smooth happiness." Until my father showed me this picture, I did not know that I had an aunt.

My aunt was not a pretty girl. You can see that she was born with a large, dark birthmark shaped like a bat on her face that disfigured her. Like most girls in her village, she never went to school and was illiterate. But she was very gentle and kind and clever, and she did all of the cooking and cleaning in the house starting at the age of eight. My grandparents worked in the fields all day, and as the big sister, Changyi was like a mother to my father. She bathed him, fed him, changed his swaddling clothes, played with him, and protected him from the other kids in the village. At the time this picture was taken, she was sixteen.

What happened to her? I asked my father.

She was taken, he said. The Japanese came to our village on January 5, 1941, because they wanted to make an example of it so that other villages would not dare to support the guerrillas. I was eleven at the time and Changyi was seventeen. My parents told me to hide in the hole under the granary. After the soldiers bayoneted our parents, I saw them drag Changyi to a truck and drive her away.

Where was she taken?

They said they were taking her to a place called Pingfang, south of Harbin.

What kind of place was it?

Nobody knew. At the time the Japanese said the place was a lumber mill. But trains passing by there had to pull down their curtains, and the Japanese evicted all the villages nearby and

395

patrolled the area heavily. The guerrillas who saved me thought it was probably a weapons depot or a headquarters building for important Japanese generals. I think maybe she was taken there to serve as a sex slave for the Japanese soldiers. I do not know if she survived. And so I picked my *biǎozì* to be Changyi (長憶) to honor my aunt, who was like a mother to my father. My name sounds like hers but it is written with different characters, and instead of "smooth happiness," it means "long remembrance." We prayed that she had survived the War and was still alive in Manchuria.

The next year, in 1981, the Japanese author Morimura Seiichi published *The Devil's Gluttony*, which was the first Japanese publication ever to talk about the history of Unit 731. I read the Chinese translation of the book, and the name Ping-fang suddenly took on a different meaning. For years, I had nightmares about what happened to my aunt.

My father died in 2002. Before his death, he asked that if I ever found out for sure what happened to my aunt, I should let him know when I made my annual visit to his grave. I promised him that I would.

This is why, a decade later, I volunteered to undertake the journey when Dr. Wei offered this opportunity. I wanted to know what happened to my aunt. I hoped against hope that she had survived and escaped, even though I knew there were no Unit 731 survivors.

Chung-Nian Shih, Director, Department of Archaeology, National Independent University of Taiwan:

I was one of the first to question Evan's decision to prioritize sending volunteers who are relatives of the victims of Unit 731 rather than professional historians or journalists. I understand that he wanted to bring peace to the victims' families, but it also meant large segments of history were consumed in private grief and are now lost forever to the world. His technique, as you know, is destructive. Once he has sent an observer to a particular place at a particular time, the Bohm-Kirino particles are gone, and no one can ever go back there again.

There are moral arguments for and against his choice: is the suffering of the victims above all a private pain? Or should it primarily be seen as a part of our shared history?

It's one of the central paradoxes of archaeology that in order to excavate a site so as to study it, we must consume it and destroy it in that process. Within the profession we are always debating over whether it's better to excavate a site now or to preserve it *in situ* until less destructive techniques could be developed. But without such destructive excavations, how can new techniques be developed?

Perhaps Evan should also have waited until they developed a way to record the past without erasing it in the process. But by then it may have been too late for the families of the victims, who would benefit from those memories the most. Evan was forever struggling with the competing claims between the past and the present.

Lillian C. Chang-Wyeth:

I took my first trip five years ago, just as Dr. Wei first began to send people back.

I went to January 6, 1941, the day after my aunt was captured.

I arrived on a field surrounded by a complex of brick buildings. It was very cold. I don't know exactly how cold, but Harbin in January usually stayed far below zero degrees Fahrenheit. Dr. Wei had taught me how to move with my mind only, but it was still shocking to suddenly find yourself in a place with no physical presence while feeling everything, a ghost. I was still getting used to moving around when I heard a loud *whack, whack* sound behind me.

I turned around and saw a line of Chinese prisoners standing in the field. They were chained together by their legs and wore just a thin layer of rags. But what struck me was that their arms were left bare, and they held them out in the freezing wind.

A Japanese officer walked in front of them, striking their frozen arms with a short stick. *Whack, whack.*

*Interview with Shiro Yamagata, former member of
Unit 731, courtesy of Nippon Broadcasting Co.*

[*Yamagata and his wife sit on chairs behind a long folding table. He is in his nineties. His hands are folded in front of him on the table, as are his wife's. He keeps his face placid and does not engage in any histrionics. His voice is frail but clear underneath that of the translator's.*]

We marched the prisoners outside with bare arms so that the arms would freeze solid quicker in the Manchurian air. It was very cold, and I did not like the times when it was my duty to march them out.

We sprayed the prisoners with water to create frostbite quicker. To make sure that the arms have been frozen solid, we would hit them with a short stick. If we heard a crisp *whack*, it meant that the arms were frozen all the way through and ready for the experiments. It sounded like whacking against a piece of wood.

I thought that was why we called the prisoners *maruta*, wood logs. *Hey, how many logs did you saw today?* We'd joke with each other. *Not many, just three small logs.*

We performed those experiments to study the effects of frostbite and extreme temperatures on the human body. They were valuable. We learned that the best way to treat frostbite is to immerse the limb in warm water, not rubbing it. It probably saved many Japanese soldiers' lives. We also observed the effects of gangrene and disease as the frozen limbs died on the prisoners.

I heard that there were experiments where we increased the

pressure in an airtight room until the person inside exploded, but I did not personally witness them.

I was one of a group of medical assistants who arrived in January 1941. In order to practice our surgery techniques, we performed amputations and other surgery on the prisoners. We used both healthy prisoners and prisoners from the frostbite experiments. When all the limbs had been amputated, the survivors were used to test biological weapons.

Once, two of my friends amputated a man's arms and reattached them to opposite sides of his body. I watched but did not participate. I did not think it was a useful experiment.

Lillian C. Chang-Wyeth:

I followed the line of prisoners into the compound. I walked around to see if I could find my aunt.

I was very lucky, and after only about half an hour, I found where the women prisoners were kept. But when I looked through all the cells, I did not see a woman that looked like my aunt. I then continued walking around aimlessly, looking into all the rooms. I saw many specimen jars with preserved body parts. I remember that in one of the rooms I saw a very tall jar in which one half of a person's body, cleaved vertically in half, was floating.

Eventually, I came to an operating room filled with young Japanese doctors. I heard a woman scream, and I went in. One doctor was raping a Chinese woman on the operating table. There were several other Chinese women in the room, all of them naked and they were holding the woman on the table down so that the Japanese doctor could focus on the rape.

The other doctors looked on and spoke in a friendly manner with each other. One of them said something, and everybody laughed, including the doctor who was raping the woman on the table. I looked at the women who were holding her down and saw that one of them had a bat-shaped birthmark that covered half of her face. She was talking to the woman on the table, trying to comfort her.

What truly shocked me wasn't the fact that she was naked, or what was happening. It was the fact that she looked so young. Seventeen, she was a year younger than I was when I left for college. Except for the birthmark, she looked just like me from back then, and just like my daughter.

[*She stops*]

Representative Kotler: Ms. Chang, would you like to take a break? I'm sure the Subcommittee would understand—

Lillian C. Chang-Wyeth: No, thank you. I'm sorry. Please let me continue.

After the first doctor was done, the woman on the table was brought away. The group of doctors laughed and joked amongst themselves. In a few minutes two soldiers returned with a naked Chinese man walking between them. The first doctor pointed to my aunt, and the other women pushed her onto the table without speaking. She did not resist.

The doctor then pointed to the Chinese man and gestured toward my aunt. The man did not at first understand what was wanted of him. The doctor said something, and the two soldiers prodded the man with their bayonets, making him jump. My aunt looked up at him.

They want you to fuck me, she said.

Shiro Yamagata:

Sometimes we took turns raping the women and girls. Many of us had not ever been with a woman or seen a live woman's organs. It was a kind of sex education.

One of the problems the army faced was venereal disease. The military doctors examined the comfort women weekly and gave them shots, but the soldiers would rape the Russian and Chinese women and got infected all the time. We needed to understand better the development of syphilis, in particular, and to devise treatments.

In order to do so, we would inject some prisoners with syphilis and make the prisoners have sex with each other so that they could be infected the regular way. Of course we would not then touch these infected women. We could then study the effects of the disease on body organs. It was all research that had not been done before.

Lillian C. Chang-Wyeth:

The second time I went back was a year later, and this time I went back to June 8, 1941, about five months after my aunt's capture. I thought that if I picked a date much later my aunt might have already been killed. Dr. Wei was facing a lot of opposition, and he was concerned that taking too many trips to the era would destroy too much of the evidence. He explained that it would have to be my last trip.

I found my aunt in a cell by herself. She was very thin, and I saw that her palms were covered with a rash, and there were bumps around her neck from inflamed lymph nodes. I could also tell that she was pregnant. She must have been very sick because she was lying on the floor, her eyes open and making a light moan—*"aiya, aiya"*—the whole time I was with her.

I stayed with her all day, watching her. I kept on trying to comfort her, but of course she couldn't hear me or feel my touch. The words were for my benefit, not hers. I sang a song for her, a song that my father used to sing to me when I was little:

萬里長城萬里長，長城外面是故鄉
高粱肥，大豆香，遍地黃金少災殃。

The Great Wall is ten thousand li *long, on the other side is my hometown*

401

> Rich sorghum, sweet soybeans, happiness spreads like
> gold on the ground.

I was getting to know her and saying good-bye to her at the same time.

Shiro Yamagata:

To study the progress of syphilis and other venereal diseases, we would vivisect the women at various intervals after they were infected. It was important to understand the effects of the disease on living organs, and vivisection also provided valuable surgical practice. The vivisection was sometimes done with chloroform, sometimes not. We usually vivisected the subjects for the anthrax and cholera experiments without use of anesthesia since anesthesia might have affected the results, and it was felt that the same would be true with the women with syphilis.

I do not remember how many women I vivisected.

Some of the women were very brave, and would lie down on the table without being forced. I learned to say, *"bútòng, bútòng"* or "it won't hurt" in Chinese to calm them down. We would then tie them to the table.

Usually the first incision, from thorax to stomach, would cause the women to scream horribly. Some of them would keep on screaming for a long while during the vivisection. We used gags later because the screaming interfered with discussion during the vivisections. Generally the women stayed alive until we cut open the heart, and so we saved that for last.

I remember once vivisecting a woman who was pregnant. We did not use chloroform initially, but then she begged us, "Please kill me, but do not kill my child." We then used chloroform to put her under before finishing her.

None of us had seen a pregnant woman's insides before, and it was very informative. I thought about keeping the fetus for some experiment, but it was too weak and died soon after being removed. We tried to guess whether the fetus was from the seed of a Japanese doctor or one of the Chinese prisoners, and I think most of us agreed in the end that it was probably one of the prisoners due to the ugliness of the fetus.

I believed that the work we did on the women was very valuable and gained us many insights.

I did not think that the work we did at Unit 731 was particularly strange. After 1941, I was assigned to northern China, first in Hebei Province and then in Shanxi Province. In army hospitals, we military doctors regularly scheduled surgery practice sessions with live Chinese subjects. The army would provide the subjects on the announced days. We practiced amputations, cutting out sections of intestines and suturing together the remaining sections, and removing various internal organs.

Often the practice surgeries were done without anesthesia to simulate battlefield conditions. Sometimes a doctor would shoot a prisoner in the stomach to simulate war wounds for us to practice on. After the surgeries, one of the officers would behead the Chinese subject or strangle him. Sometimes vivisections were also used as anatomy lessons for the younger trainees and to give them a thrill. It was important for the army to produce good surgeons quickly, so that we could help the soldiers.

"John," last name withheld, high school teacher, Perth, Australia:

You know old people are very lonely, so when they want attention, they'll say anything. They would confess to these ridiculous made-up stories about what they did. It's really sad. I'm sure I can find some old Australian soldier who'll confess to cutting up some abo woman if you put out an ad asking about it. The people who tell these stories just want attention, like those Korean prostitutes who claim to have been kidnapped by the Japanese Army during the War.

Patty Ashby, homemaker, Milwaukee, Wisconsin:

I think it's hard to judge someone if you weren't there. It was during the War, and bad things happen during wars. The Christian thing to do is to forget and forgive. Dragging up things like this is uncharitable. And it's wrong to mess with time like that. Nothing good can come of it.

Sharon, actress, New York, New York:

You know, the thing is that the Chinese have been very cruel to dogs, and they even eat dogs. They have also been very mean to the Tibetans. So it makes you think, was it karma?

Shiro Yamagata:

On August 15, 1945, we heard that the Emperor had surrendered to America. Like many other Japanese in China at that time, my unit decided that it was easier to surrender to the Chinese Nationalists. My unit was then reformed and drafted into a unit of the Nationalist Army under Chiang Kai-Shek, and I continued to work as an army doctor assisting the Nationalists against the Communists in the Chinese Civil War. As the Chinese had almost no qualified surgeons, my work was very much needed, and I was treated well.

The Nationalists were no match for the Communists, however, and in January, 1949, the Communists captured the army field hospital I was staffed in and took me prisoner. For the first month, we were not allowed to leave our cells. I tried to make friends with the guards. The Communists soldiers were very young and thin, but they seemed to be in much better spirits than their Nationalist counterparts.

After a month, we, along with the guards, were given daily lessons on Marxism and Maoism.

The War was not my fault and I was not to be blamed, I was told. I was just a soldier, deceived by the Shōwa Emperor and

Hideki Tōjō into fighting a war of invasion and oppression against the Chinese. Through studying Marxism, I was told, I would come to understand that all poor men, the Chinese and Japanese alike, were brothers. We were expected to reflect on what we did to the Chinese people and to write confessions about the crimes we committed during the War. Our punishment would be lessened, we were told, if our confessions showed sincere hearts. I wrote confessions, but they were always rejected for not being sincere enough.

Still, because I was a doctor, I was allowed to work at the provincial hospital to treat patients. I was the most senior surgeon at the hospital and had my own staff.

We heard rumors that a new war was about to start between the United States and China in Korea. *How could China win against the United States?* I thought. *Even the mighty Japanese Army could not stand against America. Perhaps I will be captured by the Americans next.* I suppose I was never very good at predicting the outcomes of wars.

Food became scarce after the Korean War began. The guards ate rice with scallions and wild weeds, while prisoners like me were given rice and fish.

Why is this? I asked.

You are prisoners, my guard, who was only sixteen, said. You are from Japan. Japan is a wealthy country, and you must be treated in a manner that matched as closely as possible the conditions in your home country.

I offered the guard my fish, and he refused.

You do not want to touch the food that had been touched by a Japanese Devil? I joked with him. I was also teaching him how to read, and he would sneak me cigarettes.

I was a very good surgeon, and I was proud of my work. Sometimes I felt that despite the War, I was doing China a great deal of good, and I helped many patients with my skills.

One day, a woman came to see me in the hospital. She had broken her leg, and because she lived far from the hospital, by the time her family brought her to me, gangrene had set in, and the leg had to be amputated.

She was on the table, and I was getting ready to administer anesthesia. I looked into her eyes, trying to calm her. *"Bútòng, bútòng."*

Her eyes became very wide, and she screamed. She screamed and screamed, and scrambled off the table, dragging her dead leg with her until she was as far away from me as possible.

I recognized her then. She had been one of the Chinese girl prisoners that we had trained to help us as nurses at the army hospital during the War with China. She had helped me with some of the practice surgery sessions. I had slept with her a few times. I didn't know her name. She was just "#4" to me, and some of the younger doctors had joked about cutting her open if Japan lost and we had to retreat.

[*Interviewer (off-camera): Mr. Yamagata, you cannot cry. You know that. We cannot show you being emotional on film. We have to stop if you cannot control yourself.*]

I was filled with unspeakable grief. It was only then that I understood what kind of a life and career I had. Because I wanted to be a successful doctor, I did things that no human being should do. I wrote my confession then, and when my guard read my confession, he would not speak to me.

I served my sentence and was released and allowed to return to Japan in 1956.

I felt lost. Everyone was working so hard in Japan. But I didn't know what to do.

"You should not have confessed to anything," one of my friends, who was in the same unit with me, told me. "I didn't, and they released me years ago. I have a good job now. My son is going to be a doctor. Don't say anything about what happened during the War."

I moved here to Hokkaido to be a farmer, as far away from

the heart of Japan as possible. For all these years I stayed silent to protect my friend. And I believed that I would die before him and so take my secret to the grave.

But my friend is now dead, and so, even though I have not said anything about what I did all these years, I will not stop speaking now.

Lillian C. Chang-Wyeth:

I am speaking only for myself, and perhaps for my aunt. I am the last connection between her and the living world. And I am turning into an old woman myself.

I don't know much about politics, and don't care much for it. I have told you what I saw, and I will remember the way my aunt cried in that cell until the day I die.

You ask me what I want. I don't know how to answer that.

Some have said that I should demand that the surviving members of Unit 731 be brought to justice. But what does that mean? I am no longer a child. I do not want to see trials, parades, spectacles. The law does not give you real justice.

What I really want is for what I saw to never have happened. But no one can give me that. And so I resort to wanting to have my aunt's story remembered, to have the guilt of her killers and torturers laid bare to the gaze of the world, the way that they laid her bare to their needle and scalpel.

I do not know how to describe those acts other than as crimes against humanity. They were denials against the very idea of life itself.

The Japanese government has never acknowledged the actions of Unit 731, and it has never apologized for them. Over the years, more and more evidence of the atrocities committed during those years have come to life, but always the answer is the same: there is not enough evidence to know what happened.

Well, now there is. I have seen what happened with my own

eyes. And I will speak about what happened, speak out against the denialists. I will tell my story as often as I can.

The men and women of Unit 731 committed those acts in the name of Japan and the Japanese people. I demand that the government of Japan acknowledge these crimes against humanity, that it apologize for them, and that it commit to preserving the memory of the victims and condemning the guilt of those criminals so long as the word *justice* still has meaning.

I am also sorry to say, Mr. Chairman and Members of the Subcommittee, that the government of the United States has also never acknowledged or apologized for its role in shielding these criminals from justice after the War or in making use of the information bought at the expense of torture, rape, and death. I demand that the government of the United States acknowledge and apologize for these acts.

That is all.

Representative Hogart:

I would like to again remind members of the public that they must maintain order and decorum during this hearing or risk being forcibly removed from this room.

Ms. Chang-Wyeth, I am sorry for whatever it is you think you have experienced. I have no doubt that it has deeply affected you. I thank the other witnesses as well for sharing their stories.

Mr. Chairman, and Members of the Subcommittee, I must again note for the record my objection to this hearing and to the resolution that has been proposed by my colleague, Representative Kotler.

The Second World War was an extraordinary time during which the ordinary rules of human conduct did not apply, and there is no doubt that terrible events occurred and terrible suffering resulted. But whatever happened—and we have no definitive proof of anything other than the results of some sensational high-energy physics that no one present, other than

Dr. Kirino herself, understands—it would be a mistake for us to become slaves to history, and to subject the present to the control of the past.

The Japan of today is the most important ally of the United States in the Pacific, if not the world, while the People's Republic of China takes daily steps to challenge our interests in the region. Japan is vital in our efforts to contain and confront the Chinese threat.

It is ill-advised at best, and counterproductive at worst, for Representative Kotler to introduce his resolution at this time. The resolution will no doubt embarrass and dishearten our ally and give encouragement and comfort to our challengers at a time when we cannot afford to indulge in theatrical sentiments, premised upon stories told by emotional witnesses who may have been experiencing "illusions," and I am quoting the words of Dr. Kirino, the creator of the technology involved.

Again, I must call upon the Subcommittee to stop this destructive, useless process.

Representative Kotler:

Mr. Chairman, and Members of the Subcommittee, thank you for giving me the chance to respond to Representative Hogart.

It's easy to hide behind intransitive verbal formulations like "terrible events occurred" and "suffering resulted." And I am sorry to hear my honored colleague, a member of the United States Congress, engage in the same shameful tactics of denial and evasion employed by those who denied that the Holocaust was real.

Every successive Japanese government, with the encouragement and complicity of the successive administrations in this country, has refused to even acknowledge, let alone apologize for, the activities of Unit 731. In fact, for many years, the Unit's very existence was unacknowledged. These denials and refusals to face Japanese atrocities committed during the Second World War form a pattern of playing-down and denial of the war record, whether we are talking about the so-called "comfort women," The Nanjing Massacre, or the forced slave laborers of Korea and China. This pattern has harmed the relationship of Japan with its Asian neighbors.

The issue of Unit 731 presents its unique challenges. Here, the United States is not an uninterested third party. As an ally and close friend of Japan, it is the duty of the United States to point out where our friend has erred. But more than that, the United States played an active role in helping the perpetrators of the crimes of Unit 731 escape justice. General MacArthur granted the men of Unit 731 immunity to get their experimental data. We are in part responsible for the denials and the cover-ups because we valued the tainted fruits of those atrocities more than we valued our own integrity. We have sinned as well.

What I want to emphasize is that Representative Hogart has misunderstood the resolution. What the witnesses and I are asking for, Mr. Chairman, is not some admission of guilt by the present government of Japan or its people. What we are asking for is a declaration from this body that it is the belief of the United States Congress that the victims of Unit 731 should be honored and remembered, and that the perpetrators of these heinous crimes be condemned. There is no bill of attainder here, no corruption of blood. We are not calling on Japan to pay compensation. All we are asking for is a commitment to truth, a commitment to remember.

Like memorials to the Holocaust, the value of such a declaration is simply a public affirmation of our common bond of humanity with the victims and our unity in standing against the ideology of evil and barbarity of the Unit 731 butchers and the Japanese militarist society that permitted and ordered such evil.

Now, I want to make it clear that "Japan" is not a monolithic thing, and it is not just the Japanese government. Individual Japanese citizens have done heroic work in bringing these atrocities to light throughout the years, almost always against government resistance and against the public's wish to forget and move on. And I offer them my heartfelt thanks.

The truth cannot be brushed away, and the families of the victims and the people of China should not be told that justice is not possible, that because their present government is repugnant to the government of the United States, that a great injustice should be covered up and hidden from the judgment of the world. Is there any doubt that this *nonbinding* resolution, or even much more stringent versions of it, would have passed without trouble if the victims were a people whose government has the favor of the United States? If we, for "strategic" reasons, sacrifice the truth in the name of gaining something of value for short-term advantage, then we will have simply repeated the errors of our forefathers at the end of the War.

It is not who we are. Dr. Wei has offered us a way to speak the truth about the past, and we must ask the government of Japan and our government to stand up and take up our collective responsibility to history.

Li Ruming, Director of the Department of History, Zhejiang University, the People's Republic of China:

When I was finishing my doctorate in Boston, Evan and Akemi often had my wife and me over to their place. They were very friendly and helpful and made us feel the enthusiasm and warmth that America is rightly famous for. Unlike many Chinese Americans I met, Evan did not give off a sense that he felt he was superior to the Chinese from the mainland. It was wonderful to have him and Akemi as lifelong friends and not have every interaction between us filtered through the lens of the politics between our two countries, as is so often the case between Chinese and American scholars.

Because I am his friend and I am also Chinese, it is difficult for me to speak about Evan's work with objectivity, but I will try my best.

When Evan first announced his intention to go to Harbin and try to travel to the past, the Chinese government was cautiously supportive. As none of it had been tried before, the full implications of Evan's destructive process for time travel were not yet clear. Due to destruction of evidence at the end of the War and continuing stonewalling by the Japanese government, we do not have access to large archives of documentary evidence and artifacts from Unit 731, and it was felt that Evan's work would help fill in the gap by providing firsthand accounts of what happened. The Chinese government granted Evan and Akemi visas under the assumption that their work would help promote Western understanding of China's historical disputes with Japan.

But they wanted to monitor his work. The War is deeply emotional for my compatriots, its unhealed wounds exacerbated by years of postwar disputes with Japan, and as such, it was not politically feasible for the government to not be involved. World War Two was not the distant past, involving ancient peoples, and China could not permit two foreigners to go traipsing through that recent history like adventurers through ancient tombs.

But from Evan's point of view—and I think he was justified in his belief—any support, monitoring, or affiliation with the Chinese government would have destroyed all credibility for his work in Western eyes.

He thus rejected all offers of Chinese involvement and even called for intervention by American diplomats. This angered many Chinese and alienated him from them. Later, when the Chinese government finally shut down his work after the storm of negative publicity, very few Chinese would speak up for him because they felt that he and Akemi had—perhaps even intentionally—done more damage to China's history and her people. The accusations were unfair, and I'm sorry to say that I do not feel that I did enough to defend his reputation.

Evan's focus throughout his project was both more universal

and more atomistic than the people of China. On the one hand, he had an American devotion to the idea of the individual, and his commitment was first and foremost to the individual voice and memory of each victim. On the other hand, he was also trying to transcend nations, to make people all over the world empathize with these victims, condemn their torturers, and affirm the common humanity of us all.

But in that process, he was forced to distance his effort from the Chinese people in order to preserve the political credibility of his project in the West. He sacrificed their goodwill in a bid to make the West care. Evan tried to appease the West and Western prejudices against China. Was it cowardly? Should he have challenged them more? I do not know.

History is not merely a private matter. Even the family members of the victims understand that there is a communitarian aspect to history. The War of Resistance Against the Japanese Invasion is the founding story of modern China, much as the Holocaust is the founding story of Israel and the Revolution and the Civil War are the founding stories of America. Perhaps this is difficult to understand for a Westerner, but to many Chinese, Evan, because he feared and rejected their involvement, was *stealing* and erasing their history. He sacrificed the history of the Chinese people, without their consent, for a Western ideal. I understand why he did it, but I cannot agree that his choice was right.

As a Chinese, I do not share Evan's utter devotion to the idea of a personalized sense of history. Telling the individual stories of all the victims, as Evan sought to do, is not possible and in any event would not solve all problems.

Because of our limited capacity for empathy for mass suffering, I think there's a risk that his approach would result in sentimentality and only selective memory. More than sixteen million civilians died in China from the Japanese invasion. The great bulk of this suffering did not occur in death factories like Pingfang or killing fields like Nanjing, which grab headlines and shout for our attention; rather, it occurred in the countless quiet villages, towns, remote outposts, where men and women were slaughtered and raped and slaughtered again, their screams fading with the chill wind, until even their names became blanks and forgotten. But they also deserve to be remembered.

It is not possible that every atrocity would find a spokesperson as eloquent as Anne Frank, and I do not believe that we should seek to reduce all of history to a collection of such narratives.

But Evan always told me that an American would rather work on the problem that he could solve rather than wring his hands over the vast realm of problems that he could not.

It was not an easy choice that he made, and I would not have chosen the same way. But Evan was always true to his American ideals.

Bill Pacer, Professor of Modern Chinese Language and Culture, University of Hawaii at Manoa:

It has often been said that since everybody in China knew about Unit 731, Dr. Wei had nothing useful to teach the Chinese and was only an activist campaigning against Japan. That's not quite right. One of the more tragic aspects of the dispute between China and Japan over history is how much their responses have mirrored each other. Wei's goal was to rescue history from both.

In the early days of the People's Republic, between 1945 and 1956, the Communists' overall ideological approach was to treat the Japanese invasion as just another historical stage in mankind's unstoppable march toward socialism. While Japanese militarism was condemned and the Resistance celebrated, the Communists also sought to forgive the Japanese individually if they showed contrition—a surprisingly Christian/ Confucian approach for an atheistic regime. In this atmosphere of revolutionary zeal, the Japanese prisoners were treated, for the most part, humanely. They were given Marxist classes and told to write confessions of their crimes. (These classes became the basis for the Japanese public's belief that any man who would confess to horrible crimes during the War must have been brainwashed by the Communists.) Once they were deemed sufficiently reformed through "re-education," They were released back to Japan. Memories of the War were then suppressed in China as the country feverishly moved to build a socialist utopia, with well-known disastrous consequences.

Yet, this generosity toward the Japanese was matched by Stalinist harsh treatment of landowners, capitalists, intellectuals, and the Chinese who collaborated with the Japanese. Hundreds of thousands of people were killed, often on little evidence and with no effort given to observe legal forms.

Later, during the 1990s, the government of the People's Republic began to invoke memories of the War in the context of patriotism to legitimize itself in the wake of the collapse of Communism. Ironically, this obvious ploy prevented large segments of the populace from being able to come to terms with the War—distrust of the government infected everything it touched.

And so the People's Republic's approach to historical memory created a series of connected problems. First, the leniency they showed the prisoners became the ground for denialists to later question the veracity of confessions by Japanese soldiers. Second, yoking patriotism to the memory of the War invited charges that any effort to remember was politically motivated. And lastly, individual victims of the atrocities became symbols, anonymized to serve the needs of the state.

However, it has rarely been acknowledged that behind Japan's postwar silence regarding wartime atrocities lay the same impulses that drove the Chinese responses. On the left, the peace movement attributed all suffering during the War to the concept of war itself and advocated universal forgiveness and peace among all nations without a sense of blame. In the center, focus was placed on material development as a bandage to cover the wounds of the War. On the right, the question of wartime guilt became inextricably yoked to patriotism. In contrast to Germany, which could rely on Nazism—distinct from the nation itself—to absorb the blame, it was impossible to acknowledge the atrocities committed by the Japanese during the War without implicating a sense that Japan itself was under attack.

And so, across a narrow sea, China and Japan unwittingly converged on the same set of responses to the barbarities of World War Two: forgetting in the name of universal ideals like "peace" and "socialism"; welding memories of the War to patriotism; abstracting victims and perpetrators alike into symbols to serve the state. Seen in this light, the abstract, incomplete, fragmentary memories in China and the silence in Japan are flip sides of the same coin.

The core of Wei's belief is that without real memory, there can be no real reconciliation. Without real memory, the individual persons of each nation have not been able to empathize with and remember and experience the suffering of the victims. An individualized story that each of us can tell ourselves about what happened is required before we can move beyond the trap of history. That, all along, was what Wei's project was about.

Crosstalk, January 21, 20XX, courtesy of FXNN

Amy Rowe: Thank you, Ambassador Yoshida and Dr. Wei, for agreeing to come on to *Cross-Talk* tonight. Our viewers want to have their questions answered, and I want to see some fireworks!

Ambassador Yoshida, let's start with you. Why won't Japan apologize?

Yoshida: Amy, Japan has apologized. This is the whole point.

Japan has apologized many many times for World War Two. Every few years we have to go through this spectacle where it's said that Japan needs to apologize for its actions during World War Two. But Japan has done so, repeatedly. Let me read you a few quotes.

This is from a statement by Prime Minister Tomiichi Murayama, on August 31, 1994. "Japan's actions in a certain period of the past not only claimed numerous victims here in Japan but also left the peoples of neighboring Asia and elsewhere with scars that are painful even today. I am thus taking this opportunity to state my belief, based on my profound remorse for these acts of aggression, colonial rule, and the like caused such unbearable suffering and sorrow for so many people, that Japan's future path should be one of making every effort to build world peace in line with my no-war commitment. It is imperative for us Japanese to look squarely to our history with the peoples of neighboring Asia and elsewhere."

And again, from a statement by the Diet, on June 9, 1995: "On the occasion of the 50th anniversary of the end of World War II, this House offers its sincere condolences to those who fell in action and victims of wars and similar actions all over the world. Solemnly reflecting upon many instances of colonial rule and acts of aggression in the modern history of the world, and recognizing that Japan carried out those acts in the past, inflicting pain and suffering upon the peoples of other countries, especially in Asia, the Members of this House express a sense of deep remorse."

I can go on and read you dozens of other quotes like this. Japan *has* apologized, Amy.

Yet, every few years, the propaganda organs of certain regimes hostile to a free and prosperous Japan try to dredge up settled historical events to manufacture controversy. When is this going to end? And some men of otherwise good intellect have allowed themselves to become the tools of propaganda. I wish they would wake up and see how they are being used.

Rowe: Dr. Wei, I have to say, those do sound like apologies to me.

Wei: Amy, it is not my aim or goal to humiliate Japan. My commitment is to the victims and their memory, not theater. What I'm asking for is for Japan to acknowledge the truth of what happened at Pingfang. I want to focus on specifics, and acknowledgment of specifics, not empty platitudes.

But since Ambassador Yoshida has decided to bring up the issue of apologies, let's look closer at them, shall we?

The statements quoted by the ambassador are grand and abstract, and they refer to vague and unspecified sufferings. They are apologies only in the most watered-down sense. What the ambassador is not telling you is the Japanese government's continuing refusal to admit many specific war crimes and to honor and remember the real victims.

Moreover, every time one of these statements quoted by the ambassador is made, it is matched soon after by another statement from a prominent Japanese politician purporting to cast doubt upon what happened in World War Two. Year after year, we are treated to this show of the Japanese government as a Janus speaking with two faces.

Yoshida: It's not that unusual to have differences of opinion when it comes to matters of history, Dr. Wei. In a democracy it's what you would expect.

Wei: Actually, Ambassador, Unit 731 *has* been consistently handled by the Japanese government: For more than fifty years the official position was absolute silence regarding Unit 731, despite the steady accumulation of physical evidence, including human remains, from Unit 731's activities. Even the Unit's existence was not admitted until the 1990s, and the government consistently denied that it had researched or used biological weapons during the War.

It wasn't until 2005, in response to a lawsuit by some relatives of Unit 731's victims for compensation, that the Tokyo High Court finally acknowledged Japan's use of biological weapons during the War. This was the first time that an official voice of the Japanese government admitted to that fact. Amy, you'll notice that this was a decade after those lofty statements read by Ambassador Yoshida. The Court denied compensation.

Since then the Japanese government has consistently stated that there is insufficient evidence to confirm exactly what experiments were carried out by Unit 731 or the details of their conduct. Official denial and silence continue despite the dedicated efforts of some Japanese scholars to bring the truth to light.

But numerous former members of Unit 731 have come forward since the 1980s to testify and confess to the grisly acts they committed. And we have confirmed and expanded upon those accounts with new eyewitness accounts by volunteers who have traveled to Pingfang. Everyday, we are finding out more about Unit 731's crimes. We will tell the world all the victims' stories.

Yoshida: I am not sure that "telling stories" is what historians should be doing. If you want to make fiction, go ahead, but do not tell people that it is history. Extraordinary claims require extraordinary proof. And there is insufficient proof for the accusations currently being directed against Japan.

Wei: Ambassador Yoshida, is your position really that nothing happened at Pingfang? Are you saying that these reports by the American occupational authority from immediately after the War are lies? Are you saying that these contemporaneous diary entries by the officers of Unit 731 are lies? Are you really denying all of this?

There is a simple solution to all this. Will you take a trip to Pingfang in 1941? Will you believe your own eyes?

Yoshida: I'm—I am not—I'm making a distinction—It was a time of war, Dr. Wei, and perhaps it is possible that some unfortunate things happened. But "stories" are not evidence.

Wei: Will you take a trip, Ambassador?

Yoshida: I will not. I see no reason to subject myself to your process. I see no reason to undergo your "time travel" hallucinations.

Rowe: Now we are seeing some fireworks!

Wei: Ambassador Yoshida, let me make this clear. The deniers are committing a fresh crime against the victims of those atrocities: Not only would they stand with the torturers and the killers, but they are also engaged in the practice of erasing and silencing the victims from history, to kill them afresh.

In the past, their task was easy. Unless the denials were actively resisted, eventually memories would dim with old age and death, and the voices of the past would fade away, and the denialists would win. The people of the present would then become exploiters of the dead, and that has always been the way history was written.

But we have now come to the end of history. What my wife and I have done is to take narrative away, and to give us all a chance to see the past with our own eyes. In place of memory, we now have incontrovertible evidence. Instead of exploiting the dead, we must look into the face of the dying. *I have seen these crimes with my own eyes.* You cannot deny that.

Archival footage of Dr. Evan Wei delivering the keynote for the Fifth International War Crimes Studies Conference in San Francisco, on November 20, 20XX. Courtesy of the Stanford University Archives

History is a narrative enterprise, and the telling of stories that are true, that affirm and explain our existence, is the fundamental task of the historian. But truth is delicate, and it has many enemies. Perhaps that is why, although we academics are supposedly in the business of pursuing the truth, the word "truth" is rarely uttered without hedges, adornments, and qualifications.

Every time we tell a story about a great atrocity, like the Holocaust or Pingfang, the forces of denial are always ready to pounce, to erase, to silence, to forget. History has always been difficult because of the delicacy of the truth, and denialists have always been able to resort to labeling the truth as fiction.

One has to be careful, whenever one tells a story about a great injustice. We are a species that loves narrative, but we have also been taught not to trust an individual speaker.

Yes, it is true that no nation, and no historian, can tell a story that completely encompasses every aspect of the truth. But it is not true that just because all narratives are constructed, that they are equally far from the truth. The Earth is neither a perfect sphere nor a flat disk, but the model of the sphere is much closer to the truth. Similarly, there are some narratives that are closer to the truth than others, and we must always try to tell a story that comes as close to the truth as is humanly possible.

The fact that we can never have complete, perfect knowledge does not absolve us of the moral duty to judge and to take a stand against evil.

Victor P. Lowenson, Professor of East Asian History, Director of the Institute of East Asian Studies, UC Berkeley:

I have been called a denialist, and I have been called worse. But I am not a Japanese right-winger who believes that Unit 731 is a myth. I do not say that nothing happened there. What I am saying is that, unfortunately, we do not have enough evidence to be able to describe with certainty all that happened there.

I have enormous respect for Wei, and he remains and will remain one of my best students. But in my view, he has abdicated the responsibility of the historian to ensure that the truth is not ensnared in doubt. He has crossed the line that divides a historian from an activist.

As I see it, the fight here isn't ideological, but methodological. What we are fighting over is what constitutes *proof*. Historians trained in Western and Asian traditions have always relied on the documentary record, but Dr. Wei is now raising the primacy of eyewitness accounts, and not even contemporaneous eyewitness accounts, mind you, but accounts by witnesses out of the stream of time.

There are many problems with his approach. We have a great deal of experience from psychology and the law to doubt the reliability of eyewitness accounts. We also have serious concerns with the single-use nature of the Kirino Process, which seems to destroy the very thing it is studying, and erases history even as it purports to allow it to be witnessed. You literally cannot ever go back to a moment of time that has already been experienced—and thus consumed—by another witness. When each eyewitness account is impossible to verify independently of *that* account, how can we rely on such a process to establish the truth of what happened?

I understand that from the perspective of supporters of Dr. Wei, the raw experience of actually seeing history unfold before your eyes makes it impossible to doubt the evidence indelibly etched in your mind. But that is simply not good enough for the rest of us. The Kirino Process requires a leap of faith: Those who have witnessed the ineffable have no doubt of its existence, but that clarity is incapable of being replicated for anyone else. And so we are stuck here, in the present, trying to make sense of the past.

Dr. Wei has ended the process of rational historical inquiry and transformed it into a form of personal religion. What one witness has seen, no one else can ever see. This is madness.

Naoki, last name withheld, clerk:

I have seen the videos of the old soldiers who supposedly confessed to these horrible things. I do not believe them. They cry and act so emotional, as though they are insane. The Communists were great brainwashers, and it is undoubtedly a result of their plot.

I remember one of those old men describing the kindness of his Communist guards. *Kind* Communist guards! If that is not evidence of brainwashing, what is?

Kazue Sato, housewife:
The Chinese are great manufacturers of lies. They have produced fake food, fake Olympics, and fake statistics. Their history is also faked. This Wei is an American, but he is also Chinese, and so we cannot trust anything he does.

Hiroshi Abe, retired soldier:
The soldiers who "confessed" have brought great shame upon their country.

Interviewer: Because of what they did?
Because of what they said.

Ienaga Ito, Professor of Oriental History, Kyoto University:
We live in an age that prizes authenticity and personalized narratives, as embodied in the form of the memoir. Eyewitness accounts have an immediacy and reality that compels belief, and we think they can convey a truth greater than any fiction. Yet, perhaps paradoxically, we are also eager to seize upon any factual deviation and inconsistency in such narratives and declare the entirety to be *mere* fiction. There's an all-or-nothing bleakness to this dynamic. But we should have conceded from the start that narratives are irreducibly subjective, though that does not mean that they do not also convey the truth.

Evan was a greater radical than most people realized. He sought to free the past from the present so that history could not be ignored, put out of our minds, or made to serve the needs of the present. The possibility of witnessing actual history and experiencing that past by all of us means that the past is not past, but alive at this very moment.

What Evan did was to transform historical investigation itself into a form of memoir writing. That kind of emotional experience is important in the way we think about history and make decisions. Culture is not merely a product of reason but also of real, visceral empathy. And I am afraid that it is primarily empathy that has been missing from the postwar Japanese responses to history.

Evan tried to introduce more empathy and emotion into historical inquiry. For this he was crucified by the academic establishment. But adding empathy and the irreducibly subjective dimension of the personal narrative to history does not detract from the truth. It enhances the truth. That we accept our own frailties and subjectivity does not free us to abdicate the moral responsibility to tell the truth, even if, and especially if, "truth" is not singular but a set of shared experiences and shared understandings that together make up our humanity.

Of course, drawing attention to the importance and primacy of eyewitness accounts unleashed a new danger. With a little money and the right equipment, anyone can eliminate the Bohm-Kirino particles from a desired era, in a specified place, and so erase those events from direct experience. Unwittingly, Evan had also invented the technology to end history forever, by denying us and future generations of that emotional experience of the past that he so cherished.

Akemi Kirino:

It was difficult during the years immediately after the Comprehensive Time Travel Moratorium was signed. Evan was denied tenure in a close vote, and that editorial in the *Wall Street Journal* by his old friend and teacher, Victor Lowenson, calling him a "tool of propaganda," deeply hurt him. Then, there were the death threats and harassing phone calls, every day.

But I think it was what they did to me that really got to him. At the height of the attacks from the denialists, the IT division of the Institute asked me if I would mind being delisted from the public faculty directory. Whenever they listed me on the website, the site would be hacked within hours, and the denialists would replace my bio page with pictures where these men, so brave and eloquent, displayed their courage and intellect by illustrating what they would do to me if they had me in their power. And you probably remember the news reports about that night when I walked home alone from work.

I don't really want to dwell on that time, if that's all right with you.

We moved away to Boise, where we tried to hide from the worst of it. We kept a low profile, got an unlisted number, and basically stayed out of sight. Evan went on medication for his depression. On the weekends we went hiking in the Sawtooth Mountains, and Evan took up charting abandoned mining sites and ghost towns from during the gold rush. That was a happy time for us, and I thought he was feeling better. The sojourn in Idaho reminded him that sometimes the world is a kind place, and all is not darkness and denial.

But he was feeling lost. He felt that he was hiding from the truth. I knew that he was feeling torn between his sense of duty to the past and his sense of loyalty to the present, to me.

I could not bear to see him being torn apart, and so I asked if he wanted to return to the fight.

We flew back to Boston, and things had grown even worse. He had sought to end history as mere *history* and to give the past living voices to speak to the present. But it did not work out the way he had intended. The past did come to life, but when faced with it, the present decided to recast history as religion.

The more Evan did, the more he felt he had to do. He would not come to bed, and fell asleep at his desk. He was writing, writing, constantly writing. He believed that he had to single-handedly refute all the lies and take on all his enemies. It was never enough, never enough for him. I stood by, helpless.

"I have to speak for them, because they have no one else," he would tell me.

By then perhaps he was living more in the past than in the present. Even though he no longer had access to our machine, in his mind he relived those trips he took, over and over again. He believed that he had let the victims down.

A great responsibility had been thrust upon him, and he had failed them. He was trying to uncover to the world a great injustice, and yet in the process he seemed to have only stirred up the forces of denial, hate, and silence.

Excerpts from the Economist,
November 26, 20XX

[*A woman's voice, flat, calm, reads out loud the article text as the camera swoops over the ocean, the beaches, and then the forests and hills of Manchuria. From the shadow of a small plane racing along the ground beneath us we can tell that the camera is shooting from the open door of the airplane. An arm, the hand clenched tight into a fist, moves into the foreground from off-frame. The fingers open. Dark ashes are scattered into the air beneath the airplane.*]

We will soon come upon the ninetieth anniversary of the Mukden Incident, the start of the Japanese invasion of China. To this day, that war remains the alpha and omega of the relationship between the two countries.

. . .

[*A series of photographs of the leaders of Unit 731 are shown. The reader's voice fades out and then fades back in.*]

. . .

The men of Unit 731 then moved on to prominent careers in postwar Japan. Three of them founded the Japan Blood Bank (which later became the Green Cross, Japan's largest pharmaceutical company) and used their knowledge of methods for freezing and drying blood derived from human experiments during the War to produce dried-blood products for sale to the United States Army at great profit. General Shiro Ishii, the commander of Unit 731, may have spent some time after the War working in Maryland, researching biological weapons. Papers were published using data obtained from human subjects, including babies (sometimes the word "monkey" was substituted as a cover-up)—and it is possible that medical papers published today still contain citations traceable to these results, making all of us the unwitting beneficiaries of these atrocities.

. . .

[*The reading voice fades out as the sound of the airplane's engine cuts in. The camera shifts to images of clashing protestors waving Japanese flags and Chinese flags, some of the flags on fire.*

Then the voice fades in again.]

. . .

Many inside and outside Japan objected to the testimonies by the surviving members of Unit 731: The men are old, they point out, with failing memories; they may be seeking attention; they may be mentally ill; they may have been brainwashed by the Chinese Communists. Reliance on oral testimony alone is an unwise way to construct a solid historical case. To the Chinese this sounded like more of the same excuses issued by the deniers of the Nanjing Massacre and other Japanese atrocities.

Year after year, history grew as a wall between the two peoples.

[*The camera switches to a montage of pictures of Evan Wei and Akemi Kirino throughout their lives. In the first pictures, they smile for the camera. In later pictures, Kirino's face is tired, withdrawn, impassive. Wei's face is defiant, angry, and then full of despair.*]

Evan Wei, a young Chinese-American specialist on Heian Japan, and Akemi Kirino, a Japanese-American experimental physicist, did not seem like the kind of revolutionary figures who would bring the world to the brink of war. But history has a way of mocking our expectations.

If lack of evidence was the issue, they had a way to provide irrefutable evidence: You could watch history as it occurred, like a play.

The governments of the world went into a frenzy. While Wei sent relatives of the victims of Unit 731 into the past to bear witness to the horrors committed in the operating rooms and prison cells of Pingfang, China and Japan waged a bitter war in courts and in front of cameras, staking out their rival claims to the past. The United States was reluctantly drawn into the fight, and, citing national security reasons, finally shut down Wei's machine when he unveiled plans to investigate the truth of America's alleged use of biological weapons (possibly derived from Unit 731's research) during the Korean War.

Armenians, Jews, Tibetans, Native Americans, Indians, the Kikuyu, the descendants of slaves in the New World—victim groups around the world lined up and demanded use of the machine, some out of fear that their history might be erased by the groups in power, others wishing to use their history for present political gain. As well, the countries who initially advocated access to the machine hesitated when the implications became clear: Did the French wish to relive the depravity of their own people under Vichy France? Did the Chinese want to re-experience the self-inflicted horrors of the Cultural Revolution? Did the British want to see the genocides that lay behind their Empire?

With remarkable alacrity, democracies and dictatorships around the world signed the Comprehensive Time Travel Moratorium while they wrangled over the minutiae of the rules for how to divide up jurisdiction of the past. Everyone, it seemed, preferred not to have to deal with the past just yet.

Wei wrote, "All written history shares one goal: to bring a coherent narrative to a set of historical facts. For far too long we have been mired in controversy over facts. Time travel will make truth as accessible as looking outside the window."

But Wei did not help his case by sending large numbers of Chinese relatives of Unit 731 victims, rather than professional historians, through his machine. (Though it is also fair to ask if things really would have turned out differently had he sent more professional historians. Perhaps accusations would still have been made that the visions were mere fabrications of the machine or historians partisan to his cause.) In any event, the relatives, being untrained observers, did not make great witnesses. They failed to correctly answer observational questions posed by skeptics. ("Did the Japanese doctors wear uniforms with breast pockets?" "How many prisoners in total were in the compound at that time?") They did not understand the Japanese they heard on their trips. Their rhetoric had the unfortunate habit of echoing that of their distrusted government. Their accounts contained minor discrepancies between one retelling and the next. Moreover, as they broke down on camera, their emotional testimonies simply added to the skeptics' charge that Wei was more interested in emotional catharsis rather than historical inquiry.

The criticisms outraged Wei. A great atrocity had occurred in Pingfang, and it was being willfully forgotten by the world through a cover-up. Because China's government was despised, the world was countenancing Japan's denial. Debates over whether the doctors vivisected all or only some of the victims without use of anesthesia, whether most of the victims were political prisoners, innocent villagers caught on raids, or common criminals, whether the use of babies and infants in experiments was known to Ishii, and so forth, seemed to him beside the point. That the questioners would focus on inconsequential details of the uniform of the Japanese doctors as a way to discredit his witnesses did not seem to him to deserve a response.

As he continued the trips to the past, other historians who saw the promise of the technology objected. History, as it turned out, was a limited resource, and each of Wei's trips took out a chunk of the past that could never be replaced. He was riddling the past with holes like Swiss cheese. Like early archaeologists who destroyed entire sites as they sought a few precious artifacts, thereby consigning valuable information about the past to oblivion, Wei was destroying the very history that he was trying to save.

When Wei jumped onto the tracks in front of a Boston subway train last Friday, he was undoubtedly haunted by the past. Perhaps he was also despondent over the unintended boost his work had given to the forces of denial. Seeking to end controversy in history, he succeeded only in causing more of it. Seeking to give voice to the victims of a great injustice, he succeeded only in silencing some of them forever.

[*Dr. Kirino speaks to us from in front of Evan Wei's grave. In the bright May sunlight of New England, the dark shadows beneath her eyes make her seem older, more frail.*]
Akemi Kirino:

I've kept only one secret from Evan. Well, actually two.

The first is my grandfather. He died before Evan and I met. I never took Evan to visit his grave, which is in California. I just told him that it wasn't something I wanted to share with him, and I never told Evan his name.

The second is a trip I took to the past, the only one I've ever taken personally. We were in Pingfang at the time, and I went to July 9, 1941. I knew the layout of the place pretty well from the descriptions and the maps, and I avoided the prison cells and the laboratories. I went to the building that housed the command center.

I looked around until I found the office for the Director of Pathology Studies. The Director was inside. He was a very handsome man: tall, slim, and he held his back very straight. He was writing a letter. I knew he was thirty-two, which was the same age as mine at that time.

I looked over his shoulder at the letter he was writing. He had beautiful calligraphy.

I have now finally settled into my work routine, and things are going well. Manchukuo is a very beautiful place. The sorghum fields spread out as far as the eye can see, like an ocean. The street vendors here make wonderful tofu from fresh soybeans, which smells delicious. Not quite as good as the Japanese tofu, but very good nonetheless.

You will like Harbin. Now that the Russians are gone, the streets of Harbin are a harmonious patchwork of the five races: the Chinese, Manchus, Mongolians, and Koreans bow as our beloved Japanese soldiers and colonists pass by, grateful for the liberation and wealth we have brought to this beautiful land. It has taken a decade to pacify this place and eliminate the Communist bandits, who are but an occasional and minor nuisance now. Most of the Chinese are very docile and safe.

But all that I really can think about these days when I am not working are you and Naoko. It is for her sake that you and I are apart. It is for her sake and the sake of her generation that we make our sacrifices. I am sad that I will miss her first birthday, but it gladdens my heart to see the Greater East Asia Co-Prosperity Sphere blossom in this remote but rich hinterland. Here, you truly feel that our Japan is the light of Asia, her salvation.

Take heart, my dear, and smile. All our sacrifices today

will mean that one day, Naoko and her children will see Asia take its rightful place in the world, freed from the yoke of the European killers and robbers who now trample over her and desecrate her beauty. We will celebrate together when we finally chase the British out of Hong Kong and Singapore.

> Red sea of sorghum
> Fragrant bowls of crushed soybeans
> I see only you
> And her, our treasure
> Now, if only you were here.

This was not the first time I had read this letter. I had seen it once before, as a little girl. It was one of my mother's treasured possessions, and I remember asking her to explain all the faded characters to me.

"He was very proud of his literary learning," my mother had said. "He always closed his letters with a *tanka*."

By then Grandfather was well into his long slide into dementia. Often he would confuse me with my mother and call me by her name. He would also teach me how to make origami animals. His fingers were very dextrous—the legacy of being a good surgeon.

I watched my grandfather finish his letter and fold it. I followed him out of the office to his lab. He was getting ready for an experiment, his notebook and instruments laid out neatly along the workbench.

He called to one of the medical assistants. He asked the assistant to bring him something for the experiment. The assistants returned about ten minutes later, holding a bloody mess on a tray, like a dish of steaming tofu. It was a human brain, still so warm from the body from which it was taken that I could see the heat rising from it.

"Very good," my grandfather said, nodding. "Very fresh. This will do."

Akemi Kirino:

There have been times when I wished Evan weren't Chinese, just as there have been times when I wished I weren't Japanese. But these are moments of passing weakness. I don't mean them. We are born into strong currents of history, and it is our lot to swim or sink, not to complain about our luck.

Ever since I became an American, people have told me that America is about leaving your past behind. I've never understood that. You can no more leave behind your past than you can leave behind your skin.

The compulsion to delve into the past, to speak for the dead, to recover their stories: that's part of who Evan was, and why I loved him. Just the same, my grandfather is part of who I am, and what he did, he did in the name of my mother and me and my children. I am responsible for his sins, in the same way that I take pride in inheriting the tradition of a great people, a people who, in my grandfather's time, committed great evil.

In an extraordinary time, he faced extraordinary choices, and maybe some would say this means that we cannot judge him. But how can we really judge anyone except in the most extraordinary of circumstances? It's easy to be civilized and display a patina of orderliness in calm times, but your true character only emerges in darkness and under great pressure: is it a diamond or merely a lump of the blackest coal?

Yet, my grandfather was not a monster. He was simply a man of ordinary moral courage whose capacity for great evil was revealed to his and my lasting shame. Labeling someone a monster implies that he is from another world, one which has nothing to do with us. It cuts off the bonds of affection and fear, assures us of our own superiority, but there's nothing learned, nothing gained. It's simple, but it's cowardly. I know now that only by empathizing with a man like my grandfather can we understand the depth of the suffering he caused. There are no monsters. The monster is us.

Why didn't I tell Evan about my grandfather? I don't know.

I suppose I was a coward. I was afraid that he might feel that something in me would be tainted, a corruption of blood. Because I could not then find a way to empathize with my grandfather, I was afraid that Evan could not empathize with me. I kept my grandfather's story to myself, and so I locked away a part of myself from my husband. There were times when I thought I would go to the grave with my secret and so erase forever my grandfather's story.

I regret it, now that Evan is dead. He deserved to know his wife whole, complete, and I should have trusted him rather than silenced my grandfather's story, which is also my story. Evan died believing that by unearthing more stories, he caused people to doubt their truth. But he was wrong. The truth is not delicate and it does not suffer from denial—the truth only dies when true stories are untold.

This urge to speak, to tell the story, I share with the aging and dying former members of Unit 731, with the descendants of the victims, with all the untold horrors of history. The silence of the victims of the past imposes a duty on the present to recover their voices, and we are most free when we willingly take up that duty.

[*Dr. Kirino's voice comes to us off-camera, as the camera pans to the star-studded sky.*]

It has been a decade since Evan's death, and the Comprehensive Time Travel Moratorium remains in place. We still do not know quite what to do with a past that is transparently accessible, a past that will not be silenced or forgotten. For now, we hesitate.

Evan died thinking that he had sacrificed the memory of the Unit 731 victims and permanently erased the traces that their truth left in our world, all for nought, but he was wrong. He was forgetting that even with the Bohm-Kirino particles gone, the actual photons forming the images of those moments of unbearable suffering and quiet heroism are still out there, traveling as a sphere of light into the void of space.

Look up at the stars, and we are bombarded by light generated on the day the last victim at Pingfang died, the day the last train arrived at Auschwitz, the day the last Cherokee walked out of Georgia. And we know that the inhabitants of those distant worlds, if they are watching, will see those moments, in time, as they stream from here to there at the speed of light. It is not possible to capture all of those photons, to erase all of those images. They are our permanent record, the testimony of our existence, the story that we tell the future. Every moment, as we walk on this earth, we are watched and judged by the eyes of the universe.

For far too long, historians, and all of us, have acted as exploiters of the dead. But the past is not dead. It is with us. Everywhere we walk, we are bombarded by fields of Bohm-Kirino particles that will let us see the past like looking through a window. The agony of the dead is with us, and we hear their screams and walk among their ghosts. We cannot avert our eyes or plug up our ears. We must bear witness and speak for those who cannot speak. We have only one chance to get it right.

This story is dedicated to the memory of Iris Chang and all the victims of Unit 731.

I first got the idea for writing a story in the form of a documentary after reading Ted Chiang's "Liking What You See: a Documentary."

The following sources were consulted during the research for this story. Their help is hereby gratefully acknowledged, though any errors in relating their facts and insights are entirely my own.

For the phrase "exploiters of the dead" and the history of Heian and premodern Japan:

Totman, Conrad. *A History of Japan, Second Edition*. Malden, MA: Blackwell Publishing, 2005.

For the history of Unit 731 and the experiments performed by Unit 731 personnel:

Gold, Hal. *Unit 731 Testimony*, Tokyo: Tuttle Publishing, 1996.

Harris, Sheldon H. *Factories of Death: Japanese Biological Warfare 1932–45 and the American Cover-Up*, New York: Routledge, 1994.

(Numerous other newspaper and journal articles, interviews, and analyses were also consulted. Their authors include, among others, Keiichi Tsuneishi, Doug Struck, Christopher Reed, Richard Lloyd Parry, Christopher Hudson, Mark Simkin, Frederick Dickinson, John Dower, Tawara Yoshifumi, Yuki Tanaka, Takashi Tsuchiya, Tien-wei Wu, Shane Green, Friedrich Frischknecht, Nicholas Kristof, Jun Hongo, Richard James Havis, Edward Cody, and Judith Miller. I thank these authors and regret that the sources are not listed here individually for space reasons.)

For descriptions of the vivisections and practice surgery sessions with live Chinese victims conducted by Japanese doctors, their treatment as prisoners after the War, and Japan's postwar responses to memories of the War:

Noda, Masaaki. "Japanese Atrocities in the Pacific War: One Army Surgeon's Account of Vivisection on Human Subjects in China," *East Asia: An International Quarterly*, 18:3 (2000) 49–91.

Note that based on testimonies and other documentation, the Japanese doctors of Unit 731 typically infected their victims while wearing protective suits to avoid the possibility that resisting prisoners would infect the doctors by struggling.

Aspects of Shiro Yamagata's post-Unit 731 recollections are modeled on the experiences of Ken Yuasa (a Japanese military doctor who was *not* a member of Unit 731), described in the Noda article.

The obituary for Evan Wei is modeled upon the *Economist*'s November 25, 2004 obituary for Iris Chang.

The hearing of the Subcommittee on Asia, the Pacific, and the Global Environment is modeled upon the February 15, 2007, hearing before that same Subcommittee on House Resolution 121, concerning Japan's wartime enslavement of women for sexual purposes (known as "comfort women").

Austin Yoder provided pictures from modern-day Pingfang, Harbin, and the Unit 731 War Crimes Museum.

The various denialist statements attributed to "men in the street" are modeled on Internet forum comments, postings, and direct communication to the author from individuals who hold such views.

About The Author

Ken Liu is one of the most lauded authors in the field of American literature. A winner of the Nebula, Hugo, World Fantasy, Sidewise, and Science Fiction & Fantasy Translation Awards, he has also been nominated for the Sturgeon and Locus Awards. His short story, "The Paper Menagerie," is the first work of fiction to win the Nebula, Hugo, and World Fantasy Awards within the same year. He also translated the 2015 Hugo Award–winning novel *The Three-Body Problem*, written by Cixin Liu, which was the first translated work to ever win the Hugo Award.

The Grace of Kings, Ken's debut novel, is the first volume in a silkpunk epic fantasy series set in a universe he and his wife, artist Lisa Tang Liu, created together. He lives with his family near Boston.

You can find out more about Ken's upcoming publications, appearances, and sneak previews of new books by signing up for his mailing list at kenliu.name/mailing-list.